ETHELYN'S MIST...

BY

Mary Jane Holmes

ETHELYN'S MISTAKE

Published by Silver Scroll Publishing

New York City, NY

First published circa 1907

Copyright © Silver Scroll Publishing, 2015

All rights reserved

ABOUT SILVER SCROLL PUBLISHING

Silver Scroll Publishing is a digital publisher that brings the best historical fiction ever written to modern readers. Our comprehensive catalogue contains everything from historical novels about Rome to works about World War I.

CHAPTER I: ETHELYN

There was a sweet odor of clover blossoms in the early morning air, and the dew stood in great drops upon the summer flowers, and dropped from the foliage of the elm trees which skirted the village common. There was a cloud of mist upon the meadows, and the windings of the river could be distinctly traced by the white fog which curled above it. But the fog and the mists were rolling away as the warm June sun came over the eastern hills, and here and there signs of life were visible in the little New England town of Chicopee, where our story opens. The mechanics who worked in the large shoe-shop halfway down Cottage Row had been up an hour or more, while the hissing of the steam which carried the huge manufactory had been heard since the first robin peeped from its nest in the alders down by the running brook; but higher up, on Bellevue Street, where the old inhabitants lived, everything was quiet, and the loamy road, moist and damp with the dews of the previous night, was as yet unbroken by the foot of man or rut of passing wheel.

The people who lived there, the Mumfords, and the Beechers, and the Grangers, and the Thorns, did not strictly belong to the working class. They held stocks in railroads, and mortgages on farms, and so could afford to sleep after the shrill whistle from the manufactory had wakened the echoes of the distant hills and sounded across the waters of Pordunk Pond. Only one dwelling here showed signs of life, and that the large square building, shaded in front with elms and ornamented at the side with a luxuriant queen of the prairie, whose blossoms were turning their blushing faces to the rising sun. This was the Bigelow house, the joint property of Mrs. Dr. Van Buren, née Sophia Bigelow, who lived in Boston, and her sister, Miss Barbara Bigelow, the quaintest and kindest-hearted woman who ever bore the sobriquet of an old maid, and was aunt to everybody. She was awake long before the whistle sounded across the river and along the meadow lands, where some of the workmen lived, and just as the robin, whose nest for four summers had been under the eaves where neither boy nor cat could reach it, brought the first worm to its clamorous young, she pushed the fringed curtain from her open window, and with her broad frilled cap still on her head, stood for a moment looking out upon the morning as it crept up the eastern sky. "She will have a nice day for her wedding. May her future life be as fair," Aunt Barbara whispered softly, then kneeling before the window with her head bowed upon the sill, she prayed earnestly for God's blessing on the bridal to take place that night beneath her roof, and upon the young girl who had been both a care and a comfort since the Christmas morning eighteen years before, when her half-sister Julia had come home to die, bringing with her the little Ethelyn, then but two years old.

Aunt Barbara's prayers were always to the point. She said what she had to say in the fewest possible words, wasting no time in repetition, and on this occasion she was briefer than usual, for the good woman had many things upon her mind this morning. First, there was Betty to rouse and get into a state of locomotion, a good half hour's work, as Aunt Barbara knew from a three years' experience. There was the "sponge" put to rise the previous night. She must see if that had risen, and with her own hands mold the snowy breakfast rolls which Ethelyn liked so much.

There were the chambers to be inspected a second time, to ascertain if everything was in its place, and dinner to be prepared for the "Van Buren set" expected up from Boston, while last, though far from least, there was Ethelyn herself to waken when the clock should chime the hour of six, and this was a pleasure which good Aunt Barbara would not for the world have foregone. Every morning for the last sixteen years, when Ethelyn was at home, she had gone to the pleasant, airy chamber where her darling slept, and bending over her had kissed her fair, glowing cheek, and so called her back from the dreamless slumber which otherwise might have been prolonged to an indefinite time, for Ethelyn did not believe in the maxim, "Early to bed and early to rise," and always begged for a little more indulgence, even after the brown eyes unclosed and flashed forth a responsive greeting to the motherly face bending above them.

This morning, however, it was not needful that Aunt Barbara should waken her, for long before the robin sang, or the white-fringed curtain had been pushed aside from Aunt Barbara's window, she was awake, and the brown eyes, which had in them a strange expression for a bride's eyes to wear, had scanned the eastern horizon wistfully, aye, drearily it may be, to see if it were morning, and when the clock in the kitchen struck four, the quivering lip had whispered, oh, so sadly, "Sixteen hours more, only sixteen," and with a little shiver the bed-clothes had been drawn more closely around the plump shoulders, and the troubled face had nestled down among the pillows to smother the sigh which never ought to have come from a maiden's lips upon her wedding day. The chamber of the bride-elect was a pleasant one, large and airy and high, with windows looking out upon the Chicopee hills, and from which Ethelyn had many a time watched the fading of the purplish twilight as, girl-like, she speculated upon the future and wondered what it might have in store for her. One leaf of the great book had been turned and lay open to her view, but she shrank away from what was written there, and wished so much that the record were otherwise. Upon the walls of Ethelyn's chamber many pictures were hung, some in water colors, which she had done herself in the happy schooldays which now seemed so far away, and some in oil, mementos also of those days. Pictures, too, there were of people, one of dear Aunt Barbara, whose kindly face was the first to smile on Ethelyn when she woke, and whose patient, watchful eyes seemed to keep guard over her while she slept. Besides Aunt Barbara's picture there was another one, a fair, boyish face, with a look not wholly unlike Ethelyn, herself, save that it lacked the firmness and decision which were so apparent in the proud curve of her lip and the flash of her brown eyes. Fair-haired and blue-eyed, with something feminine in every feature, it seemed preposterous that the original could ever make a young girl's heart ache as Ethelyn Grant's was aching that June morning, when, taking the small oval frame from the wall, she kissed it passionately, and then thrust it away into the bureau drawer, which held other relics than the oval frame. It was, in fact, the grave of Ethelyn's buried hopes--the tomb she had sworn never to unlock again; but now, as her fingers lingered a moment amid the mementos of the years when, in her girlish ignorance, she had been so happy, she felt her resolution giving way, and sitting down upon the floor, with her long hair unfastened and falling loosely about her, she bowed her head over buried treasures, and dropped into their grave the bitterest tears she had ever shed. Then, as there swept over her some better impulse, whispering of the wrong she was doing to her promised husband, she said:

"I will not leave them here to madden me again some other day. I will burn them, every one."

There were matches within her reach, while the little fireplace was not far away, and, sitting just where she was, Ethelyn Grant burned one after another, letters and notes, some directed in schoolboy style, and others showing a manlier hand, as the dates grew more recent and the envelopes bore a more modern and fashionable look. Over one, the freshest and the last, Ethelyn lingered a moment, her eyes growing dark with passion, and her lips twitching nervously as she read:

"BOSTON, April--

"Dear Ethie: I reckon mother is right, after all. She generally is, you know, so we may as well be resigned, and believe it wicked for cousins to marry each other. Of course I can never like Nettie as I have liked you, and I feel a twinge every time I remember the dear old times. But what must be must, and there's no use fretting. Do you remember old Colonel Markham's nephew from out West--the one who wore the short pants and the rusty crape on his hat when he visited his uncle, in Chicopee, some years ago? I mean the chap who helped you over the fence the time you stole the colonel's apples. He has become a member of Congress, and quite a big gun for the West, at least, mother thinks. He called on her to-day with a message from Mrs. Woodhull, but I did not see him. He goes up to Chicopee to-morrow, I believe. He is looking for a wife, they say, and mother thinks it would be a good match for you, as you could go to Washington next winter and queen it over them all. But don't, Ethie, don't for thunder's sake! It fairly makes me faint to think of you belonging to another, even though you may never belong to me. Yours always, Frank."

There was a dark, defiant look in Ethelyn's face as she applied the match to this letter, and then watched it blacken and crisp upon the hearth. How well she remembered the day when she received it--the dark, dismal April day, when the rain which dropped so fast from the leaden clouds, seemed weeping for her, who could not weep then, so complete was her humiliation, so utter her desolation. That was not quite three months ago, and so much had happened since then as the result of that M.C.'s visit to Chicopee. He was there again, this morning, an inmate of the great yellow house, with the large, old-fashioned brass knocker, and, by just putting aside her curtain, Ethelyn could see the very window of the chamber where he slept. But Ethelyn had other matters in hand, and if she thought at all of that window whose shutters were rarely opened except when Colonel Markham had, as now, an honored guest, it was with a faint shudder of terror, and she went on destroying mementos which were only a mockery of the past. One little note, the first ever received from Frank, after a, memorable morning in the huckleberry hills, she could not burn. It was only a line, and, if read by a stranger, would convey no particular meaning; so she laid it aside with the lock of light, soft hair, which clung to her fingers with a kind of caressing touch, and brought to her hot eyelids a mist which cooled their feverish heat. And now nothing remained of the treasures but a tiny tortoise-shell box, where, in its bed of pink cotton, lay a little ring, with "Ethie" marked upon it. It was too small for the finger it once encircled, for Ethel was but a child when first she wore it. Her hands were larger; plumper, now, and it would not pass the second joint of her finger, though she exerted all her strength to push it on, taking a kind of savage delight in the pain it caused her, and feeling that she was thus revenging herself on someone, she hardly knew or cared whom. At last, however, with a quick, jerking motion she drew it off, and covering her face with her hands, moaned bitterly:

"It hurts! it hurts! just as the bonds hurt which are closing around my heart. Oh! Frank, Frank, it was cruel to serve me so."

There was a step in the hall below. Aunt Barbara was coming to waken Ethelyn, and, with a spring, the young girl bounded to her feet, swept her hands twice across her face, and, shedding back from her forehead her wealth of bright brown hair, laughingly confronted the good woman, who, in the same breath, expressed her surprise that her niece was once up without being called, and her wonder at the peculiar odor pervading the apartment.

"Smells if all the old newspapers in the barrel up garret had been burnt at once," she said; but the fireplace, which lay in shadow, told no tales, and Aunt Barbara never suspected the pain tugging at the heart of the girl, whose cheeks glowed with an unnatural red as she dashed hot water over neck, and arms, and face, playfully plashing a few large drops upon her aunt's white apron, and asking if there was not an old adage, "Blessed is the bride the sun shines on." "If so, I must be greatly blessed," she said, pushing open the eastern shutter, and letting in a flood of yellow sunlight.

"The day bids fair to be a scorcher. I hope it will grow cool this evening. A crowded party is so terrible when one feels hot and uncomfortable, and the millers and horn-bugs come in so thickly, and I always get so red in the face. Please, auntie, you twist up my hair in a flat knot--no matter how. I don't seem to have any strength in my arms this morning, and my head is all in a whirl. It must be the weather," and, with a long, panting breath, Ethelyn sank, half fainting, into a chair, while her frightened aunt ran for water, and camphor, and cologne, hoping Ethelyn was not coming down with fever, or any other dire complaint, on this her wedding day.

"It is the weather, most likely, and the awful amount of sewing you've done these last few weeks," said Aunt Barbara; and Ethelyn suffered her to think so, though she herself had a far different theory with regard to that almost fainting fit, which served as an excuse for her unusual pallor, for her listless apathy, and her want of appetite, even for the flaky rolls, and the delicious strawberries, and thick, yellow cream which Aunt Barbara put before her.

She was not hungry, she said, as she turned over the berries with her spoon, and pecked at the snowy rolls. By and by she might want something, perhaps, and then Betty would make her a slice of toast to stay her stomach till the late dinner they were to have on Aunt Van Buren's account--that lady always professing to be greatly shocked at the early dinners in Chicopee, and generally managing, during her visits home, to change entirely the ways and customs of Aunt Barbara Bigelow's well-ordered household.

"I wish she was not coming, or anybody else. Getting married is a bore!" Ethelyn exclaimed, while Aunt Barbara looked curiously enough at her, wondering, for the first time, if the girl's heart were really in this marriage, which for weeks had been agitating the feminine portion of Chicopee, and for which so great preparations had been made.

Wholly honest and truthful and sincere herself, Aunt Barbara seldom suspected wrong in others, and so when Ethelyn, one April night, after a drive around the road which encircles Pordunk Pond, came to her and said, "Congratulate me, auntie, I am to be Mrs. Judge Markham," she had believed all was well, and that as sister Sophia Van Buren, of Boston, had so often averred, there was not, nor ever had been, anything serious between dandyish Frank, Mrs. Van Buren's only son, who parted his curly hair in the middle, and the high-spirited, impulsive Ethelyn, whose eyes shone like stars as she told of her engagement, and whose hand was icy cold as she held it up to the lamp-light to show the large diamond which flashed from the fourth finger as proof of what she said. The stone itself was of the first water, but the setting was old, so old that a connoisseur in such matters might wonder why Judge Markham had chosen such a ring as the seal of his betrothal. Ethelyn knew why, and the softest, kindliest feeling she had experienced for her promised husband was awakened when he told her of the fair young sister whose name was Daisy, and who for many years had slept on the Western prairie beneath the blossoms whose name she bore. This young girl, loving God with all her soul, loved too all the beautiful things he had made, and rejoiced in them as so much given her to enjoy. Brought up in the far West, where the tastes of the people were simpler than those of our Eastern neighbors, it was strange, he said, how strong a passion she possessed for gems and precious stones, especially the diamond. To have for her own a ring like one she once saw upon a grand Chicago lady was her great ambition, and knowing this the brother hoarded carefully his own earnings, until enough was saved to buy the coveted ring, which he brought to his young sister on her fourteenth birthday. But death even then had cast its shadow around her, and the slender fingers soon grew too small for the ring, which she nevertheless kept constantly by her, admiring its brilliancy, and flashing it in the sunlight for the sake of the rainbow hues it gave. And when, at last, she lay dying in her brother's arms, with her golden head upon his breast, she had given back the ring, and said, "I am going, Richard, where there are far more beautiful things than this: 'for eye hath not seen, neither hath it entered into the heart of man, the things prepared for those who love Him,' and I do love Him, brother, oh! so much, and feel His arms around me now as sensibly as I feel yours. His will stay after yours are removed, and I am done with earth; but keep the ring, Brother Dick, and when in after years you love some pure young girl as well as you love me, only different--some girl who will prize such things, and is worthy of it--give it to her, and tell her it was Daisy's; tell her for me, and that I bade her love you, as you deserve to be loved."

All this Richard Markham had said to Ethelyn as they stood for a few minutes upon the beach of the pond, with its waters breaking softly upon the sands at their feet, and the young spring moon shining down upon them like Daisy's eyes, as the brother described them when they last looked on him. There was a picture of Daisy in their best room at home, an oil painting made by a traveling artist, Richard said, and some day Ethelyn would see it, for she had promised to be his wife, and the engagement ring--Daisy's ring--was on her finger, sparkling in the moonbeam, just as it used to sparkle when the dead girl held it in the light. It was a superb diamond--even Frank, with all his fastidiousness, would admit that, Ethelyn thought, her mind more, alas! on

Frank and his opinion than on what her lover was saying to her, of his believing that she was pure and good as Daisy could have desired, that Daisy would approve his choice, if she only knew, as perhaps she did; he could not help feeling that she was there with them, looking into their hearts--that the silvery light resting so calmly on the silent water was the halo of her invisible presence blessing their betrothal. This was a good deal for Richard Markham to say, for he was not given to poetry, or sentiment, or imagery, but Ethelyn's face and Ethelyn's eyes had played strange antics with the staid, matter-of-fact man of Western Iowa, and stirred his blood as it had never been stirred before. He did fancy his angel-sister was there; but when he said so to Ethelyn she started with a shiver, and asked to be driven home, for she did not care to have even dead eyes looking into her heart, where the fires of passion were surging and swelling, like some hidden volcano, struggling to be free. She knew she was doing wrong--knew she was not the pure maiden whom Daisy would have chosen--was not worthy to be the bride of Daisy's brother; but she must do something or die, and as she did not care to die, she pledged her hand with no heart in it, and hushing the voice of conscience clamoring so loudly against what she was doing, walked back across the yellow sand, beneath the spring moonlight, to where the carriage waited, and, in comparative silence, was driven to Aunt Barbara's gate.

This was the history of the ring, and here, as well as elsewhere, we may tell Ethelyn's history up to the time when, on her bridal day, she sat with Aunt Barbara at the breakfast table, idly playing with her spoon and occasionally sipping the fragrant coffee. The child of Aunt Barbara's half-sister, she inherited none of the so-called Bigelow estate which had come to the two daughters, Aunt Barbara and Aunt Sophia, from their mother's family. But the Bigelow blood of which Aunt Sophy Van Buren was so proud was in her veins, and so to this aunt she was an object of interest, and even value, though not enough so to warrant that lady in taking her for her own when, eighteen years before our story opens, her mother, Mrs. Julia Bigelow Grant, had died. This task devolved on Aunt Barbara, whose great motherly heart opened at once to the little orphan who had never felt a mother's loss, so faithful and true had Aunt Barbara been to her trust. Partly because she did not wish to seem more selfish than her sister, and partly because she really liked the bright, handsome child who made Aunt Barbara's home so cheery, Mrs. Dr. Van Buren of Boston, insisted upon superintending the little Ethelyn's education, and so, when only twelve years of age, Ethelyn was taken from the old brick house under the elms, which Mrs. Dr. Van Buren of Boston despised as the "district school where Tom, Dick, and Harry congregated," and transplanted to the highly select and very expensive school taught by Madame--, in plain sight of Beacon Street and Boston Common. And so, as Ethelyn increased in stature, she grew also in wisdom and knowledge, both of books and manners, and the style of the great world around her. Mrs. Dr. Van Buren's house was the resort both of the fashionable and literary people, with a sprinkling of the religious, for the great lady affected everything which could effect her interest. Naturally generous, her name was conspicuous on all subscription lists and charitable associations, while the lady herself owned a pew in ---- Church, where she was a regular attendant, together with her only son, Frank, who was taught to kneel and respond in the right places and bow in the creed, and then, after church, required to give a synopsis of the sermon, by way of proving that his mind had not been running off after the dancing school he attended during the week, under his mother's watchful supervision. Mrs. Van Buren meant to be a model mother, and bring up her boy as a model man, and so she gave him every possible advantage of books and teachers, while far in the future floated the possibility that she might some day reign at the White House, not as the President's wife--this could not be, she knew, for the man who had made her Mrs. Dr. Van Buren of Boston slept in the shadow of a very tall monument out at Mount Auburn, and the turf was growing fresh and green over his head. So if she went to Washington, as she fondly hoped she might, it would be as the President's mother; but when examination after examination found Frank at the foot of his class, and teacher after teacher said he could not learn, she gave up the presidential chair, and contenting herself with a seat in Congress, asked that great pains should be taken to bring out the talent for debate and speech-making which she was sure Frank possessed; but when even this failed, and nineteen times out of twenty Frank could get no farther than "My name is Norval, on the Grampian Hills," she yielded the M.C. too, and set herself to make him a gentleman, polished, refined, and cultivated--one, in short, who was au fait with all that fashionable society required; and here she succeeded better. Frank was perfectly at home on the dancing floor or in the saloons of gaiety, or the establishment of a fashionable tailor, so that when Ethelyn, at twelve, went down to Boston, she found her tall, slender, light-haired cousin of sixteen a perfect dandy, with a capability and a disposition to criticise and laugh at whatever there was of gaucherie in her country manners and country dress. In some things the two were of mutual benefit to each other. Ethelyn, who could conquer any lesson however difficult, helped thick-headed, indolent Frank in his studies, translating his hard passages in Virgil, working out his problems in mathematics, and even writing, or at least revising and correcting, his compositions, while he in return gave her lessons in etiquette as practiced by the Boston girls, teaching her how to polka a waltz gracefully, so he would not be ashamed to introduce her as his cousin, he said, at the children's parties which they attended together. It was not strange that Frank Van Buren should admire a girl as bright and piquant and pretty as his cousin Ethelyn, but it was strange that she should idolize him, bearing patiently with all his criticisms, trying hard to please him, and feeling more than repaid for her exertions by a word of praise or commendation from her exacting teacher, who, viewing her at first as a poor relation, was inclined to be exacting, if not overbearing, in his demands. But as time passed on all this was changed, and the well-developed girl of fifteen, whom so many noticed and admired, would no longer be patronized by the young man Frank, who, finding himself in danger of being snubbed, as he termed Ethelyn's grand way of putting him down, suddenly awoke to the fact that he loved his high-spirited cousin, and he told her so one hazy day, when they were in Chicopee, and had wandered up to a ledge of rocks in the huckleberry hills which overlooked the town.

"They might as well make a sure thing of it," he said, in his off-hand way. "If she liked him and he liked her, they would clinch the bargain at once, even if they were so young." And so, when they went down the hill back to the shadow of the elm trees, where Mrs. Dr. Van Buren sat cooling herself and reading "Vanity Fair," there was a tiny ring on Ethelyn's finger, and she had pledged herself to be Frank's wife some day in the future.

Frank had promised to tell his mother, for Ethelyn would have no concealment; and so, holding up her hand and pointing to the ring, he said, more in jest than earnest:

"Look, mother, Ethie and I are engaged. If you have any objections, state them now, or ever after hold your peace."

He did not think proper to explain either to his mother or Ethie that this was his second serious entanglement, and that the ring had been bought before for a pretty milliner girl, at least six years his senior, whose acquaintance he had made at Nahant the summer previous, and whom he had forgotten when he learned that to her taste his mother was indebted for the stylish bonnet she sported every season. Frank generally had some love affair in hand--it was a part of his nature; and as he was not always careful in his choice, the mother had occasionally felt a twinge of fear lest, after all her care, some terrible mésalliance should be thrust upon her by her susceptible son. So she listened graciously to the news of his betrothal--nay, she was pleased with it, as for the time being it would divert his mind and keep him out of mischief. That he would eventually marry Ethelyn was impossible, for his bride must be rich; but Ethelyn answered the purpose now, and could easily be disposed of when other and better game appeared. So the scheming woman smiled, and said "it was not well for cousins to marry and even if it were, they were both too young to know their minds, and would do well to keep their engagement a secret for a time," and then returned to Becky Sharp, while Frank went to sleep upon the lounge, and Ethelyn stole off upstairs to dream over her happiness, which was as real to her as such a thing could well be to an impulsive, womanly girl of fifteen summers. She, at least, was in earnest, and as time passed on Frank seemed to be in earnest, too, devoting himself wholly to his cousin, whose influence over him was so great that he was fast becoming what Aunt Barbara called a man, while his mother began again to have visions of a seat in Congress, and brilliant speeches, which would find their way to Boston and be read and admired in the circles in which she moved.

And so the days and years wore on until Frank was a man of twenty-four--a third-rate practitioner, too, whose sign, "Frank Van Buren, Attorney-at-law," etc., looked very fresh and respectable in front of the office on Washington Street, and Frank himself began to have thoughts of claiming Ethelyn's promise and having a home of his own. He would not live with his mother, he said; it was more independent to be alone; and then, from some things he had discovered in his bride-elect, he had an uneasy feeling that possibly the brown of Ethelyn's eyes might not wholly harmonize with the gray of his mother's, "for Ethie was spunky as the old Nick," he argued with himself, while "for perversity and self-conceit his mother could not be beaten." It was better they should keep up two households, his mother seeing to both, and if need be, supplying the wants of both. To do Frank justice, he had some very correct notions with regard to domestic happiness, and had he been poor and dependent upon his own exertions he might have been an average husband; at least he would have gotten on well with Ethelyn, whose stronger nature would have upheld his and been like a supporting prop to a feeble timber. As it was, he drew many pleasing pictures of the home which was to be his and Ethie's. Now it was in the city, near to his mother's and Mrs. General Tophevie, his mother's intimate friend, whose house was the open sesame to the crême de la crême of Boston society; but oftener it was a rose-embowered cottage, of easy access to the city, where he could have Ethie all to himself when his day's labor was over, and where the skies would not be brighter than Ethie's eyes as she welcomed him home at night, leaning over the gate in the pale buff muslin he liked so much, with rosebuds in her hair.

He had seen her thus so often in fancy, that the picture had become a reality, and refused to be erased at once from the mental canvas, when, in January, Miss Nettie Hudson, niece to Mrs. General Tophevie, came from Philadelphia, and at once took prestige of everything on the strength of the one hundred thousand dollars of which she was sole heiress. The Hudson blood was a mixture of blacksmith's and shoemaker's, and peddler's too, it was said; but that was far back in the past. The Hudsons of the present day scarcely knew whether peddler were spelled with two d's or one. They bought their shoes at the most fashionable shops, and could, if they chose, have their horses shod with gold, and so the handsome Nettie reigned supreme as belle. The moment Mrs. Dr. Van Buren saw her, she recognized her daughter-in-law, the future Mrs. Frank, and Ethie's fate was sealed. There had been times when Mrs. Dr. Van Buren thought it possible that Ethelyn might, after all, be the most favored of women, the wife of her son. These times were at Saratoga, and Newport, and Nahant, where Ethelyn Grant was more sought after than any young lady there, and where the proud woman herself took pride in talking of "my niece," hinting once, when Ethelyn's star was at its height, of a childish affaire du coeur between the young lady and her son, and insinuating that it might yet amount to something. She changed her mind when Nettie came with her one hundred thousand dollars, and showed a willingness to be admired by Frank. That childish affaire du coeur was a very childish affair, indeed; she never gave it a moment's thought herself--she greatly doubted if Frank had ever been in earnest, and if Ethelyn had led him into an entanglement, she would not, of course, hold him to his promise if he wished to be released. He must have a rich wife to support him in his refined tastes and luxurious habits, for her own fortune was not so great as many supposed. She might need it all herself, as she was far from being old, and then again it was wicked for cousins to marry each other. It did not matter if the mothers were only half-sisters; there was the same blood in the veins of each, and it would not do at all, even if Ethelyn's affections were enlisted, which Mrs. Van Buren greatly doubted.

This was what Mrs. Dr. Van Buren said to Ethelyn, after a stormy interview with Frank, who had at first sworn roundly that he would not give Ethie up, then had thanked his mother not to meddle with his business, then bidden her "go to thunder," and finally, between a cry and a blubber, said he should always like Ethie best if he married a hundred Netties. This was in the morning, and the afternoon train had carried Mrs. Dr. Van Buren to Chicopee, where Ethelyn's glowing face flashed a bright welcome when she came, but was white and pallid as the face of a corpse when the voluminous skirts of Mrs. Van Buren's poplin dress passed through the gate next day and disappeared in the direction of the depot. Aunt Barbara was not at home--she had gone to visit a friend in Albany; and so Ethelyn met and fought with her pain alone, stifling it as best she could, and succeeding so well that Aunt Barbara, on her return, never suspected the fierce storm which Ethelyn had passed through during her absence, or dreamed how anxiously the young girl watched and waited for some word from Frank which should say that he was ready to defy his mother, and abide by his first promise. But no such letter came, and at last, when she could bear the suspense no longer, Ethelyn wrote herself to her recreant lover, asking if it were really so that hereafter their lives lay apart from each other. If such was his wish, she was content, she said, and Frank Van Buren, who could not detect the air of superb scorn which breathed in every line of that letter, felt somehow aggrieved that "Ethie should take it so easy," and relieved too, that with her he should have no trouble, as he had anticipated. He was getting used to Nettie, and getting to like her, too, for her manner toward him was far more agreeable than Ethie's brusque way of manifesting her impatience at his lack of manliness. It was inexplicable how Ethie could care for one so greatly her inferior, both mentally and physically, but it would seem that she loved him all the more for the very weakness which made her nature a necessity of his, and the bitterest pang she had ever felt came with the answer which Frank sent back to her letter, and which the reader has seen.

It was all over now, settled, finished, and two days after she hunted up Aunt Barbara's spectacles for her, and then sat very quiet while the old lady read Aunt Sophia's letter, announcing Frank's engagement with Miss Nettie Hudson, of Philadelphia. Aunt Barbara knew of Ethelyn's engagement with Frank, but like her sister at the time of its occurrence, she had esteemed it mere child's play. Later, however, as she saw how they clung to each other, she had thought it possible that something might come of it, but as Ethelyn was wholly reticent on that subject, it had never been mentioned between them. When, however, the news of Frank's second engagement came, Aunt Barbara looked over her spectacles straight at the girl, who, for any sign she gave, might have been a block of marble, so rigid was every muscle of her face, and even the tone of her voice as she said:

"I am glad Aunt Sophia is suited. Frank will be pleased with anything."

"She does not care for him and I am glad, for he is not half smart enough for her," was Aunt Barbara's mental comment, as she laid the letter by for a second reading, and then told her niece, as the last item of news, that old Captain Markham's nephew had come, and they were making a great ado over him now that he was a member of Congress, and a Judge, too. They had asked the Howells and Grangers and the Carters there to tea for the next day, she said, adding that she and Ethelyn were also invited. "They want to be polite to him," old Mrs. Markham said. Aunt Barbara continued, "but for my part, if I were he, I should not care much for politeness that comes so late. I remember when he was here ten years ago, on such a matter, and they fairly acted as if they were ashamed of him then; but titles make a difference. He's an Honorable now, and the old Captain is mighty proud of him."

What Aunt Barbara had said was strictly true, for there had been a time when proud old Captain Markham ignored his brother's family living on the far prairies of the West; but when the eldest son, Richard, called for him, had become a growing man, as boys out West are apt to do, rising from justice of the peace to a member of the State Legislature, then to a judgeship, and finally to a seat in Congress, and all before he was quite thirty-two, the Captain's tactics changed, and a most cordial letter, addressed to "My dear nephew," and signed "Your affectionate uncle," was sent to Washington, urging a visit from the young man ere he returned to Iowa.

And that was how Richard Markham, M.C., came to be in Chicopee at the precise time when Ethelyn's heart was bleeding at every pore, and ready to seize upon any new excitement which would divert it from its pain. She remembered well the time he had once before visited Chicopee. She was a little girl of ten, fleeing across the meadow-land from a maddened cow, when a tall, athletic young man had come to her rescue, standing between her and danger, helping her over the fence, picking up the apron full of apples which she had been purloining from the Captain's orchard, and even pinning together a huge rent made in her dress by catching it upon a protruding splint as she sprang to the ground. She was too much frightened to know whether he had been wholly graceful in his endeavors to serve her, and too thankful for her escape to think that possibly her torn dress was the result of his rather awkward handling. She remembered only the dark, handsome face which bent so near to hers, the brown, curly head actually bumping against her own, as he stooped to gather the stolen apples. She remembered, too, the kindly voice which asked if "her aunt would scold," while the large, red hands pinned together the unsightly seam, and she liked the Westerner, as the people of Chicopee called the stranger who had recently come among them. Frank was in Chicopee then, fishing on the river, when her mishaps occurred; and once after that, when walking with him, she had met Richard Markham, who bowed modestly and passed on, never taking his hands from his pockets where they were planted so firmly, and never touching his hat as Frank said a gentleman would have done.

"Isn't he handsome?" Ethelyn had asked, and Frank had answered, "Looks well enough, though anybody with half an eye would know he was a codger from the West. His pants are a great deal too short; and look at his coat--at least three years behind the fashion; and such a hat, with that rusty old band of crape around it. Wonder if he is in mourning for his grandmother. Oh, my! we boys would hoot him in Boston. He's what I call a gawky."

That settled it with Ethelyn. If fourteen-year-old Frank Van Buren, whose pants and coats and neckties and hats were always the latest make, said that Richard Markham was a gawky, he was one, and henceforth during his stay in Chicopee, the Western young man was regarded by Ethelyn with a feeling akin to pity for his benighted condition. Aunt Barbara's pew was very near to Captain Markham's, and Richard, who was not much of a churchman, and as often as any way lounged upon the faded damask curtains, instead of standing up, often met Ethelyn's brown eyes fixed curiously upon him, but never dreamed that she regarded him as a species of heathen, whom it would be a pious act to Christianize. Richard rarely thought of himself at all, or if he did, it was with a feeling that he "was well enough "; that if his mother and "the neighbors" were satisfied with him, as he knew they were, he ought to be satisfied with himself. So he had no suspicion of the severe criticism passed upon him by the little girl who read the service so womanly, he thought, eating caraway and lozenges between times, and whose face he carried in memory back to his prairie home, associating her always with the graceful dark-brown heifer bearing so strong a resemblance to the cow which had so frightened Ethelyn on the day of his first introduction to her.

But he forgot her in the excitement which followed, when he began to grow rapidly, as only Western men can grow, and we doubt if she had been in his mind for years until her name was mentioned by Mrs. Dr. Van Buren, who saw in him a most eligible match for her niece. He was well connected--own nephew to Captain Markham, and first cousin to Mrs. Senator Woodhull, of New York, who kept a suite of servants for herself and husband, and had the finest turn-out in the Park. Yes, he would do nicely for Ethelyn and by way of quieting her conscience, which kept whispering that she had not been altogether just to her niece, Mrs. Dr. Van Buren packed her trunk and took the train for Chicopee the very day of Mrs. Captain Markham's tea party.

Ethelyn was going, and she looked very pretty in her dark-green silk, with the bit of soft, rich lace at the throat and the scarlet ribbon in her hair. She was not dressed for effect. She cared very little, in fact, what impression she made upon the Western Judge, though she did wonder if, as a Judge, he was much improved from the raw young man whom Frank had called a "gawky." He was standing with his elbow upon the mantel talking to Susie Granger, when Ethelyn entered Mrs. Markham's parlor; one foot was carelessly crossed over the other, so that only the toe of the boot touched the carpet, while his hand grasped his large handkerchief rather awkwardly. He was not at ease with the ladies; he had never been very much accustomed to their society. He did not know what to say to them, and Susie's saucy black eyes and sprightly manner evidently embarrassed and abashed him. That vocabulary of small talk so prevalent in society, and a limited knowledge of which is rather necessary to one's getting on well with everybody, were unknown to him, and he was casting about for some way to escape from his companion, when Ethelyn was introduced, and his mind went back to the stolen apples and the torn dress which he had pinned together.

Judge Markham was a tall, finely formed man, with deep hazel eyes, which could be very stern or very soft in their expression, just as his mood happened to be. But the chief attraction of his face was his smile, which changed his entire expression, making him very handsome, as Ethelyn thought, when he stood for a moment holding her hand between both his broad palms and chatting familiarly with her as with an old acquaintance. He could talk to her better than to Susie Granger, for Ethie, though neither very deep nor learned, was fond of books and tolerably well versed in the current literature of the day. Besides that, she had a faculty of seeming to know more than she really did and so the impression left upon the Judge's mind, when the little party was over and he had returned from escorting Ethelyn to her door, was that Miss Grant was far superior to any girl he had ever met since Daisy died, and like the Judge in Whittier's "Maud Muller," he whistled snatches of an old love tune he had not whistled in years, as he went slowly back to his uncle's, and thought strange thoughts for him, the grave old bachelor who had said he should never marry. He was not looking for a wife, as rumor intimated, but he dreamed of Ethelyn Grant that night, and called upon her the next day, and the next, until the village began to gossip, and Mrs. Dr. Van Buren was in an ecstasy of delight, talking openly of the delightful time her niece would have in Washington the next winter, and predicting for her a brilliant career as reigning belle, and even hinting the possibility of her taking a house so as to entertain her Boston friends.

And Ethelyn herself had many and varied feelings on the subject, the strangest of which was a perverse desire to let Frank know that she did not care--that her heart was not broken by his desertion, and that there were those who prized her even if he did not. She had criticised Judge Markham very severely. She had weighed him in the balance with Frank, and found him sadly, wanting in all those little points which she considered as marks of culture and good breeding. He was not a ladies' man; he was even worse than that, for he was sometimes positively rude and ungentlemanly, as she thought, when he would open a gate or a door and pass through it first himself instead of holding it deferentially for her, as Frank would have done. He did not know how to swing his cane, or touch his hat, or even bow as Frank Van Buren did; while the cut of his coat, if not six, was at least two years behind the times, and he did not seem to know it either. All these things Ethelyn wrote against him; but the account was more than balanced by the seat in Congress, the anticipated winter in Washington, the great wealth he was said to possess, the high estimation in which she knew he was held, and the keen pang of disappointment from which she was suffering. This last really did the most to turn the scale in Richard's favor, for, like many a poor, deluded girl, she fancied that marrying another was the surest way to forget a past which it was not pleasant to remember. She respected Judge Markham highly, and knew that in everything pertaining to a noble manhood he was worth a dozen Franks, even if he never had been to dancing school, and did not obsequiously pick up the handkerchief which she purposely dropped to see what he would do. And so, when Aunt Sophia had gone back to the city, and Judge Markham was in a few days to return to his Western home, she rode with him around the Pond, and when she came back the dead Daisy's ring was upon her finger and she was a promised wife. A dozen times since then she had been tempted to write to Richard Markham, asking to be released from her engagement; for, bad as she has thus far appeared to the reader, there were many noble traits in her character, and she shrank from wronging the man of whom she knew she was not worthy.

But the deference paid her as Mrs. Judge Markham-elect, the delight of Aunt Sophia, the approbation of Aunt Barbara, the letter of congratulation sent her by Mrs. Senator Woodhull, Richard's cousin, and more than all, Frank's discomfiture, as evinced by the complaining note he sent her, prevailed to keep her to her promise, and the bridegroom, when he came in June to claim her hand, little guessed how heavy was the heart which lay in the bosom of the young girl so passively suffering his caresses, but whose lips never moved in response to the kiss he pressed upon them.

She was very shy, he thought--more so, even, than when he saw her last; but he loved her just as well, and never suspected that, when on the first evening of his arrival he sat with his arm around her, wondering a little what made her so silent, she was burning with mortification because the coat he wore was the very same she had criticised last spring, hoping in her heart of hearts that long before he came to her again it might find its proper place, either in the sewing society or with some Jewish vender of old clothes. Yet here it was again, and her head was resting against it, while her heart beat almost audibly, and her voice was even petulant in its tone as she answered her lover's questions. Ethelyn was making a terrible mistake, and she knew it, hating herself for her duplicity, and vaguely hoping that something would happen to save her from the fate she so much dreaded. But nothing did happen, and it was now too late to retract herself. The bridal trousseau was prepared under Mrs. Van Buren's supervision, the bridal guests were bidden, the bridal tour was planned, the bridegroom had arrived, and she would keep her word if she died in the attempt.

And so we find her on her bridal morning wishing nobody was coming, and denouncing getting married "a bore," while Aunt Barbara looked at her in surprise, wondering if everything were right. In spite of her ill humor, she was very handsome that morning in her white cambric wrapper, with just a little color in her cheeks and her heavy hair pushed back in behind her ears and twisted under the silk net. Ethelyn cared little for her looks--at least not then; by and by she might, when it was time for Mrs. Dr. Van Buren to arrive with Frank and Nettie Hudson, whom she had never seen. She should want to look her very best then, but now it did not matter, even if her bridegroom was distant not an eighth of a mile, and would in all probability be coming in ere long. She wished he would stay away--she would rather not see him till night; and she experienced a feeling of relief when, about nine o'clock, Mrs. Markham's maid brought her a little note which read as follows:

"DARLING ETHIE:

"You must not think it strange if I do not come to you this morning, for I am suffering from one of my blinding headaches, and can scarcely see to write you this. I shall be better by night. Yours lovingly,

"RICHARD MARKHAM."

Ethelyn was sitting upon the piazza steps, arranging a bouquet, when the note was brought to her; and as it was some trouble to put all the roses from her lap, she sent the girl for a pencil, and on the back of the note wrote hastily:

"It does not matter, as you would only be in the way, and I have something of a headache, too. "E. GRANT."

"Take this back to Judge Markham," she said to the girl, and then resumed her bouquet-making, wondering if every bride-elect were as wretched as herself, or if to any other maiden of twenty the world had ever looked so desolate and dreary, as it did to her this morning.

CHAPTER II: THE VAN BUREN SET

Captain Markham's carryall, which Jake, the hired man, had brushed up wonderfully for the occasion, had gone over to West Chicopee after the party from Boston--Mrs. Dr. Van Buren, with Frank, and his betrothed, Miss Nettie Hudson, from Philadelphia. Others had been invited from the city, but one after another their regrets had come to Ethelyn, who would gladly have excused the entire set, Aunt Van Buren, Frank and all, though she confessed to herself a great deal of curiosity with regard to Miss Nettie, whom she had never seen; neither had she met Frank since the dissolution of their engagement, for though she had been in Boston, where most of her dresses were made, Mrs. Dr. Van Buren had wisely arranged that Frank should be absent from home. She was herself not willing to risk a meeting between him and Ethelyn until matters were too well adjusted to admit of a change, for Frank had more than once shown signs of rebellion. He was in a more quiescent state now, having made up his mind that what could not be cured must be endured, and as he had sensibility enough to feel very keenly the awkwardness of meeting Ethelyn under present circumstances, and as Miss Nettie was really very fond of him, and he, after a fashion, was fond of her, he was in the best of spirits when he stepped from the train at West Chicopee and handed his mother and Nettie into the spacious carryall of which he had made fun as a country ark, while they rode slowly toward Aunt Barbara Bigelow's. Everything was in readiness for them. The large north chamber was aired and swept and dusted, and only little bars of light came through the closed shutters, and the room looked very cool and nice, with its fresh muslin curtains looped back with blue, its carpet of the same cool shade, its pretty chestnut furniture, its snowbank of a bed, and the tasteful bouquets which Ethelyn had arranged--Ethelyn, who lingered longer in this room than the other one across the hall, the bridal chamber, where the ribbons which held the curtains were white, and the polished marble of the bureau and washstand, sent a shiver through her veins whenever she looked in there. She was in her own cozy chamber now, and the silken hair, which in the early morning had been twisted under her net, was bound in heavy braids about her head, while a pearl comb held it in its place, and a half-opened rose was fastened just behind her ear. She had hesitated some time in her choice of a dress, vacillating between a pale buff, which Frank had always admired, and a delicate blue muslin, in which Judge Markham had once said she looked so pretty. The blue had won the day, for Ethelyn felt that she owed some concession to the man whose kind note she had treated so cavalierly that morning, and so she wore the blue for him, feeling glad of the faint, sick feeling which kept the blood from rushing too hotly to her face, and made her fairer and paler than her wont. She knew that she was very handsome when her toilet was made, and that was one secret of the assurance with which she went forward to meet Nettie Hudson when at last the carryall stopped before the gate.

Mrs. Dr. Van Buren was tired, and hot, and dusty, and as she was always a little cross when in this condition, she merely kissed Ethelyn once, and shaking hands with Aunt Barbara, went directly to the north chamber, asking that a cup of tea might be made for her dinner instead of the coffee whose fragrant odor met her olfactories as she stepped into the house. First, however, she introduced Nettie, who after glancing at Ethelyn, turned her eyes wonderingly upon Frank, thinking his greeting of his cousin rather more demonstrative than was exactly becoming even if they were cousins, and had been, as Mrs. Dr. Van Buren affirmed, just like brother and sister. That was no reason why Frank should have wound his arm around her waist, and kept it there, while he kissed her twice, and brought such a bright color to her cheeks. Miss Nettie cared just enough for Frank Van Buren to be jealous of him. She wanted all his attentions herself, and so the little blonde was in something of a pet as she followed on into the house, and twisted her hat strings into a hard knot, which Frank had to disentangle for her, just as he had to kiss away the wrinkle which had gathered on her forehead. She was a beautiful little creature, scarcely larger than a child of twelve, with a pleading, helpless look in her large, blue eyes which seemed to be saying: "Look at me; speak to me, won't you?--notice me a little."

She was just the one to be made a tool of; and Ethelyn readily saw that she had been as clay in Mrs. Van Buren's skillful hands.

"Pretty, very pretty, but decidedly a nonentity and a baby," was Ethelyn's mental comment, and she felt something like contempt for Frank, who, after loving and leaning on her, could so easily turn to weak little Nettie Hudson.

At the sight of Frank and the sound of his voice, she had felt all the olden feeling rushing back to her heart; but when, after Nettie had followed Mrs. Van Buren to her chamber, and she stood for a moment alone with him, he felt constrained to say something, and stammered out, "It's deuced mean, Ethie, to serve you so, and mother ought to be indicted. I hope you don't care much," all her pride and womanliness was roused and she answered promptly: "Of course, I don't care; do you think I would wish to marry Judge Markham if I were not all over that childish affair? You have not seen him yet. He is a splendid man."

Ethelyn felt better after paying this tribute to Richard Markham, and she liked him better, too, now that she had spoken for him, but Frank's reply, "Yes, mother told me so, but said there was a good deal of your Westernism about him yet," jarred on her feelings as she plucked the roses growing at the end of the piazza and crushed them, thorns and all, in her hands, feeling the smart less than the dull, heavy throbbing at her heart. Frank did not seem to her just as he used to be; he was the same polished dandy as of old, and just as careful to perform every little act of gallantry, but the something lacking which she had always felt to a certain extent was more perceptible now, and to herself she accused him of having degenerated since he had passed from her influence. She never dreamed of charging it to her interviews with Judge Markham, whose topics of conversation were so widely different from Frank's. She was not generous enough to concede anything in his favor, though she felt glad that Frank was not quite the same he had been--it would make the evening bridal before her easier to bear; and Ethelyn's eyes were brighter and her smiles more frequent as she sat down to dinner and answered Mrs. Van Buren's question: "Where is the Judge that he does not dine with us?"

"Sick, is he?" Mrs. Van Buren said, when told of his headache, while Frank remarked, "Sick of his bargain, maybe," laughing loudly at his own joke, while the others laughed in unison; and so the dinner passed off without that stiffness which Ethelyn had so much dreaded.

After it was over, Mrs. Dr. Van Buren felt better, and began to talk of the "Judge," and to ask if Ethelyn knew whether they would board or keep house in Washington the coming winter. Ethelyn did not know. She had never mentioned Washington to Richard Markham, and he had never guessed how much that prospective season at the capital had to do with her decision. That it would be hers to enjoy she had no shadow of doubt, but as she felt then she did not particularly care to keep up a household for the sake of entertaining her aunt, and possibly Frank and his wife, so she replied that she presumed "they should board, as it would be the short session--if he was re-elected they might consider the house."

"There may be a still higher honor in store for him than a re-election," Mrs. Van Buren said, and then proceeded to speak of a letter which she had received from a lady in Camden, who had once lived in Boston, and who had written congratulating her old friend upon her niece's good fortune. "There was no young man more popular in that section of the country than Judge Markham," she said, "and there had been serious talk of nominating him for governor. Some, however, thought him too young, and so they were waiting for a few years when he would undoubtedly be elected to the highest office in the State."

This piece of intelligence had greatly increased Mrs. Van Buren's respect for the lady-elect of Iowa's future governor, and she gave the item of news with a great deal of satisfaction, but did not tell that her correspondent had added, "It is a pity, though, that he does not know more of the usages of good society. Ethelyn is so refined and sensitive that she will be often shocked, no doubt, with the manners of the husband and his family."

This clause had troubled Mrs. Dr. Van Buren. She really liked Ethelyn, and now that she was out of Frank's way she liked her very much, and would do a good deal to serve her. She did not wish her to be unhappy, as she feared she might be from the sundry rumors which had reached her concerning that home out West, whither she was going. So, when, after dinner, they were alone for a few moments, she endeavored to impress upon her niece the importance of having an establishment of her own as soon as possible.

"It is not well for sons' wives to live with the mother," she said. "She did not mean that Nettie should live with her; and Ethelyn should at once insist upon a separate home; then, if she should see any little thing in her husband's manners which needed correcting, she could do it so much better away from his mother. I do not say that there is anything wrong in his manners," she continued, as she saw how painfully red Ethelyn was getting, "but it is quite natural there should be, living West as he does. You cannot expect prairie people to be as refined as Bostonians are; but you must polish him, dear. You know how; you have had Frank for a model so long; and even if he does not improve, people overlook a great deal in a member of Congress, and will overlook more in a governor, so don't feel badly, darling," and Mrs. Van Buren kissed tenderly the poor girl, before whom all the dreary loneliness of the future had arisen like a mountain, and whose heart even at that late hour would fain have drawn back if possible.

But when, by the way of soothing her, Mrs. Van Buren talked of the winter in Washington, and the honors which would always be accorded to her as the wife of an M.C., and then dwelt upon the possibility of her one day writing herself governor's lady, Ethelyn's girlish ambition was roused, and her vanity flattered, so that the chances were that even Frank would have been put aside for the future greatness, had he been offered to her.

It was five o'clock now, in the afternoon, nearly time for the bridal toilet to commence, and Mrs. Van Buren began to wonder "why the Judge had not appeared." He was better of his headache and up and around, the maid had reported, when at four she brought over the remainder of Mrs. Captain Markham's silver, which had not been sent in the morning, and then went back for extra napkins. There was no need to tell Ethelyn that "he was up and around," for she had known it ever since a certain shutter had been opened, and a man in his shirt-sleeves had appeared before the window and thrown water from the wash bowl upon the lilac bushes below. Ethelyn knew very well that old Mrs. Markham's servants were spoiled, that her domestic arrangements were not of the best kind, and that probably there was no receptacle for the dirty water except the ground; but she did not consider this, or reflect that aside from all other considerations the act was wholly like a man; she only thought it like him, Judge Markham, and feelings of shame and mortification, such as no woman likes to entertain with regard to her husband, began to rise and swell in her heart. In the excitement of her toilet, however, she forgot everything, even the ceremony for which she was dressing, and which came to her with a shiver when a bridesmaid announced that Captain Markham's carriage had just left his yard with a gentleman in it.

Judge Markham was on his way to his bridal.

CHAPTER III: RICHARD MARKHAM

He preferred to be called Richard by his friends and Mr. Markham by strangers--not that he was insensible to the prestige which the title of Judge or Honorable gave him, but he was a plain, matter-of-fact man, who had not been lifted off his balance, or grown dizzy by the rapidity with which he had risen in public favor. At home he was simply Dick to his three burly brothers, who were at once so proud and fond of him, while his practical, unpretending mother called him Richard, feeling, however, that it was very proper for the neighbors to give him the title of Judge. Of Mrs. Markham we shall have occasion to speak hereafter, so now we will only say that she saw no fault in her gifted son, and she was ready to do battle with anyone who should suggest the existence of a fault. Richard's wishes had never been thwarted, but rather deferred to by the entire family, and, as a natural consequence, he had come to believe that his habits and opinions were as nearly correct as they well could be. He had never mingled much in society--he was not fond of it; and the "quilting bees" and "sugar pulls" and "apple parings" which had prevailed in his neighborhood were not at all to his taste. He greatly preferred his books to the gayest of frolics, and thus he early earned for himself the sobriquet of "the old bachelor who hated girls"; all but Abigail Jones, the shoemaker's daughter, whose black eyes and bright red cheeks had proved too much for the grave, sober Richard. His first act of gallantry was performed for her, and even after he grew to be Judge his former companions never wearied of telling how, on the occasion of his first going home with the fair Abigail Jones from spelling school, he had kept at a respectful distance from her, and when the lights from her father's window became visible he remarked that "he guessed she would not be afraid to go the rest of the way alone," and abruptly bidding her good-night, ran back as fast as he could run. Whether this story were true or not, he was very shy of the girls, though the dark-eyed Abigail exerted over him so strong an influence that, at the early age of twenty he had asked her to be his wife, and she had answered yes, while his mother sanctioned the match, for she had known the Joneses in Vermont, and knew them for honest, thrifty people, whose daughter would make a faithful, economical wife for any man. But death came in to separate the lovers, and Abigail's cheeks grew redder still, and her eyes were strangely bright as the fever burned in her veins, until at last when the Indian-summer sun was shining down upon the prairies, they buried her one day beneath the late summer flowers, and the almost boy-widower wore upon his hat the band of crape which Ethelyn remembered as looking so rusty when, the year following, he came to Chicopee. Richard Markham believed that he had loved Abigail truly when she died, but he knew now that she was not the one he would have chosen in his mature manhood. She was suitable for him, perhaps, as he was when he lost her, but not as he was now, and it was long since he had ceased to visit her grave, or think of her with the feelings of sad regret which used to come over him when, at night, he lay awake listening to the moaning of the wind as it swept over the prairies, or watching the glittering stars, and wondering if she had found a home beyond them with Daisy, his only sister. There was nothing false about Richard Markham, and when he stood with Ethelyn upon the shore of Pordunk Pond, and asked her to be his wife, he told her of Abigail Jones, who had been two years older than himself, and to whom he was once engaged.

"But I did not give her Daisy's ring," he said; and he spoke very reverently as he continued, "Abigail was a good, sensible girl, and even if she hears what I am saying she will pardon me when I tell you that it did not seem to me that diamonds were befitting such as she; Daisy, I am sure, had a different kind of person in view when she made me keep the ring for the maiden who would prize such things, and who was worthy of it. Abigail was worthy, but there was not a fitness in giving it to her, neither would she have prized it; so I kept it in its little box with a curl of Daisy's hair. Had she become my wife, I might eventually have given it to her, but she died, and it was well. She would not have satisfied me now, and I should--"

He was going to add "should not have been what I am," but that would have savored too much of pride, and possibly of disrespect for the dead; so he checked himself, and while his rare, pleasant smile broke all over his beaming face, and his hazel eyes grew soft and tender in their expression, he said: "You, Ethelyn, seem to me the one Daisy would have chosen for a sister. You are quiet, and gentle, and pure like her, and I am so glad of the Providence which led me to Chicopee. They said I was looking for a wife, but I had no such idea. I never thought to marry until I met you that afternoon when you wore the pretty delaine, with the red ribbon in your hair. Do you remember it, Ethelyn?"

Ethelyn did not answer him at once. She was looking far off upon the water, where the moonlight lay sleeping, and revolving in her mind the expediency of being equally truthful with her future husband, and saying to him, "I, too, have loved, and been promised to another." She knew she ought to tell him this and she would, perhaps, have done so, for Ethie meant to be honest, and her heart was touched and softened by Richard's tender love for his sister; but when he was so unfortunate as to call the green silk which Madame--, in Boston, had made, a pretty delaine, and her scarlet velvet band a "red ribbon," her heart hardened, and her secret remained untold, while her proud lip half curled in scorn at the thought of Abigail Jones, who once stood, perhaps, as she was standing, with her hand on Richard Markham's and the kiss of betrothal wet upon her forehead. Ah, Ethie, there was this difference: Abigail had kissed her lover back, and her great black eyes had looked straight into his with an eager, blissful joy, as she promised to be his wife, and when he wound his arm around her, she had leaned up to the bashful youth, encouraging his caresses, while you--gave back no answering caress, and shook lightly off the arm laid across your neck. Possibly Richard thought of the difference, but if he did he imputed Ethelyn's cold impassiveness to her modest, retiring nature, so different from Abigail's. It was hardly fair to compare the two girls, they were so wholly unlike, for Abigail had been a plain, simple-hearted, buxom country girl of the West, whose world was all contained within the limits of the neighborhood where she lived, while Ethie was a high-spirited, petted, impulsive creature, knowing but little of such people as Abigail Jones, and wholly unfitted to cope with any world outside that to which she had been accustomed. But love is blind, and so was Richard; for with his whole heart he did love Ethelyn Grant; and, notwithstanding his habits of thirty years, she could then have molded him to her will, had she tried, by the simple process of love. But, alas! there was no answering throb in her heart when she felt the touch of his hand or his breath upon her cheek. She was only conscious of a desire to avoid his caress, if possible, while, as the days went by, she felt a growing disgust for "Abigail Jones," whose family, she gathered from her lover, lived near to, and were quite familiar with, his mother.

In happy ignorance of her real feelings, so well did she dissemble them, and so proper and ladylike was her deportment, Richard bade her good-by early in May, and went back to his Western home, writing to her often, but not such letters, it must be confessed, as were calculated to win a maiden's heart, or keep it after it was won. If he was awkward at love-making, and only allowed himself to be occasionally surprised into flashes of tenderness, he was still more awkward in letter-writing; and Ethelyn always indulged in a headache, or a fit of blues, after receiving one of his short, practical letters, which gave but little sign of the strong, deep affection he cherished for her. Those were hard days for Ethelyn--the days which intervened between her lover's bidding her adieu and his return to claim her hand--and only her deeply wounded pride, and her great desire for a change of scene and a winter in Washington, kept her from asking a release from the engagement she knew never ought to have been. Aside, however, from all this, there was some gratification in knowing that she was an object of envy to Susie Graham, and Anna Thorn, and Carrie Bell, either of whom would gladly have taken her place as bride-elect of an M.C., while proud old Captain Markham's frequent mention of "my nephew in Congress, ahem!" and Mrs. Dr. Van Buren's constant exultation over the "splendid match," helped to keep up the glamour of excitement, so that her promise had never been revoked, and now he was there to claim it. He had not gone at once to Miss Bigelow's on his arrival in Chicopee, for the day was hot and sultry, and he was very tired with his forty-eight hours' constant travel, and so he had rested a while in his chamber, which looked toward Ethelyn's, and then sat upon the piazza with his uncle till the heat of the day was past, and the round red moon was showing itself above the eastern hills as the sun disappeared in the west. Then, in his new linen coat, cut and made by Mrs. Jones, mother to Abigail, deceased, he had started for the dwelling of his betrothed. Ethelyn had seen him as he came from the depot in Captain Markham's carriage, and her cheek had crimsoned, and then grown pale at sight of the ancient-looking hair trunk swinging behind the carriage, all unconscious of the indignation it was exciting, or of the vast difference between itself and the two huge Saratoga trunks standing in Aunt Barbara Bigelow's upper hall, and looking so clean and nice in their fresh coverings. Poor Ethelyn! That hair trunk, which had done its owner such good service in his journeys to and from Washington, and which the mother had packed with so much care, never dreaming how very, very far it was behind the times, brought the hot blood in torrents to her face, and made the white hands clasp each other spasmodically, as she thought "Had I known of that hair trunk, I would certainly have told him no."

Even Abigail Jones, the shoemaker's daughter, faded into insignificance before this indignity, and it was long before Ethelyn could recover her composure or her pulse resume its regular beat. She was in no haste to see him; but such is the inconsistency of perverse girlhood that, because he delayed his coming, she felt annoyed and piqued, and was half tempted to have a headache and go to bed, and so not see him at all. But he was coming at last, linen coat and all; and Susie Graham, who had stopped for a moment by the gate to speak with Ethelyn, pronounced him "a magnificent-looking fellow," and said to Ethelyn, "I should think you would feel so proud."

Susie did not observe the linen coat, or if she had, she most likely thought it a very sensible arrangement for a day when the thermometer stood no degrees in the shade; but Susie was not Boston finished. She had been educated at Mount Holyoke, which made a difference, Ethelyn thought. Still, Susie's comment did much towards reconciling her to the linen coat; and, as Richard Markham came up the street, she did feel a thrill of pride and even pleasure, for he had a splendid figure and carried himself like a prince, while his fine face beamed all over with that joyous, happy expression which comes only from a kind, true heart, as he drew near the house and his eye caught the flutter of a white robe through the open door. Ethelyn was very pretty in her cool, cambric dress, with a bunch of sweet English violets in her hair; and at sight of her the man usually so grave and quiet, and undemonstrative with those of the opposite sex, felt all his reserve give way, and there was a world of tenderness in his voice and a misty look in his eye, as he bent over her, giving her the second kiss he had ever given to her, and asking, "How is my darling to-night?"

She did not take his arm from her neck this time--he had a right to keep it there--and she suffered the caress, feeling no greater inconvenience than that his big hand was very warm and pressed a little too hard sometimes upon her shoulders. He spoke to her of the errand on which he had come, and the great, warm hand pressed more heavily as he said, "It seems to me all a dream that in a few days you will be my own Ethie, my wife, from whom I need not be parted"; and then he spoke of his mother and his three brothers, James, and John, and Anderson, or Andy, as he was called. Each of these had sent kindly messages to Richard's bride--the mother saying she should be glad to have a daughter in her home, and the three brothers promising to love their new sister so much as to make "old Dick" jealous, if possible.

These messages "old Dick" delivered, but wisely refrained from telling how his mother feared he had not chosen wisely, that a young lady with Boston notions was not the wife to make a Western man very happy. Neither did he tell her of an interview he had with Mrs. Jones, who had always evinced a motherly care over him since her daughter's death, and to whom he had dutifully communicated the news of his intended marriage. It was not what Mrs. Jones had expected. She had watched Richard's upward progress with all the pride of a mother-in-law, lamenting often to Mrs. Markham that poor Abigail could not have lived to share his greatness, and during the term of his judgeship, when he stayed mostly in Camden, the county seat, she had, on the occasion of her going to town with butter and eggs, and chickens, taken a mournful pleasure in perambulating the streets, and selecting the house where Abigail might, perhaps, have resided, and where she could have had her cup of young hyson after the fatigue of the day, instead of eating her dry lunch of cheese and fried cakes in the rather comfortless depot, while waiting for the train. Richard's long-continued bachelorhood had given her peculiar pleasure, inasmuch as it betokened a continual remembrance of her daughter; and as her youngest child, the blooming Melinda, who was as like the departed Abigail as sisters ever are to each other ripened into womanhood, and the grave Richard spoke oftener to her than to the other maidens of the prairie village, she began to speculate upon what might possibly be, and refused the loan of her brass kettle to the neighbor whose husband did not vote for Richard when he ran for member of Congress. Melinda, too, had her little ambitions, her silent hopes and aspirations, and even her vague longings for a winter in Washington. As the Markham house and the Jones house were distant from each other only half a mile, she was a frequent visitor of Richard's mother, always assisting when there was more work than usual on hand and on the occasion of Richard's first going to Washington ironing his shirts and packing them herself in the square hair trunk which had called forth Ethelyn's ire. Though she did not remember much about "Abby," she knew that, had she lived, Richard would have been her brother; and somehow he seemed to her just like one now, she said to Mrs. Markham, as she hemmed his pocket handkerchiefs, working his initials in the corner with pink floss, and upon the last and best, the one which had cost sixty-two and a half cents, venturing to weave her own hair, which was long, and glossy, and black, as Abigail's had been. Several times a week during Richard's absence, she visited Mrs. Markham, inquiring always after "the Judge," and making herself so agreeable and useful, too, in clear-starching and doing up Mrs. Markham's caps, and in giving receipts for sundry new and economical dishes, that the good woman herself frequently doubted if Richard could do better than take the black-eyed Melinda; and when he told her of Ethelyn Grant, she experienced a feeling of disappointment and regret, doubting much if a Boston girl, with Boston notions, would make her as happy as the plainer Melinda, who knew all her ways. Something of this she said to her son, omitting, of course, that part of her thoughts which referred to Melinda. With Mrs. Jones, however, it was different. In her surprise and disappointment she let fall some remarks which opened Richard's eyes a little, and made him look at her half amused and half sorry, as, suspending her employment of paring apples for the dinner pie she put the corner of her apron to her eyes, and "hoped the new bride would not have many airs, and would put up with his mother's ways.

"You," and here the apron and hand with the knife in it came down from her eyes--"you'll excuse me, Richard, for speaking so plain, but you seem like my own boy, and I can't help it. Your mother is the best and cleverest woman in the world, but she has some peculiarities which a Boston girl may not put up with, not being used to them as Melin--I mean, as poor Abigail was."

It was the first time it had ever occurred to Richard that his mother had peculiarities, and even now he did not know what they were. Taking her all in all, she was as nearly perfect, he thought, as a woman well could be, and on his way home from his interview with Mrs. Jones he pondered in his mind what she could mean, and then wondered if for the asking he could have taken Melinda Jones to the fireside where he was going to install Ethelyn Grant. There was a comical smile about his mouth as he thought how little either Melinda or Abigail would suit him now; and then, by way of making amends for what seemed disrespect to the dead, he went round to the sunken grave where Abigail had slept for so many years, and stood again just where he had stood that day when he fancied the light from his heart had gone out forever. But he could not bring back the olden feeling, or wish that Abigail had lived.

"She is happy now--happier than I could have made her. It is better as it is," he said, as he walked away to Daisy's grave, where his tears dropped just as they always did when he stood by the sod which covered the fairest, brightest, purest being he had ever known, except his Ethie.

She was just as pure and gentle and good as blue-eyed Daisy had been, and on the manly face turned so wistfully to the eastward there was a world of love and tenderness for the Ethie who, alas, did not deserve it then, and to whom a few weeks later he gave his mother's kindly message. Then, remembering what Mrs. Jones had said, he felt in duty bound to add:

"Mother has some peculiarities, I believe most old people have; but I trust to your good sense to humor them as much as possible. She has had her own way a long time, and though you will virtually be mistress of the house, inasmuch as it belongs to me, it will be better for mother to take the lead, as heretofore."

There was a curl on Ethelyn's lip as she received her first lesson with regard to her behavior as daughter-in-law; but she made no reply, not even to ask what the peculiarities were which she was to humor. She really did not care what they were, as she fully intended having an establishment of her own in the thriving prairie village, just half a mile from her husband's home. She should probably spend a few weeks with Mrs. Markham, senior, whom she fancied a tall, stately woman, wearing heavy black silk dresses and thread lace caps on great occasions, and having always on hand some fine lamb's-wool knitting work when she sat in the parlor where Daisy's picture hung. Ethelyn could not tell why it was that she always saw Richard's mother thus, unless it were what Mrs. Captain Markham once said with regard to her Western sister-in-law, sending to Boston for a black silk which cost three dollars per yard--a great price for those days--and for two yards of handsome thread lace, which she, the Mrs. Captain, had run all over the city to get, "John's wife was so particular to have it just the pattern and width she described in her letter."

This was Richard's mother as Ethelyn saw her, while the house on the prairie, which she knew had been built within a few years, presented a very respectable appearance to her mind's eye, being large, and fashioned something after the new house across the Common, which had a bay window at the side, and a kind of cupola on the roof. It would be quite possible to spend a few weeks comfortably there, especially as she would have the Washington gayeties in prospect, but in the spring, when, after a winter of dissipation she returned to the prairies, she should go to her own home, either in Olney or Camden; the latter, perhaps, as Richard could as well live there as elsewhere. This was Ethelyn's plan, but she kept it to herself, and changing the conversation from Richard's mother and her peculiarities, she talked instead of the places they were to visit-- Quebec and Montreal, the seaside and the mountains, and lastly that great Babel of fashion, Saratoga, for which place several of her dresses had been expressly made.

Ethelyn had planned this trip herself, and Richard, though knowing how awfully he should be bored before the summer was over, had assented to all that she proposed, secretly hoping the while that the last days of August would find him safe at home in Olney among his books, his horses, and his farming pursuits. He was very tired that night, and he did not tarry longer than ten, though a word from Ethelyn would have kept him for hours at her side, so intoxicated was he with her beauty, and so quiet and happy he felt with her; but the word was not spoken, and he left her standing on the piazza, where he could see the gleaming of her white robes when he looked back, as he more than once did ere reaching his uncle's door.

The next three days passed rapidly, bringing at last the eventful one for which all others were made, it seemed to him, as he looked out upon the early, dewy morning, thinking how pleasant it was there in that quiet New England town, and trying to fight back the unwelcome headache which finally drove him back to his bed, from which he wrote the little note to Ethelyn, who might think strange at his non-appearance when he had been accustomed to go to her immediately after breakfast. He never dreamed of the relief it was to her not to have him come, as he lay flushed and heated upon his pillow, the veins upon his forehead swelling with their pressure of hot blood, and his ear strained to catch the first sound of the servant's returning step. Ethelyn would either come herself to see him, or send some cheerful message, he was sure. How, then, was he disappointed to find his own note returned, with the assurance that "it did not matter, as he would only be in the way."

Several times he read it over, trying to extract some comfort from it, and finding it at last in the fact that Ethelyn had a headache, too. This was the reason for her seeming indifference; and in wishing himself able to go to her, Richard forgot in part his own pain, and fell into a quiet sleep, which did him untold good. It was three o'clock when at last he rose, knowing pretty well all that had been doing during the hours of his seclusion in the darkened room. The "Van Buren set" had come, and he overheard Mrs. Markham's Esther saying to Aunt Barbara's Betsy, when she came for the silver cake-basket, that "Mr. Frank seemed in mighty fine spirits, considering all the flirtations he used to have with Miss Ethelyn."

This was the first intimation Richard had received of a flirtation, and even now it did not strike him unpleasantly. They were cousins, he reflected, and as such had undoubtedly been very familiar with each other. It was natural, and nothing for which he need care. He did not care, either, as he deliberately began to make his wedding toilet, thinking himself, when it was completed, that he was looking unusually well in the entire new suit which his cousin, Mrs. Woodhull, had insisted upon his getting in New York, when on his way home in April he had gone that way and told her of his approaching marriage. It was a splendid suit, made after the most approved style, and costing a sum which he had kept secret from his mother, who, nevertheless, guessed somewhere near the truth, and thought the Olney tailor would have suited him quite as well at a quarter the price, or even Mrs. Jones, who, having been a tailoress when a young girl in Vermont, still kept up her profession to a limited extent, retaining her "press-board" and "goose," and the mammoth shears which had cut Richard's linen coat after a Chicago pattern of not the most recent date Richard thought very little about his personal appearance--too little, in fact--but he felt a glow of satisfaction now as he contemplated himself in the glass, feeling only that Ethelyn would be pleased to see him thus.

And Ethelyn was pleased. She had half expected the old coat of she did not know how many years' make, and there was a fierce pang of pain in her heart as she imagined Frank's cool criticisms, and saw, in fancy, the contrast between the two men. So when Judge Markham alighted at the gate, and from her window she took in at a glance his tout ensemble, the revulsion of feeling was so great that the glad tears sprang to her eyes, and a brighter, happier look broke over her face than had been there for many weeks. She was not present when Frank was introduced to him; but when next she met her cousin, he said to her, in his usual off-hand way, "I say, Ethie, he is pretty well got up for a Westerner. But for his eyes and teeth I should never have known him for the chap who wore short pants and stove-pipe hat with the butternut-colored crape. Who was he in mourning for anyway?"

It was too bad to be reminded of Abigail Jones, just as she was beginning to feel more comfortable; but Ethelyn bore it very well, and laughingly answered, "For his sweetheart, I dare say," her cheeks flushing very red as Frank whispered slyly, "You are even, then, on that score."

No man of any delicacy of feeling or true refinement would have made this allusion to the past, with his first love within a few hours of her bridal, and his own betrothed standing near. But Frank had neither delicacy of feeling nor genuine refinement, and he even felt a secret gratification in seeing the blood mount to Ethelyn's cheeks as he thus referred to the past.

CHAPTER IV: THE BRIDAL

There was a great deal of sincere and tender interest in Richard's manner when, in reply to his inquiries for Ethelyn's headache, Aunt Barbara told him of the almost fainting fit in the morning and her belief that Ethelyn was not as strong this summer as she used to be.

"The mountain air will do her good, I trust," casting wistful glances up the stairs and toward the door of the chamber, where girlish voices were heard, Nettie Hudson and Susie Granger chatting gayly and uttering exclamations of delight as they arranged and adjusted Ethelyn's bridal robes.

Once during the period of his judgeship Richard had attended a large and fashionable bridal party, but when, on his return to Olney, Melinda Jones questioned him with regard to the dresses of the bride and the guests, he found himself utterly unable to give either fabric, fashion, or even color, so little attention had he given to the subject. He never noticed such things, he said, but he believed some of the dresses were made of something flimsy, for he could see through them, and he knew they were very long, for he had stepped on some half dozen. And this was all the information the inquisitive Melinda could obtain. Dress was of little consequence, he thought, so it was clean and whole.

This was his theory; but when, as the twilight deepened on the Chicopee hills, and the lamps were lighted in Aunt Barbara's parlors, and old Captain Markham began to wonder "why the plague the folks did not come," as he stalked up and down the piazza in all the pride and pomposity of one who felt himself to all intents and purposes the village aristocrat, and when the mysterious door of Ethie's room, which had been closed so long, was opened, and the bridegroom told that he might go in, he started in surprise at the beautiful tableau presented to his view as he stepped across the threshold. As was natural, he fancied that never before had he seen three young girls so perfectly beautiful as the three before him--Ethie, and Susie, and Nettie.

As a matter of course, he gave the preference to Ethelyn, who was very, very lovely in her bridal robes, with the orange wreath resting like a coronet upon her marble brow. There were pearls upon her fair neck and pearls upon her arms, the gift of Mrs. Dr. Van Buren, who had waited till the very last, hoping the Judge would have forethought enough to buy them himself. But the Judge had not. He knew something of diamonds, for they had been Daisy's favorites; but pearls were novelties to him, and Ethelyn's pale cheeks would have burned crimson had she known that he was thinking "how becoming those white beads were to her."

Poor, ignorant Richard! He will know more by and by of what constitutes a fashionable lady's toilet; but now he is in blissful ignorance of minutiae, and sees only the tout ensemble, which he pronounces perfect. He was half afraid of her, though, she seemed so cold, so passive, so silent, and when in the same breath Susie Granger asks if he ever saw anyone so lovely as Ethelyn and bids him kiss her quick, he starts and hesitates, and finally kisses Susie instead. He might, perhaps, have done the same with Ethelyn if she had not stepped backward to avoid it, her long train sweeping across the hearth where that morning she had knelt in such utter desolation, and where now was lying a bit of blackened paper, which the housemaid's broom had not found when, early in the day, the room was swept and dusted. So Ethelyn's white satin brushed against the gossamer thing, which floated upward for a moment, and then settled back upon the heavy, shining folds. It was Richard who saw it first, and Richard's hand which brushed away the skeleton of Frank's letter from the skirts of his bride, leaving a soiled, yellowish stain, which Susie Granger loudly deplored, while Ethelyn only drew her drapery around her, saying coldly, that "it did not matter in the least. She would as soon have it there as not."

It was meet, she thought, that the purity of her bridal garments should be tarnished; for was not her heart all stained, and black, and crisp with cruel deception? That little incident, however, affected her strangely, bringing back so vividly the scene on the ledge of rocks beneath the New England laurels, where Frank had sat beside her and poured words of boyish passion into her ear. There was for a moment a pitiful look of anguish in her eyes as they went out into the summer night toward the huckleberry hills, where lay that ledge of massy rock, and then come back to the realities about her. Frank saw the look of pain, and it awoke in his own breast an answering throb as he wondered if, after all, Ethie would not have preferred that he were standing by her instead of the grave Judge, fitting on his gloves with an awkwardness which said that such articles were comparative strangers to his large, red hands.

It was time now to go down. The guests had all arrived, the clergyman was waiting, and Captain Markham had grown very red in the face with his impatience, which his wife tried in vain to quiet. If at this last moment there arose in Ethelyn's bosom any wild impulse to break away from the dreadful scene, and rush out into the darkness which lay so softly upon the hills, she put it aside, with the thought, "too late now--forever too late"; and taking the arm which Richard offered her, she went mechanically down the staircase into the large parlor where the wedding guests were assembled. Surely, surely, she did not know what she was doing, or realize the solemn words: "I charge and require you both, as ye shall answer at the great day, when the secrets of all hearts shall be disclosed, that if either of you know any impediment why ye may not be lawfully joined together in matrimony, ye do now confess it, for be ye well assured," and so forth. She did not even hear them; for the numb, dead feeling which crept over her, chilling her blood, and making her hand, which Richard took in his while he fitted the wedding ring, so cold and clammy to the touch, that Richard felt tempted to hold and chafe it in his own warm, broad palms; but that was not in accordance with the ceremony, and so he let it fall, wondering that Ethelyn could be so cold when the sweat was standing in great drops upon his own face, and moistening his wavy hair, which clustered in short, thick curls around his brow, making him look so handsome, as more than one maiden thought, envying Ethelyn her good fortune, and marveling at the pallor of her lips and the rigidity of her form.

The ceremony was ended, and Ethelyn Grant was Mrs. Richard Markham; but the new name brought no blushes to her cheek, nor yet the kiss her husband gave her, nor the congratulations of the guests, nor Aunt Barbara's tears, which dropped upon the forehead of her darling as the good woman bent over her and thought how she had lost her; but when Frank Van Buren stooped down to touch her lips the sluggish blood quickened and a thrill went through and through her veins, sending the bright color to her cheeks, which burned as with a hectic flush. Frank saw the power he held, but to his credit he did not then exult; he only felt that it was finished, that Ethie was gone past his recall; and for the first time in his life he experienced a genuine pang of desolation, such as he had never felt before, and he fought hard to master his emotions while he watched the bride receiving the bridal guests. Another than Frank was watching her, too-- Mrs. Dr. Van Buren--who at one time feared lest Ethelyn should faint, and who, as soon as an opportunity offered, whispered to her niece, "Do, Ethie, put some animation in your manner or people will think you an unwilling bride."

For a moment a gleam of anger flashed from the eyes which looked unflinchingly into Mrs. Van Buren's, and the pale lips quivered with passion. But Ethelyn had too much pride to admit of her letting the people know what she was suffering, and so with great effort she rallied her fainting spirits, and twice ere the evening was at a close her merry laugh was heard even above Susie Granger's, as a knot of her gay companions gathered round her with their merry jokes and gay repartees.

Susie Granger was in her happiest mood, and her lively spirits seemed to pervade the whole party. Now that he knew her better, Richard was more at ease with her, and returned her playful sallies until even Ethelyn wondered to see him so funny. He never once forgot her, however, as was evinced by the loving glances he bent upon her, and by his hovering constantly at her side, as if afraid to lose her.

Once, when they were standing together and Frank was near to them, Richard laid his hand upon Ethelyn's shoulder which the cut of the wedding dress left bare. It was a very beautiful neck--white, and plump, and soft--and Richard's hand pressed somewhat heavily; but with a shiver Ethelyn drew herself away, and Frank, who was watching her, fancied he saw the flesh creep backward from the touch. Perhaps it was a feeling of pity, and perhaps it was a mean desire to test his own influence over her, which prompted him carelessly to take her hand to inspect the wedding-ring. It was only her hand, but as Frank held it in his own, he felt it growing warm and flushed, while the color deepened on Ethelyn's cheeks, and then died suddenly away at Frank's characteristic remark, spoken for her ear alone, "You feel like thunder, Ethie, and so do I."

The speech did Ethelyn good. No matter how she felt, it was not Frank's place to speak to her thus. She was now a wife, and she meant to be true to her marriage vow, both in look and deed; so, with an impatient gesture, she flung aside Frank's hand, repelling him fiercely with the reply, "You are mistaken, sir--at least, so far as I am concerned."

After that she stayed more with Richard, and once, of her own accord, she put her arm in his and stood half leaning against him with both hands clasped together, while he held the bouquet which Mrs. Senator Woodhull had sent by express from New York. It is true that Richard smelled and breathed upon the flowers oftener than was desirable; and once Ethelyn saw him extracting leaves from the very choicest blossoms; but on the whole he did very well, considering that it was the first time he had ever held a lady's bouquet in such an expensive holder.

As Ethelyn had predicted, the evening was hot and sultry; but the bugs and beetles and millers she had dreaded did not come in to annoy her, and when, as the clock struck twelve, the company dispersed, they were sincere in their assertions of having passed a delightful evening, and many were the good wishes expressed for Mrs. Judge Markham's happiness as the guests took their way to their respective homes.

An hour later and the lights had disappeared from Miss Barbara Bigelow's windows, and the summer stars looked down upon the quiet house where that strange bridal had been.

CHAPTER V: THE HONEYMOON

From Mrs. Senator Woodhull's elegant house--where Mrs. Judge Markham had been petted, and flattered, and caressed, and Mr. Judge Markham had been adroitly tutored and trained without the least effect--the newly wedded pair went on to Quebec and Montreal, and thence to the White Mountains, where Ethelyn's handsome traveling dress was ruined and Richard's linen coat, so obnoxious to his bride, was torn past repair and laid away in one of Ethelyn's trunks, with the remark that "Mother could mend it for Andy, who always took his brother's cast-off clothes." The hair trunk had been left in Chicopee, and so Ethelyn had not that to vex her.

Noticed everywhere, and admired by all whom she met, the first part of her wedding trip was not as irksome as she had feared it might be. Pleased, as a boy, with his young bride, Richard was all attention, and Ethelyn had only to express a wish to have it gratified, so that casual lookers-on would have pronounced her supremely happy. And Ethelyn's heart did not ache one-half so hard as on that terrible day of her bridal. In the railway car, on the crowded steamboat, or at the large hotels, where all were entire strangers, she forgot to watch and criticise her husband, and if any dereliction from etiquette did occur, he yielded so readily to her suggestion that to him seemed an easy task. The habits of years, however, are not so easily broken, and by the time Saratoga was reached, Richard's patience began to give way beneath Ethelyn's multifarious exactions and the ennui consequent upon his traveling about so long. Still he did pretty well for him, growing very red in the face with his efforts to draw on gloves a size too small, and feeling excessively hot and uncomfortable in his coat, which he wore even in the retirement of his own room, where he desired so much to indulge in the cool luxury of shirt-sleeves--a suggestion which Ethelyn heard with horror, openly exclaiming against the glaring vulgarity, and asking, a little contemptuously, if that were the way he had been accustomed to do at home.

"Why, yes," he answered. "Out West upon the prairies we go in for comfort, and don't mind so small a matter as shirt-sleeves on a sweltering August day."

"Please do not use such expressions as sweltering and go in--they do not sound well," Ethelyn rejoined. "And now I think of it, I wish you would talk more to the ladies in the parlor. You hardly spoke to Mrs. Cameron last evening, and she directed most of her conversation to you, too. I was afraid she would either think that you were rude, or else that you did not know what to say."

"She hit it right, if she came to the latter conclusion," Richard said, good-humoredly, "for the fact is, Ethie, I don't know what to say to such women as she. I am not a ladies' man, and it's no use trying to make me over. You can't teach old dogs new tricks."

Ethie fairly groaned as she clasped her bracelets upon her arms and shook down the folds of her blue silk; then after a moment she continued: "You can talk to me, and why not to others?"

"You are my wife, Ethie, and I love you, which makes a heap of difference," Richard said, and winding his arms around Ethie's waist he drew her face toward his own and kissed it affectionately.

They had been three days at Saratoga when this little scene occurred and their room was one of those miserable little apartments in the Ainsworth block which look out upon nothing but a patch of weeds and the rear of a church. Ethelyn did not like it at all, and liked it the less because she felt that to some extent her husband was to blame. He ought to have written and engaged rooms beforehand--Aunt Van Buren always did, and Mrs. Col. Tophevie, and everybody who understood the ins and outs of fashionable life. But Richard did not understand them. He believed in taking what was offered to him without making a fuss, he said. He had never been to Saratoga before, and he secretly hoped he should never come again, for he did not enjoy those close, hot rooms and worm-eaten furniture any better than Ethelyn did, but he accepted it with a better grace, saying, when he first entered it, that "he could put up with 'most anything, though to be sure it was hotter than an oven."

His mode of expressing himself had never suited Ethelyn. Particular, and even elegant in her choice of language, it grated upon her sensitive ear, and forgetting that she had all her life heard similar expressions in Chicopee, she charged it to the West, and Iowa was blamed for the faults of her son more than she deserved. At Saratoga, where they met many of her acquaintances, all of whom were anxious to see the fastidious Ethelyn's husband, it seemed to her that he was more remiss than ever in those little things which make up the finished gentleman, while his peculiar expressions sometimes made every nerve quiver with pain. The consequence of this was that Ethelyn became a very little cross, as Richard thought, though she had never so openly attacked him as on that day, the third after their arrival, when to her horror he took off his coat, preparatory to a little comfort, while she was dressing for dinner. At Ethelyn's request, however, he put it on again, saying as he did so, that he was "sweating like a butcher," which remark called out his wife's contemptuous inquiries concerning his habits at home. Richard was still too much in love with his young wife to feel very greatly irritated. In word and deed she had done her duty toward him thus far, and he had nothing to complain of. It is true she was very quiet and passive, and undemonstrative, never giving him back any caress as he had seen wives do. But then he was not very demonstrative himself, and so he excused it the more readily in her, and loved her all the same. It amused him that a girl of twenty should presume to criticise him, a man of thirty-two, a Judge, and a member of Congress, to whom the Olney people paid such deference, and he bore with her at first just as a mother would bear with the little child which assumed a superiority over her.

This afternoon, however, when she said so much to him, he was conscious of a very little irritation, for he was naturally high-spirited. But he put the feeling down, and gayly kissed his six-weeks bride, who, touched with his forbearance, kissed him back again, and suffered him to hold her cool face a moment between his hot, moist hands, while he bent over her.

She did respect him in spite of his vulgarism; nor was she unconscious of the position which, as his wife, she held. It was very pleasant to hear people say of her when she passed by:

"That is Mrs. Judge Markham, of Iowa--her husband is a member of Congress."

Very pleasant, too, to meet with his friends, other M. C.'s, who paid her deference on his account. Had they stayed away from Saratoga all might have been well; but alas, they were there, and so was all of Ethelyn's world--the Tophevies, the Hales, the Hungerfords and Van Burens, with Nettie Hudson, opening her great blue eyes at Richard's mistakes and asking Frank in Ethelyn's hearing, "if that Judge Markham's manners were not a little outré."

They certainly were outré, there was no denying it, and Ethelyn's blood tingled to her finger tips as she wondered if it would always be so. It is a pitiable thing for a wife to blush for her husband, to watch constantly lest he depart from those little points of etiquette which women catch intuitively, but which some of our most learned men fail to learn in a lifetime. And here they greatly err, for no man, however well versed he may be in science and literature, is well educated, or well balanced, or excusable, if he neglects the little things which good breeding and common politeness require of him, and Richard was somewhat to be blamed. It did not follow because his faults had never been pointed out to him that they did not exist, or that others did not observe them besides his wife. Ethelyn, to be sure, was more deeply interested than anyone else, and felt his mistakes more keenly, while at the same time she was over-fastidious, and had not the happiest faculty for correcting him. She did not love him well enough to be very careful of wounding him, but the patience and good humor with which he received her reprimand that hot August afternoon, when the thermometer was one hundred in the shade, and any man would have been excusable for retorting upon his wife who lectured him, awoke a throb of something nearer akin to love than anything she had felt since the night when she stood upon the sandy beach and heard the story of Daisy.

Richard was going to do better. He would wear his coat all the time, both day and night, if Ethelyn said so, He would not lean his elbow on the table while waiting for dessert, as he had more than once been guilty of doing; he would not help himself to a dish before passing it to the ladies near him; he would talk to Mrs. Cameron in the evening, and would try not to be so absorbed in his own thoughts as to pay no attention when Mrs. Tophevie was addressing herself directly to him; he would laugh in the right place, and, when spoken to, would answer in something besides monosyllables; he would try to keep his hands out of his pockets and his handkerchief out of his hand, or at least he would not "snap it," as Ethie said he had done on the first evening of his arrival at Saratoga. In short, he promised a complete reformation, even saying that if Ethelyn would select some person who was an fait in those matters in which he was so remiss, he would watch and copy that man to the letter. Would she name someone? And Ethelyn named her cousin Frank, while Richard felt a flush of something like resentment that he should be required to imitate a person whom in his secret heart he despised as dandyish, and weak, and silly, and "namby-pamby," as he would probably have expressed it if he had not forsworn slang phrases of every kind. But Richard had pledged his word, and meant to keep it; and so it was to all appearances a very happy and loving couple which, when the dinner gong sounded, walked into the dining room with Mrs. Dr. Van Buren's set, Ethelyn's handsome blue silk sweeping far behind her, and her white bare arm just touching the coat-sleeve of her husband, who was not insensible to the impression made by the beautiful woman at his side.

There were no lectures that night, for Richard had done his best, talking at least twenty times with both Mrs. Cameron and Mrs. Colonel Tophevie, whom he found more agreeable than he had supposed. Then he had held Ethelyn's white cloak upon his arm, and stood patiently against the wall, while up at the United States she danced set after set--first, the Lancers, with young Lieutenant Gray, then a polka with John Tophevie, and lastly, a waltz with Frank Van Buren, who whirled his fair partner about the room with a velocity which made Richard dizzy and awoke sundry thoughts not wholly complimentary to that doubtful dance, the waltz. Richard did not dance himself, at least not latterly. In his younger days, when he and Abigail Jones attended the quilting-frolics together and the "paring bees," he had with other young men, tried his feet at Scotch reels, French fours, "The Cheat," and the "Twin Sisters," with occasionally a cotillion, but he was not accomplished in the art. Even the Olney girls called him awkward, preferring almost anyone else for a partner, and so he abandoned the floor and cultivated his head rather than his heels. He liked to see dancing, and at first it was rather pleasant watching Ethelyn's lithe figure gliding gracefully through the intricate movements of the Lancers; but when it came to the waltz, he was not so sure about it, and he wondered if it were necessary for Frank Van Buren to clasp her as tightly about the waist as he did, or for her to lean so languidly upon his shoulder.

Richard was not naturally jealous--certainly not of Frank Van Buren; but he would rather his wife should not waltz with him or any other man, and so he said to her, asking this concession on her part in return for all he had promised to attempt; and to Ethelyn's credit we record that she yielded to her husband's wishes, and, greatly to Frank's surprise, declined the waltz which he had proposed the following evening. But she made amends in other dances, keeping poor Richard waiting for her night after night, until he actually fell asleep and dreamed of the log cabin on the prairie, where he had once danced a quadrille with Abigail Jones to the tune of Money-musk, as played by the Plympton brothers--the one on a cracked violin, and the other on an accordion.

A tap of Mrs. Tophevie's fan brought him back to consciousness, and he was almost guilty of a sigh as the log cabin faded from his vision, with the Plymptons and Abigail Jones, leaving instead that heated ballroom, with its trained orchestra, its bevy of fair young girls, its score of white-kidded dandies with wasp-like waists and perfumed locks, and Ethie smiling in their midst.

Saratoga did not agree with Richard. He grew sick first of the water; then of the fare; then of the daily routine of fashionable follies; then of the people; and then, oh! so sick of the petty lectures which Ethelyn gradually resumed as he failed in his attempts to imitate Frank Van Buren and appear perfectly at ease in everybody's presence. Saratoga was a "confounded bore," he said, and though he called himself a brute, and a savage, and a heathen, he was only very glad when toward the last of August Ethelyn became so seriously indisposed as to make a longer stay in Saratoga impossible. Newport, of course, was given up, and Ethelyn's desire was to go back to Chicopee and lie down again in the dear old room which had been hers from childhood. Aunt Barbara's toast, Aunt Barbara's tea, and Aunt Barbara's nursing, would soon bring her all right again, she said; but in this she was mistaken, for although the toast, and the tea, and the nursing each came in its turn, the September flowers had faded, and the trees on the Chicopee hills were beginning to flaunt their bright October robes ere she recovered from the low, nervous fever, induced by the mental and bodily excitement through which she had passed during the last three or four months.

Although he knew it was necessary that he should be at home if he would transact any business before the opening of his next session in Washington, Richard put aside all thoughts of self, and nursed his wife with a devotedness which awakened her liveliest gratitude.

Richard was not awkward in the sick-room. It seemed to be his special providence, and as he had once nursed and cared for Daisy and the baby brother who died, so he now cared for Ethelyn, until she began to miss him when he left her side, and to listen for his returning step when he went out for an hour or so to smoke and talk politics with his uncle, Captain Markham. With Mrs. Dr. Van Buren and Frank and the fashionable world all away, Richard's faults were not so perceptible, and Ethelyn even began to look forward with considerable interest to the time when she should be able to start for her Western home, about which she had built many delusive castles. Her piano had already been sent on in advance, she saying to Susie Granger, who came in while it was being boxed, that as they were not to keep house till spring she should not take furniture now. Possibly they could find what they needed in Chicago; if not, they could order from Boston.

Richard, who overheard this remark, wondered what it meant, for he had not the most remote idea of separating himself from his mother. She was very essential to his happiness; and he was hardly willing to confess to himself how much during the last summer he had missed her. She had a way of petting him and deferring to his judgment and making him feel that Richard Markham was a very nice kind of man, far different from Ethelyn's criticisms, which had sometimes led him seriously to inquire whether he were a fool or not. No, he could not live apart from his mother--he was firm upon that point; but there was time enough to say so when the subject should be broached to him. So he went on nailing down the cover to the pine box, and thinking as he nailed what a nice kitchen cupboard the box would make when once it was safely landed at his home in the prairie, and wondering, too, how his mother--who was not very fond of music--would bear the sound of the piano and if Ethie would be willing for Melinda Jones to practice upon it. He knew Melinda had taken lessons at Camden, where she had been to school, and he had heard her express a wish that someone nearer than the village had an instrument, as she should soon forget all she had learned. Somehow Melinda was a good deal in Richard's mind, and when a button was missing from his shirts, or his toes came through his socks--as was often the case at Saratoga--he found himself thinking of the way Melinda had of helping "fix his things" when he was going from home, and of hearing his mother say what a handy girl she was, and what a thrifty, careful wife she would make. He meant nothing derogatory to Ethelyn in these reminiscences; he would not have exchanged her for a thousand Melindas, even if he had to pin his shirt bosoms together and go barefoot all his life. But Melinda kept recurring to his mind much as if she had been his sister, and he thought it would be but a simple act of gratitude for all she had done for him to give her the use of the piano for at least one hour each day.

In blissful ignorance of all that was meditated against her, Ethelyn saw her piano taken away from the sitting room, where it would never stand again, and saw the tears which rolled down Aunt Barbara's faded cheeks as she, too, watched its going, and tried to fill up the vacancy it left by moving a chair and a table and a footstool into the gap. Those were hard days for Aunt

Barbara, harder than for Ethelyn, who liked the excitement of traveling, and was almost glad when the crisp October morning came on which she was to say good-by to the home which was hers no longer. Her two huge trunks stood in the hall, together with the square hair trunk which held Richard's wardrobe, and the three tin cans of peaches Mrs. Captain Markham was sending to her sister-in-law, with the injunction to be sure and get that particular patent for cans if she wished her fruit to keep. In addition to these, an immense box had been forwarded by express, containing, besides Ethelyn's wearing apparel, many little ornaments and pictures and brackets, which, during the winter, might perhaps adorn the walls of the parlor where Daisy's picture hung, and where, Richard had said, was also an oil-painting of Niagara, omitting to add that it was the handiwork of Melinda Jones, that young lady having dabbled in paints as well as music during her two terms schooling at Camden. Tucked away in various parts of the box were also sundry presents, which, at Mrs. Dr. Van Buren's suggestion, Ethelyn had bought for her husband's family. For James, who, she had heard Richard say, was an inveterate smoker, there was a handsome velvet smoking-cap which, having been bought at Saratoga, had cost an enormous sum; for John, an expensive pair of elaborately wrought slippers had been selected; but when it came to Anderson, as Ethelyn persisted in calling the brother whom Richard always spoke of as Andy, she felt a little perplexed as to what would be appropriate. Richard had talked very little of him--so little, in fact, that she knew nothing whatever of his tastes, except from the scrap of conversation she once accidentally overheard when the old captain was talking to Richard of his brothers.

"Does Andy like busts as well as ever?" the captain had asked, but Richard's reply was lost as Ethelyn walked on.

Still, she had heard enough to give her some inkling with regard to the mysterious Andy. Probably he was more refined than either James or John--at all events, he was evidently fond of statuary, and his tastes should be gratified. Accordingly, Boston was ransacked by Mrs. Dr. Van Buren for an exquisite head of Schiller, done in marble, and costing thirty dollars. Richard did not see it. The presents were a secret from him, all except the handsome point-lace coiffure which Aunt Barbara sent to Mrs. Markham, together with a letter which she had sat up till midnight to write, and in which she had touchingly commended her darling to the new mother's care and consideration.

"You will find my Ethie in some respects a spoiled child--[she wrote] but it is more my fault than hers. I have loved her so much, and petted her so much, that I have doubt if she knows what a harsh word or cross look means. She has been carefully and delicately brought up, but has repaid me well for all my pains by her tender love. Please, dear Mrs. Markham, be very, very kind to her, and you will greatly oblige, your most obedient servant,

"BARBARA BIGELOW.

"P.S. I dare say your ways out West are not exactly like our ways at the East, and Ethie may not fall in with them at once, perhaps never with some of them, but I am sure she will do what is right, as she is a sensible girl. Again, yours with regret, B.B."

The writing of this letter was not perhaps the wisest thing Aunt Barbara could have done, but she was incited to it by what her sister Sophia told her of the rumors concerning Mrs. Markham, and her own fears lest Ethelyn should not be as comfortable with the new mother-in-law as was wholly desirable. To Richard himself she had said that she presumed that his mother's ways were not like Ethie's--old people were different from young ones--the world had improved since their day, and instead of trying to bring young folks altogether to their modes of thinking, it was well for both to yield something. That was the third time Richard had heard his mother's ways alluded to; first by Mrs. Jones, who called them queer; second, by Mrs. Dr. Van Buren, who, for Ethie's sake had also dropped a word of caution, hinting that his mother's ways might possibly be a little peculiar; and lastly by good Aunt Barbara, who signalized them as different from Ethelyn's.

What did it mean, and why had he never discovered anything amiss in his mother? He trusted that Mrs. Jones, and Mrs. Van Buren, and Aunt Barbara were mistaken. On the whole, he knew they were; and even if they were not his mother could not do wrong to Ethie, while Ethie would, of course, be willing to conform to any request made by a person so much older than herself as his mother was. So Richard dismissed that subject from his mind, and Ethelyn--having never heard it agitated, except that time when, with Mrs. Jones on his mind, Richard had thought proper to suggest the propriety of her humoring his mother--felt no fears of Mrs. Markham, senior, whom she still associated in her mind with heavy black silk, gold-bowed spectacles, handsome lace and fleecy crochet-work.

The October morning was clear and crisp and frosty, and the sun had not yet shown itself above the eastern hills, when Captain Markham's carryall drove to Aunt Barbara's gate, followed by the long democratic-wagon which was to take the baggage. Ethelyn's spoiled traveling dress had been replaced by a handsome poplin, which was made in the extreme of fashion, and fitted her admirably, as did every portion of her dress, from her jaunty hat and dotted lace veil to the Alexandre kids and fancy little gaiters which encased her feet and hands. She was prettier even than on her bridal day, Richard thought, as he kissed away the tears which dropped so fast even after the last good-by had been said to poor Aunt Barbara, who watched the flutter of Ethie's veil and ribbons as far as they could be seen, and then in the secrecy of her own room knelt and prayed that God would bless and keep her darling, and make her happy in the new home to which she was going.

It was very quiet and lonely in the Bigelow house that day, Aunt Barbara walking softly and speaking slowly, as if the form of someone dead had been borne from her side, while on the bed, which the housemaid Betty had made so plump and round there was a cavity made by Aunt Barbara's head, which hid itself there many times as the good woman went repeatedly to God with the pain gnawing so at her heart. But in the evening, when a cheerful wood fire was kindled on the hearth of her pleasant sitting room, while Mrs. Captain Markham came in with her knitting work, to sit until the Captain called for her on his return from the meeting where he was to oppose with all his might the building of a new schoolhouse, to pay for which he would be heavily taxed, she felt better, and could talk composedly of the travelers, who by that time were nearing Rochester, where they would spend the night.

Although very anxious to reach home, Richard had promised that Ethelyn should only travel through the day, as she was not as strong as before her illness. And to this promise he adhered, so that it was near the middle of the afternoon of the fifth day that the last change was made, and they took the train that would in two hours' time deposit them at Olney. At Camden, the county seat, they waited for a few moments. There was always a crowd of people here going out to different parts of the country, and as one after another came into the car Richard seemed to know them all, while the cordial and rather noisy greeting which they gave "the Judge" struck Ethelyn a little oddly--it was so different from the quiet, undemonstrative manner to which she had been accustomed. With at least a dozen men in shaggy overcoats and slouched hats she shook hands with a tolerably good grace, but when there appeared a tall, lank, bearded young giant of a fellow, with a dare-devil expression in his black eyes and a stain of tobacco about his mouth, she drew back, and to his hearty "How are ye, Miss Markham? Considerable tuckered out, I reckon?" she merely responded with a cool bow and a haughty stare, intended to put down the young man, whom Richard introduced as "Tim Jones," and who, taking a seat directly in front of her, poured forth a volley of conversation, calling Richard sometimes "Dick," sometimes "Markham," but oftener "Squire," as he had learned to do when Richard was justice of the peace in Olney. Melinda, too, or "Melind," was mentioned as having been over to the "Squire's house helping the old lady to fix up a little," and then Ethelyn knew that the "savage" was no other than brother to Abigail Jones, deceased. The discovery was not a pleasant one, and did not tend to smooth her ruffled spirits or lessen the feeling of contempt for Western people in general, and Richard's friends in particular, which had been growing in her heart ever since the Eastern world was left behind and she had been fairly launched upon the great prairies of the Mississippi Valley. Richard was a prince compared with the specimens she had seen, though she did wonder that he should be so familiar with them, calling them by their first names, and even bandying jokes with the terrible Tim Jones spitting his tobacco juice all over the car floor and laughing so loudly at all the "Squire" said. It was almost too dreadful to endure, and Ethelyn's head was beginning to ache frightfully when the long train came to a pause, and the conductor, who also knew Judge Markham, and called him "Dick," screamed through the open door "O-l-ney!"

Ethelyn was at home at last.

CHAPTER VI: MRS. MARKHAM'S WAYS

They were very peculiar, and no one knew this better than Mrs. Jones and her daughter Melinda, sister and mother to the deceased Abigail and the redoubtable Tim. Naturally bright and quick-witted, Melinda caught readily at any new improvement, and the consequence was that the Jones house bore unmistakable signs of having in it a grown-up daughter whose new ideas of things kept the old ideas from rusting. After Melinda came home from boarding-school the Joneses did not set the table in the kitchen close to the hissing cook stove, but in the pleasant dining room, where there gradually came to be crocheted tidies on the backs of the rocking-chairs, and crayon sketches on the wall, and a pot of geraniums in the window, with a canary bird singing in his cage near by. At first, Mrs. Markham, who felt a greater interest in the Joneses than in any other family--Mrs. Jones being the only woman in the circle of her acquaintance to whom she would lend her copper boiler--looked a little askance at these "new-fangled notions," wondering how "Miss Jones expected to keep the flies out of her house if she had all the doors a-flyin' three times a day," and fearing lest Melinda was getting "stuck-up notions in her head, which would make her fit for nothing."

But when she found there were no more flies buzzing in Farmer Jones' kitchen than in her own, and that Melinda worked as much as ever, and was just as willing to lend a helping hand when there was need of haste at the Markham house, her anxiety subsided, and the Joneses were welcome to eat wherever they chose, or even to have to wait upon the table, when there was company, the little black boy Pete, whom Tim had bought at a slave auction in New Orleans, whither he had gone on a flatboat expedition two or three years before. But she never thought of introducing any of Melinda's notions into her own household. She "could not fuss" to keep so many rooms clean. If in winter time she kept a fire in the front room, where in one corner her own bed was curtained off, and if in summer she always sat there when her work was done, it was all that could be required of her, and was just as they used to do at her father's, in Vermont, thirty years ago. Her kitchen was larger than Mrs. Jones', which was rather uncomfortable on a hot day when there was washing to be done; the odor of the soap-suds was a little sickening then, she admitted, but in her kitchen it was different; she had had an eye to comfort when they were building, and had seen that the kitchen was the largest, airiest, lightest room in the house, with four windows, two outside doors, and a fireplace, where, although they had a stove, she dearly loved to cook just as her mother had done in Vermont, and where hung an old-fashioned crane, with iron hooks suspended from it. Here she washed, and ironed, and ate, and performed her ablutions in the bright tin basin which stood in the sink near to the pail, with the gourd swinging in the top, and wiped her face on the rolling towel and combed her hair before the clock, which served the double purpose of looking-glass and timepiece. When company came--and Mrs. Markham was not inhospitable--the east room, where the bed stood, was opened; and if the company, as was sometimes the case, chanced to be Richard's friends, she used the west room across the hall, where the chocolate-colored paper and Daisy's picture hung, and where, upon the high mantel, there was a plaster image of little Samuel, and two plaster vases filled with colored fruit. The carpet was a very pretty Brussels, but it did not quite cover the floor on either side. It was a small pattern, and on this account had been offered a shilling cheaper a yard, and so the economical Mrs. Markham had bought it, intending to eke out the deficiency with drugget of a corresponding shade; but the merchant did not bring the drugget, and the carpet was put down, and time went on, and the strips of painted board were still uncovered, save by the straight row of haircloth chairs, which stood upon one side, and the old-fashioned sofa, which had cost fifty dollars, and ought to last at least as many years. There was a Boston rocker, and a center table, with the family Bible on it, and a volume of Scott's Commentaries, and frosted candlesticks on the mantel and two sperm candles in them, with colored paper, pink and green, all fancifully notched and put around them, and a bureau in the corner, which held the boys' Sunday shirts and Mrs. Markham's black silk dress, with Daisy's clothes in the bottom drawer, and the silver plate taken from her coffin. There was a gilt-framed looking-glass on the wall, and blue paper curtains at the windows, which were further ornamented with muslin drapery. This was the great room-- the parlor--where Daisy had died, and which, on that account, was a kind of sacred place to those who held the memory of that sweet, little prairie blossom as the dearest memory of their lives. Had she lived, with her naturally refined tastes, and her nicety of perceptions, there was no guessing what that farmhouse might have been, for a young girl makes a deal of difference in any family. But she died, and so the house, which when she died, was not quite finished, remained much as it was--a large, square building, minus blinds, with a wide hall in the center opening in front upon a broad piazza, and opening back upon a stoop, the side entrance to the kitchen. There was a picket fence in front; but the yard was bare of ornament, if we except the lilac bushes under the parlor windows, the red peony in the corner, and the clumps of violets and daisies, which grew in what was intended for borders to the walk, from the front gate to the door. Sometimes the summer showed here a growth of marigolds, with sweet peas and china asters, for Andy was fond of flowers, and when he had leisure he did a little floral gardening; but this year, owing to Richard's absence, there had been more to do on the farm, consequently the ornamental had been neglected, and the late autumn flowers which, in honor of Ethelyn's arrival, were standing in vases on the center table and the mantel, were contributed by Melinda Jones, who had been very busy in other portions of the house working for the bride.

She could do this now without a single pang of jealousy, for she was a sensible girl, and after a night and a day of heaviness, and a vague sense of disappointment, she had sung as merrily as ever, and no one was more interested in the arrival of Richard's bride than she, from the time when Richard started eastward for her. Between herself and her mother there had been a long, confidential conversation, touching Mrs. Markham's ways and the best means of circumventing them, so that the new wife might not be utterly crushed with homesickness and surprise when she first arrived. No one could manage Mrs. Markham as well as Melinda, and it was owing to her influence wholly that the large, pleasant chamber, which had been Richard's ever since he became a growing man, was renovated and improved until it presented a very inviting appearance. The rag carpet which for years had done duty, and bore many traces of Richard's muddy boots, had been exchanged for a new ingrain--not very pretty in design, or very stylish either, but possessing the merit of being fresh and clean. To get the carpet Melinda had labored assiduously, and had enlisted all three of the brothers, James, and John, and Andy in the cause before the economical mother consented to the purchase. The rag carpet, if cleaned and mended, was as good as ever, she insisted; and even if it were not, she could put on one that had not seen so much actual service. It was Andy who finally decided her to indulge in the extravagance urged by Melinda Jones. There were reasons why Andy was very near to his mother's heart, and when he offered to sell his brown pony, which he loved as he did his eyes, his mother yielded the point, and taking with her both Mrs. Jones and Melinda, went to Camden, and sat two mortal hours upon rolls of carpeting while she decided which to take.

Mrs. Markham was not stingy with regard to her table; that was always loaded with the choicest of everything, while many a poor family blessed her as an angel. But the articles she ate were mostly the products of their large, well-cultivated farm; they did not cost money directly out of her hand, and it was the money she disliked parting with, so she talked and dickered, and beat the Camden merchant down five cents on a yard, and made him cut it a little short, to save a waste, and made him throw in the thread and binding and swear when she was gone, wondering who "the stingy old woman was." And yet the very day after her return from Camden "the stingy old woman" had sent to her minister a loaf of bread and a pail of butter, and to a poor sick woman, who lived in a leaky cabin off in the prairie, a nice, warm blanket for her bed, with a basket of delicacies to tempt her capricious appetite.

In due time the carpet had been made, Melinda Jones sewing up three of the seams, while Andy, who knew how to use the needle almost as well as a girl, claimed the privilege of sewing at least half a seam on the new sister's carpet. Adjoining Richard's chamber was a little room where Mrs. Markham's flour and meal and corn were kept, but which, with a little fitting up, would answer nicely for a bedroom, and after an amount of engineering, which would have done credit to the general of an army, Melinda succeeded in coaxing Mrs. Markham to move her barrels and bags, and give up the room for Ethelyn's bed, which looked very nice and inviting, notwithstanding that the pillows were small, and the bedstead a high poster, which had been in use for twenty years. Mrs. Markham knew all about the boxes, as she called them. There was one in Mrs. Jones' front chamber, but she had never bought one, for what then would she do with her old ones--"with them laced cords," so greatly preferable to the hard slats, which nearly broke her back the night she slept on some at a friend's house in Olney.

Richard was fond of books, and had collected from time to time a well-selected library, which was the only ornament in his room when Melinda first took it in hand; but when she had finished her work--when the carpet was down, and the neat, white shades were up at the windows; when the books which used to be on the floor and table, and chairs, and mantel, and window sills, and anywhere, were neatly arranged in the very respectable shelves which Andy made and James had painted; when the little sewing chair designed for Ethelyn was put before one window, and Richard's arm-chair before the other, and the drab lounge was drawn a little into the room, and the bureau stood corner-ways, with a bottle of cologne upon it, which John had bought, and a pot of pomade Andy had made, and two little pink and white mats Melinda had crocheted, the room was very presentable. Great, womanish Andy was sure Ethelyn would be pleased, and rubbed his hands jubilantly over the result of his labors, while Melinda was certainly pardonable for feeling that in return for what she had done for Richard's wife she might venture to suggest that the huge box, marked piano, which for ten days had been standing on the front piazza, be opened and the piano set up, so that she could try its tone. This box had cost Andy a world of trouble, keeping him awake nights, and taking him from his bed more than once, as he fancied he heard a mysterious sound, and feared someone might be stealing the ponderous thing, which it took four men to lift. With the utmost alacrity he helped in the unpacking, nearly bursting a blood-vessel as he tugged at the heaviest end, and then running to the village with all his speed, to borrow Mrs. Crandall's piano key, which, fortunately, fitted Ethelyn's, so that Melinda Jones was soon seated in state, and running her fingers over the superb five-hundred dollar instrument, Ethelyn's gift from Aunt Barbara on her nineteenth birthday.

Melinda's fingers were strained and cut with carpet thread, and pricked with carpet tacks, and red with washing dishes, but they moved nimbly over the keys, striking out with a will the few tunes she had learned during her two quarters' instruction. She had acquired a great deal of knowledge in a short time, for she was passionately fond of music, and every spare moment had been devoted to it, so that she had mastered the scales with innumerable exercises, besides learning several pieces, of which Money-musk was one. This she now played with a sprightliness and energy which brought Andy to his feet, while the cowhides moved to the stirring music in a fashion which would have utterly confounded poor Ethelyn could she have seen them. But Ethelyn was miles and miles away. She was not coming for a week or more, and in that time Andy tried his hand at Yankee Doodle, playing with one finger, and succeeding far beyond his most sanguine expectations. Andy was delighted with the piano, and so was Eunice, the hired girl, who left her ironing and her dishes, standing with wiping towel or flatiron in hand, humming an accompaniment to Andy's playing, and sometimes helping to find the proper key to touch next.

Eunice was not an Irish girl, nor a German, nor a Scotch, but a full-blooded American, and "just as good as her employers," with whom she always ate and sat. It was not Mrs. Markham's custom to keep a girl the year round, but when she did it was Eunice Plympton, the daughter of the drunken fiddler who earned his livelihood by playing for the dances the young people of Olney sometimes got up. He was anticipating quite a windfall from the infair it was confidently expected would be given by Mrs. Markham in honor of her son's marriage; and Eunice herself had washed and starched and ironed the white waist she intended to wear on the same occasion. Of course she knew she would have to wait and tend and do the running, she said to Melinda, to whom she confided her thoughts, but after the supper was over she surely might have one little dance, if with nobody but Andy.

This was Eunice, and she had been with Mrs. Markham during the past summer; but her time was drawing to a close. All the heavy work was over, the harvests were gathered in, the soap was made, the cleaning done, the house made ready for Richard's wife, and it was the understanding that when that lady came and was somewhat domesticated, Miss Eunice was to leave. There was not much to do in the winter, Mrs. Markham said, and with Richard's wife's help she should get along. Alas! how little Ethelyn was prepared for the home which awaited her, and for the really good woman, who, on the afternoon of her son's arrival, saw into the oven the young turkey which Andy had been feeding for so very long with a view to this very day, and then helped Eunice set the table for the expected guests.

It did occur to Mrs. Markham that there might be a great propriety in Eunice's waiting for once, inasmuch as there were plates to change, and custard pie and minced, and pudding, to be brought upon the table, for they were having a great dinner, but the good woman did not dare hint at such a thing, so the seven plates were put upon the table, and the china cups brought from the little cupboard at the side of the chimney, and the silver teapot, which was a family heirloom, and had been given Mrs. Markham by her mother, was brought also and rubbed up with what Eunice called a "shammy," and the pickles, and preserves, and honey, and cheese and jellies, and the white raised biscuits and fresh brown bread, and shredded cabbage and cranberry sauce, with golden butter, and pitchers of cream, were all arranged according to Eunice's ideas. The turkey was browning nicely, the vegetables were cooking upon the stove, the odor of silver-skinned onions pervading the entire house. Eunice was grinding the coffee, and the clock said it wanted but half an hour of car-time, when Mrs. Markham finally left the kitchen and proceeded to make her toilet.

Eunice's had been made some time ago, and the large-sized hoop she wore had already upset a pail and dragged a griddle from the stove hearth, greatly to the discomfiture of Mrs. Markham, who did not fancy hoops, though she wore a small one this afternoon under her clean and stiffly-starched dress of purple calico. St. Paul would have made her an exception in his restrictions with regard to women's apparel, for neither gold nor silver ornaments, nor braided hair, found any tolerance in her. She followed St. Paul strictly, except at such times as the good people in the Methodist church at the east end of the village held a protracted meeting, when she deviated so far from his injunction as to speak her mind and tell her experience.

She was a good and conscientious woman, practicing what she preached, and believing more in the inner than the outer adorning; but she looked very neat this afternoon in her purple calico, with a motherly white apron tied around her waist, and her soft, silvery hair combed smoothly back from her forehead and twisted in a knot behind, about the size of a half dollar. This knot however, was hidden by the headdress which Melinda had made from bits of black lace and purple ribbon, and which, though not at all like Aunt Barbara's Boston caps, was still very respectable, and even tasteful-looking. Almost too tasteful, Mrs. Markham thought, as she glanced at the tiny artificial flower tucked in among the bows of ribbon. But Mrs. Markham did not remove the flower, for it was a daisy, and it made her think of the Daisy who died fourteen years ago, and who, had she lived till now, would have been twenty-eight.

"A married woman, most likely, and I might have been grandmother," Mrs. Markham sighed, and then, as she heard in fancy the patter of little feet at her side, and saw before her little faces with a look like Daisy in them, her thoughts went softly out to Richard's bride, through whom this coveted blessing might come to her quiet household, and her heart throbbed with a quick sudden yearning for the young daughter-in-law, now just alighting at the Olney station, for the Eastern train had come, and James was there with the democrat-wagon to meet it.

CHAPTER VII: GETTING HOME

Olney was a thriving, busy little town, numbering five hundred inhabitants or thereabouts. It had its groceries, its dry goods stores, and its two houses for public worship--the Methodist and Presbyterian--while every other Sunday a little band of Episcopalians met for their own service in what was called the Village Hall, where, during week days, a small, select school was frequently taught by some Yankee schoolmistress. It had its post office, too; and there was also talk of a bank after the railroad came that way, and roused the people to a state of still greater activity. On the whole, it was a pretty town, though different from Chicopee, where the houses slept so aristocratically under the shadow of the old elms, which had been growing there since the day when our national independence was declared.

At home Ethelyn's pride had all been centered in Boston, and she had sometimes thought a little contemptuously of Chicopee and its surroundings; but the farther she traveled west the higher Chicopee rose in her estimation, until she found herself comparing every prairie village with that rural town among the hills, which seemed to give it dignity, and made it so greatly superior to the dead levels of which she was getting so weary. She had admired the rolling prairies at first, but, tired and jaded with her long journey, nothing looked well to her now--nothing was like Chicopee--certainly not Olney, where the dwellings looked so new and the streets were minus sidewalks.

Ethelyn had a good view of it as the train approached it and even caught a passing glimpse of the white house in the distance which Richard pointed out as home, his face lighting up with all the pleasure of a schoolboy as he saw the old familiar waymarks and felt that he was home at last.

Dropping her veil over her face Ethelyn arose to follow her husband, who in his eagerness to grasp the hand of the tall, burly young man he had seen from the window, forgot to carry her shawl and her satchel, which last being upon the car-rack, she tugged at it with all her strength, and was about crying with vexation at Richard's thoughtlessness, when Tim Jones, who while rolling his quid of tobacco in his great mouth, had watched her furtively, wondering how she and Melind would get along, gallantly came to her aid, and taking the satchel down kept it upon his arm.

"Take care of that air step. Better let me help you out. Dick is so tickled to see Jim that he even forgets his wife, I swan!" Tim said, offering to assist her from the train; but with a feeling of disgust too deep to be expressed, Ethelyn declined the offer and turned away from him to meet the curious gaze of the young man whom Richard presented as brother James.

He was younger than his brother by half a dozen years, but he looked quite as old, if not older. His face and hands were sunburnt and brown, his clothes were coarse, his pants were tucked into his tall, muddy boots, and he held in his hands the whip with which he had driven the shining bays, pricking up their ears behind the depot and eyeing askance the train just beginning to move away. The Markhams were all good-looking, and James was not an exception. The Olney girls called him very handsome, when on Sunday he came to church in his best clothes and led the

Methodist choir; but Ethelyn only thought him rough, and coarse, and vulgar, and when he bent down to kiss her she drew back haughtily.

"Ethelyn!" Richard said, in the low, peculiar tone, which she had almost unconsciously learned to fear, just as she did the dark expression which his hazel eyes assumed as he said the single word "Ethelyn!"

She was afraid of Richard when he looked and spoke that way, and putting up her lip, she permitted the kiss which the warm-hearted James gave to her. He was naturally more demonstrative than his brother, and more susceptible, too; a pretty face would always set his heart to beating and call out all the gallantry of his nature. Wholly unsophisticated, he never dreamed of the gulf there was between him and the new sister, whom he thought so beautiful-- loving her at once, because she was so pretty, and because she was the wife of Dick, their household idol. He was more of a ladies' man than Richard, and when on their way to the democratic-wagon they came to a patch of mud, through which Ethelyn's skirts were trailing, he playfully lifted her in his strong arms, and set her down upon the wagon-box, saying, as he adjusted her skirts: "We can't have that pretty dress spoiled, the very first day, with Iowa mud."

All this time Tim Jones had been dutifully holding the satchel, which he now deposited at Ethelyn's feet, and then, at James' invitation, he sprang into the hinder part of the wagon-box, and sitting down, let his long limbs dangle over the backboard, while James sat partly in Richard's lap and partly in Ethelyn's. It had been decided that the democrat must come down again for the baggage; and so, three on a seat, with Tim Jones holding on behind, Ethelyn was driven through the town, while face after face looked at her from the windows of the different dwellings, and comment after comment was made upon her pretty little round hat, with its jaunty feather, which style had not then penetrated so far west as Olney. Rumors there were of the Eastern ladies wearing hats which made them look at least ten years younger than their actual age; but Ethelyn was the first to carry the fashion to Olney, and she was pronounced very stylish, and very girlish, too, by those who watched her curiously from behind their curtains and blinds.

It was the close of a chill October day, and a bank of angry clouds hung darkly in the western sky, while the autumn wind blew across the prairie; but colder, blacker, chillier far than prairie winds, or threatening clouds, or autumnal day was the shadow resting on Ethelyn's heart, and making her almost cry out with loneliness and homesickness, as they drew near the house where the blue paper curtains were hanging before the windows and Eunice Plympton's face was pressed against the pane. The daisies and violets and summer grass were withered and dead, and the naked branches of the lilac bush brushed against the house with a mournful, rasping sound, which reminded her of the tall sign-post in Chicopee, which used to creak so in the winter wind, and keep her Aunt Barbara awake. To the right of the house, and a little in the rear, were several large, square corn-cribs, and behind these an inclosure in which numerous cattle, and horses, and pigs were industriously feeding, while the cobs, stripped, and soiled, and muddy, were scattered everywhere. Ethelyn took it all in at a glance, exclaiming, in a smothered voice, as the wagon turned into the lane which led to the side door, "Not here, Richard; surely, not here!"

But Richard, if he heard her, did not heed her. He could not comprehend her utter desolation and crushing disappointment. Her imaginings of his home had never been anything like this reality, and for a moment she felt as if in a kind of horrible nightmare, from which she struggled to awake.

"Oh! if it were only a dream," she thought; but it was no dream, though as Richard himself lifted her carefully from the wagon, and deposited her upon the side stoop, there came a mist before her eyes, and for an instant sense and feeling forsook her; but only for an instant, for the hall door was thrown open, and Richard's mother came out to greet her son and welcome her new daughter.

But alas for Ethelyn's visions of heavy silk and costly lace! How they vanished before this woman in purple calico, with ruffles of the same standing up about the throat, and the cotton lace coiffure upon her head! She was very glad to see her boy and wound both her arms around his neck, but she was afraid of Ethelyn. She, too, had had her ideal, but it was not like this proud-looking beauty, dressed so stylishly, and, as it seemed to her so extravagantly, with her long, full skirt of handsome poplin trailing so far behind her, and her basque fitting her graceful figure so admirably. Neither did the hat, rolled so jauntily on the sides, and giving her a coquettish appearance, escape her notice, nor the fact that the dotted veil was not removed from the white face, even after Richard had put the little, plump hand in hers, and said:

"This, mother, is Ethie, my wife. I hope you will love each other for my sake."

In her joy at seeing her pet boy again, Mrs. Markham would have done a great deal for his sake, but she could not "kiss a veil," as she afterwards said to Melinda Jones, when she reached the point where she talked straight out about her daughter-in-law. No, she could not kiss a veil, and so she only held and pressed Ethelyn's hand, and leading her into the house, told her she was very welcome, and bade her come to the fire and take off her things, and asked if she was not tired, and cold and hungry.

And Ethelyn tried to answer, but the great lumps were swelling in her throat, and so keen a pain was tugging at her heart that when at last, astonished at her silence, Richard said, "What is the matter, Ethie--why don't you answer mother?" she burst out in a pitiful cry:

"Oh, Richard, I can't, I can't; please take me back to Aunt Barbara."

This was the crisis, the concentration of all she had been suffering for the last hour, and it touched Mrs. Markham's heart, for she remembered just how wretched she had been when she first landed at the rude log cabin which was so long her Western home, and turning to Richard, she said, in an aside:

"She is homesick, poor child, as it's natural she should be at first. She'll be better by and by, so don't think strange of it. She seems very young."

In referring to her youth, Mrs. Markham meant nothing derogatory to her daughter-in-law, though Ethelyn did strike her as very young, in her pretty hat with her heavy hair low in her neck. She was finding an excuse for her crying, and did not mean that Ethelyn should hear. But she did hear, and the hot tears were dashed aside at once. She was too proud to be petted or patronized by Mrs. Markham, or apologized for by her, so she dried her eyes, and lifting her head, said proudly:

"I am tired to-night, and my head is aching so hard that I lost my self-control. I beg you will excuse me. Richard knows me too well to need an excuse."

A born duchess could not have assumed a loftier air, and in some perplexity Mrs. Markham glanced from her to Richard, as if asking what to do next. Fortunately for all parties, Andy just then came in with his brother John, who approached his new sister with some little hesitation. He had heard Tim Jones' verdict, "Stuck up as the old Nick," while even cautious James had admitted his fears that Dick had made a mistake, and taken a wife who would never fit their ways. And this was why John had been so late with his welcome. He had crept up the back stairs, and donned his best necktie, and changed his heavy boots for a pair of shoes, which left exposed to view a portion of his blue yarn socks. He had before changed his coat and vest, and tied on a handkerchief, but it was not his best; not the satin cravat, with the pretty bow Melinda Jones had made, and in which was stuck a rather fanciful pin he wore on great occasions. He was all right now, and he shook hands with his new sister, and asked if she were pretty well, and told her she was welcome, and then stepped back for Andy, who had been making his toilet when the bride arrived, and so was late with his congratulations.

CHAPTER VIII: ANDY

Andy was a character in his way. A fall from his horse upon the ground had injured his head when he was a boy, and since that time he had been what his mother called a little queer, while the neighbors spoke of him as simple Andy, or Mrs. Markham's half-wit, who did the work of a girl and knit all his own socks. He was next to Richard in point of age, but he looked younger than either of his brothers, for his face was round and fair, and smooth as any girl's. It is true that every Sunday of his life he made a great parade with lather and shaving-cup, standing before the glass in his shirt-sleeves, just as the other boys did, and flourishing his razor around his white throat and beardless face, to the amusement of anyone who chanced to see him for the first time.

In his younger days, when the tavern at the Cross Roads was just opened, Andy had been a sore trial to both mother and brothers, and many a night, when the rain and sleet were driving across the prairies, Richard had left the warm fireside and gone out in the storm after the erring Andy, who had more than once been found by the roadside, with his hat jammed into every conceivable shape, his face scratched, and a tell-tale smell about his breath which contradicted his assertion "that somebody had knocked him down."

Andy had been intemperate, and greatly given to what the old Captain in Chicopee had designated as "busts"; but since the time when the church missionary, young Mr. Townsend, had come to Olney, and held his first service in the log schoolhouse, Andy had ceased to frequent the Cross Roads tavern, and Richard went no more in the autumnal storms to look for his wayward brother. There was something in the beautiful simplicity of the church service which went straight to Andy's heart, and more than all, there was something in Mr. Townsend's voice, and manner, and face, which touched a responsive chord in the breast of the boyish Andy, and when at last the bishop came to that section of Iowa, his hands were first laid in blessing on the bowed head of Andy, who knelt to receive the rite of confirmation in the presence of a large concourse of people, to most of whom the service and ceremony were entirely new.

While rejoicing and thanking God for the change, which she felt was wholly sincere, Mrs. Markham had deeply deplored the pertinacity with which Andy had clung to his resolve to join "Mr. Townsend's church or none." She did not doubt Mr. Townsend's piety or Andy's either, but she doubted the Episcopalians generally because they did not require more than God himself requires, and it hurt her sore that Andy should go with them rather than to her church across the brook, where Father Aberdeen preached every Sunday against the pride, and pomp, and worldliness generally of his Episcopal brethren. Andy believed in Mr. Townsend, and in time he came to believe heart and soul in the church doctrines as taught by him, and the beautiful consistency of his daily life was to his mother like a constant and powerful argument in favor of the church to which he belonged, while to his brothers it was a powerful argument in favor of the religion he professed.

That Andy Markham was a Christian no one doubted. It showed itself in every act of his life; it shone in his beaming, good-natured face, and made itself heard in the touching pathos of his voice, when he repeated aloud in his room the prayers of his church, saying to his mother, when she objected that his prayers were made up beforehand: "And for the land's sake, ain't the sams and hims, which are nothing but prayers set to music, made up beforehand? A pretty muss you'd have of it if everybody should strike out for himself, a singin' his own words just as they popped into his head."

Mrs. Markham was not convinced, but she let Andy alone after that, simply remarking that "the prayer-book would not always answer the purpose; there would come a time when just what he wanted was not there."

Andy was willing to wait till that time came, trusting to Mr. Townsend to find for him some way of escape; and so the matter dropped, and he was free to read his prayers as much as he pleased. He had heard from Richard that his new sister was of his way of thinking--that though not a member of the church except by baptism, she was an Episcopalian, and would be married by that form.

It was strange how Andy's great, warm heart went out toward Ethelyn after that. He was sure to like her; and on the evening of the bridal, when the clock struck nine, he had taken his tallow candle to his room, and opening his prayer-book at the marriage ceremony, had read it carefully through, even to the saying: "I, Richard, take thee, Ethelyn," etc., kneeling at the proper time, and after he was through even venturing to improvise a prayer of his own, in which he asked, not that Ethelyn might be happy with his brother--there was no doubt on that point, for Richard was perfect in his estimation--but that "old Dick" might be happy with her--that he, Andy, might do his whole duty by her, and that, if it was right to ask it, she might bring him something from that famous Boston, which seemed to him like a kind of paradise, and also that she need not at once discover that he did not know as much as "old Dick."

This was Andy's prayer, which he had confessed to Mr. Townsend; and now, all shaven and shorn, with his best Sunday coat and a large bandanna in his hand, he came in to greet his sister. It needed but a glance for Ethelyn to know the truth, for Andy's face told what he was; but there was something so kind in his expression and so winning in his voice, as he called her "Sister Ethie," that she unbent to him as she had unbent to no one else; and when he stooped to kiss her, she did not draw back as she had from James and John, but promptly put up her lips, and only winced a very little at the second loud, hearty smack which Andy gave her, his great mouth leaving a wet spot on her cheek, which she wiped away with her handkerchief.

Richard had dreaded the meeting between his polished wife and his simple brother more than anything else, and several times he had tried to prepare Ethelyn for it, but he could not bring himself to say, "Andy is foolish"; for when he tried to do it Andy's pleading face came up before him just as it looked on the morning of his departure from home in June, when Andy had said to him: "Don't tell her what a shaller critter I am. Let her find it out by her learning."

So Richard had said nothing particular of Andy, and now he watched him anxiously, to see the impression he was making, and, as he saw Ethelyn's manner, marveling greatly at this new phase in her disposition. She did not feel half so desolate after seeing Andy, and she let him hold her hand, which he stroked softly, admiring its whiteness, and evidently comparing it with his own. All the Markhams had large hands and feet, just as they were all good-looking. Even Andy had his points of beauty, for his soft brown hair was handsomer, if possible, than Richard's, and more luxuriant, while many a city dandy might have coveted his white, even teeth, and his dark eyes were very placid and gentle in their expression.

"Little sister" he called Ethelyn, who though not very short in stature, seemed to him so much younger than he had expected Dick's wife to be that he applied the term "little" as he would to anything which he wished to pet.

Ethelyn's hat was laid aside by this time, and the basquine, too, which Andy thought the prettiest coat he had ever seen, and which Eunice, who was bidden to carry Ethelyn's things away, tried on before the glass in Ethelyn's chamber, as she did also the hat, deciding that Melinda Jones could make her something like them out of a gray skirt she had at home and one of Tim's palm-leaf hats.

CHAPTER IX: DINNER, AND AFTER IT

Eunice had not fully seen the stranger, and so, when dinner was announced and Richard led her out, with Andy hovering at her side, she stood ready to be introduced, with the little speech she had been rehearsing about "I hope to see you well," etc., trembling on the tip of her tongue. But her plans were seriously disarranged. Six months before Richard would have presented her himself, as a matter of course; but he had learned some things since then, and he tried not to see his mother's meaning as she glanced from him to Eunice and then to Ethelyn, whose proud, dignified bearing awed and abashed even her. Eunice, however, had been made quite too much of to be wholly ignored now, and Mrs. Markham felt compelled to say, "Ethelyn, this--ah, this is--Eunice--Eunice Plympton."

That Eunice Plympton was the hired girl Ethelyn did not for a moment dream; but that she was coarse and vulgar, like the rest of Richard's family, she at once decided, and if she bowed at all it was not perceptible to Eunice, who mentally resolved "to go home in the morning if such a proud minx was to live there."

Mrs. Markham saw the gathering storm, and Richard knew by the drop of her chin that Ethelyn had not made a good impression. How could she with that proud cold look, which never for an instant left her face, but rather deepened in its expression as the dinner proceeded, and one after the other Mrs. Markham and Eunice left the table in quest of something that was missing, while Andy himself, being nearest the kitchen, went to bring a pitcher of hot water for Ethelyn's coffee, lifting the kettle with the skirt of his coat, and snapping his fingers, which were slightly burned with the scalding steam. From the position she occupied at the table Ethelyn saw the whole performance, and had it been in any other house she would have smiled at Andy's grotesque appearance as he converted his coat skirts into a holder; but now it only sent a colder chill to her heart as she reflected that these were Richard's people and this was Richard's home. Sadly and vividly there arose before her visions of dear Aunt Barbara's household, where Betty served so quietly and where, except that they were upon a smaller scale, everything was as well and properly managed as in Mrs. Dr. Van Buren's family. It was several hours since she had tasted food, but she could scarcely swallow a morsel for the terrible homesick feeling swelling in her throat. She knew the viands before her were as nicely cooked as even Aunt Barbara or Betty could have cooked them--so much she conceded to Mrs. Markham and Eunice; but had her life depended upon it she could not have eaten them and the plate which James had filled so plentifully scarcely diminished at all. She did pick a little with her fork at the white, tender turkey, and tried to drink her coffee, but the pain in her head and the pain at her heart were both too great to allow of her doing more, and Mrs. Markham and Eunice both felt a growing contempt for a dainty thing who could not eat the dinner they had been at so much pains to prepare.

Ethelyn knew their opinion of her as well as if it had been expressed in words; but they were so very far beneath her that whatsoever they might think was not of the slightest consequence. They were a vulgar, ignorant set, the whole of them, she mentally decided, as she watched their manners at table, noticing how James and John poured their coffee into their saucers, blowing it until it was cool, while Richard, feeling more freedom now that he was again under his mother's wing, used his knife altogether, even to eating jelly with it. Ethelyn was disgusted, and once, as Richard's well-filled knife was moving toward his mouth, she gently touched his foot with her own; but if he understood her he did not heed her, and went quietly on with his dinner. Indeed, it might be truly said of him that "Richard was himself again," for his whole manner was that of a petted child, which, having returned to the mother who spoiled it, had cast off the restraint under which for a time it had been laboring. Richard was hungry, and would have enjoyed his dinner hugely but for the cold, silent woman beside him, who, he knew, was watching and criticising all he did; but somehow at home he did not care so much for her criticisms as when alone with her at fashionable hotels or with fashionable people. Here he was supreme, and none had ever disputed his will. Perhaps if Ethelyn had known all that was in his heart she might have changed her tactics and tried to have been more conciliatory on that first evening of her arrival at his home. But Ethelyn did not know--she only felt that she was homesick and wretched--and pleading a headache, from which she was really suffering, she asked to go to her room as soon as dinner was over.

It was very pleasant up there, for a cheerful wood fire was blazing on the hearth, and a rocking-chair drawn up before it, with a footstool which Andy had made and Melinda covered, while the bed in the little room adjoining looked so fresh, and clean, and inviting, that with a great sigh of relief, as the door closed between her and the "dreadful people below," Ethelyn threw herself upon it, and burying her face in the soft pillows, tried to smother the sobs which, nevertheless, smote heavily upon Richard's ear when he came in, and drove from him all thoughts of the little lecture he had been intending to give Ethelyn touching her deportment toward his folks. It would only be a fair return, he reflected, for all the Caudles he had listened to so patiently, and duly strengthened for his task by his mother's remark to James, accidentally overheard, "Altogether too fine a lady for us. I wonder what Richard was thinking of," he mounted the stairs resolved at least to talk with Ethie and ask her to do better.

Richard could be very stern when he tried, and the hazel of his eye was darker than usual, and the wrinkle between his eyebrows was deeper as he thus meditated harm against his offending wife. But the sight of the crushed form lying so helplessly upon the bed and crying in such a grieved, heart-sick way, drove all thoughts of discipline from his mind. He could not add one iota to her misery. She might be cold, and proud, and even rude to his family, as she unquestionably had been, but she was still Ethie, his young wife, whom he loved so dearly; and bending over her, he smoothed the silken bands of her beautiful hair and said to her softly, "What is it, darling? Anything worse than homesickness? Has anyone injured you?"

No one had injured her. On the contrary, all had met, or tried to meet her with kindness, which she had thrust back upon them. Ethelyn knew this as well as anyone, and Mrs. Markham, washing her dishes below stairs, and occasionally wiping her eyes with the corner of the check apron as she thought how all her trouble had been thrown away upon a proud, ungrateful girl, could not think less of Ethie than Ethie thought of herself, upstairs sobbing among the pillows.

The family were ignorant and ill bred, as she counted ignorance and ill breeding; but they did mean to be kind to her, and she hated herself for her ingratitude in not at least seeming pleased with their endeavors to please her. Added to this was a vague remembrance of a certain look seen in Richard's eye--a look which made her uneasy as she thought, "What if he should hate me, too?"

Richard was all Ethelyn had to cling to now. She respected, if she did not love him, and when she heard his step upon the stairs, her heart, for an instant, throbbed with dread lest he was coming to chide her as she deserved. When, then, he bent so kindly over her, and spoke to her so tenderly, all her better nature went out toward him in a sudden gush of something akin to love, and lifting her head, she laid it upon his bosom, and drawing his arm around her neck, held it there with a sense of protection, while she said: "No one has injured me; but, oh, I am so homesick, and they are all so different, and my head aches so hard."

He knew she was homesick and it was natural that she should be; and he knew, too, that, as she said, they were "so different," and though on this point he could not fully appreciate her feelings he was sorry for her, and he soothed her aching head, and kissed her forehead, and told her she was tired; she would feel better by and by, and get accustomed to their ways, and when, as he said this, he felt the shiver with which she repelled the assertion, he repressed his inclination to tell her that she could at least conceal her aversion to whatever was disagreeable, and kissing her again, bade her lie down and try to sleep, as that would help her sooner than anything else, unless it were a cup of sage tea, such as his mother used to make for him when his head was aching. Should he send Eunice up with a cup?

"No; oh, no," and Ethelyn's voice expressed the disgust she felt for the young lady with red streamers in her hair, who had stared so at her and called her husband Richard.

Ethelyn had not yet defined Eunice's position in the family--whether it was that of cousin, or niece, or companion--and now that Richard had suggested her, she said to him:

"Who is this Eunice that seems so familiar?"

Richard hesitated a little and then replied:

"She is the girl who works for mother when we need help."

"Not a hired girl--surely not a hired girl!" and Ethelyn opened her brown eyes wide with surprise and indignation, wondering aloud what Aunt Sophia or Aunt Barbara would say if they knew she had eaten with and been introduced to a hired girl.

Richard did not say, "Aunt Sophia or Aunt Barbara be hanged, or be--anything," but he thought it, just as he thought Ethelyn's ideas particular and over-nice. Eunice Plympton was a respectable, trusty girl, and he believed in doing well for those who did well for him; but that was no time to argue the point, and so he sat still and listened to Ethelyn's complaint that Eunice had called him Richard, and would undoubtedly on the morrow address her as Ethelyn. Richard thought not, but changed his mind when, fifteen minutes later, he descended to the kitchen and heard Eunice asking Andy if he did not think "Ethelyn looked like the Methodist minister's new wife."

This was an offense which even Richard could not suffer to pass unrebuked, and sending Andy out on some pretext or other, he said that to Eunice Plympton which made her more careful as to what she called his wife, but he did it so kindly that she could not be offended with him, though she was strengthened in her opinion that "Miss Ethelyn was a stuck-up, an upstart, and a hateful. Supposin' she had been waited on all her life, and brought up delicately, as Richard said, that was no reason why she need feel so big, and above speaking to a poor girl when she was introduced." She guessed that "Eunice Plympton was fully as respectable and quite as much thought on by the neighbors, if she didn't wear a frock coat and a man's hat with a green feather stuck in it."

This was the substance of Eunice's soliloquy, as she cleaned the potatoes for the morrow's breakfast, and laid the kindlings by the stove, ready for the morning fire. Still Eunice was not a bad-hearted girl, and when Andy, who heard her mutterings, put in a plea for Ethelyn, who he said "had never been so far away from home before, and whose head was aching enough to split," she began to relent, and proposed, of her own accord, to take up to the great lady a foot-bath together with hot water for her head.

It was so long since Richard had been at home, and there was so much to hear of what had happened during his absence that instead of going back to Ethelyn he yielded to his mother's wish that he should stay with her, and sitting down in his arm-chair by the blazing fire, he found it so pleasant to be flattered and caressed and deferred to again, that he was in some danger of forgetting the young wife who was thus left to the tender mercies of Andy and Eunice Plympton. Andy had caught eagerly at Eunice's suggestion of the foot-bath, and offered to carry it up himself, while Eunice followed with her towels and basin of hot water. It never occurred to either of them to knock for admittance, and Ethelyn was obliged to endure their presence, which she did at first with a shadow on her brow; but when Andy asked so pleadingly that she try the hot water, and Eunice joined her entreaties with his, Ethelyn consented, and lay very quiet while Eunice Plympton bathed the aching head and smoothed the long, bright hair, which both she and Andy admired so much, for Andy, when he found that Ethelyn declined the foot-bath, concluded to remain a while, and sitting down before the fire, he scrutinized the form and features of his new sister, and made remarks upon the luxuriant tresses which Eunice combed so carefully.

It was something to have the homage of even such subjects as these, and Ethelyn's heart grew softer as the pain gradually subsided beneath Eunice's mesmeric touch, so that she answered graciously the questions propounded by her as to whether that sack, or great-coat, or whatever it was called, which she wore around her, was the very last style, how much it took to cut it, and if Miss Markham had the pattern. On being told that "Miss Markham" had not the pattern, Eunice presumed Melinda Jones could cut one, and then, while the cooled water was heating on the coals which Andy raked out upon the hearth, Eunice asked if she might just try on the "vasquine" and let Miss Markham see how she looked in it.

For a moment Ethelyn hesitated, but Eunice had been so kind, and proffered her request so timidly, that she could not well refuse, and gave a faint assent. But she was spared the trial of seeing her basquine strained over Eunice's buxom figure by the entrance of Richard, who came to say that Melinda Jones was in the parlor below. In spite of all Tim had said about madam's airs, and his advice that "Melinda should keep away," that young lady had ventured upon a call, thinking her intimacy with the family would excuse any unseemly haste, and thinking, too, it may be, that possibly Mrs. Richard Markham would be glad to know there was someone in Olney more like the people to whom she had been accustomed than Mrs. Markham, senior, and her handmaid, Eunice Plympton. Melinda's toilet had been made with direct reference to what Mrs. Ethelyn would think of it, and she was looking very well indeed in her gray dress and sack, with plain straw hat and green ribbons, which harmonized well with her high-colored cheeks. But Melinda's pains had been for naught, just as Richard feared, when she asked if "Mrs. Markham" was too tired to see her.

Richard was glad to see Melinda, and Melinda was glad to see Richard--so glad that she gave him a hearty kiss, prefacing the act with the remark, "I can kiss you, now you are a married man."

Richard liked the kiss, and liked Melinda's frank, open manner, which had in it nothing Van Burenish, as he secretly termed the studied elegance of Mrs. Richard Markham's style. Melinda was natural, and he promptly kissed her back, feeling that in doing so he was guilty of nothing wrong, for he would have done the same had Ethelyn been present. She had a terrible headache, he said, in answer to Melinda's inquiry, and perhaps she did not feel able to come down. He would see.

The hot water and Eunice's bathing had done Ethelyn good, and, with the exception that she was very pale, she looked bright and handsome, as she lay upon the pillows, with her loose hair forming a dark, glossy frame about her face.

"You are better, Ethie," Richard said, bending over her, and playfully lifting her heavy hair. "Eunice has done you good. She's not so bad, after all."

"Eunice is well enough in her place," was Ethelyn's reply; and then there was a pause, while Richard wondered how he should introduce Melinda Jones.

Perhaps it was vain in him, but he really fancied that the name of Jones was distasteful to Ethelyn, just as the Van Buren name would have been more distasteful to him than it already was had he known of Frank's love affair. And to a certain extent he was right. Ethelyn did dislike to hear of the Joneses, whom she heartily despised, and her brow grew cloudy at once when Richard said, bunglingly, and as if it were not at all what he had come up to say: "Oh, don't you remember hearing me speak of Melinda Jones, whom I hoped you would like? She is very kind to mother--we all think a great deal of her; and though she knows it is rather soon to call, she has come in for a few minutes, and would like to see you. I should be so glad if you would go down, for it will gratify her, I know, and I really think we owe her something--she has always been so kind."

But Ethelyn was too tired, and her head ached too hard to see visitors, she said; and besides that, "Miss Jones ought to have known that it was not proper to call so soon. None but a very intimate friend could presume upon such a thing."

"And Melinda is an intimate friend," Richard answered, a little warmly, as he left his wife, and went back to Melinda with the message, that "some time she should be happy to make Miss Jones' acquaintance, but to-night she really must be excused, as she was too tired to come down."

All this time Andy had been standing with his back to the fire, his coat-skirts taken up in his arms, his light, soft hat on his head, and his ears taking in all that was transpiring. Andy regarded his stylish sister-in-law as a very choice gem, which was not to be handled too roughly, but he was not afraid of her; he was seldom afraid of anybody, and when Richard was gone, he walked boldly up to Ethelyn and said:

"I don't want to be meddlesome, but 'pears to me if you'd spoke out your feelings to Dick, you'd said, 'Tell Melinda Jones I don't want to see her, neither to-night nor any time.' Mebby I'm mistaken, but honest, do you want to see Melinda?"

There was something so straightforward in his manner that, without being the least offended, Ethelyn replied:

"No, I do not. I am sure I should not like her if she at all resembles her brother^ that terrible Timothy."

Andy did not know that there was anything so very terrible about Tim. He liked him, because he gave him such nice chews of tobacco, and was always so ready to lend a helping hand in hog-killing time, or when a horse was sick; neither had he ever heard him called Timothy before, and the name sounded oddly, but he classed it with the fine ways of his new sister, who called him Anderson, though he so much wished she wouldn't. It sounded as if she did not like him; but he said nothing on that subject now--he merely adhered to the Jones question, and without defending Tim, replied:

"Gals are never much like their brothers, I reckon. They are softer, and finer, and neater; leastways our Daisy was as different from us as different could be, and Melinda is different from Tim. She's been to Camden high-school, and has got a book that she talks French out of; and didn't you ever see that piece she wrote about Mr. Baldwin's boy, who fell from the top of the church when it was building, and was crushed to death? It was printed, all in rhyme, in the Camden Sentinel, and Jim has a copy of it in his wallet, 'long with a lock of Melinda's hair. I tell you she's a team."

Andy was warming up with his subject, and finding Ethelyn a good listener, he continued:

"I want you to like her, and I b'lieve you orter, for if it hadn't been for her this room wouldn't of been fixed up as 'tis. Melinda coaxed mother to buy the carpet, and the curtings, and to put your bed in there. Why, that was the meal room, where you be, and we used to keep beans there, too; but Melinda stuck to it till mother moved the chest and the bags, and then we got some paint, and me and the boys and Melinda painted, and worked, hopin' all the time that you'd be pleased, as I guess you be. We wanted to have you like us."

And simple-hearted Andy drew near to Ethelyn, who was softened more by what he said than she could have been by her husband's most urgent appeal. The thought of the people to whom she had been so cold, and even rude, working and planning for her comfort, touched a very tender chord, and had Richard then proffered his request for her to go down, it is very possible she might have done so; but it was too late now, and after Andy left her she lay pondering what he had said and listening to the sound of voices which came up to her from the parlor directly beneath her room where James, and John, and Andy, and the mother, with Melinda, and Eunice, were talking to Richard, who was conscious of a greater feeling of content, sitting there in their midst again, than he had known in many a day. Melinda had been more than disappointed at Mrs. Richard's non-appearance, for aside from a curiosity to see the great lady, there was a desire to be able to report that she seen her to other females equally curious, whom she would next day meet at church. It would have added somewhat to her self-complacency as well as importance in their eyes, could she have quoted Mrs. Richard's sayings, and, described Mrs. Richard's dress, the very first day after her arrival. It would look as if the intimacy, which many predicted would end with Mrs. Ethelyn's coming, was only cemented the stronger; but no such honor was in store for her. Ethelyn declined coming down, and with a good-humored smile Melinda said she was quite excusable; and then, untying her bonnet, she laid it aside, just as she did the indescribable air of stiffness she had worn while expecting Mrs. Richard.

How merrily they all laughed and chatted together! and how handsome James' eyes grew as they rested admiringly upon the sprightly girl, who perfectly conscious of his gaze, never looked at him, but confined her attention wholly to Richard, until Andy asked "if they could not have a bit of a tune."

Then, for the first time, Richard discovered that Ethelyn's piano had been unpacked, and was now standing between the south windows, directly under Daisy's picture. It was open, too, and the sheet of music upon the rack told that it had been used. Richard did not care for himself, but he was afraid of what Ethelyn might say, and wondered greatly why she had not spoken of the liberty they had taken.

Ethelyn had not observed the piano; or if she did she had paid no attention to it. Accustomed as she had always been to seeing one in the room, she would have missed its absence more than she noticed its presence. But when, as she lay half dozing and thinking of Aunt Barbara, the old familiar air of "Money-musk," played with a most energetic hand, came to her ear, she started, for she knew the tone of her own instrument--knew, too, that Melinda Jones' hands were sweeping the keys--and all that Melinda Jones had done for her comfort was forgotten in the deep resentment which heated her blood and flushed her cheek as she listened to "Old Zip Coon," which followed "Money-musk," a shuffling sound of feet telling that somebody's boots were keeping time after a very unorthodox fashion. Next came a song--"Old Folks at Home"-- and in spite of her resentment Ethelyn found herself listening intently as James' rich, deep bass, and John's clear tenor, and Andy's alto joined in the chorus with Melinda's full soprano. The Markham boys were noted for their fine voices; and even Richard had once assisted at a public concert; but to-night he did not sing--his thoughts were too intent upon the wife upstairs and what she might be thinking of the performance, and he was glad when the piano was closed and Melinda Jones had gone.

It was later than he supposed, and the clock pointed to almost eleven when he at last said good-night to his mother and went, with a half-guilty feeling, to his room. But there were no chidings in store for him; for, wearied with her journey and soothed by the music, Ethelyn had forgotten all her cares and lay quietly sleeping, with one hand beneath her cheek and the other resting outside the white counterpane. Ethie was very pretty in her sleep, and the proud, restless look about her mouth was gone, leaving an expression more like a child's than like a girl of twenty. And Richard, looking at her, felt supremely happy that she was his, forgetting all of the past which had been unpleasant, and thinking only that he was blessed above his fellow mortals that he could call the beautiful girl before him his Ethelyn--his wife.

CHAPTER X: FIRST DAYS IN OLNEY

There were a great many vacant seats in the Methodist church the morning following Ethelyn's arrival, while Mr. Townsend was surprised at the size of his congregation. It was generally known that Mrs. Judge Markham was an Episcopalian, and as she would of course patronize the Village Hall, the young people of Olney were there en masse, eager to see the new bride. But their curiosity was not gratified. Ethelyn was too tired to go out, Andy said, when questioned on the subject, while Eunice Plympton, who was also of Andy's faith, and an attendant of the Village Hall, added the very valuable piece of information that "Miss Markham's breakfast had been taken to her, and that when she [Eunice] came away she was still in bed, or at all events had not yet made her appearance below." This, together with Eunice's assertion that she was handsome, and Tim Jones' testimony that she was "mighty stuck-up, but awful neat," was all the disappointed Olneyites knew of Mrs. Richard Markham, who, as Eunice reported, had breakfasted in bed, and was still lying there when the one bell in Olney rang out its summons for church. She did not pretend to be sick--only tired and languid, and indisposed for any exertion; and then it was much nicer taking her breakfast from the little tray covered with the snowy towel which Richard brought her, than it was to go down stairs and encounter "all those dreadful people," as she mentally styled Richard's family; so she begged for indulgence this once, and Richard could not refuse her request, and so excused her to his mother, who said nothing, but whose face wore an expression which Richard did not like.

Always strong and healthy herself, Mrs. Markham had but little charity for nervous, delicate people, and she devoutly hoped that Richard's wife would not prove to be one of that sort. When the dishes were washed, and the floor swept, and the broom hung up in its place, and the sleeves of the brown, dotted calico rolled down, she went herself to see Ethelyn, her quick eye noticing the elaborate night-gown, with its dainty tucks and expensive embroidery, and her thoughts at once leaping forward to ironing day, with the wonder who was to do up such finery. "Of course, though, she'll see to such things herself," was her mental conclusion, and then she proceeded to question Ethelyn as to what was the matter, and where she felt the worst. A person who did not come down to breakfast must either be sick or very babyish and notional, and as Ethelyn did not pretend to much indisposition, the good woman naturally concluded that she was "hypoey," and pitied her boy accordingly.

Ethelyn readily guessed the opinion her mother-in-law was forming of her, and could hardly steady her voice sufficiently to answer her questions or repress her tears, which gushed forth the moment Mrs. Markham had left the room, and she was alone with Richard. Poor Richard! it was a novel position in which he found himself--that of mediator between his mother and his wife; but he succeeded very well, soothing and caressing the latter, until when, at three o'clock in the afternoon, the bountiful dinner was ready, he had the pleasure of taking her downstairs, looking very beautiful in her handsome black silk, and the pink coral ornaments Aunt Barbara had given her. There was nothing gaudy about her dress; it was in perfect taste, and very plain too, as she thought, even if it was trimmed with lace and bugles. But she could not help feeling it was out of keeping when James, and John, and Eunice stared so at her, and Mrs. Markham asked her if she hadn't better tie on an apron for fear she might get grease or something on her. With ready alacrity Eunice, who fancied her young mistress looked like a queen, forgetting in her admiration that she had ever thought her proud, ran for her own clean, white apron, which she offered to the lady.

But Ethelyn declined it, saying, "My napkin is all that I shall require."

Mrs. Markham, and Eunice, and Andy glanced at each other. Napkins were a luxury in which Mrs. Markham had never indulged. She knew they were common in almost every family of her acquaintance; but she did not see of what use they were, except to make more washing, and as her standard of things was the standard of thirty years back she was not easily convinced; and even Melinda Jones had failed on the napkin question. Ethelyn had been too much excited to observe their absence the previous night, and she now spoke in all sincerity, never dreaming that there was not such an article in the house. But there was a small square towel of the finest linen, and sacred to the memory of Daisy, who had hemmed it herself and worked her name in the corner. It was lying in the drawer, now, with her white cambric dress, and, at a whispered word from her mistress, Eunice brought it out and laid it in Ethelyn's lap, while Richard's face grew crimson as he began to think that possibly his mother might be a very little behind the times in her household arrangements.

Ethelyn's appetite had improved since the previous night, and she did ample justice to the well-cooked dinner; but her spirits were ruffled again when, on returning to her room an hour or so after dinner, she found it in the same disorderly condition in which she had left it. Ethelyn had never taken charge of her own room, for at Aunt Barbara's Betty had esteemed it a privilege to wait upon her young mistress, while Aunt Van Buren would have been horror-stricken at the idea of any one of her guests making their own bed. Mrs. Markham, on the contrary, could hardly conceive of a lady too fine to do that service herself, and Eunice was not the least to blame for omitting to do what she had never been told was her duty to do. A few words from Richard, however, and the promise of an extra quarter per week made that matter all right, and neither Betty nor Mrs. Dr. Van Buren's trained chambermaid, Mag, had ever entered into the clearing-up process with greater zeal than did Eunice when once she knew that Richard expected it of her. She was naturally kind-hearted, and though Ethelyn's lofty ways annoyed her somewhat, her admiration for the beautiful woman and her elegant wardrobe was unbounded, and she felt a pride in waiting upon her which she would once have thought impossible to feel in anything pertaining to her duties as a servant.

The following morning brought with it the opening of the box where the family presents were; but Ethelyn did not feel as much interest in them now as when they were purchased. She knew how out of place they were, and fully appreciated the puzzled expression on James' face when he saw the blue velvet smoking cap. It did not harmonize with the common clay pipe he always smoked on Sunday, and much less with the coarse cob thing she saw him take from the kitchen mantel that morning just after he left the breakfast table and had donned the blue frock he wore upon the farm. He did not know what the fanciful-tasseled thing was for; but he reflected that

Melinda, who had been to boarding school, could enlighten him, and he thanked his pretty sister with a good deal of gentlemanly grace. He was naturally more observing than Richard, and with the same advantages would have polished sooner. Though a little afraid of Ethelyn, there was something in her refined, cultivated manners very pleasing to him, and his soft eyes looked down upon her kindly as he took the cap and carried it to his room, laying it carefully away in the drawer where his Sunday shirts, and collars, and "dancing pumps," and fishing tackle, and paper of chewing tobacco were.

Meanwhile, John, who was even more shy of Ethelyn than James, had been made the recipient of the elegantly embroidered slippers, which presented so marked a contrast to his heavy cowhides, and were three sizes too small for his mammoth feet. Ethelyn saw the discrepancy at once, and the effort it was for John to keep from laughing outright, as he took the dainty things into which he could but little more than thrust his toes.

"You did not know what a Goliath I was, nor what stogies I wore; but I thank you all the same," John said, and with burning blushes Ethelyn turned next to her beautiful Schiller--the exquisite little bust--which Andy, in his simplicity mistook for a big doll, feeling a little affronted that Ethelyn should suppose him childish enough to care for such toys.

But when Richard, who stood looking on, explained to his weak brother what it was, saying that people of cultivation prized such things as these, and that some time he would read to him of the great German poet, Andy felt better, and accepted his big doll with a very good grace.

The coiffure came next, Mrs. Markham saying she was much obliged, and Eunice asking if it was a half-handkerchief, to be worn about the neck.

Taken individually and collectively, the presents were a failure--all but the pretty collar and ribbon-bow, which, as an afterthought, Ethelyn gave to Eunice, whose delight knew no bounds. This was something she could appreciate, while Ethelyn's gifts to the others had been far beyond them, and but for the good feeling they manifested might as well have been withheld. Ethelyn felt this heavily, and it did not tend to lessen the bitter disappointment which had been gnawing in her heart ever since she had reached her Western home. Everything was different from what she had pictured it in her mind--everything but Daisy's face, which, from its black-walnut frame above her piano, seemed to look so lovingly down upon her. It was a sweet, refined face, and the soft eyes of blue were more beautiful than anything Ethelyn had ever seen. She did not wonder that every member of that family looked upon their lost Daisy as the household angel, lowering their voices when they spoke of her, and even retarding their footsteps when they passed near her picture. She did wonder, however, that they were not more like what Daisy would have been, judging from the expression of her face and all Richard had said of her.

Between Mrs. Markham and Ethelyn there was from the first a mutual feeling of antagonism, and it was in no degree lessened by Aunt Barbara's letter, which Mrs. Markham read three times on Sunday, and then on Monday very foolishly talked it up with Eunice, whom she treated with a degree of familiarity wholly unaccountable to Ethelyn.

"What did that Miss Bigelow take her for that she must ask her to be kind to Ethelyn? Of course she should do her duty, and she guessed her ways were not so very different from other people's, either," and the good woman gave an extra twist to the tablecloth she was wringing, and shaking it out rather fiercely, tossed it into the huge clothes-basket standing near.

The wash was unusually large that day and as the unpacking of the box had taken up some time, the clock was striking two just as the last clothespin was fastened in its place, and the last brown towel hung upon the currant bushes. It was Mrs. Markham's weakness that her wash should be fluttering in the wind before that of Mrs. Jones, which could be plainly seen from her kitchen window. But to-day Mrs. Jones was ahead, and Melinda's pink sun-bonnet was visible in the little back-yard as early as eleven, at which time the Markham garments had just commenced to boil. The bride had brought with her a great deal of extra work, and what with waiting breakfast for her until the coffee was cold and the baked potatoes "all soggy," and then cleaning up the litter of "that box," Mrs. Markham was dreadfully behind with her Monday's work. And it did not tend to improve her temper to know that the cause of all her discomposure was "playing lady" in a handsome cashmere morning gown, with heavy tassels knotted at her side, while she was bending over the washtub in a faded calico pinned about her waist, and disclosing the quilt patched with many colors, and the black yarn stockings footed with coarse white. Not that Mrs. Markham cared especially for the difference between her dress and Ethelyn's--neither did she expect Ethelyn to "help" that day--but she might at least have offered to wipe the dinner dishes, she thought. It would have shown her good will at all events. But instead of that she had returned to her room the moment dinner was over, and Eunice, who went to hunt for a missing sock of Richard's, reported that she was lying on the lounge with a story book in her hand.

"Shiffless," was the word Mrs. Markham wanted to use, but she repressed it, for she would not talk openly against Richard's wife so soon after her arrival, though she did make some invidious remarks concerning the handsome underclothes, wondering "what folks were thinking of to put so much work where it was never seen. Puffs, and embroidery, and lace, and, I vum, if the ruffles ain't tucked too," she continued, in a despairing voice, hoping Ethelyn knew "how to iron such filagree herself, for the mercy knew she didn't."

Now these same puffs, and embroidery, and ruffles, and tucks had excited Eunice's liveliest admiration, and her fingers fairly itched to see how they would look hanging on the clothes bars after passing through her hands. That Ethelyn could touch them she never once dreamed. Her instincts were truer than Mrs. Markham's and it struck her as perfectly proper that one like Ethelyn should sit still while others served, and to her mistress' remarks as to the ironing, she hastened to reply: "I'd a heap sight rather do them up than to iron the boys' coarse shirts and pantaloons. Don't you mind the summer I was at Camden working for Miss Avery, who lived next door to Miss Judge Miller, from New York? She had just such things as these, and I used to go in sometimes and watch Katy iron 'em, so I b'lieve I can do it myself. Anyways, I want to try."

Fears that Eunice might rebel had been uppermost in Mrs. Markham's mind when she saw the pile of elegant clothes, for she had a suspicion that Mrs. Ethelyn would keep as much aloof from the ironing-board as she did from the dish-washing; but if Eunice was willing and even glad of the opportunity, why, that made a difference, and the good woman began to feel so much better that by the time the last article was on the line, the kitchen floor cleared up, and the basin of water heating on the stove for her own ablutions, she was quite amiably disposed toward her grand daughter-in-law, who had not made her appearance since dinner. Ethelyn liked staying in her chamber better than anywhere else, and it was especially pleasant there to-day, for Eunice had taken great pains to make it so, sweeping, and dusting and putting to rights, and patting the pillows and cushions just as she remembered seeing Melinda do, and then, after the collar and ribbon had been given to her, going down on her hands and knees before the fire to wash the hearth with milk, which gave to the red bricks a polished, shining appearance, and added much to the cheerfulness of the room. Ethelyn had commended her pleasantly, and, in the seventh heaven of delight, Eunice had returned to her washing, taking greater pains than ever with the dainty puffs and frills, and putting in a stitch where one was needed.

It was very evident that Eunice admired Ethelyn, and Ethelyn in return began to appreciate Eunice; and when, after dinner, she went to her room, and, wearied with her unpacking, lay down upon the lounge, she felt happier than she had since her first sight of Olney. It was pleasant up there, and the room looked very pretty with the brackets and ornaments, and pictures she had hung there instead of in the parlor, and she decided within herself that though disappointed in every respect, she could be quite comfortable for the few weeks which must intervene before she went to Washington. She should spend most of the time in the retirement of her room, mingling as little as possible with the family, and keeping at a respectful distance from her mother-in-law, whom she liked less than any of Richard's relations.

"I trust the Olney people will not think it their duty to call," she thought. "I suppose I shall have to endure the Joneses for Abigail's sake. Melinda certainly has some taste; possibly I may like her," and while cogitating upon Melinda Jones and the expected gayeties in Washington, she fell asleep; nor did Richard's step arouse her, when, about three o'clock, he came in from the village in quest of some law documents he wished to see.

Frank Van Buren would probably have kissed her as she lay there sleeping so quietly; but Richard was in a great hurry. He had plunged at once into business. Once there were forty men waiting to see and consult "the Squire," whose reputation for honesty and ability was very great, and whose simple assertion carried more weight than the roundest oath of some lawyers, sworn upon the biggest Bible in Olney. Waylaid at every corner, and plied with numberless questions, he had hardly found an opportunity to come home to dinner, and now he had no time to waste in love-making. He saw Ethelyn, however, and felt that his room had never been as pleasant as it was with her there in it, albeit her coming was the cause of his books and papers being disturbed and tossed about and moved where he had much trouble to find them. He felt glad, too, that she was out of his mother's way, and feeling that all was well, he found his papers and hurried off to the village again, while Ethelyn slept on till Eunice Plympton came up to say that "Miss Jones and Melinda were both in the parlor and wanted her to come down."

CHAPTER XI: CALLS AND VISITING

Mrs. Jones had risen earlier than usual that Monday morning, and felt not a little elated when she saw her long line of snowy linen swinging in the wind before that of her neighbor, whom she excused on the score of Richard's wife. But when twelve o'clock, and even one o'clock struck, and still the back yard gave no sign, she began to wonder "if any of 'em could be sick"; and never was flag of truce watched for more anxiously than she watched for something which should tell that it was all well at Sister Markham's.

The sign appeared at last, and with her fears quieted, Mrs. Jones pursued the even tenor of her way until everything was done and her little kitchen was as shining as soap and sand and scrubbing brush could make it. Perhaps it was washing the patchwork quilt which Abigail had pieced that brought the deceased so strongly to Mrs. Jones' mind, and made her so curious to see Abigail's successor. Whatever it was, Mrs. Jones was very anxious for a sight of Ethelyn; and when her work was done she donned her alpaca dress, and tying on her black silk apron, announced her intention of "running into Mrs. Markham's just a minute. Would Melinda like to go along?"

Melinda had been once to no purpose, and she had inwardly resolved to wait a while before calling again; but she felt that she would rather be with her mother at her first interview with Ethelyn, for she knew she could cover up some defects by her glibber and more correct manner of conversing. So she signified her assent, but did not wear her best bonnet as she had on Saturday night. This was only a run in, she said, never dreaming that, "for fear of what might happen if she was urged to stay to tea," her mother had deposited in her capacious pocket the shirt-sleeve of unbleached cotton she was making for Tim.

And so about four o'clock the twain started for the house of Mrs. Markham, who saw them coming and welcomed them warmly. She was always glad to see Mrs. Jones, and she was doubly glad to-day, for it seemed to her that some trouble had come upon her which made neighborly sympathy and neighborly intercourse more desirable than ever. Added to this, there was in her heart an unconfessed pride in Ethelyn and a desire to show her off. "Miss Jones was not going to stir home a step till after supper," she said, as that lady demurred at laying off her bonnet. "She had got to stay and see Richard; besides that, they were going to have waffles and honey, with warm gingerbread."

Nobody who had once tested them, could withstand Mrs. Markham's waffles and gingerbread. Mrs. Jones certainly could not; and when Eunice went up for Ethelyn, that worthy woman was rocking back and forth in a low rocking-chair, her brass thimble on her finger and Tim's shirt-sleeve in progress of making; while Melinda, in her pretty brown merino and white collar, with her black hair shining like satin, sat in another rocking-chair, working at the bit of tatting she chanced to have in her pocket. Ethelyn did not care to go down; it was like stepping into another sphere leaving her own society for that of the Joneses; but there was no alternative, and with a yawn she started up and began smoothing her hair.

"This wrapper is well enough," she said, more to herself, than Eunice, who was still standing by the door looking at her.

Eunice did not think the wrapper well enough. It was pretty, she knew, but not as pretty as the dresses she had seen hanging in Ethelyn's closet when she arranged the room that morning; so she said, hesitatingly: "I wish you wouldn't wear that down. You were so handsome yesterday in the black gown, with them red earrings and pin, and your hair brushed up, so."

Ethelyn liked to look well, even here in Olney, and so the wrapper was laid aside, the beautiful brown hair was wound in heavy coils about the back of the head, and brushed back from her white forehead after a fashion which made her look still younger and more girlish than she was. A pretty plaid silk, with trimmings of blue, was chosen for to-day, Eunice going nearly wild over the short jaunty basque, laced at the sides and the back. Eunice had offered to stay and assist at her young mistress' toilet, and as Ethelyn was not unaccustomed to the office of waiting-maid, she accepted Eunice's offer, finding, to her surprise, that the coarse red fingers, which that day had washed and starched her linen, were not unhandy even among the paraphernalia of a Boston lady's toilet.

"You do look beautiful," Eunice said, standing back to admire Ethelyn, when at last she was dressed. "I have thought Melinda Jones handsome, but she can't hold a candle to you, nor nobody else I ever seen, except Miss Judge Miller, in Camden. She do act some like you, with her gown dragglin' behind her half a yard."

Thus flattered and complimented, Ethelyn shook out her skirts, which "draggled half a yard behind," and went downstairs to where Mrs. Jones sat working on Timothy's shirt, and Melinda was crocheting, while Mrs. Markham, senior, clean and neat, and stiff in her starched, purple calico, sat putting a patch on a fearfully large hole in the knee of Andy's pants. As Ethelyn swept into the room there fell a hush upon the inmates, and Mrs. Jones was almost guilty of an exclamation of surprise. She had expected something fine, she said--something different from the Olney quality--but she was not prepared for anything as grand and queenly as Ethelyn, when she sailed into the room, with her embroidered handkerchief held so gracefully in her hands, and in response to Mrs. Markham's introduction, bowed so very low, and slowly, too, her lips scarcely moving at all, and her eyes bent on the ground. Mrs. Jones actually ran the needle she was sewing with under her thumb in her sudden start, while Melinda's crocheting dropped into her lap. She, too, was surprised, though not as much as her mother. She, like Eunice, had seen Mrs. Judge Miller, from New York, whose bridal trousseau was imported from Paris, and whose wardrobe was the wonder of Camden. And Ethelyn was very much like her, only younger and prettier.

"Very pretty," Melinda thought, while Mrs. Jones fell to comparing her, mentally, with the deceased Abigail; wondering how Richard, if he had ever loved the one, could have fancied the other, they were so unlike.

Of course, the mother's heart gave to Abigail the preference for all that was good and womanly, and worthy of Richard Markham; but Ethelyn bore off the palm for style, and beauty, too.

"Handsome as a doll, but awfully proud," Mrs. Jones decided, during the interval in which she squeezed her wounded thumb, and got the needle again in motion upon Timothy's shirt-sleeve.

Ethelyn was not greatly disappointed in Mrs. Jones and her daughter; the mother especially was much like what she had imagined her to be, while Melinda was rather prettier--rather more like the Chicopee girls than she expected. There was a look on her face like Susie Granger, and the kindly expression of her black eyes made Ethelyn excuse her for wearing a magenta bow, while her cheeks were something the same hue. They were very stiff at first, Mrs. Jones saying nothing at all, and Melinda only venturing upon common-place inquiries--as to how Ethelyn bore her journey, if she was ever in that part of the country before, and how she thought she should like the West. This last question Ethelyn could not answer directly.

"It was very different from New England," she said, "but she was prepared for that, and hoped she should not get very homesick during the few weeks which would elapse before she went to Washington."

At this point Mrs. Markham stopped her patching and looked inquiringly at Ethelyn. It was the first she had heard about Ethelyn's going to Washington; indeed, she had understood that Richard's wife was to keep her company during the winter, a prospect which since Ethelyn's arrival had not looked so pleasing to her as it did before. How in the world they should get on together without Richard, she did not know, and if she consulted merely her own comfort she would have bidden Ethelyn go. But there were other things to be considered--there was the great expense it would be for Richard to have his wife with him. Heretofore he had saved a good share of his salary, but with Ethelyn it would be money out of his pocket all the time; besides that, there were reasons why it was not proper for Ethelyn to go; her best place was at home.

Thus reasoned Mrs. Markham, and when next her needle resumed its work on Andy's patch, Ethelyn's fate with regard to Washington was decided, for as thought the mother on that point, so eventually would think the son, who deferred so much to her judgment. He came in after a little, looking so well and handsome that Ethelyn felt proud of him, and had he then laid his hand upon her shoulder, or put his arm around her waist, as he sometimes did when they were alone, she would not have shaken it off, as was her usual custom. Indeed, such is the perversity of human nature, and so many contradictions are there in it, that Ethelyn rather wished he would pay her some little attention. She could not forget Abigail, with Abigail's mother and sister sitting there before her, and she wanted them to see how fond her husband was of her, hoping thus to prove how impossible it was that Abigail could ever have been to him what she was. But Richard was shy in the presence of others, and would sooner have put his arm around Melinda than around his wife, for fear he should be thought silly. He was very proud of her, though, and felt a thrill of satisfaction in seeing how superior, both in look and manner, she was to Melinda Jones, whose buxom, healthy face grew almost coarse and homely from comparison with Ethelyn's.

As Ethelyn's toilet had occupied some time, it was five when she made her appearance in the parlor, consequently she had not long to wait ere the announcement of supper broke up the tediousness she endured from that first call, or visit. The waffles and the gingerbread were all they had promised to be, and the supper passed off quietly, with the exception of a mishap of poor, awkward Andy, who tipped his plate of hot cakes and honey into his lap, and then in his sudden spring backward, threw a part of the plate's contents upon Ethelyn's shining silk. This was the direst calamity of all, and sent poor Andy from the table so heart-broken and disconsolate that he did not return again, and Eunice found him sitting on the wood-house steps, wiping away with his coat-sleeve the great tears which rolled down his womanish face.

"Ethelyn never would like him again," he said, calling himself "a great blundering fool, who never ought to eat at the same table with civilized folks."

But when Ethelyn, who heard from Eunice of Andy's distress, went out to see him, assuring him that but little damage had been done, that soft water and magnesia would make the dress all right again, he brightened up, and was ready to hold Mr. Harrington's horse when, after dark, that gentleman drove over from Olney with his wife and sister to call on Mrs. Richard. It would almost seem that Ethelyn held a reception that evening, for more than the Harringtons knocked at the front door, and were admitted by the smiling Eunice. It was rather early to call, the Olneyites knew, but there on the prairie they were not hampered with many of Mrs. Grundy's rules, and so curious to see the "Boston lady," several of the young people had agreed together between the Sunday services to call at Mrs. Markham's the following night. They were well-meaning, kind-hearted people, and would any one of them gone far out of their way to serve either Richard or his young wife; but they were not Eastern bred, and feeling somewhat awed by Ethelyn's cold, frigid manner, they appeared shy and awkward--all except Will Parsons, the young M.D. of Olney, who joked, and talked and laughed so loudly, that even Richard wondered he had never before observed how noisy Dr. Parsons was, while Andy, who was learning to read Ethelyn's face, tried once or twice, by pulling the doctor's coat-skirts and giving him a warning glance, to quiet him down a little. But the doctor took no hints, and kept on with his fun, finding a splendid coadjutor in the "terrible Tim Jones," who himself came over to call on Dick and his woman.

Tim was rigged out in his best, with a bright red cravat tied around his neck, and instead of his muddy boots with his pants tucked in the tops, he wore coarse shoes tied with strings and flirted his yellow silk handkerchief for the entire evening. It was dreadful to Ethelyn, for she could see nothing agreeable in Richard's friends; indeed, their presence was scarcely bearable, and the proud look on her face was so apparent that the guests felt more or less ill at ease, while Richard was nearer being angry with Ethelyn than he had ever been. Will Parsons and Tim Jones seemed exceptions to the rest of the company, especially the latter, who, if he noticed Ethelyn's evident contempt, was determined to ignore it, and make himself excessively familiar.

As yet, the open piano had been untouched, no one having the courage to ask Ethelyn to play; but Tim was fond of music, and unhesitatingly seating himself upon the stool, thrust one hand in his pocket, and with the other struck the keys at random, trying to make out a few bars of "Hail, Columbia!" Then turning to Ethelyn he said, with a good-humored nod, "Come, old lady, give us something good."

Ethelyn's eyes flashed fire, while others of the guests looked their astonishment at Tim, who knew he had done something, but could not for the life of him tell what.

"Old lady" was a favorite title with him. He called his mother so, and Melinda, and Eunice Plympton, and Maria Moorehouse, whose eyes he thought so bright, and whom he always saw home from meeting on Sunday nights; and so it never occurred to him that this was his offense. But Melinda knew, and her red cheeks burned scarlet as she tried to cover her brother's blunder by modestly urging Ethelyn to favor them with some music.

Of all the Western people whom she had seen, Ethelyn liked Melinda the best. She had thought her rather familiar, and after the Olneyites came in and put her more at her ease, she fancied her a little flippant and forward; but, in all she did or said, there was so much genuine sincerity and frankness, that Ethelyn could not dislike her as she had thought she should dislike a sister of Abigail Jones and the terrible Tim. She had not touched her piano since her arrival, for fear of the homesickness which its familiar tones might awaken, and when she saw Tim's big red hands fingering the keys, in her resentment at the desecration she said to herself that she never would touch it again; but when in a low aside Melinda added to her entreaties: "Please, Mrs. Markham, don't mind Tim--he means well enough, and would not be rude for the world, if he knew it," she began to give way, and it scarcely needed Richard's imperative, "Ethelyn," to bring her to her feet. No one offered to conduct her to the piano--not even Richard, who sat just where he was; while Tim, in his haste to vacate the music stool, precipitated it to the floor, and got his leather shoes entangled in Ethelyn's skirts.

Tim, and Will Parsons, and Andy all hastened to pick up the stool, knocking their heads together, and raising a laugh in which Ethelyn could not join. Thoroughly disgusted and sick at heart, she felt much as the Jewish maidens must have felt when required to give a song. Her harp was indeed upon the willows hung, and her heart was turning sadly toward her far-off Jerusalem as she sat down and tried to think what she should play to suit her audience. Suddenly it occurred to her to suit herself rather than her hearers, and her snowy fingers--from which flashed Daisy's diamond and a superb emerald--swept the keys with a masterly grace and skill. Ethelyn was perfectly at home at the piano, and dashing off into a brilliant and difficult overture, she held her hearers for a few minutes astonished both at her execution and the sounds she made. To the most of them, however, the sounds were meaningless; their tastes had not yet been cultivated up to Ethelyn's style. They wanted something familiar--something they had heard before; and when the fine performance was ended terrible Tim electrified her with the characteristic exclamation: "That was mighty fine, no doubt, for them that understand such; but, now, for land's sake, give us a tune."

Ethelyn was horror-stricken. She had cast her pearls before swine; and with a haughty stare at the offending Timothy, she left the stool, and walking back to her former seat, said:

"I leave the tunes to your sister, who, I believe, plays sometimes."

Somewhat crestfallen, but by no means browbeaten, Tim insisted that Melinda should give them a jig; and, so, crimsoning with shame and confusion, Melinda took the vacant stool and played her brother a tune--a rollicking, galloping tune, which everybody knew, and which set the feet to keeping time, and finally brought Tim and Andy to the floor for a dance. But Melinda declined playing for a cotillion which her brother proposed, and so the dancing arrangement came to naught, greatly to the delight of Ethelyn, who could only keep back her tears by looking up at the sweet face of Daisy smiling down upon her from the wall. That was the only redeeming point in that whole assembly, she thought. She would not even except Richard then, so intense was her disappointment and so bitter her regret for the mistake she made when she promised to go where her heart could never be.

It was nine o'clock when the company dispersed. Each of the ladies cordially invited Ethelyn to call as soon as convenient, and Mrs. Harrington, a lady of some cultivation, whose husband was the village merchant, saying encouragingly to her, as she held her hand a moment, "Our Western manners seem strange to you, I dare say; but we are a well-meaning people, and you will get accustomed to us by and by."

She never should--no, never, thought Ethelyn, as she went up to her room, tired and homesick, and disheartened with this, her first introduction to the Olney people. It was a very cross wife that slept at Richard's side that night, and the opinion expressed of the Olneyites was anything but complimentary to the taste of one who had known them all his life and liked them so well. But Richard was getting accustomed to such things. Lectures did not move him now as they had at first, and overcome with fatigue from his day's work and the evening's excitement, he fell asleep, while Ethelyn was enlarging upon the merits of the terrible Tim, who had addressed her as "old lady" and asked her to "play a tune."

CHAPTER XII: SOCIETY

In the course of two weeks all the people in Olney called upon Ethelyn, who would gladly have refused herself to them all. But after the morning when Andy stood outside the door of her room, wringing his hands in great distress at the tone of Richard's voice, and Ethelyn stayed in bed all day with the headache, and was nursed by Eunice and Melinda, Ethelyn did better, and was at least polite to those who called. She had said she would not see them, and Richard had said she should; and as he usually made people do as he liked, Ethelyn was forced to submit, but cried herself sick. It was very desolate and lonely upstairs that day, for Richard was busy in town, and the wind swept against the windows with a mournful, moaning sound, which made Ethelyn think of dear old Chicopee, and the lofty elms through whose swaying branches the same October wind was probably sighing on this autumnal day. But, oh! how vast the difference, she thought; for what would have been music if heard at home among the New England hills, was agony here upon the Western prairie.

Ethelyn was very wretched and hailed with delight the presence of Melinda Jones, who came in the afternoon, bringing a basket of delicious apples and a lemon tart she had made herself. Melinda was very sorry for Ethelyn, and her face said as much as she stood by her side and laid her hand softly upon the throbbing temples, pitying her so much, for she guessed just how homesick she was there with Mrs. Markham, whose ways had never seemed so peculiar, even to her, as since Ethelyn's arrival. "And still," she thought, "I do not see how she can be so very unhappy, in any circumstances, with a husband like Richard." But here Melinda made a mistake; for though Ethelyn respected her husband, and had learned to miss him when he was gone, and the day whose close was not to bring him back would have been very long, she did not love him as a husband should be loved; and so there was nothing to fall back upon when other props gave way.

Wholly unsuspicious, Melinda sat down beside her, offering to brush her hair, and while she brushed and combed, and braided, and admired the glossy brown locks, she talked on the subject she thought most acceptable to the young wife's ear--of Richard, and the great popularity he had achieved, not only in his own county, but in neighboring ones, where he stood head and shoulders above his fellows. There was talk once of making him governor, she said, but some thought him too young. Lately, however, she had heard that the subject was again agitated, adding that her father and Tim both thought it more than probable that the next election would take him to the gubernatorial mansion.

"Tim would work like a hero for Richard," she said. "He almost idolizes him, and when he was up for Judge Tim's exertions alone procured for him a hundred extra votes. Tim is a rough, half-savage fellow, but he has the kindest of hearts, and is very popular with a certain class of men who could not be reached by one more polished and cultivated."

So much Melinda said, by way of excusing Tim's vulgarities; and then, with the utmost tact, she led the conversation back to Richard and the governorship, hinting that Ethelyn could do much toward securing that office for her husband. A little attention, which cost nothing, would go a great ways, she said; and it was sometimes worth one's while to make an effort, even if they did not feel like it. More than one rumor had reached Melinda's ear touching the pride of Dick Markham's wife--a pride which the Olney people felt keenly, and it the more keenly knowing that they had helped to give her husband a name; they had made him Judge, and sent him to Congress, and would like to make him governor, knowing well that that no office, however high, would change him from the plain, unpretending man, who, even in the Senate Chamber, would shake drunken Ike Plympton's hand, and slap Tim Jones on the back if need be. They liked their Dick, who had been a boy among them, and they thought it only fair that his wife should unbend a little, and not freeze them so with her lofty ways.

"She'll kick the whole thing over if she goes on so," Tim had said to his father, in Melinda's hearing, and so, like a true friend to Richard, Melinda determined to try and prevent the proud little feet from doing so much mischief.

Nor was she unsuccessful. Ethelyn saw the drift of the conversation, and though for an instant her cheek crimsoned with resentment that she should be talked at by Melinda Jones, she was the better for the talking, and the Olney people, when next they come in contact with her, changed their minds with regard to her being so very proud. She was homesick at first, and that was the cause of her coldness, they said, excusing her in their kind hearts, and admiring her as something far superior to themselves. Even Tim Jones got now and then a pleasant word, for Ethelyn had not forgotten the hundred extra votes. She would have repelled the insinuation that she was courting favor or that hopes of the future governorship for Richard had anything to do with her changed demeanor. She despised such things in others; but Ethelyn was human, and it is just possible that had there been nothing in expectancy she would not have submitted with so good a grace to the familiarities with which she so constantly came in contact. At home she was cold and proud as ever, for between her mother-in-law and herself there was no affinity, and they kept as far apart as possible, Ethelyn staying mostly in her room, and Mrs. Markham, senior, staying in the kitchen, where Eunice Plympton still remained.

Mrs. Markham had fully expected that Eunice would go home within a few days after Ethelyn's arrival; but when the days passed on, Ethelyn showed no inclination for a nearer acquaintance with the kitchen--"never even offering to wipe the teacups on washing days," as Mrs. Markham complained to James, and John, and Andy--the good woman began to manifest some anxiety on the subject, and finally went to Richard to know if "he expected to keep a hired girl all winter or was Ethelyn going to do some light chores."

Richard really did not know; but after a visit to his room, where Ethie sat reading in her handsome crimson wrapper, with the velvet trimmings, he decided that she could "not do chores," and Eunice must remain. It was on this occasion that Washington was broached, Mrs. Markham repeating what she heard Ethelyn saying to Melinda, and asking Richard if he contemplated such a piece of extravagance as taking his wife to Washington would be. In Richard's estimation there were other and weightier reasons why Ethelyn should remain quietly at home that winter. He did not especially mind the expense she might be to him, and he owned to a weak desire to see her queen it over all the reigning belles, as he was certain she would.

Unbiased by his mother, and urged by Ethelyn, he would probably have yielded in her favor; but the mother was first in the field, and so she won the day, and Ethie's disappointment was a settled thing. But Ethie did not know it, as Richard wisely refrained from being the first to speak of the matter. That she was going to Washington Ethelyn had no doubt, and this made her intercourse with the Olneyites far more endurable. Some of them she found pleasant, cultivated people--especially Mr. Townsend, the clergyman, who, after the Sunday on which she appeared at the Village Hall in her blue silk and elegant basquine, came to see her, and seemed so much like an old friend when she found that he had met at Clifton, in New York, some of her acquaintances. It was easy to be polite to him, and to the people from Camden, who hearing much of Judge Markham's pretty bride, came to call upon her--Judge Miller and his wife, with Marcia Fenton and Miss Ella Backus, both belles and blondes, and both some-bodies, according to Ethelyn's definition of that word. She liked these people, and Richard found no trouble in getting her to return their calls. She would gladly have stayed in Camden altogether, and once laughingly pointed out to Richard a large, vacant lot, adjoining Mr. Fenton's, where she would like to have her new house built.

There was a decided improvement in Ethelyn; nor did her old perversity of temper manifest itself very strongly until one morning, three weeks after her arrival in Olney, when Richard suggested to her the propriety of his mother's giving them a party, or infair, as he called it. The people expected it, he said; they would be disappointed without it, and, indeed, he felt it was something he owed them for all their kindness to him. Then Ethelyn rebelled--stoutly, stubbornly rebelled--but Richard carried the point, and two days after the farmhouse was in a state of dire confusion, wholly unlike the quiet which reigned there usually. Melinda Jones was there all the time, while Mrs. Jones was back and forth, and a few of the Olney ladies dropped in with suggestions and offers of assistance. It was to be a grand affair--so far, at least, as numbers were concerned--for everybody was invited, from Mr. Townsend and the other clergy, down to Cecy Doane, who did dressmaking and tailoring from house to house. The Markhams were very democratic in their feelings, and it showed itself in the guests bidden to the party. They were invited from Camden as well--Mr. and Mrs. Miller, with Marcia Fenton and Ella Backus; and after the two young ladies had come over to ascertain how large an affair it was to be, so as to know what to wear, Ethelyn began to take some little interest in it herself and to give the benefit of her own experience in such matters. But having a party in Mrs. Dr. Van Buren's handsome house, where the servants were all so well trained, and everything necessary was so easy of access, or even having a party at Aunt Barbara's, was a very different thing from having one here under the supervision of Mrs. Markham, whose ideas were so many years back, and who objected to nearly everything which Ethelyn suggested. But by dint of perseverance on Melinda's part her scruples were finally overcome; so that when the night of the party arrived the house presented a very respectable appearance, with its lamps of kerosene, and the sperm candles flaming on the mantels in the parlor, and the tallow candles smoking in the kitchen.

Mrs. Markham's bed had been removed from the sitting room, and the carpet taken from the floor, for they were going to dance, and Eunice's mother had been working hard all day to keep her liege lord away from the Cross Roads tavern so that he might be presentable at night, and capable of performing his part, together with his eldest son, who played the flute. She was out in the kitchen now, very large and important with the office of head waiter, her hoops in everybody's way, and her face radiant with satisfaction, as she talked to Mrs. Markham about what we better do. The table was laid in the kitchen and loaded with all the substantials, besides many delicacies which Melinda and Ethelyn had concocted; for the latter had even put her hands to the work, and manufactured two large dishes of Charlotte Russe, with pretty molds of blanc-mange, which Eunice persisted in calling "corn-starch puddin', with the yallers of eggs left out," There were trifles, and tarts, and jellies, and sweetmeats, with raised biscuits by the hundred, and loaves on loaves of frosted cake; while out in the woodshed, wedged in a tub of ice, was a huge tin pail, over which James, and John, and Andy, and even Richard had sat, by turns, stirring the freezing mass. Mrs. Jones' little colored boy, who knew better how to wait on company than any person there, came over in his clean jacket, and out on the doorstep was eating chestnuts and whistling Dixie, as he looked down the road to see if anybody was coming. Melinda Jones had gone home to dress, feeling more like going to bed than making merry at a party, as she looped up her black braids of hair and donned her white muslin dress with the scarlet ribbons. Melinda was very tired, for a good share of the work had fallen upon her--or rather she had assumed it-- and her cheeks and hands were redder than usual when, about seven o'clock, Tim drove her over to Mrs. Markham's, and then went to the village after the dozen or more of girls whom he had promised "to see to the doin's."

But Melinda looked very pretty--at least James Markham thought so--when she stood up on tiptoe to tie his cravat in a better-looking bow than he had done. Since the night when Richard first told her of Ethelyn, it had more than once occurred to Melinda that possibly she might yet bear the name of Markham, for her woman nature was quick to see that James, at least, paid her the homage which Richard had withheld. But Melinda's mind was not yet made up, and as she was too honest to encourage hopes which might never be fulfilled, she would not even look up into the handsome eyes resting so admiringly upon her as she tied the bow of the cravat and felt James' breath upon her burning cheeks. She did, however, promise to dance the first set with him, and then she ran upstairs to see if Ethelyn needed her. But Eunice had been before her, and Ethelyn's toilet was made.

Had this party been at Mrs. Dr. Van Buren's, in Boston, Ethelyn would have worn her beautiful white satin with the fleecy lace; but here it would be out of place, she thought, and so she left it pinned up in towels at the bottom of her trunk, and chose a delicate lavender, trimmed with white appliqué. Lavender was not the most becoming color Ethelyn could wear, but she looked very handsome in it, with the soft pearls upon her neck and arms. Richard thought her dress too low, while modest Andy averted his eyes, lest he should do wrong in looking upon the beautiful round neck and shoulders which so greatly shocked his mother. "It was ridiculous and disgraceful for respectable wimmen folks to dress like that," she said to Melinda Jones, who spoke up for Ethelyn, saying the dress was like that of all fashionable ladies, and in fact was not as low as Mrs. Judge Miller wore to a reception when Melinda was at school in Camden.

Mrs. Markham "did not care for Miss Miller, nor forty more like her. Ethelyn looked ridickerlous, showing her shoulderblades, with that sharp point running down her back, and her skirts moppin' the floor for half a yard behind."

Any superfluity of length in Ethelyn's skirts was more than counterbalanced by Mrs. Markham's, who this night wore the heavy black silk which her sister-in-law had matched in Boston ten years before. Of course it was too narrow and too short, and too flat in front, Andy said, admiring Ethelyn far more than he did his mother, even though the latter wore the coiffure which Aunt Barbara had sent her, and a big collar made from the thread lace which Mrs. Captain Markham, of Chicopee, had also matched in Boston. Ethelyn was perfect, Andy thought, and he hovered constantly near her, noticing how she carried her hands, and her handkerchief, and her fan, and thinking Richard must be perfectly happy in the possession of such a gem.

But Richard was not happy--at least not that night--for, with Mrs. Miller, and Marcia Fenton, and Ella Backus before her mind, Ethelyn had lectured him again on etiquette, and Richard did not bear lecturing here as well as at Saratoga. There it was comparatively easy to make him believe he did not know anything which he ought to know; but at home, where the old meed of praise and deference was awarded to him, where his word was law and gospel, and he was Judge Markham, the potentate of the town, Ethelyn's criticisms were not palatable, and he hinted that he was old enough to take care of himself without quite so much dictation. Then, when he saw a tear on Ethelyn's eyelashes, he would have put his arm around her and kissed it away, if she had not kept him back, telling him he would muss her dress. Still he was not insensible to her pretty looks, and felt very proud of her, as she stood at his side and shook the hands of the arriving guests.

By eight o'clock the Olneyites had assembled in full force; but it was not until the train came in and brought the élite from Camden that the party was fairly commenced. There was a hush when the three ladies with veils on their heads went up the stairs, and a greater hush when they came down again--Mrs. Judge Miller, splendid in green moire-antique, with diamonds in her ears, while Marcia Fenton and Ella Backus figured in white tarletan, one with trimmings of blue, the other with trimmings of pink, and both with waists so much lower than Ethelyn's that Mrs. Markham thought the latter very decent by comparison.

It took the ladies a few minutes to inspect the cut of Mrs. Miller's dress, and the style of hair worn by Marcia and Ella, whose heads had been under a hairdresser's hands, and were curiosities to some of the Olneyites. But all stiffness vanished with the sound of Jerry Plympton's fiddle, and the girls on the west side of the room began to look at the boys on the opposite side, who were straightening their collars and glancing at their "pumps."

Ethelyn did not intend to dance, but when Judge Miller politely offered to lead her to the floor, saying, as he guessed her thoughts, "Remember the old adage, 'among the Romans, and so forth,'" she involuntarily assented, and even found herself leading the first cotillion to the sound of Jerry Plympton's fiddle. Mrs. Miller was dancing, too, as were both Marcia and Ella, and that in a measure reconciled her to what she was doing. They knew something of the lancers there on the prairie, and terrible Tim Jones offered to call off "if Miss Markham would dance with him and kind of keep him goin' straight."

Tim had laid a wager with a companion as rough as himself, that he would dance with the proud beauty, and this was the way he took to win the bet. The ruse succeeded, too, Richard's eyes and low-toned "Ethelyn!" availing more than aught else to drive Ethelyn to the floor with the dreadful Tim, who interlarded his directions with little asides of his own, such as "Go it, Jim," "Cut her down there, Tom," "Hurry up your cakes."

Ethelyn could have screamed out with disgust, and the moment the set was over she said to Richard, "I shall not dance again to-night."

And she kept her word, until toward the close of the party when poor Andy, who had been so unfortunate as to find everybody engaged or too tired, came up to her as she was playing an accompaniment to Jerry's "Money-musk," and with a most doleful expression, said to her, timidly:

"Please, sister Ethie, dance just once with me; none of the girls wants to, and I hain't been in a figger to-night."

Ethelyn could not resist Andy, whose face was perfectly radiant as he led her to the floor, and bumped his head against hers in bowing to her. Eunice was in the same set--her partner the terrible Tim--who cracked jokes and threw his feet about in the most astounding fashion. And Ethelyn bore it all, feeling that by being there with such people she had fallen from the pedestal on which Ethelyn Grant once stood. Her lavender dress was stepped upon, and her point appliqué caught and torn by the big pin Andy had upon his coat cuff. Taken as a whole, that party was the most dreadful of anything Ethelyn had endured and she could have cried for joy when the last guest had said good-night, and she was at liberty to lay her aching head upon her pillow.

Four days after there was a large and fashionable party at Mrs. Judge Miller's, in Camden, and Ethelyn went over in the cars, taking Eunice with her as dressing-maid, and stopping at the Stafford House. That night she wore her bridal robes, receiving so much attention that her head was nearly turned with flattery. She could dance with the young men of Camden, and flirt with them, too--especially with Harry Clifford, who, she found, had been in college with Frank Van Buren. Harry Clifford was a fast young man, but pleasant to talk with for a while and Ethelyn found him very agreeable, saving that his mention of Frank made her heart throb unpleasantly; for she fancied he might know something of that page of her past life which she had concealed from Richard. Nor were her fears without foundation, for once when they were standing together near her husband, Harry said:

"It seems so strange that you are the Ethie about whom Frank used to talk so much, and a lock of whose hair he kept so sacred. I remember I tried to buy a part of it from him, but could not succeed until once, when his funds from home failed to come, and he was so hard up, as we used to say, that he actually sold, or rather pawned, half of the shining tress for the sum of five dollars. As the pawn was never redeemed, I have the hair now, but never expected to meet with its fair owner, who needs not to be told that the tress is tenfold more valuable since I have met her, and know her to be the wife of our esteemed Member," and young Clifford bowed toward Richard, whose face wore a perplexed, dissatisfied expression.

He did not fancy Harry Clifford much, and he certainly did not care to hear that he had in his possession a lock of Ethelyn's hair, while the allusions to Frank Van Buren were anything but agreeable to him. Neither did he like Ethelyn's painful blushes, and her evident desire for Harry to stop. It looked as if the hair business meant more than he would like to suppose. Naturally bright and quick, young Clifford detected Richard's thoughts, and directly began to wonder if there were not something somewhere which Judge Markham did not understand.

"I mean to find out," he thought, and watching an opportunity, when Ethelyn was comparatively alone, he crossed to her side and said in a low tone, "Excuse me, Mrs. Markham. If in my illusions to Frank Van Buren I touched a subject which has never been discussed between yourself and your husband, I meant no harm, I assure you."

Instead of rebuking the impertinent young man, Ethelyn turned very red, and stammered out something about its being of no consequence; and so Harry Clifford held the secret which she had kept so carefully from Richard, and that party in Camden was made the stepping-stone to much of the wretchedness that afterward came to our heroine.

CHAPTER XIII: GOING TO WASHINGTON

Richard's trunk was ready for Washington. His twelve shirts, which Eunice had ironed so nicely, were packed away with his collars and new yarn socks, and his wedding suit, which he was carrying as a mere matter of form, for he knew he should not need it during his three months' absence. He should not go into society, he thought, or even attend levees, with his heart as sore and heavy as it was on this, his last day at home. Ethelyn was not going with him. She knew it now, and never did the face of a six-months wife look harder or stonier than hers as she stayed all day in her room, paying no heed whatever to Richard, and leaving entirely to Eunice and her mother-in-law those little things which most wives would have been delighted to do for their husbands' comfort. Ethelyn was very unhappy, very angry, and very bitterly disappointed. The fact that she was not going to Washington had fallen upon her like a thunderbolt, paralyzing her, as it were, so that after the first great shock was over she seemed like some benumbed creature bereft of care, or feeling, or interest in anything.

She had remained in Camden the most of the day following Mrs. Judge Miller's party, and had done a little shopping with Marcia Fenton and Ella Backus, to whom she spoke of her winter in Washington as a matter of course, saying what she had to say in Richard's presence, and never dreaming that he was only waiting for a fitting opportunity to demolish her castles entirely. Perhaps if Ethelyn had talked Washington openly to her husband when she was first married, and before his mother had gained his ear, her chances for a winter at the capital would have been far greater than they were now. But she had only taken it for granted that she was going, and supposed that Richard understood it just as she did. She had asked him several times where he intended to board and why he did not secure rooms at Willard's, but Richard's non-committal replies had given her no cue to her impending fate. On the night of her return from Camden, as she stood by her dressing bureau, folding away her point-lace handkerchief, she had casually remarked, "I shall not use that again till I use it in Washington. Will it be very gay there this winter?"

Richard was leaning his elbow upon the mantel, looking thoughtfully into the fire, and for a moment he did not answer. He hated to demolish Ethie's castles, but it could not be helped. Once it had seemed very possible that she would go with him to Washington, but that was before his mother had talked to him upon the subject. Since then the fiat had gone forth, and thinking this the time to declare it, Richard said at last, "Put down your finery, Ethelyn, and come stand by me while I say something to you."

His voice and manner startled Ethelyn, but did not prepare her for what followed after she had "dropped her finery" and was standing by her husband.

"Ethelyn," he began, and his eyes did not move from the blazing fire, "it is time we came to an understanding about Washington. I have talked with mother, whose age certainly entitles her opinion to some consideration, and she thinks that for you to go to Washington this winter would not only be improper, but also endanger your life; consequently, I hope you will readily see the propriety of remaining quietly at home where mother can care for you, and see that you are not at all imprudent. It would break my heart if anything happened to my darling wife, or--" he finished the sentence in a whisper, for he was not yet accustomed to speaking of the great hope he had in expectancy.

He was looking at Ethelyn now, and the expression of her face startled and terrified him, it was so strange and terrible.

"Not go to Washington!" and her livid lips quivered with passion, while her eyes burned like coals of fire. "I stay here all this long, dreary winter with your mother! Never, Richard, never! I'll die before I'll do that. It is all--" she did not finish the sentence, for she would not say, "It is all I married you for"; she was too much afraid of Richard for that, and so she hesitated, but looked at him intently to see if he was in earnest.

She knew he was at last--knew that neither tears, nor reproaches, nor bitter scorn could avail to carry her point, for she tried them all, even to violent hysterics, which brought Mrs. Markham, senior, into the field and made the matter ten times worse. Had she stayed away Richard might have yielded, for he was frightened at the storm he had invoked; but Richard was passive in his mother's hands, and listened complacently while in stronger, plainer language than he had used she repeated in substance all he had said about the impropriety of Ethelyn's mingling with the gay throng at Washington. Immodesty, Mrs. Markham called it, with sundry reflections upon the time when she was young, and what young married women did then. And while she talked poor Ethelyn lay upon the lounge writhing with pain and passion, wishing that she could die, and feeling in her heart that she hated the entire Markham race, from Richard down to the innocent Andy, who heard of the quarrel going on between his mother and Ethelyn, and crept cautiously to the door of their room, wishing so much that he could mediate between them.

But this was a matter beyond Andy's ken. He could not even find a petition in his prayer-book suited to that occasion. Mr. Townsend had assured him that it would meet every emergency; but for once Mr. Townsend was at fault, for with the sound of Ethelyn's angry voice ringing in his ears, Andy lighted his tallow candle and creeping up to his chamber knelt down by his wooden chair and sought among the general prayers for one suited "to a man and his wife quarreling." There was a prayer for the President, a prayer for the clergy, a prayer for Congress, a prayer for rain, a prayer for the sick, a prayer for people going to sea and people going to be hanged, but there was nothing for the point at issue, unless he took the prayer to be used in time of war and tumults, and that he thought would never answer, inasmuch as he did not really know who was the enemy from which he would be delivered. It was hard to decide against Ethelyn and still harder to decide against "Dick," and so with his brains all in a muddle Andy concluded to take the prayer "for all sorts and conditions of men," speaking very low and earnestly when he asked that all "who were distressed in mind, body, or estate, might be comforted and relieved according to their several necessities." This surely covered the ground to a very considerable extent; or if it did not, the fervent "Good Lord, deliver us," with which Andy finished his devotions, did, and the simple-hearted, trusting man arose from his knees comforted and relieved, even if Richard and Ethelyn were not.

With them the trouble continued, for Ethelyn kept her bed next day, refusing to see anyone and only answering Richard in monosyllables when he addressed himself directly to her. Once he bent over her and said, "Ethelyn, tell me truly--is it your desire to be with me, your dread of separation from me, which makes you so averse to be left behind?"

There was that in his voice which said that if this were the case he might be induced to reconsider. But though sorely tempted to do it, Ethelyn would not tell a falsehood for the sake of Washington; so she made no reply, and Richard drew from her silence any inference he pleased. He was very wretched those last days, for he could not forget the look of Ethelyn's eye or the sound of her voice when, as she finally gave up the contest, she said to him with quivering nostrils and steady tones, "You may leave me here, Richard, but remember this: not one word or line will I write to you while you are gone. I mean what I say. I shall abide by my decision."

It would be dreadful not to hear a word from Ethie during all the dreary winter, and Richard hoped she would recall her words; but Ethelyn was too sorely wounded to do that. She must reach Richard somehow, and this was the way to do it. She did not come downstairs again after it was settled. She was sick, she said, and kept her room, seeing no one but Richard and Eunice, who three times a day brought up her nicely cooked meals and looked curiously at her as she deposited her tray upon the stand and quietly left the room. Mrs. Markham did not go up at all, for Ethelyn charged her disappointment directly to her mother-in-law, and had asked that she be kept away; and so, 'mid passion and tears and bitterness, the week went by and brought the day when Richard was to leave.

CHAPTER XIV: THE FIRST DAY OF RICHARD'S ABSENCE

The gray light of a November morning was breaking over the prairies when Richard stooped down to kiss his wife, who did not think it worth her while to rise so early even to see him off. She felt that she had been unjustly dealt with, and up to the very last maintained the same cold, icy manner so painful to Richard, who would fain have won from her one smile to cheer him in his absence. But the smile was not given, though the lips which Richard touched did move a little, and he tried to believe it was a kiss they meant to give. Only the day before Ethie had heard from Aunt Van Buren that Frank was to be married at Christmas, when they would all go on to Washington, where they confidently expected to meet Ethelyn. With a kind of grim satisfaction Ethelyn showed this to her husband, hoping to awaken in him some remorse for his cruelty to her, if, indeed, he was capable of remorse, which she doubted. She did not know him, for if possible he suffered more than she did, though in a different way. It hurt him to leave her there alone feeling as she did. He hated to go without her, carrying only in his mind the memory of the white, rigid face which had not smiled on him for so long. He wanted her to seem interested in something, for her cold apathy of manner puzzled and alarmed him; so remembering her aunt's letter on the morning of his departure, he spoke of it to her and said, "What shall I tell Mrs. Van Buren for you? I shall probably see more or less of them."

"Tell nothing; prisoners send no messages," was Ethelyn's reply; and in the dim gray of the morning the two faces looked a moment at each other with such thoughts and passions written upon them as were pitiable to behold.

But when Richard was fairly gone, when the tones of his voice bidding his family good-by had ceased, and Ethelyn sat leaning on her elbow and listening to the sound of the wheels which carried him away, such a feeling of utter desolation and loneliness swept over her that, burying her face in the pillows, she wept bitterer tears of remorse and regret than she had ever wept before.

That day was a long and dreary one to all the members of the prairie farmhouse. It was lonely there the first day of Richard's absence, but now it was drearier than ever; and with a harsh, forbidding look upon her face, Mrs. Markham went about her work, leaving Ethelyn entirely alone. She did not believe her daughter-in-law was any sicker than herself. "It was only airs," she thought, when at noon Ethelyn declined the boiled beef and cabbage, saying just the odor of it made her sick. "Nothing but airs and ugliness," she persisted in saying to herself, as she prepared a slice of nice cream toast with a soft-boiled egg and cup of fragrant black tea. Ethie did not refuse this, and was even gracious enough to thank her mother-in-law for her extra trouble, but she did it in such a queenly as well as injured kind of way, that Mrs. Markham felt more aggrieved than ever, and, for a good woman, who sometimes spoke in meeting, slammed the door considerably hard as she left the room and went back to her kitchen, where the table had been laid ever since Ethelyn took to eating upstairs. So long as she ate with the family Mrs. Markham felt rather obliged to take her meals in the front room, but it made a deal more work, and she was glad to return to her olden ways once more. Eunice was gone off on an errand, and so she felt at liberty to speak her mind freely to her boys as they gathered around the table.

"It is sheer ugliness," she said, "which keeps her cooped up there to be waited on. She is no more sick than the dog; but law, I couldn't make Richard b'lieve it."

"Mother, you surely did not go to Richard with complaints of his wife," and James looked reproachfully across the table at his mother, who replied: "I told him what I thought, for I wa'n't going to have him miserable all the time thinking how sick she was, but I might as well have talked to the wind, for any good it did. He even seemed putcherky, too."

"I should be more than putcherky if you were to talk to me against my wife if I had one," James retorted, thinking of Melinda and the way she sang that solo in the choir the day before.

It was a little strange that James and John and Andy all took Ethelyn's part against their mother, and even against Richard, who they thought might have taken her with him.

"It would not have hurt her any more than fretting herself to death at home. No, nor half so much; and she must feel like a cat in a strange garret there alone with them."

It was John who said this--quiet John, who talked so little, and annoyed Ethelyn so much by coming to the table in his blue frock, with his pants tucked in his boots and his curly hair standing every way. Though very much afraid of his grand sister-in-law, he admired her beyond everything, and kept the slippers she brought him safely put away with a lock of Daisy's hair and a letter written him by the young girl whose grave was close beside Daisy's in the Olney cemetery. John had had his romance and buried it with his heroine, since which time he had said but little to womankind, though never was there a truer heart than that which beat beneath the homespun frock Ethelyn so despised. Richard had bidden him to be kind to Ethie, and John had said he would; and after that promise was given had the farmhouse been on fire the sturdy fellow would have periled life and limb to save her for Dick. To James, too, Richard had spoken a word for Ethie, and to Andy also; so that there were left to her four champions in his absence--for Eunice had had her charge, with promises of a new dress if faithful to her trust; and thus there was no one against poor Ethelyn saving the mother-in-law, who made that first dinner after Richard's absence so uncomfortable that John left the table without touching the boiled Indian pudding, of which he was so fond, while James rather curtly asked what there was to be gained by spitting out so about Ethelyn, and Andy listened in silence, thinking how, by and by, when all the chores were done, he would take a basket of kindlings up for Ethie's fire, and if she asked him to sit down, he would do so and try and come to the root of the matter, and see if he could not do something to make things a little better.

CHAPTER XV: ANDY TRIES TO FIND THE ROOT OF THE MATTER

Ethelyn was very sick with a nervous headache, and so Andy did not go in with his kindlings that night, but put the basket near the door, where Eunice would find it in the morning. It was a part of Richard's bargain with Eunice that Ethie should always have a bright, warm fire to dress by, and the first thing Ethelyn heard as she unclosed her eyes was the sound of Eunice blowing the coals and kindlings into a blaze as she knelt upon the hearth, with her cheeks and eyes extended to their utmost capacity. It was a very dreary awakening, and Ethelyn sighed as she looked from her window out upon the far-stretching prairie, where the first snows of the season were falling. There were but few objects to break up the monotonous level, and the mottled November sky frowned gloomily and coldly down upon her. Down in the back-yard James and John were feeding the cattle; the bleating of the sheep and the lowing of the cows came to her ear as she turned with a shiver from the window. How could she stay there all that long, dreary winter--there where there was not an individual who had a thought or taste in common with her own? She could not stay, she decided, and then as the question arose, "Where will you go?" the utter hopelessness and helplessness of her position rushed over her with so much force that she sank down upon the lounge which Eunice had drawn to the fire, and when the latter came up with breakfast she found her young mistress crying in a heart-broken, despairing kind of way, which touched her heart at once.

Eunice knew but little of the trouble with regard to Washington. Mrs. Markham had been discreet enough to keep that from her; and so she naturally ascribed Ethie's tears to grief at parting with her husband, and tried in her homely way to comfort her. Three months were not very long; and they would pass 'most before you thought, she said, adding that she heard Jim say the night before that as soon as he got his gray colts broken he was going to take his sister all over the country and cheer her up a little.

Ethie's heart was too full to permit her to reply, and Eunice soon left her alone, reporting downstairs how white and sick she was looking. To Mrs. Markham's credit we record that with a view to please her daughter-in-law, a fire was that afternoon made in the parlor, and Ethelyn solicited to come down, Mrs. Markham, who carried the invitation, urging that a change would do her good, as it was not always good to stay in one place. But Ethelyn preferred the solitude of her own chamber, and though she thanked her mother-in-law for her thoughtfulness, she declined going down, and Mrs. Markham had made her fire for nothing. Not even Melinda came to enjoy it, for she was in Camden, visiting a schoolmate; and so the day passed drearily enough with all, and the autumnal night shut down again darker, gloomier than ever, as it seemed to Ethelyn. She had seen no one but Mrs. Markham and Eunice since Richard went away, and she was wondering what had become of Andy, when she heard his shuffling tread upon the stairs, and a moment after, his round shining face appeared, asking if he might come in. Andy wore his best clothes on this occasion, for an idea had somehow been lodged in his brain that Ethelyn liked a person well dressed, and he was much pleased with himself in his short coat and shorter pants, and the buff and white cotton cravat tied in a hard knot around his sharp, standing collar, which almost cut the bottom of his ears.

"I wished to see you," he said, taking a chair directly in front of Ethelyn and tipping back against the wall. "I wanted to come before, but was afraid you didn't care to have me. I've got something for you now, though--somethin' good for sore eyes. Guess what 'tis?"

And Andy began fumbling in his pocket for the something which was to cheer Ethelyn, as he hoped.

"Look a-here. A letter from old Dick, writ the very first day. That's what I call real courtin' like," and Andy gave to Ethelyn the letter which John had brought from the office and which the detention of a train at Stafford for four hours had afforded Richard an opportunity to write.

It was only a few lines, meant for her alone, but Ethelyn's cheek didn't redden as she read them, or her eyes brighten one whit. Richard was well, she said, explaining to Andy the reason for his writing, and then she put the letter away, while Andy sat looking at her, wondering what he should say next. He had come up to comfort her, but found it hard to begin. Ethie was looking very pale, and there were dark rings around her eyes, showing that she suffered, even if Mrs. Markham did assert there was nothing ailed her but spleen.

At last Andy blurted out: "I am sorry for you, Ethelyn, for I know it must be bad to have your man go off and leave you all alone, when you wanted to go with him. Jim and John and me talked it up to-day when we was out to work, and we think you orto have gone with Dick. It must be lonesome staying here, and you only six months married. I wish, and the boys wishes, we could do something to chirk you up."

With the exception of what Eunice had said, these were the first words of sympathy Ethelyn had heard, and her tears flowed at once, while her slight form shook with such a tempest of sobs that Andy was alarmed, and getting down on his knees beside her, begged of her to tell him what was the matter. Had he hurt her feelings? he was such a blunderin' critter, he never knew the right thing to say, and if she liked he'd go straight off downstairs.

"No, Anderson," Ethelyn said, "you have not hurt my feelings, and I do not wish you to go, but, oh, I am so wretched and so disappointed, too!"

"About goin' to Washington, you mean?" Andy asked, resuming his chair, and his attitude of earnest inquiry, while Ethelyn, forgetting all her reserve, replied: "Yes, I mean that and everything else. It has been nothing but disappointment ever since I left Chicopee, and I sometimes wish I had died before I promised to go away from dear Aunt Barbara's, where I was so happy."

"What made you promise, then? I suppose, though, it was because you loved Dick so much," simple-minded Andy said, trying to remember if there was not a passage somewhere which read, "For this cause shall a man leave father and mother and cleave unto his wife, and they twain shall be one flesh."

Ethelyn would not wound Andy by telling him how little love had had to do with her unhappy marriage, and she remained silent for a moment, while Andy continued, "Be you disappointed here--with us, I mean, and the fixins?"

"Yes, Anderson, terribly disappointed. Nothing is as I supposed. Richard never told me what I was to expect," Ethelyn replied, without stopping to consider what she was saying.

For a moment Andy looked intently at her, as if trying to make out her meaning. Then, as it in part dawned upon him, he said sorrowfully: "Sister Ethie, if it's me you mean, I was more to blame than Dick, for I asked him not to tell you I was--a--a--wall, I once heard Miss Captain Simmons say I was Widder Markham's fool," and Andy's chin quivered as he went on: "I ain't a fool exactly, for I don't drool or slobber like Tom Brown the idiot, but I have a soft spot in my head, and I didn't want you to know it, for fear you wouldn't like me. Daisy did, though, and Daisy knew what I was and called me 'dear Andy,' and kissed me when she died."

Andy was crying softly now, and Ethelyn was crying with him. The hard feeling at her heart was giving way, and she could have put her arms around this childish man, who after a moment continued: "Dick said he wouldn't tell you, so you must forgive him for that. You've found me out, I s'pose. You know I ain't like Jim, nor John, and I can't hold a candle to old Dick, but sometimes I've hope you liked me a little, even if you do keep calling me Anderson. I wish you wouldn't; seems as if folks think more of me when they say 'Andy' to me."

"Oh, Andy, dear Andy," Ethelyn exclaimed: "I do like you so much--like you best of all. I did not mean you when I said I was disappointed."

"Who, then?" Andy asked, in his straightforward way. "Is it mother? She is odd, I guess, though I never thought on't till you came here. Yes, mother is some queer, but she is good; and onct when I had the typhoid and lay like a log, I heard her pray for 'her poor dear boy Andy'; that's what she called me, as lovin' like as if I wasn't a fool, or somethin' nigh it."

Ethelyn did not wish to leave upon his mind the impression that his mother had everything to do with her wretchedness, and so cautiously as she could she tried to explain to him the difference between the habits and customs of Chicopee and Olney. Warming up with her theme as she progressed, she said more than she intended, and succeeded in driving into Andy's brain a vague idea that his family were not up to her standard, but were in fact a long way behind the times. Andy was in a dilemma; he wanted to help Ethelyn and did not know how. Suddenly, however, his face brightened, and he asked, "Do you belong to the church?"

"Yes," was Ethelyn's reply.

"You do!" Andy repeated in some surprise, and Ethelyn replied, "Not the way you mean, perhaps; but when I was a baby I was baptized in the church and thus became a member."

"So you never had the Bishop's hands upon your head, and done what the Saviour told us to do to remember him by?"

Ethelyn shook her head, and Andy went on: "Oh, what a pity, when he is such a good Saviour, and would know just how to help you, now you are so sorry-like and homesick, and disappointed. If you had him you could tell him all about it and he would comfort you. He helped me, you don't know how much, and I was dreadful bad once. I used to get drunk, Ethie--drunker'n a fool, and come hiccuppin' home with my clothes all tore and my hat smashed into nothin'."

Andy's face was scarlet as he confessed to his past misdeeds, but without the least hesitation he went on: "Mr. Townsend found me one day in the ditch, and helped me up and got me into his room and prayed over me and talked to me, and never let me off from that time till the Saviour took me up, and now it's better than three years since I tasted a drop. I don't taste it even at the sacrament, for fear what the taste might do, and I used to hold my nose to keep shut of the smell. Mr. Townsend knows I don't touch it, and God knows, too, and thinks I'm right, I'm sure, and gives me to drink of his precious blood just the same, for I feel light as air when I come from the altar. If religion could make me, a fool and a drunkard, happy, it would do sights for you who know so much. Try it, Ethie, won't you?"

Andy was getting in earnest now, and Ethelyn could not meet the glance of his honest, pleading eyes.

"I can't be good, Andy," she replied; "I shouldn't know how to begin or what to do."

"Seems to me I could tell you a few things," Andy said. "God didn't want you to go to Washington for some wise purpose or other, and so he put it into Dick's heart to leave you at home. Now, instead of crying about that I'd make the best of it and be as happy as I could be here. I know we ain't starched up folks like them in Boston, but we like you, all of us--leastwise Jim and John and me do--and I don't mean to come to the table in my shirt-sleeves any more, if that will suit you, and I won't blow my tea in my sasser, nor sop my bread in the platter; though if you are all done and there's a lot of nice gravy left, you won't mind it, will you, Ethelyn?--for I do love gravy."

Ethelyn had been more particular than she meant to be with her reasons for her disappointment, and in enumerating the bad habits to which she said Western people were addicted, she had included the points upon which Andy had seized so readily. He had never been told before that his manners were entirely what they ought not to be; he could hardly see it so now, but if it would please Ethie he would try to refrain, he said, asking that when she saw him doing anything very outlandish, she would remind him of it and tell him what was right.

"I think folks is always happier," he continued, "when they forgit to please themselves and try to suit others, even if they can't see any sense in it."

Andy did not exactly mean this as a rebuke, but it had the effect of one and set Ethelyn thinking. Such genuine simplicity and frankness could not be lost upon her, and long after Andy had left her and gone to his room, where he sought in his prayer-book for something just suited to her case, she sat pondering all he had said, and upon the faith which could make even simple Andy so lovable and good.

"He has improved his one talent far more than I have my five or ten," she said, while regrets for her own past misdeeds began to fill her bosom, with a wish that she might in some degree atone for them.

Perhaps it was the resolution formed that night, and perhaps it was the answer to Andy's prayer that God would have mercy upon Ethie and incline her and his mother to pull together better, which sent Ethelyn down to breakfast the next morning and kept her below stairs a good portion of the day, and made her accept James' invitation to ride with him in the afternoon. Then when it was night again, and she saw Eunice carrying through the hall a smoking firebrand, which she knew was designed for the parlor fire, she changed her mind about staying alone upstairs with the books she had commenced to read, but brought instead the white, fleecy cloud she was knitting, and sat with the family, who had never seen her more gracious or amiable, and wondered what had happened. Andy thought he knew; he had prayed for Ethie, not only the previous night, but that morning before he left his room, and also during the day--once in the barn upon a rick of hay and once behind the smoke-house.

Andy always looked for direct answers to his prayers, and believing he had received one his face was radiant with content and satisfaction, when after supper he brushed and wet his hair and plastered it down upon his forehead, and changed his boots for a lighter pair of Richard's, and then sat down before the parlor fire with the yarn sock he was knitting for himself. Ethelyn had never seen him engaged in this feminine employment before, and she felt a strong disposition to laugh, but fearing to wound him, repressed her smiles and seemed not to look at him as he worked industriously on the heel, turning and shaping it better than she could have done. It was not often that Ethelyn had favored the family with music, but she did so that night, playing and singing pieces which she knew were familiar to them, and only feeling a momentary pang of resentment when, at the close of "Yankee Doodle," with variations, quiet John remarked that Melinda herself could not go ahead of that! Melinda's style of music was evidently preferable to her own, but she swallowed the insult and sang "Lily Dale," at the request of Andy, who, thinking the while of dear little Daisy, wiped his eyes with the leg of his sock, while a tear trickled down his mother's cheek and dropped into her lap.

"I thought Melinda Jones wanted to practice on the pianner," Eunice said, after Ethelyn was done playing; "I heard her saying so one day and wondering if Miss Markham would be willin'."

Ethelyn was in a mood then to assent to most anything, and she expressed her entire approbation, saying even that she would gladly give Melinda any assistance in her power. Ethelyn had been hard and cold and proud so long that she scarcely knew herself in this new phase of character, and the family did not know her, either. But they appreciated it fully, and James' eyes were very bright and sparkling when, in imitation of Andy, he bade his sister good-night, thinking, as she left the room how beautiful she was and how pleased Melinda would be, and hoping she would find it convenient to practice there evenings, as that would render an escort home absolutely necessary, unless "Terrible Tim" came for her.

Ethelyn had not changed her mind when Melinda came home next day, and as a matter of course called at the Markhams' in the evening. But Ethelyn's offer had come a little too late-- Melinda was going to Washington to spend the winter! A bachelor brother of her mother's, living among the mountains of Vermont, had been elected Member of Congress in the place of the regular member, who had resigned, and as the uncle was wealthy and generous, and had certain pleasant reminiscences of a visit to Iowa when a little black-eyed girl had been so agreeable to him, he had written for her to join him in Washington, promising to defray all expenses and sending on a draft for two hundred dollars, with which she was to procure whatever she deemed necessary for her winter's outfit. Melinda's star was in the ascendant, and Ethelyn felt a pang of something like envy as she thought how differently Melinda's winter would pass from her own, while James trembled for the effect Washington might have upon the girl who walked so slowly with him along the beaten path between his house and her father's, and whose eyes, as she bade him good-night, were little less bright than the stars shining down upon her. Would she come back like Ethelyn? He hoped not, for there would then be an end to all fond dreams he had been dreaming. She would despise his homely ways and look for somebody higher than plain Jim Markham in his cowhide boots. James was sorry to have Melinda go, and Ethelyn was sorry, too. It seemed as if she was to be left alone, for two days after Melinda's return, Marcia Fenton and Ella Backus came out from Camden to call, and communicated the news that they, too, were going on to Washington, together with Mrs. Judge Miller, whose father was a United States Senator. It was terrible to be thus left behind, and Ethelyn's heart grew harder against her husband for dooming her to such a fate. Every week James, or John, or Andy brought from the post a letter in Richard's handwriting, directed to Mrs. Richard Markham, and once in two weeks Andy carried a letter to the post directed in Ethelyn's handwriting to "Richard Markham, M.C.," but Andy never suspected that the dainty little envelope, with a Boston mark upon it, inclosed only a blank sheet of paper! Ethelyn had affirmed so solemnly that she would not write to her husband that she half feared to break her vow; and, besides that, she could not forgive him for having left her behind, while Marcia, Ella, and Melinda were enjoying themselves so much. She knew she was doing wrong, and not a night of her life did she go to her lonely bed that there did not creep over her a sensation of fear as she thought, "What if I should die while I am so bad?"

At home, in Chicopee, she used always to go through with a form of prayer, but she could not do that now for the something which rose up between her and Heaven, smothering the words upon her lips, and so in this dreadful condition she lived on day after day, growing more, and more desolately and lonely, and wondering sadly if life would always be as dreary and aimless as it was now. And while she pondered thus, Andy prayed on and practiced his lessons in good manners, provoking the mirth of the whole family by his ludicrous attempts to be polite, and feeling sometimes tempted to give the matter up. Andy was everything to Ethelyn, and once when her conscience was smiting her more than usual with regard to the blanks, she said to him abruptly: "if you had made a wicked vow, which would you do--keep it or break it, and so tell a falsehood?"

Andy was not much of a lawyer, he said, but "he thought he knew some scripter right to the pint," and taking his well-worn Bible he found and read the parable of the two sons commanded to work in their father's vineyard.

"If the Saviour commended the one who said he wouldn't and then went and did it, I think there can be no harm in your breaking a wicked vow: leastways I should do it."

This was Andy's advice, and that night, long after the family were in bed, a light was shining in Ethelyn's chamber, where she sat writing to her husband, and as if Andy's spirit were pervading hers, she softened, as she wrote and asked forgiveness for all the past which she had made so wretched. She was going to do better, she said, and when her husband came home she would try to make him happy.

"But, oh, Richard," she wrote, "please take me away from here to Camden, or Olney, or anywhere--so I can begin anew to be the wife I ought to be. I was never worthy of you, Richard.

I deceived you from the first, and if I could summon the courage I would tell you about it."

This letter which would have done so much good, was never finished, for when the morning came there were troubled faces at the prairie farmhouse--Mrs. Markham looking very anxious and Eunice very scared, James going for the doctor and Andy for Mrs. Jones, while up in Ethie's room, where the curtains were drawn so closely before the windows, life and death were struggling for the mastery, and each in a measure coming off triumphant.

CHAPTER XVI: WASHINGTON

Richard had not been very happy in Washington. He led too quiet and secluded a life, his companions said, advising him to go out more, and jocosely telling him that he was pining for his young wife and growing quite an old man. When Melinda Jones came, Richard brightened a little, for there was always a sense of comfort and rest in Melinda's presence, and Richard spent much of his leisure in her society, accompanying her to concerts and occasionally to a levee, and taking pains to show her whatever he thought would interest her. It was pleasant to have a lady with him sometimes, and he wished so much it had been practicable for Ethelyn to have come. "Poor Ethie," he called her to himself, pitying her because, vain man that he was, he thought her so lonely without him. This was at first, and before he had received in reply to his letter that dreadful blank, which sent such a chill to his heart, making him cold, and faint, and sick, as he began to realize what it was in a woman's power to do. He had occasionally thought of Ethelyn's threat, not to write him a line, and felt very uncomfortable as he recalled the expression of her eyes when she made it. But he did not believe she was in earnest. She surely could not hold out against the letter he wrote, telling how he missed her every moment, and how, if it had been at all advisable, he would have taken her with him. He did not know Ethelyn, and so was not prepared for the bitter disappointment in store for him when the dainty little envelope was put into his hand. It was her handwriting--so much he knew; and there lingered about the missive faint traces of the sweet perfume he remembered as pervading everything she wore or used. Ethelyn had not kept her vow; and with a throb of joy Richard tore open the envelope and removed the delicate tinted sheet inside. But the hand of the strong man shook and his heart grew heavy as lead when he turned the sheet thrice over, seeking in vain for some line or word, or syllable or sign. But there was none. Ethelyn had kept her vow, and Richard felt for a moment as if all the world were as completely a blank as that bit of gilt-edged paper he crumpled so helplessly in his hand. Anon, however, hope whispered that she would write next time; she could not hold out thus all winter; and so Richard wrote again with the same success, until at last he expected nothing, and people said of him that he was growing old, while even Melinda noticed his altered appearance, and how fast his brown hair was turning gray. Melinda was in one sense his good angel. She brought him news from home and Ethelyn, telling for one thing of Ethie's offer to teach her music during the winter; and for another, of Ethie's long drives upon the prairie, sometimes with James, sometimes with John, but oftenest with Andy, to whom she seemed to cling as to a very dear brother.

This news did Richard good, showing a better side of Ethie's character than the one presented to him. She was not cold and proud to the family at home; even his mother, who wrote to him once or twice, spoke kindly of her, while James warmly applauded her, and Andy wrote a letter, wonderful in composition, and full of nothing but Ethelyn, who made their home so pleasant with her music, and songs, and pretty face. There was some comfort in this^ and so Richard bore his burden in silence, and no one ever dreamed that the letters he received with tolerable regularity were only blank, fulfillments of a hasty vow.

With Christmas came the Van Buren set from Boston--Aunt Sophia, with Frank, and his girlish bride, who soon became a belle, flirting with every man who offered his attentions, while Frank was in no way behind in his flirtations with the other sex. Plain, matter-of-fact Melinda Jones was among the first to claim his notice after he learned that she was niece of the man who drove such splendid blacks and kept so handsome a suite of rooms at Willard's; but Melinda was more than his match, and snubbed him so unmercifully that he gave her up, and sneered at her as "that old-maidish girl from the West." Mrs. Dr. Van Buren had been profuse in her inquiries after Ethelyn, and loud in her regrets at her absence. She had also tried to patronize both Richard and Melinda, taking the latter with her to the theater and to a reception, and trying to cultivate her for the sake of poor Ethie, who was obliged to associate with her and people like her. Melinda, however, did not need Mrs. Van Buren's patronage. Her uncle was a man of wealth and mark, who stood high in Washington, where he had been before. His niece could not lack attention, and ere the season was over the two rival belles at Washington were Mrs. Frank Van Buren, from Boston, and Miss Melinda Jones, from Iowa.

But prosperity did not spoil Melinda, and James Markham's chances were quite as good when, dressed in pink silk, with camelias in her hair, she entertained some half-dozen judges and M.C.'s as when in brown delaine and magenta ribbons she danced a quadrille at some "quilting bee out West." She saw the difference, however, between men of cultivation and those who had none, and began to understand the cause of Ethelyn's cold, proud looks when surrounded by Richard's family. She began also silently to watch and criticise Richard, comparing him with other men of equal brain, and thinking how, if she were his wife, she would go to work to correct his manners. Possibly, too, thoughts of James, in his blue frock and cowhide boots, occasionally intruded themselves upon her mind; but if so, they did not greatly disturb her equanimity, for, let what might happen, Melinda felt herself equal to the emergency--whether it were to put down Frank Van Buren and the whole race of impudent puppies like him, or polish rough James Markham if need be. How she hated Frank Van Buren when she saw his neglect of his young wife, whose money was all he seemed to care for; and how utterly she loathed and despised him after the night, when, at a party given by one of Washington's magnates, he stood beside her for half an hour and talked confidently to her of Ethelyn, whom, he hinted, he could have married if he would.

"Why didn't you, then?" and Melinda turned sharply upon him, with a look in her black eyes which made him wince as he replied: "Family interference--must have money, you know! But, zounds! don't I pity her!--tied to that clown, whom--"

Frank did not finish the sentence, for Melinda's eyes fairly blazed with anger as she cut him short with "Excuse me, Mr. Van Buren; I can't listen to such abuse of one whom I esteem as highly as I do Judge Markham. Why, sir, he is head and shoulders above you, in sense and intellect and everything which makes a man," and with a haughty bow, Melinda swept away, leaving the shamefaced Frank alone in his discomfiture.

"I'd like to kick myself if I could, though I told nothing but the truth. Ethie did want me confoundedly, and I would have married her if she hadn't been poor as a church mouse," Frank muttered to himself, standing in the deep recess of the window, and all unconscious that just outside upon the balcony was a silent, motionless form, which had heard every word of his conversation with Melinda, and his soliloquy afterward.

Richard Markham had come to this party just to please Melinda, but he did not enjoy it. If Ethie had been there he might; but he could not forget the blank that day received, or the letter from James, which said that Ethelyn was not looking as well as usual, and had the morning previously asked him to turn back before they had ridden more than two miles. He could not be happy with that upon his mind, and so he stole from the gay scene out upon the balcony, where he stood watching the quiet stars and thinking of Ethelyn, when his ear had caught by the mention of her name.

He had not thought before who the couple were standing so near to him, but he knew now it was Melinda and Frank Van Buren, and became an involuntary listener to the conversation which ensued. There was a clenching of his fist, a shutting together of his teeth, and an impulse to knock the boasting Frank Van Buren down; and then, as the past flashed before him, with the thought that possibly Frank spoke the truth and Ethelyn had loved him, there swept over him such a sense of anguish and desolation that he forgot all else in his own wretchedness. It had never occurred to him that Ethelyn married him while all the time she loved another--that perhaps she loved that other still--and the very possibility of it drove him nearly wild.

He was missed from the party, but no one could tell when he left, for no one saw him as he sprang down into the garden, and taking refuge in the paths where the shades were the deepest, escaped unobserved into the street, and so back to his own room, where he went over all the past and recalled every little act of affection on Ethelyn's part, weighed it in the balance with proofs that she did not care for him and never had. So much did Richard love his wife and so anxious was he to find her guiltless that he magnified every virtue and excused every error until the verdict rendered was in her favor, and Frank alone was the delinquent--Frank, the vain, conceited coxcomb, who thought because a woman was civil to him that she must needs wish to marry him; Frank, the wretch who had presumed to pity his cousin, and called her husband a clown! How Richard's fingers tingled with a desire to thrash the insulting rascal; and how, in spite of the verdict, his heart ached with a dull, heavy fear lest it might be true in part, that Ethie had once felt for Frank something deeper than what girls usually feel for their first cousins.

"And supposing she has?" Richard's generous nature asked. "Supposing she did love this Frank once on a time well enough to marry him? She surely was all over that love before she promised to be my wife, else she had not promised; and so the only point where she is at fault was in concealing from me the fact that she had loved another first. I was honest with her. I told her of Abigail, and it was very hard to do it, for I felt that the proud girl's spirit rebelled against such as Abigail was years ago. It would have been so easy, then, for Ethelyn to have confessed to me, if she had a confession to make; though how she could ever care for such a jackanapes as that baboon of a Frank is more than I can tell."

Richard was waxing warm against Frank Van Buren, whom he despised so heartily that he put upon his shoulders all the blame concerning Ethelyn, if blame there were. He would so like to think her innocent, and he tried so hard to do it, that he succeeded in part, though frequently as the days passed on, and he sat at his post in the House, listening to some tiresome speech, or took his solitary walk toward Arlington Heights, a pang of something like jealousy and dread that all had not been open and fair between himself and his wife cut like a knife through his heart, and almost stopped his breath. The short session was wearing to a close, and he was glad of it, for he longed to be home again with Ethelyn, even if he were doomed to meet the same coldness which those terrible blanks had brought him. Anything was preferable to the life he led, and though he grew pale as ashes and his limbs quivered like a reed when, toward the latter part of February, he received a telegram to come home at once, as Ethelyn was very sick, he hailed the news as a message of deliverance, whereby he could escape from hated Washington a few days sooner. He hardly knew when or how the idea occurred to him that Aunt Barbara's presence would be more acceptable in that house, where he guessed what had happened; but occur to him it did; and Aunt Barbara, sitting by her winter fire and thinking of Ethelyn, was startled terribly by the missive which bade her join Richard Markham at Albany, on the morrow, and go with him to Iowa, where Ethie lay so ill. A pilgrimage to Mecca would scarcely have looked more formidable to the good woman than this sudden trip to Iowa; but where her duty was concerned she did not hesitate, and when at noon of the next day the New York train came up the river, the first thing Richard saw as he walked rapidly toward the Central Depot at Albany was Aunt Barbara's bonnet protruding from the car window and Aunt Barbara's hand making frantic passes and gestures to attract his notice.

CHAPTER XVII: RICHARD'S HEIR

For one whole week the windows of Ethelyn's room were darkened as dark as Mrs. Markham's heavy shawl and a patchwork quilt could make them. The doctor rode to and from the farmhouse, looking more and more concerned each time he came from the sick-room. Mrs. Jones was over almost every hour, or if she did not come Tim was sent to inquire, his voice very low and subdued as he asked, "How is she now?" while James' voice was lower and sadder still as he answered, "There is no change." Up and down the stairs Mrs. Markham trod softly, wishing that she had never harbored an unkind thought against the pale-faced girl lying so unconscious of all they were doing for her. In the kitchen below, with a scared look upon her face, Eunice washed and wiped her dishes, and wondered if Richard would get home in time for the funeral, and if he would order from Camden a metallic coffin such as Minnie Dayton had been buried in; and Eunice's tears fell like rain as she thought how terrible it was to die so young, and unprepared, too, as she heard Mrs. Markham say to the Methodist clergyman when he came over to offer consolation.

Yes, Ethelyn was unprepared for the fearful change which seemed so near, and of all the household none felt this more keenly than Andy, whose tears soaked through and through the leaf of the prayer-book, where was printed the petition for the sick, and who improvised many a touching prayer himself, kneeling by the wooden chair where God had so often met and blessed him.

"Don't let Ethie die, Good Father, don't let her die; at least not till she is ready, and Dick is here to see her--poor old Dick, who loves her so much. Please spare her for him, and take me in her place. I'm good for nothing, only I do hope I'm ready, and Ethie ain't; so spare her and take me in her place."

This was one of Andy's prayers--generous, unselfish Andy--who would have died for Ethelyn, and who had been in such exquisite distress since the night when Eunice first found Ethelyn moaning in her room, with her letter to Richard lying unfinished before her. No one had read that letter--the Markhams were too honorable for that--and it had been put away in the portfolio, while undivided attention was given to Ethelyn. She had been unconscious nearly all the time, saying once when Mrs. Markham asked, "Shall we send for Richard?" "Send for Aunt Barbara; please send for Aunt Barbara."

This was the third day of Ethelyn's danger, and on the sixth there came a change. The shawl was pinned back from the window, admitting light enough for the watchers by the bedside to see if the sufferer still breathed. Life was not extinct, and Mrs. Markham's lips moved with a prayer of thanksgiving when Mrs. Jones pointed to a tiny drop of moisture beneath the tangled hair. Ethelyn would live, the doctor said, but down in the parlor on the sofa where Daisy had lain was a little lifeless form with a troubled look upon its face, showing that it had fought for its life. Prone upon the floor beside it sat Andy, whispering to the little one and weeping for "poor old Dick, who would mourn for his lost boy."

Andy was very sorry, and to one who saw him that day, and, ignorant of the circumstances, asked what was the matter that he looked so solemn, he answered sadly, "I have just lost my little uncle that I wanted to stand sponsor for. He only lived a day," and Andy's tears flowed afresh as he thought of all he had lost with the child whose life numbered scarcely twenty-four hours in all. But that was enough to warrant its being now among the spirits of the Redeemed, and heaven seemed fairer, more desirable to Andy than it had done before. His father was there with Daisy and his baby uncle, as he persisted in calling Ethelyn's dead boy until James told him better, and pointed out the ludicrousness of the mistake. To Ethelyn Andy was tender as a mother, when at last they let him see her, and his lips left marks upon her forehead and cheek. She was perfectly conscious now, and when told they had sent for Richard, manifested a good deal of interest, and asked when he would probably be there. They were expecting him every train; but ere he came the fever, which seemed for a time to have abated, returned with double force and Ethelyn knew nothing of the kisses Richard pressed upon her lips, or the tears Aunt Barbara shed over her poor darling.

There were anxious hearts and troubled faces in the farmhouse that day, for Death was brooding there again, and they who watched his shadow darkening around them spoke only in whispers, as they obeyed the physician's orders. When Richard first came in Mrs. Markham wound her arm around his neck, and said, "I am so sorry for you, my poor boy," while the three sons, one after another, had grasped their brother's hand in token of sympathy, and that was all that had passed between them of greeting. For the rest of the day, Richard had sat constantly by Ethelyn, watching the changes of her face, and listening to her as she raved in snatches, now of himself, and the time he saved her from the maddened cow, and now of Frank and the huckleberries, which she said were ripening on the Chicopee hills. When she talked of this Richard held his breath, and once, as he leaned forward so as not to lose a word, he caught Aunt Barbara regarding him intently, her wrinkled cheek flushing as she met his eye and guessed what was in his mind. If Richard had needed any confirmation of his suspicions, that look on transparent Aunt Barbara's face would have confirmed them. There had been something between Ethelyn and Frank Van Buren more than a cousinly liking, and Richard's heart throbbed powerfully as he sat by the tossing, restless Ethelyn, moaning on about the huckleberry hills, and the ledge of rocks where the wild laurels grew. This pain he did not try to analyze; he only said to himself that he felt no bitterness toward Ethelyn. She was too near to death's dark tide for that. She was Ethie--his darling--the mother of the child that had been buried from sight before he came. Perhaps she did not love him, and never would; but he had loved her, oh! so much, and if he lost her he would be wretched indeed. And so, forgiving all the past of which he knew, and trying to forgive all he did not know, he sat by her till the sun went down, and his mother came for the twentieth time, urging him to eat. He had not tasted food that day, and faint for the want of it he followed her to where the table had been set, and supper prepared with a direct reference to his particular taste.

He felt better and stronger when supper was over, and listened eagerly while Andy and Eunice, who had been the last with Ethelyn before her sudden illness, recounted every incident as minutely and reverently as if speaking of the dead. Especially did he hang on what Andy said with reference to her questioning him about the breaking of a wicked vow, and when Eunice added her mite to the effect that, getting up for some camphor for an aching tooth, she had heard a groan from Ethelyn's room, and had found her mistress bending over a half-finished letter, which she "reckoned" was to him, and had laid away in the portfolio, he waited for no more, but hurried upstairs to the little bookcase where Eunice had put the treasure--for it was a countless treasure, that unfinished letter, which he read with the great tears rolling down his cheeks, and his heart growing tenfold softer and warmer toward the writer, who confessed to having wronged him, and wished so much that she dare tell him all. What was it she had to tell? Would he ever know? he asked himself, as he put the letter back where he found it. Yes, she would surely tell him, if she lived, as live she must. She was dearer to him now than she had ever been, and the lips unused to prayer, save as a form, prayed most earnestly that Ethie might be spared. Then, as there flashed upon him a sense of the inconsistency there was in keeping aloof from God all his life, and going to him only when danger threatened, he bowed his head in very shame, and the prayer died on his lips. But Andy always prayed--at least he had for many years; and so the wise strong brother sought the simple weaker one, and asked him to do what he had not power to do.

Andy's swollen eyes and haggard face bore testimony to his sorrow, and his voice was very low and earnest, as he replied: "Brother Dick, I'm prayin' all the time. I've said that prayer for the sick until I've worn it threadbare, and now every breath I draw has in it the petition, 'We beseech Thee to hear us, good Lord.' There's nothing in that about Ethie, it's true; but God knows I mean her, and will hear me all the same."

There was a touching simplicity in Andy's faith, which went to the heart of Richard, making him feel of how little avail was knowledge or wisdom or position if there was lacking the one thing needful, which Andy so surely possessed. That night was a long, wearisome one at the farmhouse; but when the morning broke hope and joy came with it, for Ethelyn was better, and in the brown eyes, which unclosed so languidly, there was a look of consciousness, which deepened into a look of surprise and joyful recognition as they rested upon Aunt Barbara.

"Is this Chicopee? Am I home? Oh, Aunt Barbara, I am so glad! you can't guess how glad, or know how tired and sorry your poor Ethie has been," came brokenly from the pale lips, as Ethelyn moved nearer to Aunt Barbara and laid her head upon the motherly bosom, where it had so often lain in the dear old Chicopee days.

She did not notice Richard, or seem to know that she was elsewhere than in Chicopee, back in the old home, and Richard's pulse throbbed quickly as he saw the flush come over Ethie's face, and the look of pain creep into her eyes, when a voice broke the illusion and told her she was still in Olney, with him and the mother-in-law leaning over the bed-rail saying, "Speak to her, Richard."

"Ethie, don't you know me, too?--I came with Aunt Barbara."

That was what he said, as he bent over her, seeking to take in his own one of the feverish little hands locked so fast in those of Aunt Barbara. She did know then, and remember, and her lip quivered in a grieved, disappointed way as she said, "Yes, Richard, I know now. I am not at home, I'm here;" and the intonation of the voice as it uttered the word "here," spoke volumes, and told Aunt Barbara just how homesick and weary and wretched her darling had been here. She must not talk much, the physician said, and so with one hand in Richard's and one in Aunt Barbara's she fell away to sleep again, while the family stole out to their usual avocations, Mrs. Markham and Eunice to their baking, James and John to their work upon the farm, and Andy to his Bethel in the wood-house chamber, where he repeated: "Blessed be the Lord God of Israel who has visited and redeemed his people," and added at the conclusion the Gloria Patri, which he thought suitable for the occasion.

CHAPTER XVIII: DAYS OF CONVALESCENCE

They were very pleasant to Ethelyn, for with Aunt Barbara anticipating every want, and talking of Chicopee; she could not be very weary. It was pleasant, too, having Richard home again, and Ethie was very soft and kind and amiable toward him; but she did not tell him of the letter she had commenced, or hint at the confession he longed to hear. It would have been comparatively easy to write it, but with him there where she could look into his face and watch the dark expression which was sure to come into his eyes, it was hard to tell him that Frank Van Buren had held the first place in her affections, if indeed he did not hold it now. She was not certain yet, though she hoped and tried to believe that Frank was nothing more than cousin now. He surely ought not to be, with Nettie calling him her husband, while she too was a wife. But so subtle was the poison which that unfortunate attachment had infused into her veins that she could not tell whether her nature was cleared of it or not, and so, though she asked forgiveness for having so literally kept her vow, and said that she did commence a letter to him, she kept back the most important part of all. It was better to wait, she thought, until she could truly say, "I loved Frank Van Buren once, but now I love you far better than ever I did him."

Had she guessed how much Richard knew, and how the knowledge was rankling in his bosom, she might have done differently. But she took the course she thought the best, and the perfect understanding Richard had so ardently hoped for was not then arrived at. For a time, however, there seemed to be perfect peace between them, and could Richard have forgotten Frank Van Buren's words or even those of Ethie herself when her fever was on, he would have been supremely happy. But to forget was impossible, and he often found himself wondering how much of Frank's assertion was true, and if Ethelyn would ever be as open and honest with him as he had tried to be with her. She did not get well very fast, and the color came slowly back into her lips and cheeks. She was far happier than she had been before since she first came to Olney. She could not say that she loved her husband as a true wife ought to love a man like Richard Markham, but she found a pleasure in his society which she had never experienced before, while Aunt Barbara's presence was a constant source of joy. That good woman had prolonged her stay far beyond what she had thought it possible when she left Chicopee. She could not tear herself away, when Ethie pleaded so earnestly for her to remain a little longer, and so, wholly impervious to the hints which Mrs. Markham occasionally threw out, that her services were no longer needed as nurse to Ethelyn, she stayed on week after week, seeing far more than she seemed to see, and making up her mind pretty accurately with regard to the prospect of Ethie's happiness, if she remained an inmate of her husband's family.

Aunt Barbara and Mrs. Markham did not harmonize at all. At first, when Ethie was so sick, everything had been merged in the one absorbing thought of her danger, and even the knowledge accidentally obtained that Richard had paid Miss Bigelow's fare out there and would pay it back, had failed to produce more than a passing pang in the bosom of the close, calculating, economical Mrs. Markham; but when the danger was past, it kept recurring again and again, with very unpleasant distinctness, that Aunt Barbara was an expense they could well do without.

Nobody could quarrel with Aunt Barbara--she was so mild, and gentle, and peaceable--and Mrs. Markham did not quarrel with her, but she thought about her all the time, and fretted over her, and remembered the letter she had written about her ways and her being good to Ethie, and wondered what she was there for, and why she did not go home, and asked her what time they generally cleaned house in Chicopee, and if she dared trust her cleaning with Betty. Aunt Barbara was a great annoyance, and she complained to Eunice and Mrs. Jones, and Melinda, who had returned from Washington, that she was spoiling Ethelyn, babying her so, and making her think herself so much weaker than she was.

"Mercy knew," she said, that in her day, when she was young and having children, she did not hug the bed forever. She had something else to do, and was up and around in a fortnight at the most. Her table wasn't loaded down with oranges and figs, and the things they called banannys, which fairly made her sick at her stomach. Nobody was carryin' her up glasses of milk-punch, and lemonade, and cups of tea, at all hours of the day. She was glad of anything, and got well the faster for it. Needn't tell her!--it would do Ethelyn good to stir around and take the air, instead of staying cooped up in her room, complaining that it is hot and close there in the bedroom. "It's airy enough out doors," and with a most aggrieved look on her face, Mrs. Markham put into the oven the pan of soda biscuit she had been making, and then proceeded to lay the cloth for tea.

Eunice had been home for a day or two with a felon on her thumb, and thus a greater proportion of the work had fallen upon Mrs. Markham, which to some degree accounted for her ill-humor. Mrs. Jones and Melinda were spending the afternoon with her, but the latter was up in Ethie's room. Melinda had always a good many ideas of her own, and she had brought with her several new ones from Washington and New York, where she had stayed for four weeks at the Fifth Avenue Hotel. But Melinda, though greatly improved in appearance, was not one whit spoiled. In manner, and the fit of her dress, she was more like Ethelyn and Mrs. Judge Miller, of Camden, than she once had been, and at first James was a little afraid of her, she puffed her hair so high, and wore her gowns so long, while his mother, looking at the stylish hat and fashionable sack which she brought back from Gotham, said her head was turned, and she was altogether too fine for Olney. But when, on the next rainy Sunday, she rode to church in her father's lumber wagon, holding the blue cotton umbrella over her last year's straw and waterproof--and when arrived at the church she suffered James to help her to alight, jumping over the muddy wheel, and then going straight to her accustomed seat in the choir, which had missed her strong voice so much--the son changed his mind, and said she was the same as ever; while after the day when she found Mrs. Markham making soap out behind the corn-house, and good-humoredly offered to watch it and stir it while that lady went into the house to see to the corn pudding, which Eunice was sure to spoil if left to her own ingenuity, the mother, too, changed her mind, and wished Richard had been so lucky as to have fixed his choice on Melinda. But James was far from wishing a thing which would so seriously have interfered with his hopes and wishes. He was very glad that Richard's preference had fallen where it did, and his cheery whistle was heard almost constantly, and after Tim Jones told, in his blunt way, how "Melind was tryin' to train him, and make him more like them dandies at the big tavern in New York," he, too, began to amend, and taking Richard for his pattern, imitated him, until he found that simple, loving Andy, in his anxiety to please Ethelyn, had seized upon more points of etiquette than Richard ever knew existed, and then he copied Andy, having this in his favor: that whatever he did himself was done with a certain grace inherent in his nature, whereas Andy's attempts were awkward in the extreme.

Melinda saw the visible improvement in James, and imputing it rather to Ethelyn's influence than her own, was thus saved from any embarrassment she might have experienced had she known to a certainty how large a share of James Markham's thoughts and affections she possessed. She was frequently at the farmhouse; but had not made what her mother called a visit until the afternoon when Mrs. Markham gave her opinion so freely of Aunt Barbara's petting and its effect on Ethelyn.

From the first introduction Aunt Barbara had liked the practical, straightforward Melinda, in whom she found a powerful ally whenever any new idea was suggested with regard to Ethelyn. To her Aunt Barbara had confided her belief that it was not well for Ethelyn to stay there any longer--that she and Richard both would be better by themselves; an opinion which Melinda heartily indorsed, and straightway set herself at work to form some plan whereby Aunt Barbara's idea might be carried out.

Melinda was not a meddlesome girl, but she did like to help manage other people's business, doing it so well, and evincing so little selfishness in her consideration for others, that when once she had taken charge of a person's affairs she was pretty sure to have the privilege again. When Richard ran for justice of the peace, and she was a little girl, she had refused to speak to three other little girls who flaunted the colors of the opposition candidate; and when he was nominated first for Judge and then as member for the district, she had worked for him quite as zealously as Tim himself, and through her more than one vote, which otherwise might have been lost, was cast in his favor. As she had worked for him, so she now worked for Ethelyn, approaching Richard very adroitly and managing so skillfully that when at last, on the occasion of her visit to his mother's, Aunt Barbara asked him, in her presence and Ethelyn's, if he had never thought it would be well both for himself and wife to live somewhere else than there at home, he never dreamed that he was echoing the very ideas Melinda had instilled into his mind by promptly replying that "he had recently thought seriously of a change," and then asked Ethie where she would like to live--in Olney or in Camden.

"Not Olney--no, not Olney!" Ethelyn gasped, thinking how near that was to her mother-in-law, and shrinking from the espionage to which she would surely be subjected.

Her preference was Davenport, but to this Richard would not listen. Indeed, he began to feel sorry that he had admitted a willingness to change at all, for the old home was very dear to him, and he thought he would never leave it. But he stood committed now, and Melinda followed him up so dexterously, that in less than half an hour it was arranged that early in June Ethelyn should have a home in Camden--either a house of her own, or a suite of rooms at the Stafford House, just which she preferred. She chose the latter, and, womanlike, began at once in fancy to furnish and arrange the handsome apartments which looked out upon Camden Park, and which Melinda said were at present unoccupied. Melinda knew, for only two days before she had been to Camden with her brother Tim and dined at the Stafford House, and heard her neighbor on her right inquire of his vis-à-vis how long since General Martin left the second floor of the new wing, and who occupied it now. This was a mere happen so, but Melinda was one of those to whom the right thing was always happening, the desired information always coming; and if she did contrive to ascertain the price charged for the rooms, it was only because she understood that one of the Markham peculiarities was being a little close, and wished to be armed at every point.

Richard had no idea that Melinda was managing him, or that anyone was managing him. He thought himself that Camden might be a pleasant place to live; as an ex-Judge and M.C. he could get business anywhere; and though he preferred Olney, inasmuch as it was home, he would, if Ethelyn liked, try Camden for a while. It is true the price of the rooms, which Melinda casually named, was enormous, but, then, Ethelyn's health and happiness were above any moneyed consideration; and so, while Mrs. Markham below made and molded the soda biscuit, and talked about dreading the hot weather if "Ethelyn was going to be weakly," Aunt Barbara, and Melinda, and Richard settled a matter which made her eyes open wide with astonishment when, after the exit of the Joneses and the doing up of her work, it was revealed to her. Of course, she charged it all to Aunt Barbara, wishing that good woman as many miles away as intervened between Olney and Chicopee. Had the young people been going to keep house, she would have been more reconciled, for in that case much of what they consumed would have been the product of the farm; but to board, to take rooms at the Stafford House where Ethelyn would have nothing in the world to do but to dress and gossip, was abominable. Then when she heard of the price she opposed the plan with so much energy that, but for Aunt Barbara and Melinda Jones, Richard might have succumbed; but the majority ruled, and Ethelyn's eyes grew brighter, and her thin cheeks rounder, with the sure hope of leaving a place where she had been so unhappy. She should miss Melinda Jones; and though she would be near Mrs. Miller, and Marcia Fenton, and Ella Backus, they could not be to her all Melinda had been, while Andy--Ethelyn felt the lumps rising in her throat whenever she thought of him and the burst of tears with which he had heard that she was going away.

"I can't help thinkin' it's for the wuss," he said, wiping his smooth face with the cuff of his coat-sleeve. "Something will happen as the result of your goin' there. I feel it in my bones."

Were Andy's words prophetic? Would something happen, if they went to Camden, which would not have happened had they remained in Olney? Ethelyn did not ask herself the question. She was too supremely happy, and if she thought at all, it was of how she could best accelerate her departure from the lonely farmhouse.

When Mrs. Markham found that they were really going, that nothing she could say would be of any avail, she gave up the contest, and, mother-like, set herself at work planning for their comfort, or rather for Richard's comfort. It was for him that the best and newest featherbed, weighing thirty pounds and a half to a feather, was aired and sunned three days upon the kitchen roof, the good woman little dreaming that if the thirty-pounder was used at all, it would do duty under the hair mattress Ethelyn meant to have. They were to furnish their own rooms, and whatever expense Mrs. Markham could save her boy she meant to do. There was the carpet in their chamber--they could have that; for after they were gone it was not likely the room would be used, and the old rag one would answer. They could have the curtains, too, if they liked, with the table and the chairs. Left to himself and his mother's guidance, Richard would undoubtedly have taken to Camden such a promiscuous outfit as would have made even a truckman smile; but there were three women leagued against him, and so draft after draft was drawn from his funds in the Camden bank until the rooms were furnished; and one bright morning in early June, a week after Aunt Barbara started for Chicopee, Ethie bid her husband's family good-by, and turning her back upon Olney, turned also the first leaf of her life's history in the West.

CHAPTER XIX: COMING TO A CRISIS

Richard was not happy in his new home; it did not fit him like the old. He missed his mother's petting; he missed the society of his plain, outspoken brothers; he missed his freedom from restraint, and he missed the deference so universally paid to him in Olney, where he was the only lion. In Camden there were many to divide the honors with him; and though he was perhaps unconscious of it, he had been first so long that to be one of many firsts was not altogether agreeable. With the new home and new associates more like those to which she had been accustomed, Ethelyn had resumed her training process, which was not now borne as patiently as in the halcyon days of the honeymoon, when most things wore the couleur de rose and were right because they came from the pretty young bride. Richard chafed under the criticisms to which he was so frequently subjected, and if he improved on them in the least it was not perceptible to Ethlyn, who had just cause to blush for the careless habits of her husband--habits which even Melinda observed, when in August she spent a week with Ethelyn, and then formed one of a party which went for a pleasure trip to St. Paul and Minnehaha. From this excursion, which lasted for two weeks, Richard returned to Camden in anything but an amiable frame of mind. Ethelyn had not pleased him at all, notwithstanding that she had been unquestionably the reigning belle of the party--the one whose hand was claimed in every dance, and whose company was sought in every ride and picnic. Marcia Fenton and Ella Backus faded into nothingness when she was near, and they laughingly complained to Richard that his wife had stolen all their beaux away, and they wished he would make her do better.

"I wish I could," was his reply, spoken not playfully, but moodily, just as he felt at the time.

He was not an adept in concealing his feelings, which generally showed themselves upon his face, or were betrayed in the tones of his voice, and when he spoke as he did of his wife the two young girls glanced curiously at each other, wondering if it where possible that the grave Judge was jealous. If charged with jealousy Richard would have denied it, though he did not care to have Ethelyn so much in Harry Clifford's society. Richard knew nothing definite against Harry, except that he would occasionally drink more than was wholly in accordance with a steady and safe locomotion of his body; and once since they had been at the Stafford House, where he also boarded, the young lawyer had been invisible for three entire days. "Sick with a cold" was his excuse when he appeared again at the table, with haggard face and bloodshot eyes; but in the parlor, and halls, and private rooms, there where whispers of soiled clothes and jammed hats, and the servants bribed to keep the secret that young lawyer Clifford's boots were carried dangling up to No. 94 at a very late hour of the night on which he professed to have taken his cold. After this, pretty Marcia Fenton, who, before Ethelyn came to town, had ridden oftenest after the black horses owned by Harry, tossed her curls when he came near, and arched her eyebrows in a manner rather distasteful to the young man; while Ella Backus turned her back upon him, and in his hearing gave frequent lectures on intemperance and its loathsomeness. Ethelyn, on the contrary, made no difference in her demeanor toward him. She cared nothing for him either way, except that his polite attentions and delicate deference to her tastes and opinions were complimentary and flattering, and so she saw no reason why she should shun him because he had fallen once. It might make him worse, and she should stand by him as an act of philanthropy, she said to Richard when he asked her what she saw to admire in that drunken Clifford.

Richard had no idea that Ethelyn cared in the least for Harry Clifford; he knew she did not, though she sometimes singled him out as one whose manners in society her husband would do well to imitate. Of the two young men, Harry Clifford and Frank Van Buren, who had been suggested to him as copies, Richard preferred the former, and wished he could feel as easy with regard to Frank as he was with regard to Harry. He had never forgotten that fragment of conversation overheard in Washington, and as time went on it haunted him more and more. He had given up expecting any confession from Ethelyn, though at first he was constantly expecting it, and laying little snares by way of hints and reminders; but Ethelyn had evidently changed her mind, and if there was a past which Richard ought to have known, he would now probably remain in ignorance of it, unless some chance revealed it. It would have been far better if Richard had tried to banish all thoughts of Frank Van Buren from his mind and taken Ethelyn as he found her; but Richard was a man, and so, manlike, he hugged the skeleton which he in part had dragged into his home, and petted it, and kept it constantly in sight, instead of thrusting it out from the chamber of his heart, and barring the door against it. Frank's name was never mentioned between them, but Richard fancied that always after the receipt of Mrs. Dr. Van Buren's letters Ethelyn was a little sad, and more disposed to find fault with him, and he sometimes wished Mrs. Dr. Van Buren might never write to them again. There was one of her letters awaiting Ethelyn after her return from Minnesota, and she read it standing under the chandelier, with Richard lying upon the couch near by, watching her curiously. There was something in the letter which disturbed her evidently, for her face flushed, and her lips shut firmly together, as they usually did when she was agitated. Richard already read Aunt Barbara's letters, and heretofore he had been welcome to Mrs. Van Buren's, a privilege of which he seldom availed himself, for he found nothing interesting in her talk of parties, and operas and fashions, and the last new color of dress goods, and style of wearing the hair.

"It was too much twaddle for him," he had said in reply to Ethelyn's questions as to whether he would like to see what Aunt Van Buren had written.

Now, however, she did not offer to show him the letter, but crumpled it nervously in her pocket, and going to her piano, began to play dashingly, rapidly, as was her custom when excited. She did not know that Richard was listening to her, much less watching her, as he lay in the shadow, wondering what that letter contained, and wishing so much that he knew. Ethelyn was tired that night, and after the first heat of her excitement had been thrown off in a spirited schottische, she closed her piano, and coming to the couch where Richard was lying, sat down by his side, and after waiting a moment in silence, asked "of what he was thinking."

There was something peculiar in the tone of her voice--something almost beseeching, as if she either wanted sympathy, or encouragement for the performance of some good act. But Richard did not so understand her. He was, to tell the truth, a very little cross, as men, and women, too, are apt to be when tired with sight-seeing and dissipation. He had been away from his business three whole weeks, traveling with a party for not one member of which, with the exception of his wife, Melinda, Marcia, and Ella, did he care a straw.

Hotel life at St. Paul he regarded as a bore, second only to life at Saratoga. The falls of Minnehaha "was a very pretty little stream," he thought, but what people could see about it go into such ecstasies as Ethelyn, and even Melinda did, he could not tell. Perhaps if Harry Clifford had not formed a part of every scene where Ethelyn was the prominent figure, he might have judged differently. But Harry had been greatly in his way, and Richard did not like it any more than he liked Ethelyn's flirting so much with him, and leaving him, her husband, to look about for himself. He had shown, too, that he did not like it to Marcia Fenton and Ella Backus who probably thought him a bear, as perhaps he was. On the whole, Richard was very uncomfortable in his mind, and Aunt Van Buren's letter did not tend in the least to improve his temper; so when Ethelyn asked him of what he was thinking, and accompanied her question with a stroke of her hand upon his hair, he answered her, "Nothing much, except that I am tired and sleepy."

The touch upon his hair he had felt to his finger tips, for Ethelyn seldom caressed him even as much as this; but he was in too moody a frame of mind to respond as he would once have done. His manner was not very encouraging, but, as if she had nerved herself to some painful duty, Ethelyn persisted, and said to him next: "You have not seen Aunt Van Buren's letter. Shall I read you what she says?"

Every nerve in Richard's body had been quivering with curiosity to see that letter, but now, when the coveted privilege was within his reach, he refused it; and, little dreaming of all he was throwing aside, answered indifferently: "No, I don't know that I care to hear it. I hardly think it will pay. Where are they now?"

"At Saratoga," Ethelyn replied; but her voice was not the same which had addressed Richard first; there was a coldness, a constraint in it now, as if her good resolution had been thrown back upon her and frozen up the impulse prompting her to the right.

Richard had had his chance with Ethelyn and lost it. But he did not know it, or guess how sorry and disappointed she was when at last she left him and retired to her sleeping-room. There was a window open in the parlor, and as the wind was rising with a sound of rain, Richard went to close it ere following his wife. The window was near to the piano and as he shut it something rattled at his feet. It was the crumpled letter, which Ethelyn had accidentally drawn from her dress pocket with the handkerchief she held in her hand when she sat down by Richard. He knew it was that letter, and his first thought was to carry it to Ethelyn; then, as he remembered her offer to read it to him, he said, "Surely there can be no harm in reading it for myself. A man has a right to know what is in a letter to his wife."

Thus reasoning, he sat down by the side light as far away from the bedroom door as possible and commenced Mrs. Dr. Van Buren's letter. They were stopping at the United States, and there was nothing particular at first, except her usual remarks of the people and what they wore; but on the third page Richard's eye caught Frank's name, and skipping all else, leaped eagerly forward to what the writer was saying of her son. His conduct evidently did not please his mother; neither did the conduct of Nettie, who was too insipid for anything, the lady wrote, adding that she was not half so bright and pretty as when she was first married, but had the headache and kept her own room most of the time, and was looking so faded and worn that Frank was really ashamed of her.

"You know how he likes brilliant, sparkling girls," she wrote, "and of course he has no patience with Nettie's fancied ailments. I can't say that I altogether sympathize with her myself; and, dear Ethie, I must acknowledge that it has more than once occurred to me that I did very wrong to meddle with Frank's first love affair. He would be far happier now if it had been suffered to go on, for I suspect he has never entirely gotten over it; but it is too late now for regrets. Nettie is his wife, and he must make the best of it."

Then followed what seemed the secret of the Van Buren discomfort. The bank in which most of Nettie's fortune was deposited had failed, leaving her with only the scanty income of five hundred dollars a year, a sum not sufficient to buy clothes, Mrs. Van Buren said. But Richard did not notice this--his mind was only intent upon Frank's first love affair, which ought to have gone on. He did not ask himself whether, in case it had gone on, Ethelyn would have been there, so near to him that her soft breathing came distinctly to his ear. He knew she would not; there had been something between her and Frank Van Buren, he was convinced beyond a doubt, and the fiercest pang he had ever known was that which came to him when he sat with Mrs. Dr. Van Buren's letter in his hand, wondering why Ethie had withheld the knowledge of it from him, and if she had outlived the love which her aunt regretted as having come to naught. Then, as the more generous part of his nature began to seek excuses for her, he asked himself why she offered to read the letter if she had really been concerned in Frank's first love affair, and hope whispered that possibly she was not the heroine of that romance. There was comfort in that thought: and Richard would have been comforted if jealousy had not suggested how easy it was for her to skip the part relating to Nettie and Frank, and thus leave him as much in the dark as ever. Yes, that was undoubtedly her intention. While seeming to be so open and honest, she would have deceived him all the more. This was what Richard decided, and his heart grew very hard against the young wife, who looked so innocent and pretty in her quiet sleep, when at last he sought his pillow and lay down by her side.

He was very moody and silent for days after that, and even his clients detected an irritability in his manner which they had never seen before. "There was nothing ailed him," he said to Ethelyn, when she asked what was the matter, and accused him of being positively cross. She was very gay; Camden society suited her; and as the season advanced, and the festivities grew more and more frequent, she was seldom at home more than one or two evenings in the week, while the day was given either to the arrangement of dress or taking of necessary rest, so that her husband saw comparatively little of her, except for the moment when she always came to him with hood and white cloak in hand to ask him how she looked, before going to the carriage waiting at the door. Never in her girlish days had she been so beautiful as she was now, but Richard seldom told her so, though he felt the magic influence of her brilliant beauty, and did not wonder that she was the reigning belle. He seldom accompanied her himself. Parties, and receptions, and concerts, were bores, he said; and at first he had raised objections to her going without him. But after motherly Mrs. Harris, who boarded in the next block, and was never happier than when chaperoning someone, offered to see to her and take her under the same wing which had sheltered six fine and now well-married daughters, Richard made no further objections. He did not wish to be thought a domestic tyrant; he did not wish to seem jealous, and so he would wrap Ethie's cloak around her, and taking her himself to Mrs. Harris' carriage, would give that lady sundry charges concerning her, bidding her see that she did not dance till wholly wearied out, and asking her to bring her home earlier than the previous night. Then, returning to his solitary rooms, he would sit nursing the demon which might so easily have been thrust aside. Ethie was not insensible to his kindness in allowing her to follow the bent of her own inclinations, even when it was so contrary to his own, and for his sake she did many things she might not otherwise have done. She snubbed Harry Clifford and the whole set of dandies like him, so that, though they danced, and talked, and laughed with her, they never crossed a certain line of propriety which she had drawn between them. She was very circumspect; she tried at first in various ways to atone to Richard for her long absence from him, telling him whatever she thought would interest him, and sometimes, when she found him waiting for her, and looking so tired and sleepy, playfully chiding him for sitting up for her, and telling him that though it was kind in him to do so, she preferred that he should not. This was early in the season; but after the day when Mrs. Markham, senior, came over from Olney to spend the day, and "blow Richard's wife up," as she expressed it, everything was changed, and Ethelyn stayed out as late as she liked without any concessions to Richard. Mrs. Markham, senior, had heard strange stories of Ethelyn's proceedings--"going to parties night after night, with her dress shamefully low, and going to plays and concerts bareheaded, with flowers and streamers in her hair, besides wearing a mask, and pretending she was Queen Hortense."

"A pretty critter to be," Mrs. Markham had said to the kind neighbor who had returned from Camden and was giving her the particulars in full of Ethelyn's misdoings. "Yes, a pretty critter to be! If I was goin' to turn myself into somebody else I'd take a decent woman. I wonder at Richard's lettin' her; but, law! he is so blind and she so headstrong!"

And the good woman groaned over this proof of depravity as she questioned her visitor further with regard to Ethie's departures from duty.

"And he don't go with her much, you say," she continued, feeling more aggrieved than ever when she heard that on the occasion of Ethie's personating Hortense, Richard had also appeared as a knight of the sixteenth century, and borne his part so well that Ethelyn herself did not recognize him until the mask was removed.

Mrs. Markham could not suffer such high-handed wickedness to go unrebuked, and taking as a peace offering, in case matters assumed a serious aspect, a pot of gooseberry jam and a ball of head cheese, she started for Camden the very next day.

Ethelyn did not expect her, but she received her kindly, and knowing how she hated a public table, had dinner served in her own room, and then, without showing the least impatience, waited a full hour for Richard to come in from the court-house, where an important suit was pending. Mrs. Markham was to return to Olney that night, and as there was no time to lose, she brought the conversation round to the "stories" she had heard, and little by little laid on the lash till Ethelyn's temper was roused, and she asked her mother-in-law to say out what she had to say at once, and not skirt round it so long. Then came the whole list of misdemeanors which Mrs. Markham thought "perfectly ridiculous," asking her son how he "could put up with such work."

Richard wisely forbore taking either side; nor was it necessary that he should speak for Ethie. She was fully competent to fight her own battle, and she fought it with a will, telling her mother-in-law that she should attend as many parties as she pleased and wear as many masks. She did not give up her liberty of action when she married. She was young yet, and should enjoy herself if she chose, and in her own way.

This was all the satisfaction Mrs. Markham could get, and supremely pitying "her poor boy," whom she mentally decided was "henpecked," she took the cars back to Olney, saying to Richard, who accompanied her to the train, "I am sorry for you from the bottom of my heart. It would be better if you had stayed with me."

Richard liked his mother's good opinion, but as he walked back to the hotel he could not help feeling that a mother's interference between man and wife was never very discreet, and he wished the good woman had stayed at home. If he had said so to Ethelyn, when on his return to his rooms he found her weeping passionately, there might have come a better understanding between them, and she probably would have stayed with him that evening instead of attending the whist party given by Mrs. Miller. But he had fully determined to keep silent, and when Ethelyn asked if she was often to be subjected to such insults, he did not reply. He went with her, however, to Mrs. Miller's, and knowing nothing of cards, almost fell asleep while waiting for her, and playing backgammon with another fellow-sufferer, who had married a young wife and was there on duty.

Mrs. Markham, senior, did not go to Camden again, and when Christmas came, and with it an invitation for Richard and his wife to dine at the farmhouse on the turkey Andy had fattened for the occasion, Ethelyn peremptorily declined; and as Richard would not go without her, Mrs. Jones and Melinda had their seats at table, and Mrs. Markham wished for the hundredth time that Richard's preference had fallen on the latter young lady instead of "that headstrong piece who would be his ruin."

CHAPTER XX: THE CRISIS

It was the Tuesday before Lent. The gay season was drawing to a close, for Mrs. Howard and Mrs. Miller, who led the fashionable world of Camden before Ethelyn's introduction to it, were the highest kind of church-women, and while neglecting the weightier matters of the law were strict to bring their tithes of mint, and anise, and cummin. They were going to wear sackcloth and ashes for forty days and stay at home, unless, as Mrs. Miller said to Ethelyn, they met occasionally in each other's house for a quiet game of whist or euchre. There could be no harm in that, particularly if they abstained on Fridays, as of course they should. Mr. Bartow himself could not find fault with so simple a recreation, even if he did try so hard to show what his views were with regard to keeping the Lenten fast. Mrs. Miller and Mrs. Howard intended to be very regular at the morning service, hoping that the odor of sanctity with which they would thus be permeated would in some way atone for the absence of genuine heart-religion and last them for the remainder of the year. First, however, and as a means of helping her in her intended seclusion from the world, Mrs. Howard was to give the largest party of the season--a sort of carnival, from which the revelers were expected to retire the moment the silvery-voiced clock on her mantel struck the hour of twelve and ushered in the dawn of Lent. It was to be a masquerade, for the Camdenites had almost gone mad on that fashion which Ethelyn had the credit of introducing into their midst; that is, she was the first to propose a masquerade early in the season, telling what she had seen and giving the benefit of her larger experience in such matters.

It was a fashion which took wonderfully with the people, for the curiosity and interest attaching to the characters was just suited to the restless, eager temperament of the Camdenites, and they entered into it with heart and soul, ransacking boxes and barrels and worm-eaten chests, scouring the country far and near and even sending as far as Davenport and Rock Island for the necessary costumes. Andy himself had been asked by Harry Clifford to lend his Sunday suit, that young scamp intending to personate some raw New England Yankee; and that was how Mrs. Markham, senior, first came to hear of the proceedings which, to one of her rigid views, savored strongly of the pit, especially after she heard one of the parties described by an eye-witness, who mentioned among other characters his Satanic Majesty, as enacted by Harry Clifford, who would fain have appeared next in Andy's clothes! No wonder the good woman was enraged and took the next train for Camden, giving her son and daughter a piece of her mind and winding up her discourse with: "And they say you have the very de'il himself, with hoofs and horns. I think you might have left him alone, for I reckon he was there fast enough if you could not see him."

Ethelyn had not approved of Harry Clifford's choice, and with others had denounced his taste as bad; but she enjoyed the masquerades generally, and for this last and most elaborate of all she had made great preparations. Richard had not opposed her joining it, but he did wince a little when he found she was to personate Mary, Queen of Scots, wishing that she would not always select persons of questionable character, like Hortense and Scotland's ill-fated queen. But Ethie had decided upon her role without consulting him, and so he walked over piles of ancient-looking finery and got his boots tangled in the golden wig which Ethie had hunted up, and told her he should be glad when it was over, and wished mentally that it might be Lent the year around, and was persuaded into saying he would go to the party himself, not as a masker, but in his own proper person as Richard Markham, the grave and dignified Judge whom the people respected so highly. Ethie was glad he was going. She would always rather have him with her, if possible; and the genuine satisfaction she evinced when he said he would accompany her did much toward reconciling him to the affair about which so much was being said in Camden. When, however, he came in to supper on Tuesday night complaining of a severe headache, and saying he wished he could remain quietly at home, inasmuch as he was to start early the next morning for St. Louis, where he had business to transact, Ethelyn said to him: "If you are sick, of course I will not compel you to go. Mr. and Mrs. Miller will look after me."

She meant this kindly, for she saw that he was looking pale and haggard, and Richard took it so then; but afterward her words became so many scorpions stinging him into fury. It would seem as if every box, and drawer, and bag, had been overturned, and the contents brought to light, for ribbons, and flowers, and laces were scattered about in wild confusion, while on the carpet, near the drawer where Ethie's little mother-of-pearl box was kept, lay a tiny note, which had inadvertently been dropped from its hiding-place when Ethie opened the box in quest of something which was wanted for Queen Mary's outfit. Richard saw the note just as he saw the other litter, but paid no attention to it then, and after supper was over went out as usual for his evening paper.

Gathered about the door of the office was a group of young men, all his acquaintances, and all talking together upon some theme which seemed to excite them greatly.

"Too bad to make such a fool of himself," one said, while another added, "He ought to have known better than to order champagne, when he knows what a beast a few drops will make of him, and he had a first-class character for to-night, too."

Richard was never greatly interested in gossip of any kind, but something impelled him now to ask of whom they were talking.

"Of Hal Clifford," was the reply. "A friend of his came last night to Moore's Hotel, where Hal boards, and wishing to do the generous host Hal ordered champagne and claret for supper, in his room, and got drunker than a fool. It always lasts him a day or two, so he is gone up for to-night."

Richard had no time to waste in words upon Harry Clifford, and after hearing the story started for his boarding-place. His route lay past the Moore House and as he reached it the door opened and Harry came reeling down the steps. He was just drunk enough to be sociable, and spying Richard by the light of the lamppost he hurried to his side, and taking his arm in the confidential manner he always assumed when intoxicated, he began talking in a half-foolish, half-rational way, very disgusting to Richard, who tried vainly to shake him off. Harry was not to be baffled, and with a stammer and a hiccough he began: "I say--a--now, old chap, don't be so fast to get rid of a cove. Wife waiting for you, I suppose. Deuced fine woman. Envy you; I do, 'pon honor, and so does somebody else. D'ye know her old beau that she used to be engaged to, is here?"

"Who? What do you mean?" Richard asked, turning sharply upon his companion, who continued:

"Why, Frank Van Buren. Cousin, you know; was chum with me in college, so I know all about it. Don't you remember my putting it to her that first time I met her at Mrs. Miller's? Mistrusted by her blushing there was more than I supposed; and so there was. He told me all about it last night."

Richard did not try now to shake off his comrade. There seemed to be a spell upon him, and although he longed to thrash the impudent young man, saying such things of Ethelyn, he held his peace, with the exception of the single question:

"Frank Van Buren in town? Where is he stopping?"

"Up at Moore's. Came last night; and between you and me, Judge, I took a little too much. Makes my head feel like a tub. Sorry for Frank. He and his wife ain't congenial, besides she's lost her money that Frank married her for. Serves him right for being so mean to Mrs. Markham, and I told him so when he opened his heart clear to the breast-bone and told me all about it; how his mother broke it up about the time you were down there; and, Markham, you don't mind my telling you, as an old friend, how he said she went to the altar with a heavier heart than she would have carried to her coffin. Quite a hifalutin speech for Frank, who used to be at the foot of his class."

Richard grew faint and cold as death, feeling one moment an impulse to knock young Clifford down, and the next a burning desire to hear the worst, if, indeed, he had not already heard it. He would not question Harry; but he would listen to all he had to say, and so kept quiet, waiting for the rest. Harry was just enough beside himself to take a malicious kind of satisfaction in inflicting pain upon Richard, as he was sure he was doing. He knew Judge Markham despised him, and though, when sober, he would have shrunk from so mean a revenge, he could say anything now, and so went on:

"She has not seen him yet, but will to-night, for he is going. I got him invited as my friend. She knows he is here. He sent her a note this morning. Pity I can't go, too; but I can't, for you see, I know how drunk I am. Here we part, do we?" and Harry loosed his hold of Richard's arm as they reached the corner of the street.

Wholly stunned by what he had heard, Richard kept on his way, but not toward the Stafford House. He could not face Ethelyn yet. He was not determined what course to pursue, and so he wandered on in the darkness, through street after street, while the wintry wind blew cold and chill about him; but he did not heed it, or feel the keen, cutting blast. His blood was at a boiling heat, and the great drops of sweat were rolling down his face, as, with head and shoulders bent like an aged man, he walked rapidly on, revolving all he had heard, and occasionally whispering to himself, "She carried a heavier heart to the altar than she would have taken to her coffin."

"Yes, I believe it now. I remember how white she was, and how her hand trembled when I took it in mine. Oh! Ethie, Ethie, I did not deserve this from you."

Resentment--hard, unrelenting resentment--was beginning to take the place of the deep pain he had at first experienced, and it needed but the sight of Mrs. Miller's windows, blazing with light, to change the usually quiet, undemonstrative man into a demon.

"She is to meet him here to-night, it seems, and perhaps talk over her blighted life. Never, no, never, so long as bolts and bars have the power to hold her. She shall not disgrace herself, for with all her faults she is my wife, and I have loved her so much. Oh, Ethie, I love you still," and the wretched man leaned against a post as he sent forth this despairing cry for the Ethie who he felt was lost forever.

Every little incident which could tend to prove that what Harry had said was true came to his mind; the conversation overheard in Washington between Frank and Melinda, Ethelyn's unfinished letter, to which she had never referred, and the clause in Aunt Van Buren's letter relating to Frank's first love affair. He could not any longer put the truth aside with specious arguments, for it stood out in all its naked deformity, making him cower and shrink before it. It was a very different man who went up the stairs of the Stafford House to room No-- from the man who two hours before had gone down them, and Ethelyn would hardly have known him for her husband had she been there to meet him. Wondering much at his long absence, she had at last gone on with her dressing, and then, as he still did not appear, she had stepped for a moment to the room of a friend, who was sick, and had asked to see her when she was ready. Richard saw that she was out, and sinking into the first chair, his eyes fell upon the note lying near the bureau drawer. The room had partially been put to rights, but this had escaped Ethie's notice, and Richard picked it up, glowering with rage, and almost foaming at the mouth when, in the single word, "Ethie," on the back, he recognized Frank Van Buren's writing!

He had it then--the note which his rival had sent, apprising his wife of his presence in town, and he would read it, too. He had no scruples about that, and his fingers tingled to his elbows as he opened the note, never observing how yellow and worn it looked, or that it was not dated. He had no doubt of its identity, and his face grew purple with passion as he read:

"MY OWN DARLING ETHIE: Don't fail to be there to-night, and, if possible, leave the 'old maid' at home, and come alone. We shall have so much better time. Your devoted,

"FRANK."

Words could not express Richard's emotions as he held that note in his shaking hand, and gazed at the words, "My own darling Ethie." Quiet men like Richard Markham are terrible when roused; and Richard was terrible in his anger, as he sat like a block of stone, contemplating the proof of his wife's unfaithfulness. He called it by that hard name, grating his teeth together as he thought of her going by appointment to meet Frank Van Buren, who had called him an "old maid," and planned to have him left behind if possible. Then, as he recalled what Ethelyn had said about his remaining at home if he were ill, he leaped to his feet, and an oath quivered on his lips at her duplicity.

"False in every respect," he muttered, "and I trusted her so much."

It never occurred to him that the note was a strange one for what he imagined it to portend, Frank merely charging Ethelyn to be present at the party, without even announcing his arrival or giving any explanation for his sudden appearance in Camden. Richard was too much excited to reason upon anything, and stood leaning upon the piano, with his livid face turned toward the door, when Ethie made her appearance, looking very pretty and piquant in her Mary Stuart guise.

She held her mask in her hand, but when she caught a glimpse of him she hastily adjusted it, and springing forward, "Where were you so long? I began to think you were never coming. We shall be among the very last. How do I look as Mary? Am I pretty enough to make an old maid like Elizabeth jealous of me?"

Had anything been wanting to perfect Richard's wrath, that allusion to an "old maid" would have done it. It was the drop in the brimming bucket, and Richard exploded at once, hurling such language at Ethelyn's head that, white and scared, and panting for breath, she put up both her hands to ward off the storm, and asked what it all meant. Richard had locked the door, the only entrance to their room, and stooping over Ethelyn he hissed into her ear his meaning, telling her all he had heard from Harry Clifford, and asking if it were true. Ere Ethelyn could reply there was a knock at the door, and a servant's voice called out, "Carriage waiting for Mrs. Markham."

It was the carriage sent by Mrs. Miller for Ethelyn, and quick as thought Richard stepped to the door, and unlocking it, said hastily, "Give Mrs. Miller Mrs. Markham's compliments, and say she cannot be present to-night. Tell her she regrets it exceedingly"; and Richard's voice was very bitter and sarcastic in its tone as he closed the door upon the astonished waiter; and relocking it, he returned again to Ethelyn, who had risen to her feet, and with a different expression upon her face from the white, scared look it had worn at first, stood confronting him fearlessly now, and even defiantly, for this bold step had roused her from her apathy; and in a fierce whisper, which, nevertheless, was as clear and distinct as the loudest tones could have been; she asked, "Am I to understand that I am a prisoner here in my own room? It is your intention to keep me from the party?"

"It is," and with his back against the door, as if doubly to bar her egress, Richard regarded her gloomily, while he charged her with the special reason why she wished to go. "It was to meet Frank Van Buren, your former lover," he said, asking if she could deny it.

For a moment Ethelyn stood irresolute, mentally going over all that would be said if she stayed from Mrs. Miller's, where she was to be the prominent one, and calculating her strength to stem the tide of wonder and conjecture as to her absence which was sure to follow. She could not meet it, she decided; she must go, at all hazards, even if, to achieve her purpose, she made some concessions to the man who had denounced her so harshly, and used such language as is not easily forgotten.

"Richard," she began, and her eyes had a strange glittering light in them, "with regard to the past I shall say nothing now, but that Frank was here in Camden I had not the slightest knowledge till I heard it from you. Believe me, Richard, and let me go. My absence will seem very strange, and cause a great deal of remark. Another time I may explain what would best have been explained before."

The light in her eyes was softer now, and her voice full of entreaty; for Ethie felt almost as if pleading for her life. But she might as well have talked to the wall for any good results it produced. Richard was moved from his lofty height of wrath and vindictiveness, but he did not believe her. How could he, with the fatal note in his hand, and the memory of the degrading epithet it contained, and which Ethie, too, had used against him, still ringing in his ears? The virgin queen of England was never more stony and inexorable with regard to the unfortunate Mary than was Richard toward his wife, and the expression of his face froze all the better emotions rising in Ethie's heart, as she felt that in a measure she was reaping a just retribution for her long deception.

"I do not believe you, madam," Richard said; "and if I were inclined to do so, this note, which Harry said was sent to you, and which I found upon the floor, would tell me better," and tossing into her lap the soiled bit of paper, accomplishing so much harm, he continued: "There is my proof; that in conjunction with the name of opprobrium, which you remember you insinuatingly used, asking if you were pretty enough to make the old maid, Elizabeth, jealous. You are pretty enough, madam; but it is an accursed beauty which would attract to itself men of Frank Van Buren's stamp."

Richard could not get over that epithet. He would have forgiven the other sin almost as soon as this, and his face was very dark and stern as he watched Ethelyn reading the little note. She knew in a moment what it was, and the suddenness of its appearance before her turned her white and faint. It brought back so vividly the day when she received it--six or seven years ago, the lazy September day, when the Chicopee hills wore the purplish light of early autumn, and the air was full of golden sunshine. It was a few weeks after the childish betrothal among the huckleberry hills, and Frank had come up to spend a week with a boy friend of his, who lived across the river. There was to be an exhibition in the white schoolhouse, in the river district, and Frank had written, urging her to come, and asking that Aunt Barbara should be left behind--"the old maid," he sometimes called her to his cousin, thinking it sounded smart and manlike. Aunt Barbara had stayed at home from choice, sending her niece in charge of Susie Granger's mother; but the long walk home, after the exercises were over, the lingering, loitering walk across the causeway, where the fog was riding so damply, the stopping on the bridge, and looking down into the deep, dark water, where the stars were reflected so brightly, the slow climbing of the depot hill, and the long talk by the gate beneath the elms, whose long arms began to drop great drops of dew on Ethie's head ere the interview was ended--all this had been experienced with Frank, whose arm was around the young girl's waist, and whose hand was clasping hers, as with boyish pride and a laughable effort to seem manly, he talked of "our engagement," and even leaped forward in fancy to the time "when we are married."

All this came back to Ethelyn, and she seemed to feel again the breath of the September night, and see through the clustering branches the flashing light waiting for her in the dear old room in Chicopee. She forgot for a moment the stern, dark face watching her so jealously, and so hardening toward her as he saw how pale she grew, and heard her exclamation of surprise when she first recognized the note, and remembered that in turning over the contents of the ebony box she must have dropped it upon the floor.

"Do you still deny all knowledge of Frank's presence in town?" Richard asked, and his voice recalled Ethelyn from the long ago back to the present time.

He was waiting for her answer; but Ethie had none to give. Her hot, imperious temper was in the ascendant now. She was a prisoner for the night; her own husband was the jailer, who she felt was unjust to her, and she would make no explanations, at least not then. He might think what he liked or draw any inference he pleased from her silence. And so she made him no reply, except to crush into her pocket the paper which she should have burned on that morning when, crouching on the hearthstone at home, she destroyed all other traces of a past which ought never to have been. He could not make her speak, and his words of reproach might as well have been given to the winds as to that cold, statue-like woman, who mechanically laid aside the fanciful costume in which she was arrayed, doing everything with a deliberation and coolness more exasperating to Richard than open defiance would have been. A second knock at the door, and another servant appeared, saying, apologetically, that the note he held in his hand had been left at the office for Mrs. Markham early in the morning, but forgotten till now.

"Give it to me, if you please. It is mine," Ethelyn said, and something in her voice and manner kept Richard quiet while she took the offered note and went back to the chandelier where, with a compressed lip and burning cheek, she read the genuine note sent by Frank.

"Dear cousin," he wrote, "business for a Boston firm has brought me to Camden, where they have had debt standing out. Through the influence of Harry Clifford, who was a college chum of mine, I have an invitation to Mrs. Miller's, where I hope to meet yourself and husband. I should call to-day, but I know just how busy you must be with your costume, which I suppose you wish to keep incog., even from me. I shall know you, though, at once. See if I do not. Wishing to be remembered to the Judge, I am, yours truly,

"FRANK VAN BUREN."

This is what Ethelyn read, knowing, as she read, that it would make matters right between herself and husband--at least so far as an appointment was concerned; but she would not show it to him then. She was too angry, too much aggrieved, to admit of any attempts on her part for a reconciliation; so she put that note with the other, and then went quietly on arranging her things in their proper places. Then, when this was done, she sat down by the window and peering out into the wintry darkness watched the many lights and moving figures in Mrs. Miller's house, which could be distinctly seen from the hotel. Richard still intended to take the early train for St. Louis, and so he retired at last, but Ethelyn sat where she was until the carriages taking the revelers home had passed, and the lights were out in Mrs. Miller's windows, and the bell of St. John's had ushered in the second hour of the fast. Not then did she join her husband, but lay down upon the sofa, where he found her when at six o'clock he came from his broken, feverish sleep, to say his parting words. He had contemplated the propriety of giving up his trip and remaining at home while Frank Van Buren was in town, but this he could not very well do.

"I will leave her to herself," he thought, "trusting that what has passed will deter her from any further improprieties."

Something like this he said to her when, in the gray dawn, he stood before her, equipped for his journey; but Ethelyn did not respond, and with her cold, dead silence weighing more upon him than bitter reproaches would have done, Richard left her and took his way through the chill, snowy morning to the depot, little dreaming as he went of when and how he and Ethelyn would meet again.

CHAPTER XXI: THE RESULT

The bell in the tower of St. John's pealed forth its summons to the house of prayer, and one by one, singly or in groups, the worshipers went up to keep this first solemn day of Lent--true, sincere worshipers, many of them, who came to weep, and pray, and acknowledge their past misdeeds; while others came from habit, and because it was the fashion, their pale, haggard faces and heavy eyes telling plainly of the last night's dissipation, which had continued till the first hour of the morning. Mrs. Howard was there, and Mrs. Miller, too, both glancing inquiringly at Judge Markham's pew and then wonderingly at each other. Ethelyn was not there. She had breakfast in her room after Richard left, and when that was over had gone mechanically to her closet and drawers and commenced sorting her clothes--hanging away the gayest, most expensive dresses, and laying across chairs and upon the bed the more serviceable ones, such as might properly be worn on ordinary occasions. Why she did this she had not yet clearly defined, and when, after her wardrobe was divided, and she brought out the heavy traveling trunk, made for her in Boston, she was not quite certain what she meant to do. She had been sorely wounded, and, as she thought, without just cause. She knew she was to blame for not having told Richard of Frank before she became his wife, but of the things with which he had so severely charged her she was guiltless, and every nerve quivered and throbbed with passion and resentment as she recalled the scene of the previous night, going over again with the cruel words Richard had uttered in his jealous anger, and then burning with shame and indignation as she thought of being locked in her room, and kept from attending the masquerade, where her absence must have excited so much wonder.

"What did they say, and what can I tell them when we meet?" she thought, just as Mrs. Howard's voice was heard in the upper hall.

Church was out, and several of the more intimate of Ethie's friends had stopped at the Stafford House to inquire into so strange a proceeding.

"Come to see if you were sick, or what, that you disappointed me so. I was vexed enough, I assure you," Mrs. Miller said, looking curiously enough at Ethelyn, whose face was white as ashes, save where a crimson spot burned on her cheeks, and whose lips were firmly pressed together.

She did not know what to say, and when pressed to give a reason stammered out:

"Judge Markham wished me to stay with him, and as an obedient wife I stayed."

With ready tact the ladies saw that something was wrong, and kindly forbore further remarks, except to tell what a grand affair it was, and how much she was missed. But Ethie detected in their manner an unspoken sympathy or pity, which exasperated and humiliated her more than open words would have done. Heretofore she had been the envy of the entire set, and it wounded her deeply to fall from that pedestal to the level of ordinary people. She was no longer the young wife, whose husband petted and humored her so much, but the wife whose husband was jealous and tyrannical, and even abusive, where language was concerned, and she could not rid herself of the suspicion that her lady friends knew more than they professed to know, and was heartily glad when they took their departure and left her again alone.

There was another knock at her door, and a servant handed in a card bearing Frank Van Buren's name. He was in the office, the waiter said. Should he show the gentleman up?

Ethie hesitated a moment, and then taking her pencil wrote upon the back of the card, "I am too busy to see you to-day."

The servant left the room, and Ethelyn went back to where her clothes were scattered about and the great trunk was standing open. She did not care to see Frank Van Buren now. He was the direct cause of every sorrow she had known, and bitter feelings were swelling in her heart in place of the softer emotions she had once experienced toward him. He was nothing to her now. Slowly but gradually the flame had been dying out, until Richard had nothing to dread from him, and he was never nearer to winning his wife's entire devotion than on that fatal night when, by his jealousy and rashness, he built so broad a gulf between them.

"It is impossible that we should ever live together again, after all that has transpired," Ethelyn said, as she stood beside her trunk and involuntarily folded up a garment and laid it on the bottom.

She had reached a decision, and her face grew whiter, stonier, as she made haste to act upon it. Every article which Richard had bought was laid aside and put away in the drawers and bureaus she would never see again. These were not numerous, for her bridal trousseau had been so extensive that but few demands had been made upon her husband's purse for dress, and Ethelyn felt glad that it was so. It did not take long to put them away, or very long to pack the trunk, and then Ethie sat down to think "what next?"

Only a few days before a Mr. Bailey, who boarded in the house, and whose daughter was taking music lessons, had tried to purchase her piano, telling her that so fine a player as herself ought to have one with a longer keyboard. Ethie had thought so herself, wishing sometimes that she had a larger instrument, which was better adapted to the present style of music, but she could not bring herself to part with Aunt Barbara's present. Now, however, the case was different. Money she must have, and as she scorned to take it from the bank, where her check was always honored, she would sell her piano. It was hers to do with as she liked, and when Mr. Bailey passed her door at dinner time he was asked to step in and reconsider the matter. She had changed her mind, she said. She was willing to sell it now; there was such a superb affair down at Shumway's Music Room. Had Mr. Bailey seen it?

Ethie's voice was not quite steady, for she was not accustomed to deception of this kind, and the first step was hard. But Mr. Bailey was not at all suspicious, and concluded the bargain at once; and two hours later Ethie's piano was standing between the south windows of Mrs. Bailey's apartment, and Ethie, in her own room, was counting a roll of three hundred dollars, and deciding how far it would go.

"There's my pearls," she said, "if worst comes to worst I can sell them and my diamond ring."

She did not mean Daisy's ring. She would not barter that, or take it with her, either. Daisy never intended it for a runaway wife, and Ethelyn must leave it where Richard would find it when he came back and found her gone. And then as Ethie in her anger exulted over Richard's surprise and possible sorrow when he found himself deserted, some demon from the pit whispered in her ear, "Give him back the wedding ring. Leave that for him, too, and so remove every tie which once bound you to him."

It was hard to put off Daisy's ring, and Ethelyn paused and reflected as the clear stone seemed to reflect the fair, innocent face hanging on the walls at Olney. But Ethie argued that she had no right to it, and so the dead girl's ring was laid aside, and then the trembling fingers fluttered about the plain gold band bearing the date of her marriage. But when she essayed to remove that, too, blood-red circles danced before her eyes, and such a terror seized her that her hands dropped powerless into her lap and the ring remained in its place.

It was four o'clock in the afternoon, and the cars for Olney left at seven. She was going that way as far as Milford, where she could take another route to the East. She would thus throw Richard off the track if he tried to follow her, and also avoid immediate remark in the hotel. They would think it quite natural that in her husband's absence she should go for a few days to Olney, she reasoned; and they did think so in the office when at six she asked that her trunk be taken to the station. Her rooms were all in order. She had made them so herself, sweeping and dusting, and even leaving Richard's dressing-gown and slippers by the chair where he usually sat the evenings he was at home. The vacancy left by the piano would strike him at once, she knew, and so she moved a tall bookcase up there, and put a sofa where the bookcase had been, and a large chair where the sofa had been, and pushed the center table into the large chair's place; and then her work was done--the last she would ever do in that room, or for Richard either. The last of everything is sad, and Ethie felt a thrill of pain as she whispered to herself, "It is the last, last time," and then thought of the outer world which lay all unknown before her. She would not allow herself to think, lest her courage should give way, and tried, by dwelling continually upon Richard's cruel words, to steel her heart against the good impulses which were beginning to suggest that what she was doing might not, after all, be the wisest course. What would the world say?--and dear Aunt Barbara, too? How it would wring her heart when she heard the end to which her darling had come! And Andy--simple, conscientious, praying Andy--Ethie's heart came up in her throat when she thought of him and his grief at her desertion.

"I will write to Andy," she said. "I will tell him how thoughts of him almost deterred me from my purpose," and opening her little writing desk, which Richard gave her at Christmas, she took up her pen and held it poised a moment, while something said: "Write to Richard, too. Surely you can do so much for him. You can tell him the truth at last, and let him know how he misjudged you."

And so the name which Ethie first wrote down upon the paper was not "Dear Brother Andy," but simply that of "Richard."

CHAPTER XXII: ETHIE'S LETTERS

"Stafford House, Feb.--,

"Five o'clock in the afternoon.

"RICHARD: I am going away from you forever, and When you recall the words you spoke to me last night, and the deep humiliation you put upon me, you will readily understand that I go because we cannot live together any longer as man and wife. You said things to me, Richard, which women find hard to forgive, and which they never can forget. I did not deserve that you should treat me so, for, bad as I may have been in other respects, I am innocent of the worst thing you alleged against me, and which seemed to excite you so much. Until I heard it from you, I did not know Frank Van Buren was within a thousand miles of Camden. The note from him which I leave with this letter, and which you will remember was brought to the door by a servant, who said it had been mislaid and forgotten, will prove that I tell you truly. The other note which you found, and which must have fallen from the box where I kept it, was written years ago, when I was almost a little girl, with no thought that I ever could be the humbled, wretched creature I am now.

"Let me tell you all about it, Richard--how I happened to be engaged to Frank, and how wounded and sore and sorry I was when you came the second time to Chicopee, and asked me to be your wife."

Then followed the whole story of Ethelyn's first love. Nothing was concealed, nothing kept back. Even the dreariness of the day when Aunt Van Buren came up from Boston and broke poor Ethie's heart, was described and dwelt upon with that particularity which shows how the lights, and shadows, and sunshine, and storms which mark certain events in one's history will impress themselves upon one's mind, as parts of the great joy or sorrow which can never be forgotten. Then she spoke of meeting Richard, and the train of circumstances which finally led to their betrothal.

"I wanted to tell you about Frank that night, on the shore of the pond, when you told me of Abigail, and twice I made up my mind to do so, but something rose up to prevent it, and after that it was very hard to do so."

She did not tell him how she at first shrank away from his caresses with a loathing which made her flesh creep, but she confessed that she did not love him, even when taking the marriage vow.

"But I meant to be true to you, Richard. I meant to be a good wife, and never let you know how I felt. You were different from Frank; different from most men whom I had met, and you did annoy me so at times. You will tell me I was foolish to lay so much stress on little things, and so, perhaps, I was; but little things, rather than big, make up the sum of human happiness, and, besides, I was too young to fully understand how any amount of talent and brain could atone for absence of culture of manner. Then, too, I was so disappointed in your home and family. You know how unlike they are to my own, but you can never know how terrible it was to me who had formed so different an estimate of them. I suppose you will say I did not try to assimilate, and perhaps I did not. How could I, when to be like them was the thing I dreaded most of all? I do believe they tried to be kind, especially your brothers, and I shall ever be grateful to them for their attempt to please and interest me during that dreadful winter I spent alone, with you in Washington. You did wrong, Richard, not to take me with you, when I wanted so much to go. I know that, after what happened, you and your mother think you were fully justified in what you did; but, Richard, you are mistaken. The very means you took to avert a catastrophe hastened it instead. The cruel disappointment and terrible homesickness which I endured hastened our baby's birth, and cost its little life. Had it lived, Richard, I should have been a better woman from what I am now. It would have been something for me to love, and oh, my heart did ache so for an object on which to fasten. I did not love you when I became your wife, but I was learning to do so. When you came home from Washington I was so glad to see you, and I used to listen for your step when you went to Olney and it was time for you to return. Just in proportion as I was drawn toward you, Frank fell in my estimation, and I wanted to tell you all about it, and begin anew. I was going to do so in that letter commenced the night I was taken so ill, and two or three times afterwards I thought I would do it. Do you remember that night of our return from St. Paul? I found a letter from Aunt Van Buren, and asked if you would like to hear it. You seemed so indifferent and amost cross about it, that the good angel left me, and your chance was lost again. There was something in that letter about Frank and me--something which would have called forth questions from you, and I meant to explain if you would let me. Think, Richard. You will remember the night. You lay upon the sofa, and I sat down beside you, and smoothed your hair. I was nearer to loving you then than I ever was before; but you put me off, and the impulse did not come again--that is, the impulse of confession. A little more consideration on your part for what you call my airs and high notions would have won me to you, for I am not insensible to your many sterling virtues, and I do believe that you did love me once. But all that is over now. I made a great mistake when I came to you, and perhaps I am making a greater one in going from you. But I think not. We are better apart, especially after the indignities of last night. Where I am going it does not matter to you. Pursuit will be useless, inasmuch as I shall have the start of a week. Neither do I think you will search for me much. You will he happier without me, and it is better that I should go. You will give the accompanying note to Andy. Dear Andy, my heart aches to its very core when I think of him, and know that his grief for me will be genuine. I leave you Daisy's ring. I am not worthy to keep that, so I give it back. I wish I could make you free from me entirely, if that should be your wish. Perhaps some time you will be, and then when I am nothing to you save a sad memory, you will think better of me than you do now.

"Good-by, Richard. We shall probably never meet again. Good-by.

"ETHIE."

She did not stop to read what she had written. There was not time for that, and taking a fresh sheet, she wrote:

"DEAR, DARLING ANDY: If all the world were as good, and kind, and true as you, I should not be writing this letter, with my arrangements made for flight. Richard will tell you why I go. It would take me too long. I have been very unhappy here, though none of my wretchedness has been caused by you. Dear Andy, if I could tell you how much I love you, and how sorry I am to fall in your opinion, as I surely shall when you hear what has happened. Do not hate me, Andy, and sometimes when you pray, remember Ethie, won't you? She needs your prayers so much, for she cannot pray herself. I do not want to be wholly bad--do not want to be lost forever; and I have faith that God will hear you. The beautiful consistency of your everyday life and simple trust, have been powerful sermons to me, convincing me that there is a reality in the religion you profess. Go on, Andy, as you have begun, and may the God whom I am not worthy to name, bless you, and keep you, and give you every possible good. In fancy I wind my arms around your neck, and kiss your dear, kind face, as, with scalding tears, I write you good-by.

"Farewell, Andy, darling Andy, farewell."

Ethelyn had not wept before, but now, as Andy rose up before her with the thought that she should see him no more, her tears poured like rain, and blotted the sheet on which she had written to him. It hurt her more, if possible, to lose his respect than that of any other person, and for a half-instant she wavered in the decision. But it was too late now. The piano was sold and delivered, and if she tarried she had no special excuse to offer for its sale. She must carry out her plan, even though it proved the greatest mistake of her life. So the letters were directed and put, with Daisy's ring, in the little drawer of the bureau, where Richard would be sure to find them when he came back. Perhaps, as Ethie put them there, she thought how they might be the means of a reconciliation; that Richard, after reading her note, would move heaven and earth to find her, and having done so, would thenceforth be her willing slave; possibly, too, remembering the harsh things he had so recently said to her, she exulted a little as she saw him coming back to his deserted home, and finding his domestic altar laid low in the dust. But if this was so she gave no sign, and though her face was deathly pale, her nerves were steady and her voice calm, as she gave orders concerning her baggage, and then when it was time, turned the key upon her room, and left it with the clerk, to whom she said:

"I shall not be back until my husband returns."

She was going to Olney, of course--going to see his folks, the landlady said, when she heard Mrs. Markham had gone; and so no wonder was created among the female boarders, except that Ethelyn had not said good-by to a single one of them. She was not equal to that. Her great desire was to escape unseen, and with a veil drawn closely over her face, she sat in the darkest corner of the ladies' room, waiting impatiently for the arrival of the train, and glancing furtively at the people around her. Groups of men were walking up and down upon the platform without, and among them Frank Van Buren. On his way to the cars he had called again at the Stafford House, and learned that Mrs. Markham was out.

"I'll see her when I return," he thought, and so went his way to the train, which would take him to his next point of destination.

Never once dreaming how near he was to her, Ethie drew her veil and furs more closely around her, and turning her face to the frosty window, gazed drearily out into the wintry darkness as they sped swiftly on. She hardly knew where she was going or what she could do when she was there. She was conscious only of the fact that she was breaking away from scenes and associations which had been so distasteful to her--that she was leaving a husband who had been abusive to her, and she verily believed she had just cause for going. The world might not see it so, perhaps, but she did not care for the world. She was striking out a path of her own, and with her heart as sore and full of anger as it then was, she felt able to cope with any difficulty, so that her freedom was achieved. They were skirting across the prairie now; and the lights of Olney were in sight. Perhaps she could see the farmhouse, and rubbing, with her warm palm, the moisture from the window-pane, she looked wistfully out in the direction of Richard's home. Yes, there it was, and a light shining from the sitting-room window, as if they expected her. But Ethie was not going there, and with something like a sigh as she thought of Andy so near, yet separated so widely from her, she turned from the window and rested her tired head upon her hands while they stayed at Olney. It was only a moment they stopped, but to Ethie it seemed an age, and her heart almost stopped its beating when she heard the voice of Terrible Tim just outside the car. He was not coming in, as she found after a moment of breathless waiting; he was only speaking to an acquaintance, who stepped inside and took a seat by the stove, just as the train plunged again into the darkness, leaving behind a fiery track to mark its progress across the level prairie.

CHAPTER XXIII: THE DESERTED HUSBAND

Richard had been very successful in St. Louis. The business which took him there had been more than satisfactorily arranged. He had collected a thousand-dollar debt he never expected to get, and had been everywhere treated with the utmost deference and consideration, as a man whose worth was known and appreciated. But Richard was ill at ease, and his face wore a sad, gloomy expression, which many remarked, wondering what could be the nature of the care so evidently preying upon him. Do what he might, he could not forget the white, stony face which had looked at him so strangely in the gray morning, nor shut out the icy tones in which Ethie had last spoken to him. Besides this, Richard was thinking of all he had said to her in the heat of passion, and wishing he could recall it in part at least. He was very indignant, very angry still, for he believed her guilty of planning to meet Frank Van Buren at the party and leave him at home, while his heart beat with keen throbs of pain when he remembered that Ethie's first love was not given to him--that she would have gone to her grave more willingly than she went with him to the altar; but he need not have been so harsh with her--that was no way to make her love him. Kindness must win her back should she ever be won, and impatient to be reconciled, if reconciliation were now possible, Richard chafed at the necessary delays which kept him a day longer in St. Louis than he had at first intended.

Ethie had been gone just a week when he at last found himself in the train which would take him back to Camden. First, however, he must stop at Olney; the case was imperative--and so he stepped from the train one snowy afternoon when the February light shone cold and blue upon the little town and the farmhouse beyond. His brothers were feeding their flocks and herds in the rear yard to the east; but they came at once to greet him, and ask after his welfare. The light snow which had fallen that day was lying upon the front door-steps undisturbed by any track, so Richard entered at the side. Mrs. Markham was dipping candles, and the faint, sickly odor of the hot melted tallow, which filled Richard's olfactories as he came in, was never forgotten, but remembered as part and parcel of that terrible day which would have a place in his memory so long as being lasted. Every little thing was impressed upon his mind, and came up afterward with vivid distinctness whenever he thought of that wretched time. There was a bit of oilcloth on the floor near to the dripping candles, and he saw the spots of tallow which had dropped and dried upon it--saw, too, his mother's short red gown and blue woolen stockings, as she got up to meet him, and smelled the cabbage cooking on the stove, for they were having a late dinner that day-- the boys' favorite, and what Mrs. Markham designated as a "dish of biled vittles."

Richard had seen his mother dip candles before--nay, had sometimes assisted at the dipping. He had seen her short striped gown and blue woolen stockings, and smelled the cooking cabbage, but they never struck him with so great a sense of discomfort as they did to-day when he stood, hat in hand, wondering why home seemed so cheerless. It was as if the shadow of the great shock awaiting him had already fallen upon him, oppressing him with a weight he could not well shake off. He had no thought that any harm had come to Ethie, and yet his first question was for her. Had his mother heard from her while he was away, or did she know if she was well?

Mrs. Markham's under jaw dropped, in the way peculiar to her when at all irritated, but she did not answer at once; she waited a moment, while she held the rod poised over the iron kettle, and with her forefinger deliberately separated any of the eight candles which showed a disposition to stick together; then depositing them upon the frame and taking up another rod, she said:

"Miss Plympton was down to Camden three or four days ago, and she said Ann Merrills, the chambermaid at the Stafford House, told her Ethelyn had come to Olney to stay with us while you was away; but she must have gone somewhere else, as we have not seen her here. Gone to visit that Miss Amsden, most likely, that lives over the creek."

"What makes you think she has gone there?" Richard asked, with a sudden spasm of fear, for which he could not account, and which was not in any wise diminished by his mother's reply: "Ann said she took the six o'clock train for Olney, and as Miss Amsden lives beyond us, it's likely she went there, and is home by this time."

Richard accepted this supposition, but it was far from reassuring him. The load he had felt when he first came into the kitchen was pressing more and more heavily, and he wished that he had gone straight on instead of stopping at Olney. But now there was nothing to do but to wait with what patience he could command until the next train came and carried him to Camden.

It was nine o'clock when he reached there, and a stiff northeaster was blowing down the streets with gusts of sleet and rain, but he did not think of it as he hurried on toward the Stafford House, with that undefined dread growing stronger and stronger as he drew near. He did not know what he feared, nor why he feared it. He should find Ethie there, he said. She surely had returned from her visit by this time; he should see the lights from the windows shining out upon the park, just as he had seen them many other nights when hastening back to Ethie. He would take the shortest route down that dark, narrow alley, and so gain a moment of time. The alley was traversed at last, also the square, and he turned the corner of the street where stood the Stafford House. Halting for an instant, he strained his eyes to see if he were mistaken, or was there no light in the window, no sign that Ethie was there. There were lights below, and lights above, but the second floor was dark, the shutters closed, and all about them a look of silence and desertion, which quickened Richard's footsteps to a run. Up the private staircase he went, and through the narrow hall, till he reached his door and found it locked. Ethie was surely gone. She had not expected him so soon. Mrs. Amsden had urged her to stay, and she had stayed. This was what Richard said, as he went down to the office for the key, which the clerk handed him, with the remark: "Mrs. Markham went to Olney the very day you left. I thought perhaps you would stop there and bring her home."

Richard did not reply, but hurried back to the darkened room, where everything was in order; even Ethie's work-box was in its usual place upon the little table, and Ethie's chair was standing near; but something was missing--something besides Ethie--and its absence made the room look bare and strange as the gas-light fell upon it. The piano was gone or moved. It must be the latter, and Richard looked for it in every corner, even searching in the bedroom and opening the closet door, as if so ponderous a thing could have been hidden there! It was gone, and so was Ethie's trunk, and some of Ethie's clothes, for he looked to see, and then mechanically went out into the hall, just as Mr. Bailey came upstairs and saw him.

"Ho, Judge! is that you? Glad to see you back. Have been lonesome with you and your wife both away. Do you know of the trade we made--she and I--the very day you left? She offered me her piano for three hundred dollars, and I took her up at once. A fine instrument, that, but a little too small for her. Answers very well for Angeline. It's all right, isn't it?" the talkative man continued, as he saw the blank expression on Richard's face and construed it into disapprobation of the bargain.

"Yes, all right, of course. It was her piano, not mine," Richard said huskily. Then feeling the necessity of a little duplicity, he said, "Mrs. Markham went the same day I did, I believe?"

"Really, now, I don't know whether 'twas that day or the next," Mr. Bailey replied, showing that what was so important to Richard had as yet made but little impression upon him. "No, I can't say which day it was; but here's Hal Clifford--he'll know," and Mr. Bailey stepped aside as Harry came up the hall.

He had been to call upon a friend who occupied the floor above, and seeing Richard came forward to speak to him, the look of shame upon his face showing that he had not forgotten the circumstances under which they had last met. As Harry came in Mr. Bailey disappeared, and so the two men were alone when Richard asked, "Do you know what day Mrs. Markham left Camden?"

Richard tried to be natural. But Harry was not deceived. There was something afloat-- something which had some connection with his foolish, drunken talk and Ethie's non-appearance at the masquerade. Blaming himself for what he remembered to have said, he would not now willingly annoy Richard, and he answered, indifferently: "She went the same day you did; that is, she left here on the six o'clock train. I know, for I called in the evening and found her gone."

"Was she going to Olney?"

Richard's lips asked this rather than his will, and Harry replied, "I suppose so. Isn't she there?"

It was an impudent question, but prompted purely by curiosity, and Richard involuntarily answered, "She has not been there at all."

For several seconds the two men regarded each other intently, one longing so much to ask a certain question, and the other reading that question in the wistful, anxious eyes bent so earnestly upon him.

"He left in that same train, and took the same route, too."

Harry said this, and Richard staggered forward, till he leaned upon the door-post while his face was ashy pale. Harry had disliked Richard Markham, whom he knew so strongly disapproved of his conduct; but he pitied him now and tried to comfort him.

"It cannot be they went together. I saw no indications of such an intention on the part of Frank. I hardly think he saw her, either. He was going to--, he said, and should be back in a few days. Maybe she is somewhere."

Yes, maybe she was somewhere, but so long as Richard did not know where, it was poor comfort for him. One thing, however, he could do--he could save her good name until the matter was further investigated; and pulling Harry after him into his room, he sat down by the cold, dark stove, over which he crouched shiveringly, while he said, "Ethie has gone to visit a friend, most likely--a Mrs. Amsden, who lives in the direction of Olney. So please, for her sake, do not say either now or ever who went on the train with her."

"You have my word as a gentleman that I will not," Harry replied; "and as no one but myself ever knew that they were cousins and acquaintances, their names need not be mentioned together, even if she never returns."

"But she will--she will come back, Ethie will. She has only gone to Mrs. Amsden's," Richard replied, his teeth chattering and his voice betraying all the fear and anguish he tried so hard to hide.

Harry saw how cold he seemed, and with his own hands built a quick wood fire, and then asked:

"Shall I leave you alone, or would you prefer me to stay?"

"Yes, stay. I do not like being here alone, though Ethie will come back. She's only gone to visit Mrs. Amsden," and Richard whispered the words, "gone to visit Mrs. Amsden."

It is pitiful to see a strong man cut down so suddenly, and every nerve of Harry's throbbed in sympathy as he sat watching the deserted husband walking up and down the room, now holding his cold fingers to the fire and now saying to himself: "She has only gone to Mrs. Amsden's. She will be back to-morrow."

At last the clock struck eleven, and then Richard roused from his lethargy and said: "The next train for Olney passes at twelve. I am going there, Harry--going after Ethie. You'll see her coming back to-morrow."

Richard hardly knew why he was going back to Olney, unless it were from a wish to be near his own kith and kin in this hour of sorrow. He knew that Ethie had gone, and the Mrs. Amsden ruse was thrown out for the benefit of Harry, who, frightened at the expression of Richard's face, did not dare to leave him alone until he saw him safely on board the train, which an hour later dropped him upon the slippery platform in Olney, and then went speeding on in the same direction Ethie once had gone.

Mrs. Markham's candles were finished, and in straight even rows were laid away in the candle-box, the good woman finding to her great satisfaction that there were just ten dozen besides the slim little thing she had burned during the evening, and which, with a long, crisp snuff, like the steeple of a church, was now standing on the chair by her bed. The hash was chopped ready for breakfast, the coffee was prepared, and the kindlings were lying near the stove, where, too, were hanging to dry Andy's stockings, which he had that day wet through. They had sat up later than usual at the farmhouse that night, for Melinda and her mother had been over there, and the boys had made molasses candy, and "stuck up" every dish and spoon, as Mrs. Markham said. Tim had come after his mother and sister, and as he had a good deal to say, the clock struck eleven before the guests departed, and Andy buttoned the door of the woodshed and put the nail over the window by the sink. Mrs. Markham had no suspicion of the trial in store for her, but for some cause she felt restless and nervous, and even scary, as she expressed it herself. "Worked too hard, I guess," she thought, as she tied on her high-crowned, broad-frilled nightcap, and then as a last chore, wound the clock before stepping into bed.

It was nearly midnight, and for some little time she lay awake listening to the wind as it swept past the house, or screamed through the key-hole of the door. But she did not hear the night train when it thundered through the town; nor the gate as it swung back upon its hinges; nor the swift step coming up the walk; nor the tap upon her window until it was repeated, and Richard's voice called faintly, "Mother, mother, let me in!"

Andy, who was as good as a watch-dog, was awake by this time, and with his window open was looking down at the supposed burglar, while his hand felt for some missile to hurl at the trespasser's head. With a start, Mr. Markham awoke, and, springing up, listened till the voice said again, "Mother, mother, it's I; let me in!"

The Japan candlestick Andy had secured was dropped in a trice, and adjusting his trousers as he descended the stairs, he reached the door simultaneously with his mother, and pulling Richard into the hall, asked why he was there, and what had happened. Richard did not know for certain that anything had happened. "Ethie was most probably with Mrs. Amsden. She would be home to-morrow," and Andy felt how his brother leaned against him and his hand pressed upon his shoulders as he went to the stove, and crouched down before it just as he had done in Camden. The candle was lighted, and its dim light fell upon that strange group gathered there at midnight, and looking into each other's faces with a wistful questioning as to what it all portended.

"It is very cold; make more fire," Richard said, shivering, as the sleet came driving against the window; and in an instant all the morning kindlings were thrust into the stove, which roared and crackled, and hissed, and diffused a sense of warmth and comfort through the shadowy room.

"What is it, Richard? What makes you so white and queer?" his mother asked, trying to pull on her stockings, and in her trepidation jamming her toes into the heel, and drawing her shoe over the bungle thus made at the bottom of her foot.

"Ethie was not there, and has not been since the night I left. She sold her piano, and took the money, and her trunk, and her clothes, and went to visit Mrs. Amsden."

This was Richard's explanation, which Andy thought a mighty funny reason for his brother's coming at midnight, and frightening them so terribly. But his mother saw things differently. She knew there was something underlying all this--something which would require all her skill and energy to meet--and her face was almost as white as Richard's as she asked, "Why do you think she has gone to Mrs. Amsden's?"

"You told me so, didn't you?" and Richard looked up at her in a bewildered, helpless way, which showed that all he knew upon the Amsden question was what she had said herself, and that was hardly enough to warrant a conclusion of any kind.

"Was there any reason why Ethelyn should go away?" she asked next, and Richard's head dropped, and his eyes were cast down in shame, as he replied:

"Yes; we--quar--. We differed, I mean, the night before I went away, and I kept her from the masquerade, I would not let her go. I locked the door, and now she has gone--gone to Mrs. Amsden's."

He persisted in saying that, as if he would fain make himself believe it against his better judgment.

"What is it all about? What does it mean?" Andy asked in great perplexity; and his mother answered for Richard:

"It means just this, as far as I can see: Ethelyn has got mad at Richard for keepin' her in, which he or'to have done long ago, and so, with her awful temper she has run away."

Mrs. Markham had defined it at last--had put into words the terrible thing which had happened, the disgrace which she saw coming upon them; and with this definition of it she, too, defined her own position with regard to Ethelyn, and stood bristling all over with anger and resentment, and ready to do battle for her son against the entire world.

"Mother! mother!" Andy gasped, and his face was whiter than Richard's. "It is not true. Ethie never went and done that--never! Did she, Dick? Tell me! Speak! Has Ethie run away?"

Andy was down on one knee now, and looking into Richard's face with a look which would almost have brought Ethie back could she have seen it. Andy had faith in her, and Richard clung to him rather than to the mother in denouncing her so bitterly.

"I don't know, Andy," he said, "I hope not. I think not. She must have gone to Mrs. Amsden's. We will wait till morning and see."

The sound of voices had aroused both James and John, who, half-dressed, came down to inquire what had happened, and why Dick was there at that unseemly hour of the night. James' face was very pale as he listened, and when his mother spoke of the disgrace which would come upon them all, his hard fists were clenched for a moment, while he thought of Melinda, and wondered if with her it would make any difference. Both James and John had liked Ethelyn, and as the temper about which their mother talked so much had never been exhibited to them, they were inclined even now to take her part, and cautious John suggested that it might not be so bad as his mother feared. To be sure, he didn't know how hard Dick and Ethie might have spatted it, or what had gone before; but anyway his advice would be to wait and see if she was not really at Mrs. Amsden's, or somewhere else. Richard let them manage it for him. He was powerless to act then, and stunned and silent he sat shivering by the stove, which they made red-hot with the blocks of wood they put in, hoping thus to warm him. There was no more sleep at the farmhouse that night, though James and John went back to bed, and Andy, too, crept up to his lonely room; but not to sleep. His heart was too full for that, and kneeling by his wooden chair, he prayed for Ethie--that she had not run away, but might be at Mrs. Amsden's, where he was going for her himself the moment the morning broke. He had claimed this privilege, and his mother had granted it, knowing that many allowances would be made for whatever Andy might say, and feeling that, on this account, he would do better than either of his brothers. Richard, of course, could not go. He scarcely had strength to move, and did not look up from his stooping posture by the stove, when, at day-dawn, Andy drew on his butternut overcoat, and tying a thick comforter about his neck, started for Mrs. Amsden's.

CHAPTER XXIV: THE INVESTIGATION

Richard knew she was not there--at least all the probabilities were against it; and still he clung to the vague hope that Andy would bring him some good news, and his thoughts went after the brother whose every breath was a prayer, as he galloped over the snowy ground toward Mrs. Amsden's. They were early risers there, and notwithstanding the sun was just coming up the eastern sky, the family were at breakfast when Andy's horse stopped before their gate, and Andy himself knocked at their door for admission. Andy's faith was great--so great that, in answer to his petitions, he fully expected to see Ethie herself at the table, when the door was opened, and he caught a view of the occupants of the dining room; but no Ethie was there, nor had been, as they said, in answer to his eager questionings.

"What made you think she was here? When did she go away? Was she intending to visit me?" Mrs. Amsden asked.

But Andy, while praying that Ethie might be there, had also asked that if she were not, "he needn't make a fool of himself, nor let the cat out of the bag," and he didn't; he merely replied:

"She left home a few days ago. Dick was in St. Louis, and it was lonesome stayin' alone. I'll find her, most likely, as she is somewhere else."

Andy was in his saddle now, and his fleet steed fled swiftly along toward home, where they waited so anxiously for him, Richard tottering to the window so as to read his fate in Andy's tell-tale face.

"She is not there. I knew she was not. She has gone with that villain."

Richard did not mean to say that last. It dropped from him mechanically, and in an instant his mother seized upon it, demanding what he meant, and who was the villain referred to. Richard tried to put her off, but she would know what he meant, and so to her and his three brothers he told as little as he could and make any kind of a story, and as he talked his heart hardened toward Ethie, who had done him this wrong. It seemed a great deal worse when put into words, and the whole expression of Richard's face was changed when he had finished speaking, while he was conscious of feeling much as he did that night when he denounced Ethie so terribly to her face. "Had it been a man, or half a man, or anybody besides that contemptible puppy, it would not seem so bad; but to forsake me for him!" Richard said, while the great ridges deepened in his forehead, and a hard, black look crept into his eyes, and about the corners of his mouth. He was terrible in his anger, which grew upon him until even his mother stood appalled at the fearful expression of his face.

"He would do nothing to call her back," he said, when James suggested the propriety of trying in a quiet way to ascertain where she had gone. "She had chosen her own path to ruin, and she might tread it for all of him. He would not put forth a hand to save her and if she came back, he never could forgive her."

Richard was walking up and down the room, white with rage, as he said this, and Andy, cowering in a corner, was looking on and listening. He did not speak until Richard declared his incapacity for forgiving Ethie, when he started up, and confronting the angry man, said to him rebukingly:

"Hold there, old Dick! You have gone a leetle too far. If God can forgive you and me all them things we've done, which he knows about, and other folks don't, you can, or or'to forgive sister Ethie, let her sin be what it may. Ethie was young, Dick, and childlike, and so pretty, too, and I 'most know you aggravated her some, if you talked to her as you feel now; and then, too, Dick, and mother, and all of you, I don't care who says it, or thinks it, it's a big lie! Ethie never went off with a man--never! I know she didn't. She wasn't that kind. I'll swear to it in the court. I won't hear anybody say that about her. I'll fight 'em, first, even if 'twas my own kin who did it!" And in his excitement, Andy began to shove back his wrist-bands from his strong wrists, as if challenging someone to the fight he had threatened.

Andy was splendid in his defense of Ethie, and both James and John stepped up beside him, showing their adhesion to the cause he pleaded so well. Ethie might have ran away, but she had surely gone alone, they said, and their advice was that Richard should follow her as soon as possible. But Richard would not listen to such a proposition now, and quietly aided and abetted by his mother, he declared his intention of "letting her alone." She had chosen her course, he said, and she must abide by it. "If she has gone with that villain"--and Richard ground his teeth together--"she can never again come back to me. If she has not gone with him, and chooses to return, I do not say the door is shut against her."

Richard seemed very determined and unrelenting, and, knowing how useless it was to reason with him when in so stern a mood, his brothers gave up the contest, Andy thinking within himself how many, many times a day he should pray for Ethie that she might come back again. Richard would not return to Camden that day, he said. He could not face his acquaintance there until the first shock was over and they were a little accustomed to thinking of the calamity which had fallen upon him. So he remained with his mother, sitting near the window which looked out upon the railroad track over which Ethie had gone. What his thoughts were none could fathom, save as they were expressed by the dark, troubled expression of his face, which showed how much he suffered. Perhaps he blamed himself as he went over again the incidents of that fatal night when he kept Ethelyn from the masquerade; but if he did, no one was the wiser for it, and so the first long day wore on, and the night fell again upon the inmates of the farmhouse. The darkness was terrible to Richard, for it shut out from his view that strip of road which seemed to him a part of Ethie. She had been there last, and possibly looked up at the old home--her first home after her marriage; possibly, too, she had thought of him. She surely did, if, as Andy believed, she was alone in her flight. If not alone, he wanted no thoughts of hers, and Richard's hands were clenched as he moved from the darkening window, and took his seat behind the stove, where he sat the entire evening, like some statue of despair, brooding over his ruined hopes.

The next day brought the Joneses--Melinda and Tim--the latter of whom had heard from Mrs. Amsden's son of Andy's strange errand there. There was something in the wind, and Melinda came to learn what it was. Always communicative to the Jones family, Mrs. Markham told the story without reserve, not even omitting the Van Buren part, but asking as a precaution that

Melinda would not spread a story which would bring disgrace on them. Melinda was shocked, astonished, and confounded, she did not believe in Frank Van Buren. Ethie never went with him--never. She, like Andy, would swear to that, and she said as much to Richard, taking Ethie's side as strongly as she could, without casting too much blame on him. And Richard felt better, hearing Ethie upheld and spoken for, even if it were so much against himself. Melinda was still his good angel, while Ethie, too, had just cause for thanking the kind girl who stood by her so bravely, and even made the mother-in-law less harsh in her expression.

There was a letter for Richard that night, from Harry Clifford, who wrote as follows:

"I do not know whether you found your wife at Mrs. Amsden's or not, but I take the liberty of telling you that Frank Van Buren has returned, and solemnly affirms that if Mrs. Markham was on board the train which left here on the 17th, he did not know it. Neither did he see her at all when in Camden. He called on his way to the depot that night, and was told she was out. Excuse my writing you this. If your wife has not come back, it will remove a painful doubt, and if she has, please burn and forget it. Yours,

"H. CLIFFORD."

"Thank Heaven for that!" was Richard's exclamation as in the first revulsion of feeling he sprang from his chair, while every feature of his face was irradiated with joy.

"What is it, Dick? Is Ethie found? I knew she would be. I've prayed for it fifty times to-day, and I had faith that God would hear," Andy said, the great tears rolling down his smooth, round face as he gave vent to his joy.

But Andy's faith was to be put to a stronger test, and his countenance fell a little when Richard explained the nature of the letter. Ethie was not found; she was only proved innocent of the terrible thing Richard had feared for her, and in being proven innocent, she was for a moment almost wholly restored to his favor. She would come back some time. She could not mean to leave him forever. She was only doing it for a scare, and to punish him for what he did that night. He deserved punishment, too, he thought, for he was pretty hard on her, and as he surely had been punished in all he had suffered during the last forty-eight hours, he would, when she came back, call everything even between them, and begin anew.

This was Richard's reasoning; and that night he slept soundly, dreaming that Ethie had returned, and on her knees was suing for his forgiveness, while her voice was broken with tears and choking sobs. As a man and husband who had been deserted, it was his duty to remain impassive a few moments, while Ethie atoned fully for her misdeeds: then he would forgive her, and so he waited an instant, and while he waited he woke to find only Andy, with whom he was sleeping, kneeling by the bedside, with the wintry moonlight falling on his upturned face, as he prayed for the dear sister Ethie, whose steps had "mewandered" so far away.

"Don't let any harm come to her; don't let anybody look at her for bad, but keep her--keep her--keep her in safety, and send her back to poor old Dick and me, and make Dick use her better than I 'most know he has, for he's got the Markham temper in him, and everybody knows what that is."

This was Andy's prayer, taken from no book or printed form, but the outpouring of his simple, honest heart, and Richard heard it, wincing a little as Andy thus made confession for him of his own sins; but he did not pray himself, though he was glad of Andy's prayers, and placed great hopes upon them. God would hear Andy, and if he did not send Ethie back at once, he would surely keep her from harm.

The next day Richard went back to Camden. Melinda Jones had suggested that possibly Ethie left a letter, or note, which would explain her absence, and Richard caught at it eagerly, wondering he had not thought of it before, and feeling very impatient to be off, even though he dreaded to meet some of his old friends, and be questioned as to the whereabouts of his wife. He did not know that the story of his desertion was already there--Mrs. Amsden having gone to town with her mite, which, added to the sale of the piano, Ethie's protracted absence, Richard's return to Olney at midnight, and Harry Clifford's serious and mysterious manner, were enough to set the town in motion. Various opinions were expressed, and, what was very strange, so popular were both Richard and Ethelyn that everybody disliked blaming either, and so but few unkind remarks had as yet been made, and those by people who had been jealous or envious of Ethelyn's high position. No one knew a whisper of Frank Van Buren, for Harry kept his promise well, and no worse motive was ascribed to Ethie's desertion than want of perfect congeniality with her husband. Thus they were not foes, but friends, who welcomed Richard back to Camden, watching him curiously, and wishing so much to ask where Mrs. Markham was. That she was not with him, was certain, for only Andy came--Andy, who held his head so high, and looked round so defiantly, as he kept close to Richard's side on the way to the hotel. It was very dreary going up the old, familiar staircase into the quiet hall, and along to the door of the silent room, which seemed drearier than on that night when he first came back to it and found Ethie gone. There were ashes now upon the stove-hearth where Hal Clifford had kindled the fire, and the two chairs they had occupied were standing just where they had left them. The gas had not been properly turned off, and a dead, sickly odor filled the room, making Andy heave as he hastened to open the window, and admit the fresh, pure air.

"Seems as it did the day Daisy died," Andy said, his eyes filling with tears.

To Richard it was far worse than the day Daisy died, for he had then the memory of her last loving words in his ear, and the feeling of her clinging kiss upon his lips, while now the memories of the lost one were only bitter and sad in the extreme.

"Melinda suggested a letter or something. Where do you suppose she would put it if there were one?" Richard asked in a helpless, appealing way, as he sank into a chair and looked wistfully around the room.

He had been very bold and strong in the cars and in the street; but here, in the deserted room, where Ethie used to be, and where something said she would never be again, he was weak as a girl, and leaned wholly upon Andy, who seemed to feel how much was depending upon him, and so kept up a cheery aspect while he kindled a fresh fire and cleared the ashes from the hearth by blowing them off upon the oilcloth; then, as the warmth began to make itself felt and the cold to diminish, he answered Richard's query.

"In her draw, most likely; mother mostly puts her traps there." So, to the "draw" they went--the very one where Daisy's ring was lying; and Richard saw that first, knowing now for sure that Ethelyn had fled.

He knew so before, but this made it more certain--more dreadful, too, for it showed a determination never to return.

"It was Daisy's, you know," he said to Andy, who, at his side, was not looking at the ring, but beyond it, to the two letters, his own and Richard's, both of which he seized with a low cry, for he, too, was sure of Ethie's flight.

"See, Dick, there's one for you and one for me," he exclaimed, and his face grew very red as he tore open his own note and began to devour the contents, whispering the words, and breaking down entirely amid a storm of sobs and tears as he read:

"DEAR ANDY: I wish I could tell you how much I love you, and how sorry I am to fall in your good opinion, as I surely shall when you hear what has happened. Do not hate me, Andy; and sometimes, when you pray, remember Ethie, won't you?"

He could get no farther than this, and with a great cry he buried his face in his hands and sobbed: "Yes, Ethie, I will, I will; but oh, what is it? What made you go? Why did she, Dick?" and he turned to his brother, who, with lightning rapidity, was reading Ethelyn's long letter. He did not doubt a word she said, and when the letter was finished he put it passively in Andy's hand, and then, with a bitter groan, laid his throbbing head upon the cushion of the lounge where he was sitting. There were no tears in his eyes--nothing but blood-red circles floating before them; while the aching balls seemed starting from their sockets with the pressure of pain. He had had his chance with Ethie and lost it; and though, as yet, he saw but dimly where he had been to blame, where he had made a mistake, he endured for the time all he was capable of enduring, and if revenge had been her object, Ethie had more than her desire.

Andy was stunned for a moment, and sat staring blankly at the motionless figure of his brother; then, as the terrible calamity began to impress itself fully upon him, intense pity for Richard became uppermost in his mind, and stooping over the crushed man, he laid his arm across his neck, and, tender as a sorrowing, loving mother, kissed and fondled the damp brown hair, and dropped great tears upon it, and murmured words of sympathy, incoherent at first, for the anguish choking his own utterance, but gradually gathering force and sound as his quivering lips kept trying to articulate: "Dick, poor old Dick, dear old Dick, don't keep so still and look so white and stony. She'll come back again, Ethie will. I feel it, I feel it, I know it, I shall pray for her every hour until she comes. Prayer will reach her where nothing else can find her. Poor Dick, I am so sorry. Don't look at me so; you scare me. Try to cry; try to make a fuss; try to do anything rather than that dreadful look. Lay your head on me, so," and lifting up the bowed head, which offered no resistance, Andy laid it gently on his arm, and smoothing back the hair from the pallid forehead, went on: "Now cry, old boy, cry with all your might;" and with his hand Andy brushed away the scalding tears which began to fall like rain from Richard's eyes.

"Better so, a great deal better than the other way. Don't hold up till you've had it out," he kept repeating, while Richard wept, until the fountain was dry and the tears refused to flow.

"I've been a brute, Andy," he said, when at last he could speak. "The fault was all my own. I did not understand her in the least. I ought never to have married her. She was not of my make at all."

Andy would hear nothing derogatory of Richard any more than of Ethelyn, and he answered promptly: "But, Dick, Ethie was some to blame. She didn't or'to marry you feelin' as she did. That was where the wrong began."

This was the most and the worst Andy ever said against Ethelyn, and he repented of that the moment the words were out of his mouth. It was mean to speak ill of the absent, especially when the absent one was Ethie, who had written, "In fancy I put my arms around your neck and kiss your dear, kind face." Andy deemed himself a monster of ingratitude when he recalled these lines and remembered that of her who penned them he had said, "She was some to blame." He took it all back to himself, and tried to exonerate Ethie entirely, though it was hard work to do so where he saw how broken, and stunned, and crushed his brother was, and how little he realized what was passing around him.

"He don't know much more than I do," was Andy's mental comment, when to his question, "What shall we do next?" Richard replied, in a maudlin kind of way, "Yes, that is a very proper course. I leave it entirely to you."

Andy felt that a great deal was depending upon himself, and he tried to meet the emergency. Seeing how Richard continued to shiver, and how cold he was, he persuaded him to lie down upon the bed, and piling the blankets upon him, made such a fire as he said to himself, "would roast a common ox"; then, when Hal Clifford came to the door and knocked, he kept him out, with that "Dick had been broke of his rest, and was tryin' to make it up."

But this state of things could not last long. Richard was growing ill, and talking so strangely withal, that Andy began to feel the necessity of having somebody there beside himself; "some of the wimmen folks, who knew what to do, for I'm no better than a settin' hen," he said.

Very naturally his thoughts turned to his mother as the proper person to come, "though Melinda Jones was the properest of the two. There was snap to her, and she would not go to pitchin' in to Ethie."

Accordingly, the next mail carried to Melinda Jones a note from Andy, which was as follows:

"MISS MELINDA JONES: Dear Madam--We found the letters Ethie writ, one to me, and one to Dick, and Dick's was too much for him. He lies like a punk of wood, makin' a moanin' noise, and talkin' such queer things, that I guess you or somebody or'to come and see to him a little. I send to you because there's no nonsense about you, and you are made of the right kind of stuff.

"Yours to command,

"ANDERSON MARKHAM, ESQ."

This note Melinda carried straight to Mrs. Markham, and as the result, four hours later both the mother and Melinda were on the road to Camden, where Melinda's services were needed to stem the tide of wonder and gossip, which had set in when it began to be known that Ethelyn was gone, and Richard was lying sick in his room, tended only by Andy, who would admit no one, not even the doctor, who, when urged by Harry Clifford, came to offer his services.

"He wasn't goin' to let in a lot of curious critters to hear what Dick was talkin'," he said to his mother and Melinda, his haggard face showing how much he had endured in keeping them at bay, and answering through the key-hole their numerous inquiries.

Richard did not have a fever, as was feared at first; but for several days he kept his bed, and during that time his mother and Melinda stayed by him, nursing him most assiduously, but never once speaking to each other of Ethelyn. Both had read her letter, for Mrs. Markham never thought of withholding it from Melinda, who, knowing that she ought not to have seen it, wisely resolved to keep to herself the knowledge of its contents. So, when she was asked, as she was repeatedly, "Why Mrs. Markham had gone away," she answered evasively, or not at all, and finding that nothing could be obtained from her, the people at last left her in quiet and turned to their own resources, which furnished various reasons for the desertion. They knew it was a desertion now, and hearing how sick and broken Richard was, popular opinion was in his favor mostly, though many a kind and wistful thought went after the fair young wife, who had been a belle in their midst, and a general favorite, too. Where was she now, and what was she doing, these many days, while the winter crept on into spring, and the March winds blew raw and chill against the windows of the chamber where Richard battled with the sickness which he finally overcame, so that by the third week of Ethie's absence he was up again and able to go in quest of her, if so be she might be found and won to the love she never returned.

CHAPTER XXV: IN CHICOPEE

They were having a late dinner at Aunt Barbara's, a four o'clock dinner of roast fowls with onions and tomatoes, and the little round table was nicely arranged with the silver and china and damask for two, while in the grate the fire was blazing brightly and on the hearth, the tabby cat was purring out her appreciation of the comfort and good cheer. But Aunt Barbara's heart was far too sorry and sad to care for her surroundings, or think how pleasant and cozy that little dining room looked to one who did not know of the grim skeleton which had walked in there that very day along with Mrs. Dr. Van Buren, of Boston. That lady had come up on the morning train and in her rustling black silk with velvet trimmings, and lace barb hanging from her head, she sat before the fire with a look of deep dejection and thoughtfulness upon her face, as if she too recked little of the creature comforts around her. Aunt Barbara knew nothing of her coming, and was taken by surprise when the village hack stopped at the door, and Sister Sophia's sable furs and beaver cloak alighted. That something was the matter she suspected from her sister's face the moment that lady removed her veil and gave the usual dignified kiss of greeting. Things had gone wrong again with Frank and Nettie, most likely, she thought, for she was not ignorant, of the misunderstandings and misery arising from that unfortunate marriage, and she had about made up her mind to tell her sister just where the fault lay. She would not spare Frank any longer, but would give him his just deserts. She never dreamed that the trouble this time concerned Ethie, her own darling, the child whom she had loved so well, and pitied, and thought of so much since the time she left her out West with "those Philistines," as she designated Richard's family. She had not heard from her for some time, but, in the last letter received, Ethie had written in a very cheerful strain, and told how gay and pleasant it was in Camden that winter. Surely nothing had befallen her, and the good woman stood aghast when Mrs. Dr. Van Buren abruptly asked if Ethelyn was not there, or had been there lately, or heard from either. What did it portend? Had harm come upon Ethie? And a shadow broke the placid surface of the sweet old face as Aunt Barbara put these questions, first to herself, and then to Mrs. Van Buren, who rapidly explained that Ethelyn had left her husband, and gone, no one knew whither.

"I hoped she might be here, and came up to see," Mrs. Van Buren concluded; while Aunt Barbara steadied herself against the great bookcase in the corner, and wondered if she was going out of her senses, or had she heard aright, and was it her sister Van Buren sitting there before her, and saying such dreadful things.

She could not tell if it were real until Tabby sprang with a purring, caressing sound, upon her shoulder, and rubbed her soft sides against her cap. That made it real, and brought the color back to her wrinkled face, but brought, also, a look of horror into her blue eyes, which sought Mrs. Van Buren's with an eager, and yet terribly anxious glance. Mrs. Dr. Van Buren understood the look. Its semblance had been on her own face for an instant when she first heard the news, and now she hastened to dispossess her sister's mind of any such suspicion.

"No, Barbara; Frank did not go with her, or even see her when in Camden. He is not quite so bad as that, I hope."

The mother nature was in the ascendant, and for a moment resented the suspicion against her son, even though that suspicion had been in her own mind when Frank returned from Camden with the news of Ethie's flight. That he had had something to do with it was her first fear, until convinced to the contrary; and now she blamed Aunt Barbara for harboring the same thought. As soon as possible she told all she had heard from Frank, and then went on with her invectives against the Markhams generally, and Richard in particular, and her endless surmises as to where Ethelyn had gone, and what was the final cause of her going.

For a time Aunt Barbara turned a deaf ear to what she was saying, thinking only of Ethie, gone; Ethie, driven to such strait, that she must either run away or die; Ethie, the little brown-eyed, rosy-cheeked, willful, imperious girl, whom she loved so much for the very willful imperiousness which always went hand in hand with such pretty fits of penitence, and sorrow, and remorse for the misdeed, that not to love her was impossible. Where was she now, and why had she not come at once to the dear old home, where she would have been so welcome until such time as matters could be adjusted on a more amicable basis?

For Aunt Barbara, though in taking Ethie's side altogether, had no thought that the separation should be final. She had chosen a life of celibacy because she preferred it, and found it a very smooth and pleasant one, especially after Ethie came and brought the sunshine of joyous childhood to her quiet home; but "those whom God had joined together" were bound to continue so, she firmly believed; and had Ethie come to her with her tale of sorrow, she would have listened kindly to it, poured in the balm of sympathy and love, and then, if possible, restored her to her husband. Of all this she thought during the few minutes Mrs. Dr. Van Buren talked, and she sat passive in her chair, where she had dropped, with her dumpy little hands lying so helplessly in her lap, and her cap all awry, as Tabby had made it when purring and rubbing against it.

"Then, you have not seen her, or heard a word?" Mrs. Van Buren asked; and in a kind of uncertain way, as if she wondered what they were talking about, Aunt Barbara replied:

"No, I have not seen her, and I don't know, I am sure, what made the child go off without letting us know."

"She was driven to it by the pack of heathens around her," Mrs. Dr. Van Buren retorted, feeling a good deal guilty herself for having been instrumental in bringing about this unhappy match, and in proportion as she felt guilty, seizing with avidity any other offered cause for Ethie's wretchedness. "I've heard even more about them than you told me," she went on to say. "There was Mrs. Ellis, whose cousin lives in Olney--she says the mother is the most peculiar and old-fashioned woman imaginable; actually wears blue yarn stockings, footed with black, makes her own candles, and sleeps in the kitchen."

With regard to the candles Aunt Barbara did not know; the sleeping in the kitchen she denied, and the footed stockings she admitted; saying, however, those she saw were black, rather than blue. Black or blue, it was all the same to Mrs. Dr. Van Buren, whose feet seldom came in contact with anything heavier than silk or the softest of lamb's wool; and, had there been wanting other evidence of Mrs. Markham's vulgarity, the stocking question would have settled the matter with her.

"Poor Ethie!" she sighed, as she drew her seat to the fire, and asked what they ought to do.

Aunt Barbara did not know. She was too much bewildered to think of anything just then, and after ordering the four o'clock dinner, which, she knew, would suit her sister's habits better than an earlier one, she, too, sat quietly down by the fire with her knitting lying idly in her lap, and her eyes looking dreamily through the frosty panes off upon the snowy hills where Ethelyn used to play. Occasionally, in reply to some question of her sister's, she would tell what she herself saw in that prairie home, and then look up amazed at the exasperating effect it seemed to have upon Mrs. Dr. Van Buren. That lady was terrible incensed against the whole Markham race, for through them she had been touched on a tender point. Ethie's desertion of her husband would not be wholly excused by the world; there was odium attaching to such a step, however great the provocation, and the disgrace was what Mrs. Van Buren would feel most keenly. That a Bigelow should do so was very humiliating; and, by way of fortifying herself with reasons for the step, she slandered and abused the Markhams until they would hardly have recognized the remotest relationship between themselves and the "terrible creatures" whom the great lady from Boston dissected so mercilessly that afternoon in Chicopee.

It was nearly four o'clock now, and the dinner was almost ready. Aunt Barbara had dropped her knitting upon the floor, where the ball was at once claimed as the lawful prey of Tabby, who rolled, and kicked, and tangled the yarn in a perfect abandon of feline delight. Mrs. Van Buren having exhausted herself, if not her topic, sat rocking quietly, and occasionally giving little sniffs of inquiry as to whether the tomatoes were really burned or not. If they were, there were still the silver-skinned onions left; and, as Mrs. Van Buren was one who thought a great deal of what she ate, she was anticipating her dinner with a keen relish, and wishing Barbara and Betty would hurry, when a buggy stopped before the door, and, with a start of disagreeable surprise, she recognized Richard Markham coming through the gate, and up the walk to the front door. He was looking very pale and worn, for to the effects of his recent illness were added traces of his rapid, fatiguing journey, and he almost staggered as he came into the room. It was not in kind Aunt Barbara's nature to feel resentment toward him then, and she went to him at once, as she would have gone to Ethie, and, taking his hand in hers, said softly:

"My poor boy! We have heard of your trouble. Have you found her yet? Do you know where she is?"

There was a look of anguish and disappointment in Richard's eyes as he replied:

"I thought--I hoped I might find her here."

"And that is the reason of your waiting so long before coming?" Mrs. Dr. Van Buren put in sharply.

It was three weeks now since Ethie's flight, and her husband had shown himself in no hurry to seek her, she reasoned; but Richard's reply, "I was away a week before I knew it, and I have been very sick since then," mollified her somewhat, though she sat back in her chair very stiff and very straight, eyeing him askance, and longing to pounce upon him and tell him what she thought. First, however, she must have her dinner. The tea would be spoiled if they waited longer; and when Aunt Barbara began to question Richard, she suggested that they wait till after dinner, when they would all be fresher and stronger. So dinner was brought in, and Richard, as he took his seat at the nicely-laid table, where everything was served with so much care, did think of the difference between Ethie's early surroundings and those to which he had introduced her when he took her to his mother's house. He was beginning to think of those things now; Ethie's letter had opened his eyes somewhat, and Mrs. Dr. Van Buren would open them more before she let him go. She was greatly refreshed with her dinner. The tomatoes had not been burned; the fowls were roasted to a most delicate brown; the currant jelly was just the right consistency; the pickled peaches were delicious, and the tea could not have been better. On the whole, Mrs. Van Buren was satisfied, and able to cope with a dozen men as crushed, and sore, and despondent as Richard seemed. She had scanned him very closely, deciding that so far as dress was concerned, he had improved since she saw him last. It is true, his collar was not all the style, and his necktie was too wide, and his coat sleeves too small, and his boots too rusty, and his vest too much soiled; but she made allowance for the circumstances, and his hasty journey, and so excused his tout ensemble. She had resumed her seat by the fire, sitting where she could look the culprit directly in the face; while good Aunt Barbara occupied the middle position, and, with her fat, soft hands shaking terribly, tried to pick up the stitches Tabby had pulled out. That personage, too, had had her chicken wing out in the woodshed, and, knowing nothing of Ethie's grievances, had mounted into Richard's lap, where she lay, slowly blinking and occasionally purring a little, as Richard now and then passed his hand over her soft fur.

"Now tell us: Why did Ethelyn go away?--that is, what reason did she give?"

It was Mrs. Dr. Van Buren who asked this question, her voice betokening that nothing which Richard could offer as an excuse would be received. They must have Ethie's reason or none. Richard would far rather Mrs. Dr. Van Buren had been in Boston, or Paris, or Guinea, than there in Chicopee, staring so coolly at him; but as her being there was something he could not help, he accepted it as a part of the train of calamities closing so fast about him, and answered, respectfully:

"It was no one thing which made her go, but the culmination of many. There was a mistake on my part. I thought her guilty when she was not, and charged her with it in a passion, saying things I would give much to recall. This was one night, and she went the next, before her temper had time to cool. You know she was a little hasty herself at times."

"Perhaps so, though her temper never troubled me any. On the whole, I think her temper amiable and mild in disposition as people generally are," Mrs. Van Buren replied, forgetting, or choosing to forget, the many occasions on which even she had shrunk from the fire which blazed in Ethie's eyes when that young lady was fully roused.

But Aunt Barbara had either more conscience or a better memory, and in a manner half apologetic for her interference, she said: "Yes, Sophia, Richard is right. Ethie had a temper--at least she was very decided. Don't you remember when she broke the cut glass fruit dish, because she could not have any more pineapple?"

"Barbara!" Mrs. Dr. Van Buren exclaimed, her voice indicating her surprise that her sister should so far forget herself as to reveal any secrets of the family, and especially any which could be brought to bear upon Ethelyn.

Aunt Barbara felt the implied rebuke, and while her sweet, old face crimsoned with mortification, she said: "Truth is truth, Sophia. Ethie is as dear to me as to you, but she was high-tempered, and did break the big fruit bowl, and then denied herself sweetmeats of all kinds, and even went without sugar in her coffee and butter on her bread until she had saved enough to buy another in its place. Ethie was generous and noble after it was all over, if she was a little hot at times. That's what I was going to say when you stopped me so sudden."

Aunt Barbara looked a little aggrieved at being caught up so quickly by her sister, who continued: "She was a Bigelow, and everybody knows what kind of blood that is. She was too sensitive, and had too nice a perception of what was proper to be thrown among"--heathen, she was going to add, but something in Aunt Barbara's blue eyes kept her in check, and so she abruptly turned to Richard and asked, "Did she leave no message, no reason why she went?"

Richard could have boasted his Markham blood had he chosen, and the white heats to which that was capable of being roused; but he was too utterly broken to feel more than a passing flash of resentment for anything which had yet been said, and after a moment's thought, during which he was considering the propriety of showing Mrs. Van Buren what Ethie had written of Frank, he held the letter to her, saying, "She left this. Read it if you like. It's a part of my punishment, I suppose, that her friends should know all."

With a stately bow Mrs. Van Buren took the letter and hastily read it through, her lip quivering a little and her eyelids growing moist as Ethie described the dreariness of that dreadful day when "Aunt Van Buren came up from Boston and broke her heart." And as she read how much poor Ethie had loved Frank, the cold, proud woman would have given all she had if the past could be undone and Ethie restored to her just as she was that summer nine years ago, when she came from the huckleberry hills and stood beneath the maples. With a strange obtuseness peculiar to some people who have seen their dearest plans come to naught, she failed to ascribe the trouble to herself, but charged it all to Richard. He was the one in fault; and by the time the letter was finished the Bigelow blood was at a boiling pitch, and for a polished lady, Mrs. Dr. Van Buren, of Boston, raised her voice pretty high as she asked: "Did you presume, sir, to think that my son--mine--a married man--would make an appointment with Ethie, a married woman? You must have a strange misconception of the manner in which he was brought up! But it is all of a piece with the rest of your abominable treatment of Ethelyn. I wonder the poor girl stayed with you as long as she did. Think of it, Barbara! Accused her of going to meet Frank by appointment, and then locked her up to keep her at home, and she a Bigelow!"

This was the first inkling Aunt Barbara had of what was in the letter. She was, however, certain that Frank was in some way involved in the matter, and anxious to know the worst, she said, beseechingly:

"Tell me something, do. I can't read it, for my eyes are dim-like to-night."

They were full of unshed tears--the kind old eyes, which did not grow one whit sterner or colder as Mrs. Van Buren explained, to some extent, what was in the letter; reading a little, telling a little, and skipping a little where Frank was especially concerned, until Aunt Barbara had a pretty correct idea of the whole. Matters had been worse than she supposed, Ethie more unhappy, and knowing her as she did, she was not surprised that at the last she ran away; but she did not say so--she merely sat grieved and helpless, while her sister took up the cudgels in Ethelyn's defense, and, attacking Richard at every point, left him no quarter at all. She did not pretend that Ethie was faultless or perfect, she said, but surely, if mortal ever had just provocation for leaving her husband, she had.

"Her marriage was a great mistake," she said; "and I must say, Mr. Markham, that you did very wrong to take her where you did without a word of preparation. You ought to have told her what she was to expect; then, if she chose to go, very well. But neither she nor I had any idea of the reality; and the change must have been terrible to her. For my part, I can conceive of nothing worse than to be obliged to live with people whom even sister Barbara called 'Hottentots,' when she came home from Iowa."

"Not Hottentots," mildly interposed Aunt Barbara. "Philistines was what I called them, Sophia; and in doing so; I did not mean all of them, you know."

"Well, Philistines, then, if that's a better word than Hottentots, which I doubt," Mrs. Van Buren retorted sharply.

Aunt Barbara's evident wish to smooth matters irritated her to say more than she might otherwise have done, and she went on:

"I know you made exceptions, but if my memory serves me right, your opinion of Ethie's mother-in-law was not very complimentary to that lady. A man has no business to take his wife to live with his mother when he knows how different they are."

"But I did not know," Richard said; "that is, I had never thought much of the things which tried Ethie. Mother was always a good mother to me, and I did not suppose she was so very different from other women."

"You certainly must be very obtuse, then," Mrs. Van Buren replied: "for, if all accounts which I hear are true, your mother is not the person to make a daughter-in-law happy. Neither, it seems, did you do what you could to please her. You annoyed her terribly with your codger-like ways, if I may be allowed that term. You made but little effort to improve, thinking, no doubt, that it was all nonsense and foolishness; that it was just as well to wear your hat in church, and sit with your boots on top of the stove, as any other way."

"I never wore my hat in church!" Richard exclaimed, with more warmth than he had before evinced.

"I don't suppose you did do that particular thing, but you were guilty of other low-bred habits which grated just as harshly as that. You thought because you were a judge and an M.C., and had the reputation of possessing brains, that it did not matter how you demeaned yourself; and there you were mistaken. The manners of a gentleman would sit ten times more gracefully upon you because you had brains. No one likes a boor, and no man of your ability has any business to be a clown. Even if you were not taught it at home, you could learn from observation, and it was your duty to do so. Instead of that, you took it for granted you were right because no one had ever suggested that you were wrong, while your mother had petted you to death. I have not the honor of her acquaintance, but I must say I consider her a very remarkable person, even for a Western woman."

"My mother was born East," Richard suggested, and Mrs. Van Buren continued:

"Certainly; but that does not help the matter. It rather makes it worse, for of all disagreeable people, a Western Yankee is, I think, the most disagreeable. Such an one never improves, but adheres strictly to the customs of their native place, no matter how many years have passed since they lived there, or how great the march of improvement may have been. In these days of railroads and telegraphs there is no reason why your mother should not be up to the times. Her neighbors are, it seems, and I have met quite as cultivated people from beyond the Rocky Mountains as I have even seen in Boston."

This was a great admission for Mrs. Van Buren, who verily believed there was nothing worth her consideration out of Boston unless it were a few families in the immediate vicinity of Fifth Avenue and Madison Square. She was bent upon making Richard uncomfortable, and could at the moment think of no better way of doing it than contrasting his mother's "way" with those of her neighbors. Occasionally Aunt Barbara put her feeble oar into the surging tide, hoping to check, even if she could not subdue the angry waters; but she might as well have kept silent save that Richard understood and appreciated her efforts to spare him as much as possible. Mrs. Van Buren was not to be stopped, and at last, when she had pretty fully set before Richard his own and his mother's delinquencies, she turned fiercely on her sister, demanding if she had not said "so and so" with regard to Ethie's home in the West. Thus straitened, Aunt Barbara replied:

"Things did strike me a little odd at Ethie's, and I don't well see how she could be very happy there. Mrs. Markham is queer--the queerest woman, if I must say it, that I ever saw, though I guess there's a good many like her up in Vermont, where she was raised, and if the truth was known, right here in Chicopee, too; and I wouldn't wonder if there were some queer ones in Boston. The place don't make the difference; it's the way the folks act."

This she said in defense of the West generally. There were quite as nice people there as anywhere, and she believed Mrs. Markham meant to be kind to Ethie; surely Richard did, only he did not understand her. It was very wrong to lock her up, and then it was wrong in Ethie to marry him, feeling as she did. "It was all wrong every way, but the heaviest punishment for the wrong had fallen on poor Ethie, gone, nobody knew where."

It was not in nature for Aunt Barbara to say so much without crying, and her tears were dropping fast into her motherly lap, where Tabby was now lying. Mrs. Van Buren was greatly irritated that her sister did not render her more assistance, and as a failure in that quarter called for greater exertions on her own part, she returned again to the charge, and wound up with sweeping denunciations against the whole Markham family.

"The idea of taking a young girl there, and trying to bend her to your ways of thinking--to debar her from all the refinements to which she had been accustomed, and give her for associates an ignorant mother-in-law and a half-witted brother."

Richard had borne a great deal from Mrs. Van Buren, and borne it patiently, too, as something which he deserved. He had seen himself torn to atoms, until he would never have recognized any one of the dissected members as parts of the Honorable Judge he once thought himself to be. He had heard his mother and her "ways" denounced as utterly repugnant to any person of decency, while James and John, under the head of "other vulgar appendages to the husband," had had a share in the general sifting down, and through it all he had kept quiet, with only an occasional demur or explanation; but when it came to Andy, the great, honest, true-hearted Andy, he could bear it no longer, and the Bigelow blood succumbed to the fiery gleam in Richard's eyes as he started to his feet, exclaiming:

"Mrs. Van Buren, you must stop, for were you a hundred times a woman, I would not listen to one word of abuse against my brother Andy. So long as it was myself and my mother, I did not mind; but every hair of Andy's head is sacred to us who know him, and I would take his part against the world, were it only for the sake of Ethie, who loved him so much, and whom he idolized. He would die for Ethie this very night, if need be--aye, die for you too, perhaps, if you were suffering and his life could bring relief. You don't know Andy, or you would know why we held him as dear as we do the memory of our darling Daisy; and when you taunt me with my half-witted brother, you hurt me as much as you would to tear my dead sister from her grave, and expose her dear face to the gaze of brutal men. No, Mrs. Van Buren, say what you like of me, but never again sneer at my brother Andy."

Richard paused, panting for breath, while Mrs. Van Buren looked at him with entirely new sensations from what she had before experienced. There was some delicacy of feeling in his nature, after all--something which recoiled from her unwomanly attack upon his weak-minded brother--and she respected him at that moment, if she had never done so before. Something like shame, too, she felt for her cruel taunt, which had both roused and wounded him, and she would gladly have recalled all she said of Andy if she could, for she remembered now what Aunt Barbara had told her of his kindness and the strong attachment there was between the simple man and Ethie. Mrs. Van Buren could be generous if she tried; and as this seemed a time for the trial, she did attempt to apologize, saying her zeal for Ethie had carried her too far; that she hoped Richard would excuse what she had said of Andy--she had no intention of wounding him on that point.

And Richard accepted the apology, but his face did not again assume the cowed, broken expression it had worn at first. There was a compression about the mouth, a firm shutting together of the teeth, and a dark look in the bloodshot eyes, which warned Mrs. Van Buren not to repeat much of what she had said. It would not now be received as it was at first. Richard would do much to bring Ethie back--he would submit to any humiliation, and bear anything for himself, but he would never again listen quietly while his mother and family were so thoroughly abused. Mrs. Van Buren felt this intuitively, and knowing that what she said had made an impression, and would after a time be acted upon, perhaps, she changed her tactics, and became quite as conciliating as Aunt Barbara herself, talking and consulting with Richard as to the best course to be pursued with regard to finding Ethie, and succeeding, in part, in removing from his face the expression it had put on when Andy was the subject of her maledictions.

Richard had a great dread of meeting his uncle, the old colonel, in his present trouble, and he was not quite sure whether he should go there or not. At least, he should not to-night; and when the clock struck eleven, he arose to retire.

"The room at the head of the stairs. I had a fire made for you in there," Aunt Barbara said, as she handed him the lamp.

Richard hesitated a moment, and then asked, "Does anyone occupy Ethie's old room? Seems to me I would rather go there. It would be somehow bring her nearer to me."

So to Ethie's old room he went, Aunt Barbara lamenting that he would find it so cold and comfortless, but feeling an increased kindliness toward him for this proof of love for her darling.

"There's a great deal of good about that man, after all," she said to her sister, when, after he was gone to his room, they sat together around their hearth and talked the matter over afresh; and then, as she took off and carefully smoothed her little round puffs of false hair, and adjusted her nightcap in its place, she said, timidly, "You were rather hard on him, Sophia, at times."

It needed but this for Mrs. Van Buren to explode again and charge her sister with saying too little rather than too much. "One would think you blamed Ethie entirely, or at least that you were indifferent to her happiness," she said, removing her lace barb, and unfastening the heavy switch bound about her head. "I was surprised at you, Barbara, I must say. After all your pretended affection for Ethelyn, I did expect you would be willing to do as much as to speak for her, at least."

This was too much for poor Aunt Barbara, and without any attempt at justification, except that her sister in her attack upon Richard had left her nothing to say, she cried quietly and sorrowfully, as she folded up her white apron and made other necessary preparations for the night. That she should be accused of not caring for Ethie, of not speaking for her, wounded her in a tender point; and long after Mrs. Van Buren had gone to the front chamber, where she always slept, Aunt Barbara was on her knees by the rocking chair, praying earnestly for Ethie, and then still kneeling there, with her face on the cushion, sobbing softly, "God knows how much I love her. There's nothing of personal comfort I would not sacrifice to bring her back; but when a man was feeling as bad as he could, what was the use of making him feel worse?"

CHAPTER XXVI: WATCHING AND WAITING

The pink and white blossoms of the apple trees by the pump in Aunt Barbara's back yard were dropping their snowy petals upon the clean, bright grass, and the frogs in the meadows were croaking their sad music, when Richard Markham came again to Chicopee. He had started for home the morning after his memorable interview with Mrs. Dr. Van Buren, and to Aunt Barbara had fallen the task of telling her troubles to the colonel's family, asking that the affair be kept as quiet as possible, inasmuch as Ethie might soon be found, and matters between her and Richard be made right. Every day, after the mail came from the West, the colonel rang at Aunt Barbara's door and asked solemnly, "if there was any news"--good news, he meant--and Aunt Barbara always shook her head, while her face grew thinner, and her round, straight figure began to get a stoop and a look of greater age than the family Bible would warrant.

Ethelyn had not been heard from, and search as he would, Richard could find no trace of her whatever. She had effectually covered her tracks, so that not even a clew to her whereabouts was found. No one had seen her, or any person like her, and the suspense and anxiety of those three-- Richard, Aunt Barbara, and Andy--who loved her so well, was getting to be terrible, when there came to Andy a letter--a letter in the dear, familiar handwriting. A few lines only, and they read:

"NEW YORK, May--.

"MY DARLING ANDY: I know you have not forgotten me, and I am superstitious enough to fancy that you are with me in spirit constantly. I do not know why I am writing this to you, but something impels me to do it, and tell you that I am well. I cannot say happy yet, for the sundering of every earthly relation made too deep a wound for me not to feel the pain for months and may be for years. I have employment, though--constant employment--that helps me to bear, and keeps me from dwelling too much upon the past.

"Andy, I want you to tell Richard that in thinking over my married life I see many places where I did very wrong and tried him terribly. I am sorry for that, and hope he will forgive me. I wish I had never crossed his path and left so dark a shadow on his life.

"Tell your mother that I know now I did not try to make her like me. Perhaps I could not if I had; but I might at least have tried. I am sorry I troubled her so much.

"Tell Melinda Jones, and James and John, that I remember all their kindness, and thank them so much. And Eunice, too. She was good to me, always. And oh! Andy, please get word somehow to dear Aunt Barbara that her lost Ethie is well, and so sorry to give her pain, as I know I do. I would write to her myself, but I am afraid she blames me for going away and bringing a kind of disgrace upon her and Aunt Van Buren. I cannot say yet I am sorry for the step I took, and, until I am sorry I cannot write to Aunt Barbara. But you must tell her for me how much I love her, and how every night of my life I dream I am back in the dear old home under the maples, and see upon the hills the swelling buds and leaves of spring. Tell her not to forget me, and be sure that wherever I am or whatever may befall me, she will be remembered as the dearest, most precious memory of my life. Next to her Andy, you come; my darling Andy, who was always so kind to me when my heart was aching so hard.

"Good-by, Andy, good-by."

This was the letter which Andy read with streaming eyes, while around him, on tiptoe, to look over his and each other's shoulders, stood the entire family, all anxious and eager to know what the runaway had written. It was a very conciliatory letter, and it left a sadly pleasant impression on those who read it, making even the mother wipe her eyes with the corner of her apron as she washed her supper dishes in the sink and whispered to herself, "She didn't trouble me so very much more than I did her. I might have done different, too."

Richard made no comment whatever, but, like Andy, he conned the letter over and over until he knew it by heart, especially the part referring to himself. She had cast a shadow upon his life, but she was very dear to him for all that, and he would gladly have taken back the substance, had that been possible. This letter Richard carried to Aunt Barbara, whom he found sitting in her pleasant porch, with the May moonlight falling upon her face, and her eyes wearing the look of one who is constantly expecting something which never comes. And Aunt Barbara was expecting Ethie. It could not be that a young girl like her would stay away for long. She might return at any time, and every morning the good woman said to herself, "She will be here to-day;" every night, "She will come home to-morrow." The letter, however, did not warrant such a conclusion There was no talk of coming back, but the postmark, "New York," told where she was, and that was something gained. They could surely find her now, Aunt Barbara said, and she and Richard talked long together about what he was going to do, for he was on his way then to the great city.

"Bring her to me at once. It is my privilege to have her first," Aunt Barbara said, next morning, as she bade Richard good-by, and then began to watch and wait for tidings which never came.

Richard could not find Ethelyn, or any trace of her, and after a protracted search of six long weeks, he went back to his Iowa home, sick, worn out, and discouraged. Aunt Barbara roused herself for action. "Men were good for nothing to hunt. They could not find a thing if it was right before their face and eyes. It took a woman; and she was going to see what she could do," she said to Mrs. Van Buren, who was up at the homestead for a few days, and who looked aghast at her sister's proposition, that she should accompany her, and help her hunt up Ethie.

"Was Barbara crazy, that she thought of going to New York in this hot weather, when the smallpox, and the dysentery, and the plague, and mercy knew what was there? Besides that, how did Barbara intend to manage? What was she going to do?"

Barbara hardly knew herself how she should manage, or what she should do. "Providence would direct," she said, though to be sure she had an idea. Ethie had written that she had found employment, and what was more probable than to suppose that the employment was giving music lessons, for which she was well qualified, or teaching in some gentleman's family. Taking this as her basis, Aunt Barbara intended to inquire for every governess and teacher in the city, besides watching every house where such an appendage would be likely to be found. Still her great hope was in the street and the Park. She should surely meet Ethie there some day--at least she would try the effect of her plan; and she went quietly on with her preparations, while Mrs. Van Buren tried to dissuade her from a scheme which seemed so foolish and utterly impracticable.

"Suppose Ethie was a governess, the family most likely would be out of town at that season; and what good would it do for Aunt Barbara to risk her life and health in the crowded city?"

This view of the matter was rather dampening to Aunt Barbara's zeal; but trusting that Providence would interfere in her behalf, she still insisted that she should go, and again expressed a wish that Sophia would go with her. "It would not be so lonesome, and would look better, too," she said, "while you know more of city ways than I do, and would not get imposed upon."

Mrs. Van Buren could go far beyond her sister in abusing Richard, but when it came to a sacrifice of her own comfort and pleasure, she held back. Nothing could induce her to go to New York. She preferred the cool seaside, where she was to join a party of Boston élite. Her dresses were made, her room engaged, and she must go, she said, urging that Nettie's health required the change--Nettie, who had given to her husband a sickly, puny child, which lived just long enough to warrant a grand funeral, and then was laid to rest under the shadow of the Van Buren monument, out in pleasant Mount Auburn.

So Mrs. Van Buren went back to Boston, while Aunt Barbara gave all needful directions to Betty with regard to the management of the house, and the garden, and plants, and cellar door, which must be shut nights, and the spot on the roof which sometimes leaked when it rained, and the burdocks and dandelions which must be dug up, and the grass which Uncle Billy Thompson must cut once in two weeks, and the old cat, Tabby, and the young cat, Jim, who had come to the door in a storm, and was now the pet of the house, and the canary bird, and the yeast, and look in the vinegar barrel to see that all was right, and be sure and scald the milk-pans, and turn them up in the sun for an hour, and keep the doors locked, and the silver up in the scuttle-hole; and if she heard the rat which baffled and tormented them so long, get some poison and kill it, but not on any account let it get in the cistern; and keep the door-steps clean, and the stoop, and once in a while sweep the low roof at the back of the house, and not sit up late nights, or sleep very long in the morning; and inasmuch as there would be so little to do, she might as well finish up all her new sewing, and make the pile of sheets and pillow-cases which had been cut out since March. These were Aunt Barbara's directions, which Betty, nothing appalled, promised to heed, telling her mistress not to worry an atom, as things should be attended to, even better than if she were at home to see to them herself.

Aunt Barbara knew she could trust old Betty, and so, after getting herself vaccinated in both arms, as a precaution against the smallpox, and procuring various disinfecting agents, and having underpockets put in all her dresses, by way of eluding pickpockets, the good woman started one hot July morning on her mission in search of Ethie. But, alas, finding Ethie, or anyone, in New York, was like "hunting for a needle in a hay mow," as Aunt Barbara began to think after she had been for four weeks or more an inmate of an uptown boarding house, recommended as first-class, but terrible to Aunt Barbara, from the contrast it presented to her own clean, roomy home beneath the maple trees, which came up to her so vividly, with all its delicious coolness and fragrance, and blossoming shrubs, and newly cut grass, with the dew sparkling like diamonds upon it.

Aunt Barbara was terribly homesick from the first, but she would not give up; so day after day she traversed one street after another, looking wistfully in every face she met for the one she sought, questioning children playing in the parks and squares as to whether they knew any teacher by the name of Markham or Grant, ringing the door-bells of every pretentious-looking house and putting the same question to the servants, until the bombazine dress and black Stella shawl, and brown Neapolitan hat, and old-fashioned lace veil, and large sun umbrella became pretty well known in various parts of New York, while the owner thereof grew to be a suspicious character, whom servants watched from the basement and ladies from the parlor windows, and children shunned on the sidewalk, while even the police were cautioned with regard to the strange woman who went up and down day after day, sometimes in stages, sometimes in cars, but oftener on foot, staring at everyone she met, especially if they chanced to be young or pretty, and had any children near them. Once down near Washington Square, as she was hurrying toward a group of children, in the center of which stood a figure much like Ethie's, a tall man in the blue uniform accosted her, inquiring into her reasons for wandering about so constantly.

Aunt Barbara's honest face, which she turned full toward the officer, was a sufficient voucher for her with the simple, straightforward explanation which she made to the effect that her niece had left home some time ago--run away, in fact--and she was hunting for her here in New York, where her letter was dated. "But it's wearisome work for an old woman like me, walking all over New York, as I have," Aunt Barbara said, and her lip began to quiver as she sat down upon one of the seats in the square, and looked helplessly up at the policeman. She was not afraid of him, nor of the five others of the craft who knew her by sight, and stopped to hear what she had to say. She never dreamed that they could suspect her of wrong, and they did not when they heard her story, and saw the truthful, motherly face. Perhaps they could help her, they said, and they asked the name of the runaway.

At first Aunt Barbara refused to give it, wishing to spare Ethie this notoriety; but she finally yielded so far as to say, "She might call herself either Markham or Grant," and that was all they could get from her; but after that day the bombazine dress, and black Stella shawl, and large sun umbrella were safe from the surveillance of the police, save as each had a kindly care for the owner, and an interest in the object of her search.

The light-fingered gentry, however, were not as chary of her. The sweet, motherly face, and wistful, pleading, timid eyes, did not deter them in the least. On the contrary, they saw in the bombazine and Stella shawl a fine field for their operations; and twice, on returning to her boarding house, the good soul was horrified to find her purse was missing, notwithstanding that she had kept her hand upon her pocket every instant, except once, when the man who looked like a minister had kindly opened the car window for her, and she had gathered up her dress to make more room for him at her side, and once when she got entangled in a crowd, and had to hold on to her shawl to keep it on her shoulders. Ten dollars was the entire sum purloined, so the villains did not make much out of her, Aunt Barbara reflected with a good deal of complacency; but when they stole her gold-bowed glasses from her pocket, and adroitly snatched from her hand the parcel containing the dress she had bought for Betty at Stewart's, she began to look upon herself as specially marked by a gang of thieves for one on whom to commit their depredations; and when at last a fire broke out in the very block where she was boarding, and she, with others was driven from her bed at midnight, with her bombazine only half on, and her hoops left behind, she made up her mind that the fates were against her, and wrote to Betty that she was coming home, following her letter in the next train so that both reached Chicopee the same day, the very last day of summer.

It was sooner than Betty expected her, but the clean, cool house, peeping out from the dense shadows of the maples, looked like a paradise to the tired, dusty woman, who rode down the street in the village hack and surprised Betty sitting in the back door cutting off corn to dry and talking to Uncle Billy, whose scythe lay on the grass while he drank from the gourd swimming on top of the water-pail.

Betty was glad to see her mistress, and lamented that she did not know of her coming, so as to have a nice hot cup of tea ready, with a delicate morsel of something. Aunt Barbara was satisfied to be home on any terms, though her nose did go up a little, and something which sounded like "P-shew!" dropped from her lips as she entered the dark sitting room, where the odor was not the best in the world.

"It's the rat, ma'am, I think," Betty said, opening both blinds and windows. "I put the pizen for him as you said, and all I could do he would die in the wall. It ain't as bad as it has been, and I've got some stuff here to kill it, though I think it smells worse than the rat himself," and Betty held her nose as she pointed out to her mistress the saucer of chloride of lime which, at Mrs. Col. Markham's suggestion, she had put in the sitting room.

Aside from the rat in the wall, things were mostly as Aunt Barbara could wish them to be. The vinegar had made beautifully. There was fresh yeast, brewed the day before, in the jug. The milk-pans were bright and sweet; the cellar door was fastened; the garden was looking its best; the silver was all up the scuttle-hole, Betty climbing up and risking her neck every morning to see if it were safe; the stoop and steps were scrubbed, the roof was swept, and both the cats, Tabby and Jim, were so fat that they could scarcely walk as they came up to greet their mistress. Only two mishaps Betty had to relate. Jim had eaten up the canary bird, and she had broken the kitchen tongs. She had also failed to accomplish as much sewing as she had hoped to do, and the pile of work was not greatly diminished.

"There is so many steps to take when a body is alone, and with you gone I was more particular," she said, by way of apology, as she confessed to the rat, and the canary bird, and the kitchen tongs, and the small amount of sewing she had done.

These were all the points wherein she had been remiss, and Aunt Barbara was content, and even happy, as she laid aside her Stella shawl and brown Neapolitan, and out in her pleasant dining room sat down to the hasty meal which Betty improvised, of bread and butter, Dutch cheese, baked apples, and huckleberry pie, with a cup of delicious tea, such as Aunt Barbara did not believe the people of New York had ever tasted. Most certainly those who were fortunate enough to board at first-class boarding-houses had not; and as she sipped her favorite beverage with Tabby on her dress and the criminal Tim in her lap, his head occasionally peering over the table, she felt comforted and rested, and thankful for her cozy home, albeit it lay like a heavy weight upon her that her trouble had been for nothing, and no tidings of Ethie had been obtained.

She wrote to Richard the next day, of her unsuccessful search, and asked what they should do next.

"We can do nothing but wait and hope," Richard wrote in reply, but Aunt Barbara added to it, "we can pray;" and so all through the autumn, when the soft, hazy days which Ethie had loved so well kept the lost one forever in mind, Aunt Barbara waited and hoped, and prayed and watched for Ethie's coming home, feeling always a sensation of expectancy when the Western whistle sounded and the Western train went thundering through the town; and when the hack came up from the depot and did not stop at her door, she said to herself, "She would walk up, maybe," and then waiting again she would watch from her window and look far up the quiet street, where the leaves of crimson and gold were lying upon the walk. No Ethie was to be seen. Then as the days grew shorter and the nights fell earlier upon the Chicopee hills, and the bleak winds blew across the meadow, and the waters of the river looked blue and dark and cold in the November light, she said: "She will be here sure by Christmas. She always liked that day best," and her fingers were busy with the lamb's wool stockings she was knitting for her darling.

"It won't be much," she said to Betty, "but it will show she is not forgotten;" and so the stocking grew, and was shaped from a half-worn pair which Ethelyn used to wear, and on which Aunt Barbara's tears dropped as she thought of the dear little feet, now wandered so far away, which the stockings used to cover.

Christmas came, and Susie Granger sang of Bethlehem in the old stone church, and other fingers than Ethie's swept the organ keys, and the Christmas tree was set up, and the presents were hung upon the boughs, and the names were called, and Aunt Barbara was there, but the lamb's-wool stockings were at home in the bureau drawer; there was no one to wear them, no one to take them from the tree, if they had been put there; Ethie had not come.

CHAPTER XXVII: AFFAIRS AT OLNEY

Richard could not stay in Camden, where everything reminded him so much of Ethelyn, and at his mother's earnest solicitations he went back to Olney, taking with him all the better articles of furniture which Ethie had herself selected, and which converted the plain farmhouse into quite a palace, as both Andy and his mother thought. The latter did not object to them in the least, and was even conscious of a feeling of pride and satisfaction when her neighbors came in to admire, and some of them to envy her the handsome surroundings. Mrs. Dr. Van Buren's lesson, though a very bitter one, was doing Richard good, especially as it was adroitly followed up by Melinda Jones, who, on the strength of her now being his sister-elect, took the liberty of saying to him some pretty plain things with regard to his former intercourse with Ethie.

James had finally nerved himself to the point of asking Melinda if she could be happy with such a homespun fellow as himself, and Melinda had answered that she thought she could, hinting that it was possible for him to overcome much which was homespun about him.

"I do not expect you to leave off your heavy boots or your coarse frock when your work requires you to wear them," she said, stealing her hand into his in a caressing kind of way; "but a man can be a gentleman in any dress."

James promised to do his best, and with Melinda Jones for a teacher, had no fear of his success. And so, some time in August, when the summer work at the Jones' was nearly done, Melinda came to the farmhouse and was duly installed as mistress of the chamber which James and John had occupied--the latter removing his Sunday clothes, and rifle, and fishing lines, and tobacco, and the slippers Ethie had given him, into Andy's room, which he shared with his brother. Mrs. Markham, senior, got on better with Melinda than she had with Ethelyn; Melinda knew exactly how to manage her, and, indeed, how to manage the entire household, from Richard down to Andy, who, though extremely kind and attentive to her, never loved her as he did Ethelyn.

"She was a nice, good girl," he said, "but couldn't hold a candle to Ethie. She was too dark complected, and had altogether too thumpin' feet and ankles, besides wearin' wrinkly stockings."

That was Andy's criticism, confided to his brother John, around whose grave mouth there was a faint glimmer of a smile, as he gave a hitch to his suspender and replied, "I guess her stockin's do wrinkle some."

A few of Melinda's ways Mrs. Markham designated as high-flown, but one by one her prejudices gave way as Melinda gained upon her step by step, until at last Ethelyn would hardly have recognized the well-ordered household, so different from what she had known it.

"The boys" no longer came to the table in their shirt-sleeves, for Melinda always had their coats in sight, just where it was handy to put them on, and the trousers were slipped down over the boots while the boys ate, and the soft brown Markham hair always looked smooth and shining, and Mrs. Markham tidied herself a little before coming to the table, no matter how heavy her work, and never but once was she guilty of sitting down to her dinner in her pasteboard sun-bonnet, giving as an excuse that her "hair was at sixes and sevens." She remembered seeing her mother do this fifty years before, and she had clung to the habit as one which must be right because they used to do so in Vermont. Gradually, too, there came to be napkins for tea, and James' Christmas present to his wife was a set of silver forks, while John contributed a dozen individual salts, and Andy bought a silver bell, to call he did not know whom, only it looked pretty on the table, and he wanted it there every meal, ringing it himself sometimes when anything was needed, and himself answering the call. On the whole, the Markhams were getting to be "dreadfully stuck up," Eunice Plympton's mother said, while Eunice doubted if she should like living there now as well as in the days of Ethelyn. She had been a born lady, and Eunice conceded everything to her; but, "to see the airs that Melinda Jones put on" was a little too much for Eunice's democratic blood, and she and her mother made many invidious remarks concerning "Mrs. Jim Markham," who wore such heavy silk to church, and sported such handsome furs. One hundred and fifty dollars the cape alone had cost, it was rumored, and when, to this Richard added a dark, rich muff to match, others than Eunice looked enviously at Mrs. James, who to all intents and purposes, was the same frank, outspoken person that she was when she wore a plain scarf around her neck, and rode to church in her father's lumber wagon instead of the handsome turn-out James had bought since his marriage. Nothing could spoil Melinda, and though she became quite the fashion in Olney, and was frequently invited to Camden to meet the élite of the town, she was up just as early on Monday mornings as when she lived at home, and her young, strong arms saved Mrs. Markham more work than Eunice's had done. She would not dip candles, she said, nor burn them, either, except as a matter of convenience to carry around the house; and so the tallows gave way to kerosene, and as Melinda liked a great deal of light, the house was sometimes illuminated so brilliantly that poor Mrs. Markham had either to shade her eyes with her hands, or turn her back to the lamp. She never thought of opposing Melinda; that would have done no good; and she succumbed with the rest to the will which was ruling them so effectually and so well.

Some very plain talks Melinda had with Richard with regard to Ethelyn; and Richard, when he saw how anxious James was to please his wife, even in little things which he had once thought of no consequence, regretted so much that his own course had not been different with Ethelyn. "Poor, dear Ethie," he called her to himself, as he sat alone at night in the room where she used to be. At first he had freely talked of her with his family. That was when, like Aunt Barbara, they were expecting her back, or rather expecting constantly to hear from her through Aunt Barbara. She would go to Chicopee first, they felt assured, and then Aunt Barbara would write, and Richard would start at once. How many castles he built to that second bringing her home, where Melinda made everything so pleasant, and where she could be happy for a little time, when they would go where she liked--it did not matter where. Richard was willing for anything, only he did want her to stay a little time at the farmhouse, just to see how they had improved, and to learn that his mother could be kind if she tried. She meant to be so if Ethelyn ever came back, for she had said as much to him on the receipt of Ethie's message, sent in Andy's letter, and her tears had fallen fast as she confessed to not always having felt or acted right toward the young girl. With Melinda the ruling spirit they would have made it very pleasant for Ethelyn, and they waited for her so anxiously all through the autumnal days till early winter snow covered the prairies, and the frost was on the window panes, and the wind howled dismally past the door, just as it did one year ago, when Ethelyn went away. But, alas no Ethie came, or tidings of her either, and Richard ceased to speak of her at last, and his face wore so sad a look whenever she was mentioned that the family stopped talking of her; or, if they spoke her name, it was as they spoke of Daisy, or of one that was dead.

For a time Richard kept up a correspondence with Aunt Barbara; but that, too, gradually ceased, and as his uncle, the old colonel, died in the spring, and the widow went to her friends in Philadelphia, he seemed to be cut off from any connections with Chicopee, and but for the sad, harassing memory of what had been, he was to all intents and purposes the same grave, silent bachelor as of yore, following the bent of his own inclinations, coming and going as he liked, sought after by those who wished for an honest man to transact their business, and growing gradually more and more popular with the people of his own and the adjoining counties.

CHAPTER XXVIII: THE GOVERNOR

They were to elect a new one in Iowa, and there were rumors afloat that Richard Markham would be the man chosen by his party. There had been similar rumors once before, but Mrs. Markham had regarded them as mythical, never dreaming that such an honor could be in store for her boy. Now, however, matters began to look a little serious. Crowds of men came frequently to the farmhouse and were closeted with Richard. Tim Jones rode up and down the country, electioneering for "Dick." Hal Clifford, in Camden, contributed his influence, though he belonged to the other party. Others, too, of Harry's way of thinking, cast aside political differences and "went in," as they said, for the best man--one whom they knew to be honest and upright, like Judge Markham. Each in their own way--James and John, and Andy and Melinda-- worked for Richard, who was frequently absent from home for several days, sometimes taking the stump himself, but oftener remaining quiet while others presented his cause. Search as they might, his opponents could find nothing against him, except that sad affair with his wife, who, one paper said, "had been put out of the way when she became troublesome," hinting at every possible atrocity on the husband's part, and dilating most pathetically upon the injured, innocent, and beautiful young wife. Then with a face as pale as ashes, Richard made his "great speech" in Camden court-house, asking that the whole matter be dropped at once, and saying that he would far rather live a life of obloquy than have the name, more dear to him than the names of our loved dead, bandied about from lip to lip and made the subject for newspaper paragraphs. They knew Richard in Camden, and they knew Ethelyn, too, liking both so well, that the result of that speech was to increase Richard's popularity tenfold, and to carry in his favor the entire town.

The day of election was a most exciting one, especially in Olney, where Richard had lived from boyhood. It was something for a little town like this to furnish the governor, the Olneyites thought, and though, for party's sake, there were some opponents, the majority went for Richard, and Tim Jones showed his zeal by drinking with so many that at night he stopped at the farmhouse, insisting that he had reached home, and should stay there, "for all of Melind," and hurrahing so loud for "Richud--Mark-um--Square," that he woke up the little blue-eyed boy which for six weeks had been the pride and pet and darling of the household.

Andy's tactics were different. He had voted in the morning, and prayed the rest of the day, that if it were right, "old Dick might lick the whole of 'em," adding the petition that "he need not be stuck up if he was governor," and that Ethie might come back to share his greatness. Others than Andy were thinking of Ethelyn that day, for not the faintest echo of a huzza reached Richard's ears that did not bring with it regretful thoughts of her. And when at last success was certain, and, flushed with triumph, he stood receiving the congratulations of his friends, and the Olney bell was ringing in honor of the new governor, and bonfires were lighted in the streets, the same little boys who had screamed themselves hoarse for the other candidates, stealing barrels and dry-goods boxes to feed the flames with quite as much alacrity as their opponents, there was not a throb of his heart which did not go out after the lost one, with a yearning desire to bring her back, and, by giving her the highest position in the State, atone in part for all which had been wrong. But Ethie was very, very far away--further than he dreamed--and strain ear and eye as she might, she could not see the lurid blaze which lit up the prairie till the tall grass grew red in the ruddy glow, or hear the deafening shouts which rent the sky for the new Governor Markham, elected by an overwhelming majority. Oh, how lonely Richard felt even in the first moments of his success! And how he longed to get away from all the noise and din which greeted him at every step, and be alone again, as since Ethie went away he had chosen to be so much of his time. Melinda guessed at his feelings in part, and when he came home at last, looking so pale and tired, she pitied him, and showed her pity by letting him alone; and when supper was ready, sending his tea to his room, whither he had gone as soon as his mother had unwound her arms from his neck, and told him how glad she was.

These were also days of triumph for Melinda, for it was soon known that she was to be the lady of the governor's mansion, and the knowledge gave her a fresh accession of dignity among her friends. It was human that Melinda should feel her good fortune a little, and perhaps she did. Andy thought so, and prayed silently against the pomps and vanities of the world, especially after her new purple silk was sent home, with the handsome velvet cloak and crimson morning gown. These had been made in Camden, a thing which gave mortal offense to Miss Henry, the Olney dressmaker, who wondered "what Melinda Jones was that she should put on such airs, and try to imitate Mrs. Richard Markham." They had expected such things from Ethelyn, and thought it perfectly right. She was born to it, they said; but for Melinda, whom all remembered as wearing a red woolen gown when a little girl, "for her to set up so steep was another matter." But when Melinda ordered a blue merino, and a flannel wrapper, and a blue silk, and a white cloak for baby, made at Miss Henry's, and told that functionary just how her purple was trimmed, and even offered to show it to her, the lady changed her mind, and quoted "Mrs. James Markham's" wardrobe for months afterward.

Richard, and James, and Melinda, and baby, and Eunice Plympton as baby's nurse, all went to Des Moines, and left the house so lonely that Andy lay flat upon the floor and cried, and his mother's face wore the look of one who had just returned from burying their dead. It was something, however, to be the mother and brother of a governor, and a comfort to get letters from the absent ones, to hear of Richard's immense popularity, and the very graceful manner in which Melinda discharged her duties. But to see their names in print, to find something about Governor Markham in almost every paper--that was best of all, and Andy spent half his time in cutting out and saving every little scrap pertaining to the "governor's family," and what they did at Des Moines. Andy was laid up with rheumatism toward spring; but Tim Jones used to bring him the papers, rolling his quid of tobacco rapidly from side to side as he pointed to the paragraphs so interesting to both. Tim hardly knew whether himself, or Richard, or Melinda, was the governor. On the whole, he gave the preference to "Melind," after the governor's levee, at which she had appeared in "royal purple, with ostrich feathers in her hair," and was described in the Camden Leader as the "elegant and accomplished Mrs. James Markham, who had received the guests with so much dignity and grace."

"Ain't Melind a brick? and only to think how she used to milk the cows, and I once chased her with a garter snake," Tim said, reading the article aloud to Andy, who, while assenting that she was a brick, and according all due credit to her for what she was, and what she did, never for a moment forgot Ethelyn.

She would have done so much better, and looked so much neater, especially her shoes! Andy could not quite forgive Melinda's big feet and ankles, especially as his contempt for such appendages was constantly kept in mind by the sight of the little half-worn slippers which Ethie had left in her closet when she moved to Camden, and which, now that she was gone, he kept as something almost as sacred as Daisy's hair, admiring the dainty rosettes and small high heels more than he admired the whole of Melinda's wardrobe when spread upon the bed, and tables, and chairs, preparatory to packing it for Des Moines. Richard, too, remembered Ethelyn, and never did Melinda stand at his side in any gay saloon that he did not see in her place a brown-eyed, brown-haired woman who would have moved a very queen among the people. Ethelyn was never forgotten, whether in the capitol, or the street, or at home, or awake, or asleep. Ethie's face and Ethie's form were everywhere, and if earnest, longing thoughts could have availed to bring her back, she would have come, whether across the rolling sea, or afar from the trackless desert. But they could not reach her, Ethie did not come, and the term of Richard's governorship glided away, and he declined a re-election, and went back to Olney, looking ten years older than when he left it, with an habitual expression of sadness on his face, which even strangers noticed, wondering what was the heart trouble which was aging him so fast, and turning his brown hair gray.

For a time the stillness and quiet of Olney were very acceptable to him, and then he began to long for more excitement--something to divert his mind from the harrowing fear, daily growing more and more certain, that Ethie would never come back. It was four years since she went away, and nothing had been heard from her since the letter sent to Andy from New York. "Dead," he said to himself many a time, and but for the dread of the hereafter, he, too, would gladly have lain down in the graveyard where Daisy was sleeping so quietly. With Andy it was different. Ethie was not dead--he knew she was not--and some time she would surely come back, There was comfort in Andy's strong assurance, and Richard always felt better after a talk with his hopeful brother. Perhaps she would come back, and if so he must have a place worthy of her, he said, one day, to Melinda, who seized the opportunity to unfold a plan she had long been cogitating. During the two years spent in Des Moines, James had devoted himself to the study of law, preferring it to his farming, and now he was looking out for a good locality where to settle and practice his profession.

"Let's go together somewhere and build a house," Melinda said. "You know Ethie's taste. You can fashion it as you think she would like it, and meantime we will live with you and see to you a little. You need some looking after," and Melinda laid her hand half pityingly upon the bowed head of her brother-in-law, who, but for her strong, upholding influence, and Andy's cheering faith, would have sunk ere this into hopeless despondency.

Melinda was a fine specimen of true womanhood. She had met many highly cultivated people at Des Moines and other towns, where, as the governor's sister-in-law, she had spent more or less of the last two years, and as nothing ever escaped her notice, she had improved wonderfully, until even Mrs. Van Buren, of Boston, would have been proud of her acquaintance. She had known sorrow, too; for in the cemetery at Des Moines she had left her little blue-eyed baby boy when only six months old, and her mother's heart had ached to its very core, until there came another child, a little girl, this time, whom they had christened "Ethelyn Grant," and who, on this account, was quite as dear to Richard as to either of its parents. Richard was happier with that little brown-haired girl than with anyone else, and when Melinda suggested they should go together somewhere, he assented readily, mentioning Davenport as a place where Ethelyn had many times said she would like to live. Now, as ever, Melinda's was the active, ruling voice, and almost before Richard knew it, he was in Davenport and bargaining for a vacant lot which overlooked the river and much of the country beyond. Davenport suited them all, and by September, Melinda, who had spent the summer with her mother, was located at a hotel and making herself very useful to Richard with her suggestions with regard to the palatial mansion he was building.

There was nothing in Davenport like the "governor's house," and the people watched it curiously as it went rapidly up. There was a suite of rooms which they called Ethelyn's, and to the arrangement and adorning of these Richard gave his whole attention, sparing nothing which could make them beautiful and attractive, and lavishing so much expense upon them that strangers came to inspect and comment upon them, wondering why he took so much pains, and guessing, as people will, that he was contemplating a second marriage as soon as a divorce could be obtained from his runaway wife.

The house was finished at last, and Richard took possession, installing Melinda as housekeeper, and feeling how happy he should be if only Ethie were there. Somehow he expected her now. Andy's prayers would certainly be answered even if his own were not, for he, too, had begun to pray, feeling, at times, that God was slow to hear, as weeks and weeks went by and still Ethie did not come. "Hope deferred maketh the heart sick," and the weary waiting told upon his bodily health, which began to fail so rapidly that people said "Governor Markham was going into a decline," and the physicians urged a change of air, and Mr. Townsend, who came in May for a day at Davenport, recommended him strongly to try what Clifton Springs, in Western New York, could do for him--the Clifton, whose healing waters and wonderful power to cure were famed from the shores of the Atlantic to the Californian hills.

CHAPTER XXIX: AFTER YEARS OF WAITING

The weather in Chicopee that spring was as capricious as the smiles of the most spoiled coquette could ever be. The first days of April were warm, and balmy, and placid, without a cloud upon the sky or a token of storm in the air. The crocuses and daffodils showed their heads in the little borders by Aunt Barbara's door, and Uncle Billy Thompson sowed the good woman a bed of lettuce, and peas, and onions, which came up apace, and were the envy of the neighbors. Taking advantage of the warmth and the sunshine, and Uncle Billy's being there to whip her carpets, Aunt Barbara even began her house cleaning, commencing at the chambers first--the rooms which since the last "reign of terror," had only been used when a clergyman spent Sunday there, and when Mrs. Dr. Van Buren was up for a few days from Boston, with Nettie and the new girl baby, which, like Melinda's, bore the name of Ethelyn. Still they must be renovated, and cleaned, and scrubbed, lest some luckless moth were hiding there, or some fly-speck perchance had fallen upon the glossy paint. Aunt Barbara was not an untidy house-cleaner--one who tosses the whole house into chaos, and simultaneous with the china from the closet, brings up a basket of bottles from the cellar to be washed and rinsed. She took one room at a time, settling as she went along, so that her house never was in that state of dire confusion which so many houses present every fall and spring. Her house was not hard to clean, and the chambers were soon done, except Ethie's own room, where Aunt Barbara lingered longest, turning the pretty ingrain carpet the brightest side up, rubbing the furniture with polish, putting a bit of paint upon the window sills where it was getting worn, and once revolving the propriety of hanging new paper upon the wall. But that, she reasoned, would be needless expense. Since the night Richard spent there, five years ago, no one had slept there, and no one should sleep there, either, till Ethie came back again.

"Till Ethie comes again." Aunt Barbara rarely said that now, for with each fleeting year the chance for Ethie's coming grew less and less, until now she seldom spoke of it to Betty, the only person to whom she ever talked of Ethie. Even with her she was usually very reticent, unless something brought the wanderer to mind more vividly than usual. Cleaning her room was such an occasion, and sitting down upon the floor, while she darned a hole in the carpet which the turning had brought to view, Aunt Barbara spoke of her darling, and the time when, a little toddling thing of two years old, she first came to the homestead, and was laid in that very room, and "on that very pillow," Aunt Barbara said, seeing again the round hollow left by the little brown head when the child awoke and stretched its fat arms toward her.

"Julia, her mother, died in that bed," Aunt Barbara went on, "and Ethie always slept there after that. Well put on the sheets marked with her name, Betty, and the ruffled pillow-cases. I want it to seem as if she were here," and Aunt Barbara's chin quivered, and her eyes grew moist, as her fat, creasy hands smoothed and patted the plump pillows, and tucked in the white spread, and picked up a feather, and moved a chair, and shut the blinds, and dropped the curtains, and then she went softly out and shut the door behind her.

Two weeks from that day, the soft, bland air was full of sleet, and snow, and rain, which beat down the poor daffies on the borders, and pelted the onions, and lettuce, and peas which Uncle Billy had planted, and dashed against the closed windows of Ethie's room, and came in under the door of the kitchen, and through the bit of leaky roof in the dining room, while the heavy northeaster which swept over the Chicopee hills screamed fiercely at Betty peering curiously out to see if it was going to be any kind of drying for the clothes she had put out early in the day, and then, as if bent on a mischievous frolic took from the line and carried far down the street, Aunt Barbara's short night-gown with the patch upon the sleeve. On the whole it was a bleak, raw, stormy day, and when the night shut down, the snow lay several inches deep upon the half-frozen ground, making the walking execrable, and giving to the whole village that dirty, comfortless appearance which a storm in April always does. It was pleasant, though, in Aunt Barbara's sitting room. It was always pleasant there, and it seemed doubly so to-night from the contrast presented to the world without by the white-washed ceiling, the newly whipped carpet, the clean, white curtains, and the fire blazing on the hearth, where two huge red apples were roasting. This was a favorite custom of Aunt Barbara's, roasting apples in the evening. She used to do it when Ethie was at home, for Ethie enjoyed it quite as much as she did, and when the red cheeks burst, and the white frothy pulp came oozing out, she used, as a little girl, to clap her hands and cry, "The apples begin to bleed, auntie! the apples begin to bleed!"

Aunt Barbara never roasted them now that she did not remember her darling, and many times she put one down for Ethie, feeing that the "make believe" was better than nothing at all. There was one for to-night, and Aunt Barbara sat watching it as it simmered and sputtered, and finally burst with the heat, "bleeding," just as her heart was bleeding for the runaway whose feet had wandered so long. It was after nine, and Betty had gone to bed, so that Aunt Barbara was there alone, with the big Bible in her lap. She had been reading the parable of the Prodigal, and though she would not liken Ethie to him, she sighed softly, "If she would only come, we would kill the fatted calf." Then, thoughtfully, she turned the leaves of the Good Book one by one, till she found the "Births," and read in a low whisper, "Ethelyn Adelaide, Born," and so forth. Then her eye moved on to where the marriage of Ethelyn Adelaide with Richard Markham, of Iowa, had been recorded; and then she turned to the last of "Deaths," wondering if, unseen by her, Ethie's name had been added to the list. The last name visible to mortal eye was that of Julia, wife of William Grant, who had died at the age of twenty-five.

"Just as old as Ethie is, if living," Aunt Barbara whispered, and the tears which blotted the name of Julia Grant were given to Ethie rather than the young half-sister who had been so much of a stranger.

Suddenly, as Aunt Barbara sat there, with her Bible in her lap, there was heard the distant rumbling of the New York express, as it came rolling across the plains from West Chicopee. Then as the roar became more muffled as it moved under the hill, a shrill whistle echoed on the night air, and half the people of Chicopee who were awake said to each other, "The train is stopping. Somebody has come from New York." It was not often that the New York express stopped at Chicopee, and when it did, it was made a matter of comment. To-night, however, it was too dark, and stormy, and late for anyone to see who had come; and guessing it was some of the Lewises, who now lived in Col. Markham's old house, the people, one by one, went to their beds, until nearly every light in Chicopee was extinguished save the one shining out into the darkness from the room where Aunt Barbara sat, with thoughts of Ethie in her heart. And up the steep hill, from the station, through the snow, a girlish figure toiled--the white, thin face looking wistfully down the maple-lined street when the corner by the common was turned, and the pallid lips whispering softly, "I wonder if she will know me?"

There were flecks of snow upon the face and on the smooth brown hair and travel-soiled dress; clogs of snow, too, upon the tired feet--the little feet Andy had admired so much; but the traveler kept on bravely, till the friendly light shone out beneath the maples, and then she paused, and leaning for a moment against the fence, sobbed aloud, but not sadly or bitterly. She was too near home for that--too near the darling Aunt Barbara, who did not hear gate or door unclose, or the step in the dark hall. But when the knob of the sitting room door moved, she heard it, and, without turning her head, called out, "What is it, Betty? I thought you in bed an hour ago."

The supposed Betty did not reply, but stood a brief instant taking in every feature in the room, from the two apples roasting on the hearth to the little woman sitting with her fingers on the page where possibly Ethie's death ought to be recorded. Aunt Barbara was waiting for Betty to answer, and she turned her head at last, just as a low, rapid step glided across the floor, and a voice, which thrilled every vain, first with a sudden fear, and then with a joy unspeakable, said, "Aunt Barbara, it's I. It's Ethie, come back to you again. Is she welcome here?"

Was she welcome? Answer, the low cry, and gasping sob, and outstretched arms, which held the wanderer in so loving an embrace, while a rain of tears fell upon the dear head from which the bonnet had fallen back as Ethelyn sank upon her knees before Aunt Barbara. Neither could talk much for a few moments. Certainly not Aunt Barbara, who sat bewildered and stupefied while Ethelyn, more composed, removed her hat, and cloak, and overshoes, and shook out the folds of her damp dress; and then drawing a little covered stool to Aunt Barbara's side, sat down upon it, and leaning her elbows on Aunt Barbara's lap, looked up in her face, with the old, mischievous, winning smile, and said, "Auntie, have you forgiven your Ethie for running away?"

Then it began to seem real again--began to seem as if the last six years were blotted out, and things restored to what they were when Ethie was wont to sit at her aunt's feet as she was sitting now. There was this difference, however; the bright, round, rosy face, which used to look so flushed, and eager, and radiant, and assured, was changed, and the one confronting Aunt Barbara now was pale, and thin, and worn, and there were lines across the brow, and the eyes were heavy and tired, and a little uncertain and anxious in their expression as they scanned the sweet old face above them. Aunt Barbara saw it all, and this, if nothing else, would have brought entire pardon even had she been inclined to withhold it, which she was not. Ethie was back again, and that was enough for her. She would not chide or blame her ever so little, and her warm, loving hands took the thin white face and held it while she kissed the parted lips, the blue-veined forehead, and the hollow cheeks, whispering: "My own darling. I am so glad to have you back. I have been so sad without you, and mourned for you so much, fearing you were dead. Where has my darling been that none of us could find you?"

"Did you hunt, Aunt Barbara? Did you really hunt for me?"

And something of Ethie's old self leaped into her eyes and flushed into her cheeks as she asked the question.

"Yes, darling. All the spring and all the summer long, and on into the fall, and then I gave it up."

"Were you alone, auntie? That is, did nobody help you hunt?" was Ethelyn's next query; and Richard would have read much hope for him in the eagerness of the eyes, which waited for Aunt Barbara's answer, and which dropped so shyly upon the carpet when Aunt Barbara said, "Alone, child? No; he did all he could--Richard did--but we could get no clew."

Ethelyn could not tell her story until she had been made easy on several important points, and smoothing the folds of Aunt Barbara's dress, and still looking beseechingly into her face, she said, "and Richard hunted, too. Was he sorry, auntie? Did he care because I went away?"

"Care? Of course he did. It almost broke his heart, and wasted him to a skeleton. You did wrong, Ethie, to go and stay so long. Richard did not deserve it."

It was the first word of censure Aunt Barbara had uttered, and Ethelyn felt it keenly, as was evinced by her quivering lip and trembling voice, as she said: "Don't auntie, don't you scold me, please. I can bear it better from anyone else. I want you to stand by me. I know I was hasty and did very wrong. I've said so a thousand times; but I was so unhappy and wretched at first, and at the last he made me so angry with his unjust accusations."

"Yes; he told me all, and showed me the letter you left. I know the whole," Aunt Barbara said, while Ethelyn continued:

"Where is he now? How long since you heard from him?"

"It is two years or more. He wrote the last letter. I'm a bad correspondent, you know, and as I had no good news to write, I did not think it worth while to bother him. I don't know where he is since he quit being governor."

There was a sudden lifting of Ethie's head, a quick arching of her eyebrows, which told that the governor part was news to her. Then she asked, quietly, "Has he been governor?"

"Yes, Governor of Iowa; and James' wife lived with him. She was Melinda Jones."

"Yes, yes," and Ethie's foot beat the carpet thoughtfully, while her eyes were cast-down, and the great tears gathered slowly in the long-fringed lids, then they fell in perfect showers, and laying her head in Aunt Barbara's lap she sobbed piteously.

Perhaps she was thinking of all she had thrown away, and weeping that another had taken the post she would have been so proud to fill. Aunt Barbara did not know, and she kept smoothing the bowed head until it was lifted up again, and the tears were dried in Ethie's eyes, where there was not the same hopeful expression there had been at first when she heard of Richard's hunting for her. Some doubt or fear had crossed her mind, and her hands were folded together in a hopeless kind of way as, at Aunt Barbara's urgent request, she began the story of her wanderings.

CHAPTER XXX: ETHIE'S STORY

"You say you read my letter, auntie; and if you did, you know nearly all that made me go away. I do not remember now just what was in it, but I know it was very concise, and plain, and literal; for I was angry when I wrote it, and would not spare Richard a bit. But, oh! I had been so tired and so wretched. You can't guess half how wretched I was at the farmhouse first, where they were all so different, and where one of the greatest terrors was lest I should get used to it and so be more like them. I mean Richard's mother, auntie. I liked the others--they were kind and good; especially Andy. Oh, Andy! dear old Andy! I have thought of him so much during the last five years, and bad as I am I have prayed every night that he would not forget me.

"Aunt Barbara, I did not love Richard, and that was my great mistake. I ought not to have married him, but I was so sore and unhappy then that any change was a relief. I do not see now how I ever could have loved Frank; but I did, or thought I did, and was constantly contrasting Richard with him and making myself more miserable. If I had loved Richard things would have been so much easier to bear. I was beginning to love him, and life was so much pleasanter, when he got so angry about Frank and charged me with those dreadful things, driving me frantic and making me feel as if I hated him and could do much to worry him. Don't look so shocked. I know how wicked it was, and sometimes I fear God never can forgive me; but I did not think of him then. I forgot everything but myself and my trouble, and so I went away, going first to ----, so as to mislead Richard, and then turning straight back to New York.

"Do you remember Abby Jackson, who was at school in Boston, and who once spent a week with me here? She married, and lives in New York, and believes in women's rights and wears the Bloomer dress. She would take my part, I said, and I went at once to her house and told her all I had done, and asked if I could stay until I found employment. Aunt Barbara, this is a queer world, and there are queer people in it. I thought I was sure of Abby, she used to protest so strongly against the tyranny of men, and say she should like nothing better than protecting females who were asserting their own rights. I was asserting mine, and I went to her for sympathy. She was glad to see me at first, and petted and fondled me just as she used to do at school. She was five years older than I, and so I looked up to her. But when I told my story her manner changed, and it really seemed as if she looked upon me as a suspicious person who had done something terrible. She advocated women's rights as strongly as ever, but could not advise me to continue in my present course. It would bring odium upon me, sure. A woman separated from her husband was always pointed at, no matter what cause she had for the separation. It was all wrong, she urged, that public opinion should be thus, and ere long she trusted there would be a change. Till then I would do well to return to Iowa and make it up with Richard. That was what she said, and it made me very angry, so that I was resolved to leave her the next day; but I was sick in the morning, and sick some weeks following, so that I could not leave her house.

"She nursed me carefully and tried to be kind, but I could see that my being there was a great annoyance to her. Her husband had an aunt--a rich, eccentric old lady--who came sometimes to see me, and seemed interested in me. Forgive me, auntie, if it was wrong. I dropped the name of

Markham and took yours, asking Abby to call me simply Miss Bigelow to her friends. Her husband knew my real name, but to all others I was Adelaide Bigelow. Old Mrs. Plum did not know I was married, for Abby was as anxious to keep the secret as I was myself. She was going abroad, the rich aunt, and being a nervous invalid, she wanted some young, handy person as traveling companion. So when I was better Abby asked if I was still resolved not to go home, and on learning that I was, she spoke of Mrs. Plum, and asked if I would go. I caught at it eagerly, and in May I was sailing over the sea to France. I wrote a few lines to Andy before I went, and I wanted to write to you, but I fancied you must be vexed and mortified, and I would not trouble you.

"Mrs. Plum was very nervous, and capricious, and exacting, and my life with her was not altogether an easy one. At first, before we were accustomed to each other, it was terrible. I suppose I have a high temper. She thought so, and yet she could not do without me, for she was lame in her arms, and unable to help herself readily; besides that, I spoke the French language well enough to make myself understood, and so was necessary to her. There were many excellent traits of character about her, and after a time I liked her very much, while she seemed to think of me as a willful but rather 'nicish' kind of a daughter. She took me everywhere, even into Russia and Palestine; but the last two years of our stay abroad were spent in Southern France, where the days were one long bright summer dream, and I should have been so happy if the past had been forgotten."

"And did you hear nothing from us in all that time?" Aunt Barbara asked, and Ethelyn replied: "Nothing from Richard, no; and nothing direct from you. I requested as a favor that Mrs. Plum should order the Boston Traveller and Springfield Republican to be sent to her address in Paris, which we made our headquarters. I knew you took both these papers, and if anything happened to you, it would appear in their columns. I saw the death of Col. Markham, and after that I used to grow so faint and cold, for fear I might find yours. I came across a New York paper, too, and saw that Aunt Van Buren had arrived at the Fifth Avenue Hotel, knowing then that she was just as gay as ever. Richard's name I never saw; neither did Abby know anything about him.. I called at her house yesterday. She has seven children now--five born since I went away--and her women's rights have given place to theories with regard to soothing syrups and baby-jumpers, and the best means of keeping one child quiet while she dresses the other. Mrs. Plum died six weeks ago--died in Paris; and, auntie, I was kind to her in her last sickness, bearing everything, and finding my reward in her deep gratitude, expressed not only in words, but in a most tangible form. She made her will, and left me ten thousand dollars. So you see I am not poor nor dependent. I told her my story, too--told her the whole as it was; and she made me promise to come back, to you at least, if not to Richard. Going to him would depend upon whether he wanted me, I said. Do you think he has forgotten me?"

Again the eager, anxious expression crept into Ethie's eyes, which grew very soft, and even dewy, as Aunt Barbara replied, "Forgotten you? No. I never saw a man feel as he did when he first came here, and Sophia talked to him so, as he sat there in that very willow chair."

Involuntarily Ethie's hand rested itself on the chair where Richard had sat, and Ethie's face crimsoned where Aunt Barbara asked:

"Do you love Richard now?"

"I cannot tell. I only know that I have dreamed of him so many, many times, and thought it would be such perfect rest to put my tired head in his lap, as I never did put it. When I was on the ocean, coming home, there was a fearful storm, and I prayed so earnestly to live till I could hear him say that he forgave me for all the trouble I have caused him. I might not love him if I were to see him again just as he used to be. Sometimes I think I should not, but I would try. Write to him, auntie, please, and tell him I am here, but nothing more. Don't say I want to see him, or that I am changed from the willful, high-tempered Ethie who made him so unhappy, for perhaps I am not."

A while then they talked of Aunt Van Buren, and Frank, and Nettie, and Susie Granger, who was married to a missionary and gone to heathen lands; and the clock was striking one before Aunt Barbara lighted her darling up to the old room, and kissing her good-night, went back to weep glad tears of joy in the rocking-chair by the hearth, and to thank her Heavenly Father for sending home her long lost Ethelyn.

CHAPTER XXXI: MRS. DR. VAN BUREN

She was always tossing up just when she was not wanted, Ethie used to say in the olden days, when she saw the great lady alighting at the gate in time to interfere with and spoil some favorite project arranged for the day, and she certainly felt it, if she did not say it, when, on the morning following her arrival in Chicopee she heard Betty exclaim, "If there ain't Miss Van Buren! I wonder what sent her here!"

Ethie wondered so, too, and drawing the blanket closer around her shoulders (for she had taken advantage of her fatigue and languor to lie very late in bed) she wished her aunt had stayed in Boston, for a little time at least.

It had been very delightful, waking up in the dear old room and seeing Betty's kind face bending over her--Betty, who had heard of her young mistress' return with a gush of glad tears, and then at once bethought herself as to what there was nice for the wanderer to eat. Just as she used to do when Ethie was a young lady at home, Betty had carried her pan of coals and kindlings into the chamber where Ethie was lying, and kneeling on the hearth had made the cheerfulest of fires, while Ethie, with half-closed eyes, watched her dreamily, thinking how nice it was to be cared for again, and conscious only of a vague feeling of delicious rest and quiet, which grew almost into positive happiness as she counted the days it would take for Aunt Barbara's letter to go to Iowa and for Richard to answer it in person, as he surely would if all which Aunt Barbara had said was true.

Ethie did not quite know if she loved him. She had thought of him so much during the last two years, and now, when he seemed so near, she longed to see him again--to hear his voice and look into his eyes. They were handsome eyes as she remembered them; kindly and pleasant, too--at least they had been so to her, save on that dreadful night, the memory of which always made her shiver and grow faint. It seemed a dream now--a far-off, unhappy dream--which she would fain forget just as she wanted Richard to forget her foibles and give her another chance. She had bidden Aunt Barbara write to say she was there, and so after the tempting breakfast, which had been served in her room, and which she had eaten sitting up in bed, because Betty insisted that it should be so--and she was glad to be petted and humored and made into a comfortable invalid-- Aunt Barbara brought her writing materials into the room, and bidding Ethie lie still and rest herself, began the letter to Richard.

But only the date and name were written, when Betty, coming in with a few geranium leaves and a white fuchsia which she had purloined from her mistress' house plants, announced Mrs. Van Buren's arrival, and the pleasant morning was at an end. Mrs. Dr. Van Buren had come up from Boston to borrow money from her sister for the liquidation of certain debts contracted by her son, and which she had not the ready means to meet. Aunt Barbara had accommodated her once or twice before, saying to her as she signed the check, "That money in the bank was put there for Ethie, but no one knows if she will ever need it, so it may as well do somebody some good."

It had done good by relieving Mrs. Van Buren of a load of harassing care, for money was not as plenty with her as formerly, and now she wanted more. She was looking rather old and worn, and her cloak was last year's fashion, but good enough for Chicopee, she reflected, as she hurried into the house and stamped the muddy, melting snow from her feet.

Utter amazement seemed the prevailing sensation in her mind when she learned that Ethelyn had returned, and then her selfishness began to suggest that possibly Barbara's funds, saved for Ethie, might not now be as accessible for Frank. She was glad, though, to see her niece, but professed herself shocked at her altered appearance.

"Upon my word, I would not have recognized you," she said, sitting down upon the bed and looking Ethie fully in the face.

Aunt Barbara, thinking her sister might like to have Ethie alone for a little, had purposely left the room, and so Mrs. Van Buren was free to say what she pleased. She had felt a good deal of irritation toward Ethie for some time past. In fact, ever since Richard became governor, she had blamed her niece for running away from the honor which might have been hers. As aunt to the governor's lady, she, too, would have come in for a share of the éclat; and so, as she smoothed out the folds of her stone-colored merino, she felt as if she had been sorely aggrieved by that thin, white-faced woman, who really did not greatly resemble the rosy, bright-faced Ethelyn to whom Frank Van Buren had once talked love among the Chicopee hills.

"No, I don't believe I should have known you," Mrs. Van Buren continued. "What have you been about to fade you so?"

Few women like to hear that they have faded, even if they know it to be true, and Ethie's cheek flushed a little as she asked, with a smile, "Am I really such a fright?"

"Why, no, not a fright! No one with the Bigelow features can ever be that. But you are changed; and so I am sure Richard would think. He liked beautiful girls. You know he has been governor?"

Ethie nodded, and Mrs. Van Buren continued: "You lost a great deal, Ethelyn, when you went away; and I must say that, though, of course, you had great provocation, you did a very foolish thing leaving your husband as you did, and involving us all, to a certain extent, in disgrace."

It was the first direct intimation Ethie had received that her family had suffered from mortification on her account. She had felt that they must, and knew that she deserved some censure; but as kind Aunt Barbara had withheld it, she was not quite willing to hear it from Mrs. Van Buren, and for an instant her eyes flashed, and a hot reply trembled on her lips; but she restrained herself and merely said: "I am sorry if I disgraced you, Aunt Sophia. I was very unhappy at the time,"

"Certainly; I understand that, but the world does not; and if it did, it forgot all when your husband became governor. He was greatly honored and esteemed, I hear from a friend who spent a few weeks at Des Moines, and everybody was so sorry for him."

"Did they talk of me?" Ethie asked, repenting the next minute that she had been at all curious in the matter.

Mrs. Van Buren, bent upon annoying her, replied, "Some, yes; and knowing the governor as they did, it is natural they should blame you more than him. There was a rumor of his getting a divorce, but my friends did not believe it and neither do I, though divorces are easy to get out West. Have you written to him? Are you not 'most afraid he will think you came back because he has been governor?"

"Aunt Sophia!" and Ethie looked very much like her former self, as she started from her pillow and confronted her interlocutor. "He cannot think so. I never knew he had been governor until I heard it from Aunt Barbara last night. I came back for no honors, no object. My work was taken from me; I had nothing more to do, and I was so tired, and sick, and weary, and longed so much for home. Don't begrudge it to me, Aunt Sophia, that I came to see Aunt Barbara once more. I won't stay long in anybody's way; and if--if he likes, Richard--can--get--that--divorce--as soon as he pleases."

The last came gaspingly, and showed the real state of Ethie's feelings. In all the five long years of her absence the possibility that Richard would seek to separate himself from her had never crossed her mind. She had looked upon his love for her as something too strong to be shaken--as the great rock in whose shadow she could rest whenever she so desired. At first, when the tide of angry passion was raging at her heart, she had said she never should desire it, that her strength was sufficient to stand alone against the world; but as the weary weeks and months crept on, and her anger had had time to cool, and she had learned better to know the meaning of "standing alone in the world," and thoughts of Richard's many acts of love and kindness kept recurring to her mind, she had come gradually to see that the one object in the future to which she was looking forward was a return to Aunt Barbara and a possible reconciliation with her husband. The first she had achieved, and the second seemed so close within her grasp, a thing so easy of success, that in her secret heart she had exulted that, after all, she was not to be more sorely punished than she had been--that she could not have been so very much in fault, or Providence would have placed greater obstacles in the way of restoration to all that now seemed desirable. But Ethie's path back to peace and quiet was not to be free from thorns, and for a few minutes she writhed in pain, as she thought how possible, and even probable, it was that Richard should seek to be free from one who had troubled him so much. Life looked very dreary to Ethelyn that moment--drearier than it ever had before--but she was far too proud to betray her real feelings to her aunt, who, touched by the look of anguish on her niece's face, began to change her tactics, and say how glad she was to have her darling back under any circumstances, and so she presumed Richard would be. She knew he would, in fact; and if she were Ethie, she should write to him at once, apprising him of her return, but not making too many concessions.--Men could not bear them, and it was better always to hold a stiff rein, or there was danger of a collision. She might as well have talked to the winds, for all that Ethie heard or cared. She was thinking of Richard, and the possibility that she might not be welcome to him now. If so, nothing could tempt her to intrude herself upon him. At all events, she would not make the first advances. She would let Richard find out that she was there through some other source than Aunt Barbara, who should not now write the letter. It would look too much like begging him to take her back. This was Ethie's decision, from which she could not be moved; and when, next day, Mrs. Van Buren went back to Boston with the check for $1,000 which Aunt Barbara had given her, she was pledged not to communicate with Richard Markham in any way, while Aunt Barbara was held to the same promise.

"He will find it out somehow. I prefer that he should act unbiased by anything we can do," Ethelyn said to Aunt Barbara. "He might feel obliged to come if you wrote to him that I was here, and if he came, the sight of me so changed might shock him as it did Aunt Van Buren. She verily thought me a fright," and Ethie tried to smile as she recalled her Aunt Sophia's evident surprise at her looks.

The change troubled Ethie more than she cared to confess. Nor did the villagers' remarks, when they came in to see her, tend to soothe her ruffled feelings. Pale, and thin, and languid, she moved about the house and yard like a mere shadow of her former self, having, or seeming to have, no object in life, and worrying Aunt Barbara so greatly that the good woman began at last seriously to inquire what was best to do. Suddenly, like an inspiration, there came to her a thought of Clifton, the famous water-cure in Western New York, where health, both of body and soul, had been found by so many thousands. And Ethie caught eagerly at the proposition, accepting it on one condition--she would not go there as Mrs. Markham, where the name might be recognized. She had been Miss Bigelow abroad, she would be Miss Bigelow again; and so Aunt Barbara yielded, mentally asking pardon for the deception to which she felt she was a party, and when, two weeks after, the clerk at Clifton water-cure looked over his list to see what rooms were engaged, and to whom, he found "Miss Adelaide Bigelow, of Massachusetts," put down for No. 101, while "Governor Markham of Iowa," was down for No. 102.

CHAPTER XXXII: CLIFTON

They were very full at Clifton that summer, for the new building was not completed, and every available point was taken, from narrow, contracted No. 94 in the upper hall down to more spacious No. 8 on the lower floor, where the dampness, and noise, and mold, and smell of coal and cooking, and lower bathrooms were. "A very, very quiet place, with only a few invalids too weak and languid, and too much absorbed in themselves and their 'complaints' to note or care for their neighbors; a place where one lives almost as much excluded from the world as if immured within convent walls; a place where dress and fashion and distinction were unknown, save as something existing afar off, where the turmoil and excitement of life were going on." This was Ethelyn's idea of Clifton; and when, at four o'clock, on a bright June afternoon, the heavily laden train stopped before the little brown station, and "Clifton" was shouted in her ears, she looked out with a bewildered kind of feeling upon the crowd of gayly dressed people congregated upon the platform. Heads were uncovered, and hair frizzled, and curled, and braided, and puffed, and arranged in every conceivable shape, showing that even to that "quiet town" the hairdresser's craft had penetrated. Expanded crinoline, with light, fleecy robes, and ribbons, and laces, and flowers, was there assembled, with bright, eager, healthful faces, and snowy hands wafting kisses to some departed friend, and then turning to greet some new arrival. There were no traces of sickness, no token of disease among the smiling crowd, and Ethelyn almost feared she had made a mistake and alighted at the wrong place, as she gave her checks to John, and then taking her seat in the omnibus, sat waiting and listening to the lively sallies and playful remarks around her. Nobody spoke to her, nobody stared at her, nobody seemed to think of her; and for that she was thankful, as she sat with her veil drawn closely over her face, looking out upon the not very pretentious dwellings they were passing. The scenery around Clifton is charming, and to the worn, weary invalid escaping from the noise and heat and bustle of the busy city, there seems to come a rest and a quiet, from the sunlight which falls upon the hills, to the cool, moist meadow lands where the ferns and mosses grow, and where the rippling of the sulphur brook gives out constantly a soothing, pleasant kind of music. But for the architecture of the town not very much can be said; and Ethie, who had longed to get away from Chicopee, where everybody knew her story, and all looked curiously at her, confessed to a feeling of homesickness as her eyes fell upon the blacksmith shop, the dressmaker's sign, the grocery on the corner, where were sold various articles of food forbidden by doctor and nurse; the schoolhouse to the right, where a group of noisy children played, and the little church further on, where the Methodist people worshiped. She did not see the "Cottage" then, with its flowers and vines, and nicely shaven lawn, for her back was to it; nor the handsome grounds, where the shadows from the tall trees fall so softly upon the velvet grass; and the winding graveled walks, which intersect each other and give an impression of greater space than a closer investigation will warrant.

"I can't stay here," was Ethie's thought, as it had been the thought of many others, when, like her, they first step into the matted hall and meet the wet, damp odor, as of sheets just washed, which seems to be inseparable from that part of the building.

But that was the first day, and before she had met the kindness and sympathy of those whose business it is to care for the patients, or felt the influences for good, the tendency to all the better impulses of our nature, which seems to pervade the very atmosphere of Clifton. Ethie felt this influence very soon, and her second letter to Aunt Barbara was filled with praise of Clifton, where she had made so many friends, in spite of her evident desire to avoid society and stay by herself. She had passed through the usual ordeal attending the advent of every new face, especially if that face be a little out of the common order of faces. She had been inspected in the dining room, and bathroom, and chapel, both when she went in and when she went out. She had been talked up and criticised from the way she wore her hair to the hang of her skirts, which here, as well as in Olney, trailed the floor with a sweep unmistakably aristocratic and stamped her as somebody. The sacque and hat brought from Paris had been copied by three or four, and pronounced distingué, but ugly by as many more, while Mrs. Peter Pry, of whom there are always one or two at every watering-place, had set herself industriously at work to pry into her antecedents to find out just who and what Miss Bigelow was. As the result of this research, it had been ascertained that the young lady was remotely connected with the Bigelows of Boston, and had something of her own--that she had spent several years abroad, and could speak both French and German with perfect ease; that she had been at the top of Mont Blanc, and passed part of a winter at St. Petersburg, and seen a crocodile in the river Nile, and a Moslem burying-ground in Constantinople, and had the cholera at Milan, the varioloid at Rome, and was marked between the eyes and on the chin, and was twenty-five years old, and did not wear false hair, nor use Laird's Liquid Pearl, as was at first suspected from the clearness of her complexion, and did wear crimping pins at night, and pay Annie, the bath-girl, extra for bringing up the morning bath, and was more interested in the chapel exercises when the great Head Center was there, and bought cream every morning of Mrs. King, and sat up at night long after the gas was turned off, and was there at Clifton for spine in the back and head difficulties generally. These few items, together with the surmise that she had had some great trouble--a disappointment, most likely, which affected her health--were all Mrs. Pry could learn, and she detailed them to anyone who would listen, until Ethelyn's history, from the Pry point of view, was pretty generally known and the most made of every good quality and virtue.

The Mrs. Pry of this summer was not ill-natured; she was simply curious; and as she generally said more good than evil of people, she was generally liked and tolerated by all. She was not a fashionable woman, nor an educated woman, though very popular with her neighbors at home, and she was there for numbness and swollen knees; and, having knit socks for four years for the soldiers, she now knit stockings for the soldiers' orphans, and took a dash every morning and screamed loud enough to be heard at the depot when she took it, and had a pack every afternoon, and corked her right ear with cotton, which she always took out when in a pack, so as to hear whatever might be said in the hall, her open ventilator being the medium of sound. This was Mrs. Peter Pry, drawn from no one in particular, but a fair exponent of characters found in other places than Clifton Springs. Rooming on the same floor with Ethelyn, whom she greatly admired, the good woman persisted until she overcame the stranger's shyness, and succeeded in establishing, first, a bowing, then a speaking, and finally, a calling acquaintance between them-- the calls, however, being mostly upon one side, and that the prying one.

Ethie had been at Clifton for three or four weeks, and the dimensions of No. 101 did not seem half so circumscribed, as at first. On the whole, she was contented, especially after the man who snored, and the woman who wore squeaky boots, and talked in her sleep, vacated No. 102, the large, airy, pleasant room adjoining her own. There was no one in it now but Mary, the chambermaid, who said it was soon to be occupied by a sick gentleman, adding that she believed he had the consumption, and hoped his cough would not fret Miss Bigelow. Ethie hoped so too. Nervousness, and, indeed, diseases of all kinds, seemed to develop rapidly at Clifton, where one has nothing to do but to watch each new symptom, and report to physician or nurse, and Ethie was not an exception. She was very nervous, and she found herself dreading the arrival of the sick man, wondering if his coughing would keep her awake nights, and if the light from her candle shining out into the darkened hall would annoy and worry him, as it had worried the woman opposite, who complained that she could not rest with that glimmer on the wall, showing that somebody was up, who, might at any moment make a noise. That he was a person of consequence she readily guessed, for an extra pair of pillows was taken in, and the rocking-chair possessed of two whole arms, and No. 109, also vacant just then, was rifled of its round stand and footstool, and Mrs. Pry reported that Dr. F---- himself had been up to see that all was comfortable, and Miss Clark had ordered a better set of springs, with a new hair mattress, and somebody had put a bouquet of flowers in the room and hung a muslin curtain at the window.

"A big-bug, most likely," Mrs. Peter Pry said, when, after her pack, she brought her knitting for a few moments into Ethelyn's room and wondered who the man could be.

Ethelyn did not care particularly who he was, provided he did not cough nights and keep her awake, in which case she should feel constrained to change her room, an alternative she did not care to contemplate, as she had become more attached to No. 101 than she had at first supposed possible. Ethelyn was very anxious that day, and, had she believed in presentiments, she would have thought that something was about to befall her, so heavy was the gloom weighing upon her spirits, and so dark the future seemed. She was going to have a headache, she feared, and as a means of throwing it off, she started, after ten, for a walk to Rocky Run, a distance of a mile or more. It was a cool, hazy July afternoon, such as always carried Ethie back to Chicopee and the days of her happy girlhood, when her heart was not so heavy and sad as it was now. With thoughts of Chicopee came also thoughts of Richard, and Ethie's eyes were moist with tears as she looked wistfully toward the setting sun and wondered if he ever thought of her now or had forgotten her, and was the story true of his seeking for a divorce. That rumor had troubled Ethie greatly, and was the reason why she did not improve as the physician hoped she would when she first came to Clifton. Sitting down upon the bridge across the creek, she bowed her head in her hands and went over again all the dreadful past, blaming herself now more than she did Richard, and wishing that much could be undone of all that had transpired to make her what she was, and while she sat there the Western train appeared in view, and, mechanically rising to her feet, Ethie turned her steps back toward the Cure, standing aside to let the long train go by, and feeling, when it passed her, a strange, sudden throb, as if it were fraught with more than ordinary interest to her. Usually, that Western train, the distant roll of whose wheels and the echo of whose scream quickened so many hearts waiting for news from home, had no special interest for her. It never brought her a letter. Her name was never called in the exciting distribution which took place in the parlor or on the long piazza after the eight-o'clock mail had arrived, and so she seldom heeded it; but to-night there was a difference, and she watched the long line curiously until it passed the corner by the old brown farmhouse and disappeared from view. It had left the station long ere she reached the Cure, for she had walked slowly, and lights were shining from the different rooms, and there was a sound of singing in the parlor, and the party of croquet players had come up from the lawn, and ladies were hurrying toward the bathroom, when she came in and climbed the three flights of stairs which led to the fourth floor. There was a light shining through the ventilator of No. 102, the door was partly ajar, and the doctor was there, asking some questions of the tall figure, whose outline Ethelyn dimly descried as she went into her room. There was more talking after a little--more going in and out, while Mary Ann brought up some supper on a tray, and John brought up a traveling trunk much larger than himself, and then, without Mrs. Pry's assurance, Ethie knew that the occupant of No. 102 had arrived.

CHAPTER XXXIII: THE OCCUPANT OF NO. 102

He did not cough, but he seemed to be a restless spirit, for Ethie heard him pacing up and down his room long after the gas was turned off and her own candle was extinguished. Once, too, she heard a long-drawn sigh, or groan, which made her start suddenly, for something in the tone carried her to Olney and the house on the prairie. It was late that night ere she slept, and when next morning she awoke, the nervous headache, which had threatened her the previous night, was upon her in full force, and kept her for nearly the entire day confined to her bed. Mrs. Pry was spending the day in Phelps, and with this source of information cut off, Ethelyn heard nothing of No. 102, further than the chambermaid's casual remark that "the gentleman was quite an invalid, and for the present was to take his meals and baths in his room to avoid so much going up and down stairs."

Who he was Ethelyn did not know or care, though twice she awoke from a feverish sleep with the impression that she had heard Richard speaking to her; but it was only Jim, the bath man, talking in the next room, and she laid her throbbing head again upon her pillow, while her new neighbor dreamed in turn of her and woke with the strange fancy that she was near him. Ethie's head was better that night; so much better that she dressed herself and went down to the parlor in time to hear the calling of the letters as the Western mail was distributed. Usually she felt but little interest in the affair further than watching the eager, anxious faces bending near the boy, and the looks of joy or disappointment which followed failure and success. To-night, however, it was different. She was not expecting a letter herself. Nobody wrote to her but Aunt Barbara, whose letters came in the morning, but she was conscious of a strange feeling of expectancy, and taking a step toward the table around which the excited group were congregated, she stood leaning against the column while name after name was called. First the letters, a score or two, and then the papers, matters of less account, but still snatched eagerly by those who could get nothing better. There was a paper for Mrs. More-house, and Mrs. Stone, and Mrs. Wilson, and Mrs. Turner, while Mr. Danforth had half a dozen or less, and then Perry paused a moment over a new name--one which had never before been called in the parlor at Clifton:

"Richard Markham, Esq."

The name rang out loud and clear, and Ethie grasped the pillar tightly to keep herself from falling. She did not hear Mr. Danforth explaining that it was "Governor Markham from Iowa, who came the night before." She did not know, either, how she left the parlor, for the next thing of which she was perfectly conscious was the fact that she was hurrying up the stairs and through the unfinished halls toward her own room, casting frightened glances around, and almost shrieking with excitement when through the open door of No. 102 she heard Dr. Hayes speaking to someone, and in the voice which answered recognized her husband.

He was there, then, next to her, separated by only a thin partition--the husband whom she had not seen for five long years, whom she had voluntarily left, resolving never to go back to him again, was there, where, just by crossing a single threshold, she could fall at his feet and sue for the forgiveness she had made up her mind to crave should she ever see him again. Dr. Hayes' next call was upon her, and he found her fainting upon the floor, where she had fallen in the excitement of the shock she had experienced.

"It was a headache," she said, when questioned as to the cause of the sudden attack; but her eyes had in them a frightened, startled look, for which the doctor could not account.

There was something about her case which puzzled and perplexed him. "She needed perfect quiet, but must not be left alone," he said, and so all that night Richard, who was very wakeful, watched the light shining out into the hall from the room next to his own, and heard occasionally a murmur of low voices as the nurse put some question to Ethie, who answered always in whispers, while her eyes turned furtively toward No. 102, as if fearful that its occupant would hear and know how near she was. For three whole days her door was locked against all intruders, for the headache and nervous excitement did not abate one whit. How could they, when every sound from No. 102, every footfall on the floor, every tone of Richard's voice speaking to servant or physician, quickened the rapid beats and sent the hot blood throbbing fiercely through the temple veins and down along the neck? At Clifton they are accustomed to every phase of nervousness, from spasms at the creaking of a board to the stumbling upstairs of the fireman in the early winter morning, and once when Ethie shuddered and turned her head aside at the sound of Richard's step, the attendant said to the physician:

"It's the gentleman's boots, I think, which make her nervous."

There was a deprecating gesture on Ethie's part, but it passed unnoticed, and when next the doctor went to visit Richard he said, in a half-apologetic way, that the young lady in the next room was suffering from a violent headache, which was aggravated by every sound, even the squeak of a boot--would Governor Markham greatly object to wearing slippers for a while? Dr. Hayes was sorry to trouble him, but "if they would effect a cure they must keep their patients quiet, and guard against everything tending to increase nervous irritation."

Governor Markham would do anything in his power for the young lady, and he asked some questions concerning her. Had he annoyed her much? Was she very ill? And what was her name?

"Bigelow," he repeated after Dr. Hayes, thinking of Aunt Barbara in Chicopee, and thinking of Ethelyn, too, but never dreaming how near she was to him.

He had come to Clifton at the earnest solicitation of some of his friends, who had for themselves tested the healing properties of the water, but he had little faith that anything could cure so long as the pain was so heavy at his heart. It had not lessened one jot with the lapse of years. On the contrary, it seemed harder and harder to bear, as the months went by and brought no news of Ethie. Oh, how he wanted her back again, even if she came as willful and imperious as she used to be at times, when the high spirit was roused to its utmost, and even if she had no love for him, as she had once averred. He could make her love him now, he said: he knew just where he had erred; and many a time in dreams he had strained the wayward Ethie to his bosom in the fond caress which from its very force should impart to her some faint sensation of joy. He had stroked her beautiful brown hair, and caressed her smooth round cheek, and pressed her little hands, and made her listen to him till the dark eyes flashed into his own with something of the tenderness he felt for her. Then, with a start, he had awakened to find it all a dream, and only darkness around him. Ethie was not there. The arms which had held her so lovingly were empty. The pillow where her dear head had lain was untouched, and he was alone as of old. Even that handsome house he had built for her had ceased to interest him, for Ethie did not come back to enjoy it. She would never come now, he said, and he built many fancies as to what her end had been, and where her grave could be. Here at Clifton he had thought of her continually, but not that she was alive. Andy's faith in her return was as strong as ever, but Richard's had all died out. Ethie was dead, and when asked by Dr. Hayes if he had a wife, he answered sadly:

"I had one, but I lost her."

He had no thought of deception, or how soon the story would circulate through the house that he was a widower, and so he, as ex-governor of Iowa, and a man just in his prime, became an object of speculative interest to every marriageable woman there. He had no thought, no care for the ladies, though for the Miss Bigelow, whom his boots annoyed, he did feel a passing interest, and Ethie, whose ears seemed doubly sharp, heard him in his closet adjusting the thin-soled slippers, which made no sound upon the carpet. She heard him, too, as he moved his water pitcher, and knew he was doing it so quietly for her. The idea of being cared for by him, even if he did not know who she was, was very soothing and pleasant, and she fell into a quiet sleep, which lasted several hours, while Richard, on the other side of the wall, scarcely moved, so fearful was he of worrying the young lady.

Ethie's headache spent itself at last, and she awoke at the close of the third day, free from pain, but very weak and languid, and wholly unequal to the task of entertaining Mrs. Peter Pry, who had been so distressed on her account, and was so delighted with a chance to see and talk with her again. Ethie knew she meant to be kind, and believed she was sincere in her professions of friendship. At another time she might have been glad to see her; but now, when she guessed what the theme of conversation would be, she felt a thrill of terror as the good woman came in, knitting in hand, and announced her intention of sitting through the chapel exercises. She was not going to prayer meeting that night, she said, for Dr. Foster was absent, and they were always stupid when he was away. She could not understand all Mr.---- said, his words were so learned, while the man who talked so long, and never came to the point, was insufferable in hot weather, so she remained away, and came to see her friend, who, she supposed, knew that she had a governor for next-door neighbor--Governor Markham from Iowa--and a widower, too, as Dr. Hayes had said, when she asked why his wife was not there with him.

"A widower!" and Ethie looked up so inquiringly that Mrs. Pry, mistaking the nature of her sudden interest, went on more flippantly. "Yes, and a splendid looking man, too, if he wasn't sick. I saw him in the chapel this morning--the only time he has been there--and sat where I had a good view of his face. They say he is very rich, and has one of the handsomest places in Davenport."

"Does he live in Davenport?" Ethie asked, in some surprise, and Mrs. Pry replied:

"Yes; and that Miss Owens, from New York, is setting her cap for him already. She met him in Washington, a few years ago, and the minute chapel exercises were over, she and her mother made up to him at once. I'm glad there's somebody good enough for them to notice. If there's a person I dislike it's that Susan Owens and her mother. I do hope she'll find a husband. It's what she's here for, everybody says."

Mrs. Peter had dropped a stitch while animadverting against Miss Susan Owens, from New York, and stopped a moment while she picked it up. It would be difficult to describe Ethelyn's emotions as she heard her own husband talked of as something marketable, which others than Susan Owens might covet. He was evidently the lion of the season. It was something to have a governor of Richard's reputation in the house, and the guests made the most of it, wishing he would join them in the parlor or on the piazza, and regretting that he stayed so constantly in his room. Many attempts were made to draw him out, Mrs. and Miss Owens, on the strength of their acquaintance in Washington, venturing to call upon him, and advising him to take more exercise. Miss Owens' voice was loud and clear, and Ethie heard it distinctly as the young lady talked and laughed with Richard, the hot blood coursing rapidly through her veins, and the first genuine pangs of jealousy she had ever felt creeping into her heart as she guessed what might possibly be in Miss Owens' mind. Many times she resolved to make herself known to him; but uncertainty as to how she might be received, and the remembrance of what Mrs. Van Buren had said with regard to the divorce, held her back; and so, with only a thin partition between them, and within sound of each other's footsteps, the husband and wife, so long estranged from each other, lived on, day after day, Richard spending most of his time in his room, and Ethelyn managing so adroitly when she came in and went out, that she never saw so much as his shadow upon the floor, and knew not whether he was greatly changed or not.

CHAPTER XXXIV: IN RICHARD'S ROOM

Richard had been sick for a week or more. As is frequently the case, the baths did not agree with him at first, and Mrs. Pry reported to Ethelyn that the governor was confined to his bed, and saw no one but the doctor and nurses, not even "that bold Miss Owens, who had actually sent to Geneva for a bouquet, which she sent to his room with her compliments." This Mrs. Pry knew to be a fact, and the highly scandalized woman repeated the story to Ethelyn, who scarcely heard what she was saying for the many turbulent emotions swelling at her heart. That Richard should be sick so near to her, his wife--that other hands than hers should tend his pillow and minister to his wants--seemed not as it should be; and when she recalled the love and tender care which had been so manifest that time when he came home from Washington and found her so very ill, the wish grew strong within her to do something for him. But what to do--that was the perplexing question. She dared not go openly to him, until assured that she was wanted; and so there was nothing left but to imitate Miss Owens and adorn his room with flowers. Surely she had a right to do so much, and still her cheek crimsoned like some young girl's as she gathered together the choicest flowers the little town afforded, and arranging them into a most tasteful bouquet, sent them in to Richard, vaguely hoping that at least in the cluster of double pinks, which had been Richard's favorite, there might be hidden some mesmeric power or psychological influence which should speak to the sick man of the wayward Ethie who had troubled him so much.

Richard was sitting up in bed when Mary brought the bouquet, saying, Miss Bigelow sent it, thinking it might cheer him a bit. Should she put it in the tumbler near Miss Owens'?

Miss Owens had sent a pretty vase with hers, but Ethie's was simply tied with a bit of ribbon she had worn about her neck. And Richard took it in his hand, an exclamation escaping him as he saw and smelled the fragrant pinks, whose perfume carried him first to Olney and Andy's weedy beds in the front yard, and then to Chicopee, where in Aunt Barbara's pretty garden, a large plant of them had been growing when he went after his bride. A high wind had blown them down upon the walk, and he had come upon Ethie one day trying to tie them up. He had plucked a few, he remembered, telling Ethie they were his favorites for perfume, while the red peony was his favorite for beauty. There had been a comical gleam in her brown eyes which he now knew was born of contempt for his taste with regard to flowers. Red peonies were not the rarest of blossoms--Melinda had taught him that when he suggested having them in his conservatory; but surely no one could object to these waxen, feathery pinks, whose odor was so delicious. Miss Bigelow liked them, else she had never sent them to him. And he kept the bouquet in his hand, admiring its arrangement, inhaling the sweet perfume of the delicate pinks and heliotrope, and speculating upon the kind of person Miss Bigelow must be to have thought so much of him. He could account for Miss Owens' gift--the hot-house blossoms, which had not moved him one-half so much as did this bunch of pinks. She had known him before--had met him in Washington; he had been polite to her on one or two occasions, and it was natural that she should wish to be civil, at least while he was sick. But the lady in No. 101--the Miss Bigelow for whom he had discarded his boots and trodden on tiptoe half the time since his arrival--why she should care for him he could not guess; and finally deciding that it was a part of Clifton, where everybody was so kind, he put the bouquet in the tumbler Mary had brought and placed it on the stand beside him. He was very restless that night, and Ethie heard the watchman at his door twice asking if he wanted anything.

"Nothing," was the reply, and the voice, heard distinctly in the stillness of the night, was so faint and sad that Ethie hid her face in her pillow and sobbed bitterly, while the intense longing to see him grew so strong within her that by morning the resolution was taken to risk everything for the sake of looking upon him again.

He did not require an attendant at night--he preferred being alone, she had ascertained; and she knew that his door was constantly left open for the admission of fresh air. The watchman only came into the hall once an hour or thereabouts, and while Richard slept it would be comparatively easy for her to steal into his room. Fortune seemed to favor her, for when at nine the doctor, as usual, came up to pay his round visits, she heard him say, "I will leave you something which never fails to make one sleep," and after two hours had passed she knew by the regular breathing which, standing on the threshold of her room, she could distinctly hear, that Richard was sleeping soundly. The watchman had just made the tour of that hall, and the faint glimmer of his lantern was disappearing down the stairs. It would be an hour before he came back again, and now, if ever, was her time. There was a great throb of fear at her heart, a trembling of every joint, a choking sensation in her throat, a shrinking back from what might probably be the result of that midnight visit; and then, nerving herself for the effort, she stepped out into the hall and listened. Everything was quiet, and every room was darkened, save by the moon, which, at its full, was pouring a flood of light through the southern window at the end of the hall and seemed to beckon her on. She was standing now at Richard's door, opened wide enough to admit her, and so she made no noise as she stepped cautiously across the threshold and stood within the chamber. The window faced the east, and the inside blinds were opened wide, making Ethelyn remember how annoyed she used to be at that propensity of Richard's to roll up every curtain and open every shutter so as to make the room light and airy. It was light now almost as day, for the moonlight lay upon the floor in a great sheet of silver, and showed her plainly the form and features of the sick man upon the bed. She knew he was asleep, and with a beating heart she drew near to him, and stood for a moment looking down upon the face she had not seen since that wintry morning five years before, when in the dim twilight, it had bent wistfully over her, as if the lips would fain have asked forgiveness for the angry words and deeds of the previous night. That face was pale now, and thin, and the soft brown hair was streaked with gray, making Richard look older than he was. He had suffered, and the suffering had left its marks upon him so indisputably that Ethie could have cried out with pain to see how changed he was.

"Poor Richard," she whispered softly, and kneeling by the bedside she laid her hot cheek as near as she dared to the white, wasted hand resting outside the counterpane.

She did not think what the result of waking him might be. She did not especially care. She was his wife, let what would happen--his erring but repentant Ethie. She had a right to be there with him, and so at last she took his thin hand between her own, and caressed it tenderly. Then Richard moved, and moaning in his deep sleep seemed to have a vague consciousness that someone was with him. Perhaps it was the nurse who had been with him at night on one or two occasions; but the slumber into which he had fallen was too deep to be easily broken. Something he murmured about the medicine, and Ethie's hand held it to his lips, and Ethie's arm was passed beneath his pillow as she lifted up his head while he swallowed it. Then, without unclosing his eyes, he lay back upon his pillow again, while Ethie stood over him until the glimmer of the watchman's lamp passed down the hall a second time, and disappeared around the corner. The watchman had stopped at Richard's door to listen, and then Ethie had experienced a spasm of terror at the possibility of being discovered; but with the receding footsteps her fears left her, and she waited a half-hour longer, while Richard in his dreams talked of bygone days--speaking of Olney, and then of Daisy and herself. Dead, both of them, he seemed to think; and Ethie's pulse throbbed with a strange feeling of joy as she heard herself called his poor darling, whom he wanted back again. She was satisfied now. He had not forgotten her, or even thought to separate himself from her, as Aunt Van Buren hinted. He was true to her yet, and she had acted foolishly in keeping aloof from him so long. But she would be foolish no longer. To-morrow he should know everything. If he would only awaken she would tell him now, and take the consequences. But Richard did not waken, and at last, with a noiseless step, she glided back to her own chamber. She would write to Richard, she decided. She could talk to him better on paper, and, then, if he did not care to receive her, they would both be spared much embarrassment.

Ethie's door was locked all the next morning, for she was writing to her husband a long, humble letter, in which all the blame was taken upon herself, inasmuch as she had made the great mistake of marrying without love. "But I do love you now, Richard," she said; "love you truly, too, else I should never be writing this to you, and asking you to take me back and try if I cannot make you happy."

It was a good deal for Ethie to confess that she had been so much in fault; but she did it honestly, and when the letter was finished she felt as if all that had been wrong and bitter in the past was swept away, and a new era in her life had begun. She would wait till night, she said-- wait till all was again quiet in the hall and in the sick-room, and then when the boy came around with the mail, as he was sure to do, she would hand her letter to him, and bid him leave it in Governor Markham's room. The rest she could not picture to herself; but she waited impatiently for the long August day to draw to its close, joining the guests in the parlor by way of passing the time, and appearing so bright and gay that those who had thought her proud and cold, and reticent, wondered at the brightness of her face and the glad, eager expression of her eyes. She was pretty, after all, they thought, and even Miss Owens, from New York, tried to be very gracious, speaking to her of Governor Markham, whose room adjoined hers, and asking if she had seen him. About him Ethie did not care to talk, and, making some excuse to get away, left the room without hearing a whisper of the story which was going the rounds of the Cure, and which Miss Owens was rather desirous of communicating to someone who, like herself, would be likely to believe it a falsehood.

CHAPTER XXXV: MRS. PETER PRY TAKES A PACK

Mrs. Pry was in a pack, a whole pack, too, which left nothing free but her head, and even that was bandaged in a wet napkin, so that the good woman was in a condition of great helplessness, and nervously counted the moments which must elapse ere Annie, the bath girl, would come to her relief. Now, as was always the case when in a pack, her ears were uncorked and turned toward the door, which she had purposely left ajar, so as not to lose a word, in case any of the ladies came down to that end of the hall and stood by the window while they talked together. They were there now, some half a dozen or more, and they were talking eagerly of the last fresh piece of news brought by Mrs. Carter and daughter, who had arrived from Iowa the day before, and for lack of accommodations at the Cure had gone to the hotel. Both were old patients, and well known in Clifton and so they had spent most of the day at the Cure, hunting up old acquaintances and making new ones. Being something of lion-seekers, they had asked at the office who was there worth knowing, the young lady's face wearing a very important air as she glanced round upon the guests, and remarked, "How different they seemed from those charming people from Boston and New York whom we met here last summer!"

It did not appear as if there was a single lion there this season, whether moneyed, literary, or notorious; and Miss Annie Carter thought it very doubtful whether they should remain or go on to Saratoga, as all the while she had wished to do. In great distress good Mrs. Leigh racked her brain to think who the notables were, and finally bethought herself of Governor Markham, whose name acted like magic upon the newcomers.

"Governor Markham here? Strange, I never thought of Clifton when I heard that he was going East for his health. How is he? Does he improve? It is quite desirable that he should do so, if all reports are true;" and Mrs. Carter looked very wise and knowing upon the group which gathered around her, anxious to hear all she had to tell of Governor Markham.

She did not pretend that she knew him herself, as she lived some distance from Davenport; but she had heard a great deal about him and his handsome house; and Annie, her daughter, who was visiting in Davenport, had been all over it after it was finished. Such a beautiful suite of rooms as he had fitted up for his bride; they were the envy and wonder of both Davenport and Rock Island, too.

"His bride! We did not know he had one. He passes for a widower here," several voices echoed in chorus, and then Mrs. Carter began the story which had come to her through a dozen mediums, and which circulated rapidly through the house, but had not reached Mrs. Pry up to the time when, with her blanket and patchwork quilt she had brought from New Hampshire, she lay reposing in her pack, with her ears turned toward the door and ventilator, ready to catch the faintest breath of gossip.

She heard a great deal that afternoon, for the ladies at the end of the hall did not speak very low, and when at last she was released from her bandages and had made her afternoon toilet, she hastened round to Miss Bigelow's to report what she had heard. Tired with her vigils of the previous night, Ethie was lying down, but she bade Mrs. Pry come in, and then kept very quiet while the good woman proceeded to ask if she had heard the news. Ethie had not, but her heart stood still while her visitor, speaking in a whisper, asked if she was sure Governor Markham could not hear. That the news concerned herself Ethelyn was sure, and she was glad that her face was in a measure concealed from view as she listened to the story.

Governor Markham's wife was not dead, as they had supposed. She was a shameless creature, who eight or ten years before eloped with a man a great deal younger than herself. She was very beautiful, people said, and very fascinating, and the governor worshiped the ground she trod upon. He took her going off very hard at first, and for years scarcely held up his head. But lately he had seemed different, and had been more favorable to a divorce, as advised by his friends. This, however, was after he met Miss Sallie Morton, whose father was a millionaire in Chicago, and whose pretty face had captivated the grave governor. To get the divorce was a very easy matter there in the West, and the governor was now free to marry again. As Miss Morton preferred Davenport to any other place in Iowa, he had built him a magnificent house upon a bluff, finishing it elegantly, and taking untold pains with the suite of rooms intended for his bride. As Miss Sallie objected to marrying him while he was so much of an invalid, he had come to Clifton, hoping to reestablish his health so as to bring home his wife in the autumn, for which event great preparations were making in the family of Miss Sallie.

This was the story as told by Mrs. Pry, and considering that it had only come to her through eight or ten different persons, she repeated the substance of it pretty accurately, and then stopped for Ethie's comment. But Ethie had nothing to say, and when, surprised at her silence, Mrs. Pry asked if she believed it at all, there was still no reply, for Ethelyn had fainted. The reaction was too great from the bright anticipations of the hour before, to the crushing blow which had fallen so suddenly upon her hopes. That a patient at Clifton should faint was not an uncommon thing. Mrs. Pry had often felt like it herself when just out of a pack, or a hot sulphur bath, and so Ethie's faint excited no suspicion in her mind. She was fearful, though, that Miss Bigelow had not heard all the story, but Ethie assured her that she had, and then added that if left to herself she might possibly sleep, as that was what she needed. So Mrs. Pry departed, and Ethie was alone with the terrible calamity which had come upon her. She had been at the Water Cure long enough to know that not more than half of what she heard was true, and this story she knew was false in the parts pertaining to herself and her desertion of her husband. She had never heard before that she was suspected of having had an associate in the flight, and her cheeks crimsoned at the idea, while she wondered if Richard had ever thought that of her. Not at first, she knew, else he had never sought for her so zealously as Aunt Barbara had intimated; but latterly, as he had heard no tidings from her, he might have surmised something of the kind, and that was the secret of the divorce.

"Oh, Richard! Richard!" she murmured, with her hands pressed tightly over her lips, so as to smother all sound, "I felt so sure of your love. You were so different from me. I am punished more than I can bear."

If she had never known before, Ethie knew now, how much she really loved her husband, and how the hope of eventually returning to him had been the day-star of her life. Had she heard that he was lying dead in the next room, she would have gone to him at once, and claiming him as hers, would have found some comfort in weeping sadly over him, and kissing his cold lips, but now it did indeed seem more than she could bear. She did not doubt the story of the divorce, or greatly disbelieve in the other wife. It was natural that many should seek to win his love now that he had risen so high, and she supposed it was natural that he should wish for another companion. Perhaps he believed her dead, and Ethie's heart gave one great throb of joy as she thought of going in to him, and by her bodily presence contradict that belief, and possibly win him from his purpose. But Ethie was too proud for that, and her next feeling was one of exultation that she had not permitted Aunt Barbara to write, or herself taken any measures for communicating with him. He should never know how near she had been to him, or guess ever so remotely of the anguish she was enduring, as, only a few feet removed from him, she suffered, in part, all the pain and sorrow she had brought upon him. Then, as she remembered the new house fitted for the bride, she said:

"I must see that house. I must know just what is in store for my rival. No one knows me in Davenport. Richard is not at home, and there is no chance for my being recognized."

With this decision came a vague feeling akin to hope that possibly the story was false--that after all there was no rival, no divorce. At all events, she should know for a certainty by going to Davenport; and with every nerve stretched to its utmost tension, Ethie arose from her bed and packed her trunk quietly and quickly, and then going to the office, surprised the clerk with the announcement that she wished to leave on the ten-o'clock train. She had received news which made her going so suddenly imperative, she said to him, and to the physician, whom she called upon next, and whose strong arguments against her leaving that night almost overcame her. But Ethie's will conquered at last, and when the train from the East came in she stood upon the platform at the station, her white face closely veiled, and her heart throbbing with the vague doubts which began to assail her as to whether she were really doing a wise and prudent thing in going out alone and unprotected to the home she had no right to enter, and where she was not wanted.

CHAPTER XXXVI: IN DAVENPORT

Hot, and dusty, and tired, and sick, and utterly hopeless and wretched, Ethie looked drearily out from the windows of her room at the hotel, whither she had gone on her first arrival in Davenport. Her head seemed bursting as she stood tying her bonnet before the mirror, and drawing on her gloves, she glanced wistfully at the inviting-looking bed, feeling strongly tempted to lie down there among the pillows and wait till she was rested before she went out in that broiling August sun upon her strange errand. But a haunting presentiment of what the dizziness and pain in her head and temples portended urged her to do quickly what she had to do; so with another gulp of the ice water she had ordered, and which only for a moment cooled her feverish heat, she went from her room into the hall, where the boy was waiting to show her the way to "the governor's house." He knew just where it was. Everybody knew in Davenport, and the chambermaid to whom Ethie had put some questions, had volunteered the information that the governor had gone East for his health, and the house, she believed, was shut up--not shut so that she could not effect an entrance to it. She would find her way through every obstacle, Ethie thought, wondering vaguely at the strength which kept her up and made her feel equal to most anything as she followed her conductor through street after street, onward and onward, up the hill, where the long windows and turrets of a most elegant mansion were visible. When asked at the hotel if she would not have a carriage, she had replied that she preferred to walk, feeling that in this way she should expend some of the fierce excitement consuming her like an inward fire. It had not abated one whit when at last the house was reached, and dismissing her guide she stood a moment upon the steps, leaning her throbbing head against the door post, and summoning courage to ring the bell. Never before had she felt so much like an intruder, or so widely separated from her husband, as during the moment she stood at the threshold of her home, hesitating whether to ring or go away and give the matter up. She could not go away now that she had come so far, she finally decided. She must go in and see the place where Richard lived, and so, at last, she gave the silver knob a pull, which reverberated through the entire house, and brought Hannah, the housemaid, in a trice to see who was there.

"Is Governor Markham at home?" Ethie asked, as the girl waited for her to say something.

Governor Markham was East, and the folks all gone, the girl replied, staring a little suspiciously at the stranger who without invitation, had advanced into the hall, and even showed a disposition to make herself further at home by walking into the drawing room, the door of which was slightly ajar.

"My name is Markham. I am a relative of the governor. I am from the East," Ethelyn volunteered, as she saw the girl expected some explanation.

Had Hannah known more of Ethelyn, she might have suspected something; but she had not been long in the family, and coming, as she did, from St. Louis, the story of her master's wife was rather mythical to her than otherwise. That there was once a Mrs. Markham, who, for beauty, and style, and grandeur, was far superior to Mrs. James, the present mistress of the establishment, she had heard vague rumors; while only that morning when dusting and airing

Richard's room, she had stopped her work a moment to admire the handsome picture which Richard had had painted, from a photograph of Ethie, taken when she was only seventeen. It was a beautiful, girlish face, and the brown eyes were bright and soft, and full of eagerness and joy; while the rounded cheeks and pouting lips were not much like the pale thin woman who now stood in the marbled hall, claiming to be a relative of the family. Hannah never dreamed who it was; but, accustomed to treat with respect everything pertaining to the governor, she opened the door of the little reception-room, and asked the lady to go in.

"I'll send you Mrs. Dobson the housekeeper," she said; and Ethie heard her shuffling tread as she disappeared through the hall and down the stairs to the regions where Mrs. Dobson reigned.

Ethelyn was a little afraid of that dignitary; something in the atmosphere of the house made her afraid of everything, inspiring her as it did with the feeling that she had no business there--that she was a trespasser, a spy, whom Mrs. Dobson would be justified in turning from the door. But Mrs. Dobson meditated no such act. She was a quiet, inoffensive, unsuspicious, personage, believing wholly in Governor Markham and everything pertaining to him. She was canning fruit when Hannah came with the message that some of the governor's kin had come from the East, and remembering to have heard that Richard once had an uncle somewhere in Massachusetts, she had no doubt that this was a daughter of the old gentleman and a cousin of Richard's, especially as Hannah described the stranger as youngish and tolerably good-looking. She had no thought that it was the runaway wife, of whom she knew more than Hannah, else she would surely have dropped the Spencer jar she was filling and burned her fingers worse than she did, trying to crowd in the refractory cover, which persisted in tipping up sideways and all ways but the right way.

"Some of his kin. Pity they are gone. What shall we do with her?" she said, as she finally pushed the cover to its place and blew the thumb she had burned badly.

"Maybe she don't mean to stay long; she didn't bring no baggage," Hannah said, and thus reassured, Mrs. Dobson rolled down her sleeves and tying on a clean apron, started for the reception-room, where Ethie sat like one stupefied, or one who walks in a dream from which he tries in vain to waken.

This house, as far as she could judge, was not like that home on the prairie where her first married days were spent. Everything here was luxurious and grand and in such perfect taste. It seemed a princely home, and Ethie experienced more than one bitter pang of regret that by her own act she had in all probability cut herself off from any part or lot in this earthly paradise.

"I deserve it, but it is very hard to bear," she thought, just as Mrs. Dobson appeared and bowing respectfully, began:

"Hannah tells me you are kin to the governor's folks,--his cousin, I reckon--and I am so sorry they are all, gone, and will be yet for some weeks. The governor is at a water cure down East-- strange you didn't hear of it-- and t'other Mr. Markham has gone with his wife to Olney, and St. Paul, and dear knows where. Too bad, ain't it? But maybe you'll stay a day or two and rest? We'll make you as comfortable as we can. You look about beat out," and Mrs. Dobson came nearer to Ethelyn, whose face and lips were white as ashes, and whose eyes looked almost black with her excitement.

She was very tired. The rapid journey, made without rest or food either, save the cup of tea and cracker she tried to swallow, was beginning to tell upon her, and while Mrs. Dobson was speaking she felt stealing over her the giddiness which she knew was a precursor to fainting.

"I am tired and heated," she gasped. "I could not sleep at the hotel or eat, either. I will stay a day and rest, if you please. Rich--Governor Markham will not care; I was traveling this way, and thought I would call. I have heard so much about his house."

She felt constrained to say this by way of explanation, and Mrs. Dobson accepted it all, warming up at once on the subject of the house--that was her weak point; while to show strangers through the handsome rooms was her delight. No opportunity to do this had for some time been presented, and the good woman's face glowed with the pleasure she anticipated from showing the governor's cousin his house and grounds. But first the lady must have some dinner, and bidding her lay aside her bonnet and shawl and make herself at home, she hurried back to the kitchen and dispatched Hannah for the tender lamb-chop she was going to broil, as that was something easily cooked, and the poor girl seemed so tired and feeble.

"She looks like the Markhams, or like somebody I've seen," she said, never dreaming of finding the familiar resemblance to "somebody she had seen" in the picture hanging in Richard's room.

What she would have done had she known who the stranger was is doubtful. Fortunately she did not know; but being hospitably inclined, and feeling anxious to show the governor's Eastern relatives how grand and nice they were, she broiled the tender lamb, and made the fragrant coffee, and laid the table in the cozy breakfast-room, and put on the little silver set, and then conducted her visitor out to dinner, helping her herself, and leaving the room with the injunction to ring if she wanted anything, as Hannah was within hearing. Terribly bewildered and puzzled with regard to her own identity, Ethie sat down to Richard's table, in Richard's house, and partook of Richard's food, with a strange feeling of quiet, and a constantly increasing sensation of numbness and bewilderment. Access to the house had been easier than she fancied; but she could not help feeling that she had no right to be there, no claim on Richard's hospitality. Certainly she had none, if what she had heard at Clifton were true. But was it? There was some doubt creeping into her mind, though why Richard should wish to build so large and so fine a house just for himself alone she could not understand. She never guessed how every part of that dwelling had been planned with a direct reference to her and her tastes; that not a curtain, or a carpet, or a picture had been purchased without Melinda's having said she believed Ethie would approve it. Every stone, and plank and tack, and nail had in it a thought of the Ethie whose coming back had been speculated upon and planned in so many different ways, but never in this way--never just as it had finally occurred, with Richard gone, and no one there to welcome her, save the servants in the kitchen, who, while she ate her solitary dinner, feeling more desolate and wretched than she had ever before felt in her life, wondered who she was, and how far they ought to go with their attentions and civilities. They were not suspicious, but took her for what she professed to be--a Markham, and a near connection of the governor; and as that stamped her somebody, they were inclined to be very civil, feeling sure that Mrs. James would heartily approve their course. She had rung no bell for Hannah; but they knew her dinner was over, for they heard her as she went back into the reception-room, where Mrs. Dobson ere long joined her, and asked if she would like to see the house.

"It's the only thing we can amuse you with, unless you are fond of music. Maybe you are," and Mrs. Dobson led the way to a little music-room, where, in the recess of a bow window a closed piano was standing.

At first Ethelyn did not observe it closely; but when the housekeeper opened it, and pushing back the heavy drapery, disclosed it fully to view, Ethie started forward with a sudden cry of wonder and surprise, while her face was deathly pale, and the fingers which came down with a crash upon the keys shook violently, for she knew it was her old instrument standing there before her--the one she had sold to procure money for her flight. Richard must have bought it back; for her sake, too, or rather for the sake of what she once was to him, not what she was now.

"Play, won't you?" Mrs. Dobson said. But Ethie could not then have touched a note. The faintest tone of that instrument would have maddened her and she turned away from it with a shudder, while the rather talkative Mrs. Dobson continued: "It's an old piano, I believe, that belonged to the first Mrs. Markham. There's to be a new one bought for the other Mrs. Markham, I heard them say."

Ethie's hands were tightly locked together now, and her teeth shut so tightly over her lips that the thin skin was broken, and a drop of blood showed upon the pale surface; but in so doing she kept back a cry of anguish which leaped up from her heart at Mrs. Dobson's words. The "first Mrs. Markham," that was herself, while the "other Mrs. Markham" meant, of course, her rival-- the bride about whom she had heard at Clifton. She did not think of Melinda as being a part of that household, "and the other Mrs. Markham," for whom the new piano was to be purchased-- she thought of nothing but herself, and her own blighted hopes.

"Does the governor know for certain that his first wife is dead?" she asked, at last, and Mrs. Dobson replied:

"He believes so, yes. It's five years since he heard a word. Of course she's dead. She must have been a pretty creature. Her picture is in the governor's room. Come, I will show it to you."

Mrs. Dobson had left her glasses in the kitchen, so she did not notice the white, stony face, so startling in its expression, as her visitor followed her on up the broad staircase into the spacious hall above, and on still further, till they came to the door of Richard's room, which Hannah had left open. Then for a moment Ethelyn hesitated. It seemed almost like a sacrilege for her feet to tread the floor of that private room, for her breath to taint the atmosphere of a spot where the new wife would come. But Mrs. Dobson led her on until she stood in the center of Richard's room, surrounded by the unmistakable paraphernalia of a man, with so many things around her to remind her of the past. Surely, this was her own furniture; the very articles he had chosen for the room in Camden. It was kind in Richard to keep and bring them here, where everything was so much more elegant--kind, too, in him to redeem her piano. It showed that for a time, at least, he had remembered her; but alas! he had forgotten her now, when she wanted his love so much.

There were great blurring tears in her eyes, and she could not distinctly see the picture on the walk which Mrs. Dobson said was the first Mrs. Markham, asking if she was not a beauty.

"Rather pretty, yes," Ethie said, making a great effort to speak naturally, and adding after a moment: "I suppose it will be taken down when the other Mrs. Markham comes."

In Mrs. Dobson's mind the other Mrs. Markham only meant Melinda, and she replied:

"Why should it? She knows it is here. She knew the other lady and liked her, too."

"She knew me? Who can it be?" Ethie asked herself, remembering that the name she had heard at Clifton was a strange one to her.

"This, now, is the very handsomest part of the whole house," Mrs. Dobson said, throwing open a door which led from Richard's room into a suite of apartments which, to Ethie's bewildered gaze, seemed more like fairyland than anything real she had ever seen. "This the governor fitted up expressly for his wife and I'm told he spent more money here than in all the upper rooms. Did you ever see handsomer lace? He sent to New York for them," she said, lifting up one of the exquisitely wrought curtains festooned across the arch which divided the boudoir from the large sleeping room beyond. "This I call the bridal chamber," she continued, stepping into the room where everything was so pure and white. "But, bless me, I forgot that I put on a lot of bottles to heat: I'll venture they are every one of them shivered to atoms. Hannah is so careless. Excuse me, will you, and entertain yourself a while. I reckon you can find your way back to the parlor."

Ethelyn wanted nothing so much as to be left alone and free to indulge in the emotions which were fast getting the mastery of her. Covering her face with her hands, as the door closed after Mrs. Dobson, she sat for a moment bereft of the power to think or feel. Then, as things became more real, as great throbs of heat and pain went tearing through her temples, she remembered that she was in Richard's house, up in the room which Mrs. Dobson had termed the bridal chamber, the apartments which had been fitted up for Richard's bride, whoever she might be.

"I never counted on this," she whispered, as she paced up and down the range of rooms, from the little parlor or boudoir to the dressing room beyond the bedroom, and the little conservatory at the side, where the choicest of plants were in blossom, and where the dampness was so cool to her burning brow.

It did not strike her as strange that Richard should have thought of all this, nor did she wonder whose taste had aided him in making such a home. She did not wonder at anything except at herself, who had missed so much and fallen into such depths of woe.

"Oh, Richard!" she sighed, as she went back to the bridal chamber. "You would pity me now, and forgive me, too, if you knew what I am suffering here in your home, which can never, never be mine!"

She was standing now near the low window, taking in the effect of her surroundings, from the white ground carpet covered with brilliant bouquets, to the unrumpled, snowy bed which looked so deliciously cool and inviting and seemed beckoning the poor, tired woman to its embrace. And Ethie yielded at last to the silent invitation, forgetting everything save how tired, and sorry, and fever-smitten she was, and how heavy her swollen eyelids were with tears unshed, and the many nights she had not slept. Ethie's cheeks were turning crimson, and her pulse throbbing rapidly as, loosing her long, beautiful hair, which of all her girlish beauty remained unimpaired, and putting off her little gaiters, she lay down upon the snowy bed, and pressing her aching head upon the pillows, whispered softly to her other self--the Ethelyn Grant she used to know in Chicopee, when a little twelve-year-old girl she fled from the maddened cow and met the tall young man from the West.

"Governor Markham they call him now," she said, "and I am Mrs. Governor," and a wild laugh broke the stillness of the rooms kept so sacred until now.

In the hall below Hannah overheard the laugh, and mounting the stairs cast one frightened glance into the chamber where a tossing, moaning figure lay upon the bed, with masses of brown hair falling about the face and floating over the pillows.

Good Mrs. Dobson dropped one of the jars she was filling when Hannah came with her strange tale, and leaving the scalding mass of pulp and juice upon the floor, she hastened up the stairs, and with as stern a voice as it was possible for her to assume, demanded of Ethelyn what she was doing there. But Ethie only whispered on to herself of divorces, and governors' wives-elect, and bridal chambers where she could rest so nicely. Mrs. Dobson and Mrs. Dobson's ire were nothing to her, and the good woman's wrath changed to pity as she met the bright, restless eyes, and felt the burning hands which she held for a moment in her own. It was a pretty little hand--soft and white and small almost as a child's. There was a ring upon the left hand, too; a marriage ring, Mrs. Dobson guessed, wondering now more than ever who the stranger was that had thus boldly taker possession of a room where none but the family ever came.

"She is married, it would seem," she said to Hannah, and then, as Richard's name dropped from Ethelyn's lips, she looked curiously at the flushed face so ghastly white, save where spots of crimson colored the cheeks, and at the mass of hair which Ethie had pushed up and off from the forehead it seemed to oppress with its weight.

"Go, bring me some ice-water from the cellar," Mrs. Dobson said to Hannah, who hurried away on the errand, while the housekeeper, left to herself, bent nearer to Ethelyn and closely scrutinized her face; then stepping to Richard's room, she examined the picture on the wall, where the hair was brushed back and the lips were parted like the lips and hair in that other room where the stranger was.

Mrs. Dobson was a good deal alarmed--"set back," as she afterward expressed it when telling the story to Melinda--and her knees fairly knocked together as she returned to the sick-room, and bending again over the stranger asked, "Is your name Ethelyn?"

For an instant there was a look of consciousness in the brown eyes, and Ethie whispered faintly:

"Don't tell him. Don't send me away. Let me stay here and die; it won't be long, and this pillow is so nice."

She was wandering again, and satisfied that her surmises were correct, Mrs. Dobson lifted her gently up, and to the great surprise of Hannah, who had returned with the ice, began removing the heavy dress and the skirts so much in the way.

"Bring some of Mrs. Markham's night-clothes, and ask me no questions," she said to the astonished girl, who silently obeyed her, and then assisted while Ethelyn was arrayed in Melinda's night-gown and made more comfortable and easy than she could be in her own tight-fitting dress.

"Take this to the telegraph office," was Mrs. Dobson's next order, after she had been a few moments in the library, and Hannah obeyed, reading as she ran:

The way was open for the dispatch, and in less than half an hour the operator at Olney was writing out the message which would take Melinda back to Davenport as fast as steam could carry her.

CHAPTER XXXVII: AT HOME

Mrs. James Markham had spent a few weeks with a party of Davenport friends in St. Paul and vicinity, but she was now at home in Olney with her mother, whom she helped with the ironing that morning, showing a quickness and dexterity in the doing up of Tim's shirts and best table linen which proved that, although a "mighty fine lady," as some of the Olneyites termed her, she had neither forgotten nor was above working in the kitchen when the occasion required. The day's ironing was over now, and refreshed with a bath and a half-hour's sleep after it, she sat under the shadow of the tall trees, arrayed in her white marseilles, which, being gored, made her look, as unsophisticated Andy thought, most too slim and flat. Andy himself was over at the Joneses that afternoon, and, down upon all fours, was playing bear with baby Ethelyn, who shouted and screamed with delight at the antics of her childish uncle. Mrs. James was not contemplating a return to Davenport for three or four weeks; indeed, ever since the letter received from Clifton with regard to Richard's sickness, she had been seriously meditating a flying visit to the invalid, who she knew would be glad to see her. It must be very desolate for him there alone, she said; and then her thoughts went after the wanderer whom they had long since ceased to talk about, much less than to expect back again. Melinda was sadly thinking of her, and speculating as to what her fate had been, when down the road from the village came the little messenger boy, who always made one's heart beat so fast when he handed out his missive. He had one now, and he brought it to Melinda, who, thinking of her husband, gone to Denver City, felt a thrill of fear lest something had befallen him. But no; the dispatch came from Davenport, from Mrs. Dobson herself, and read that a strange woman lay very sick in the house.

"A strange woman," that was all, but it made Melinda's heart leap up into her throat at the bare possibility as to who the strange woman might be. Andy was standing by her now reading the message, and Melinda knew by the flush upon his face, and the drops of perspiration which started out so suddenly around his mouth, that he, too, shared her suspicions. But not a word was spoken by either upon the subject agitating them so powerfully. Melinda only said, "I must go home at once--in the next train if possible," while Andy rejoined, "I am going with you."

Melinda knew why he was going, and when at last they were on the way, the sight of his honest-speaking face, glowing all over with eagerness and joyful anticipations, kept her own spirits up, and made what she so greatly hoped for seem absolutely certain. It was morning when they arrived, and were driven rapidly through the streets toward home. The house seemed very quiet; every window and shutter, so far as they could see, was closed, and both experienced a terrible fear lest "the strange woman" was gone. They could not wait for Hannah to open the door, and so they went round to the basement, surprising Mrs. Dobson as she bent over the fire, stirring the basin of gruel she was preparing for her patient. "The strange woman" was not gone. She was raving mad, Mrs. Dobson said, and talked the queerest things. "I've had the doctor, just as I knew you would have done, had you been here," she said, "and he pronounced it brain fever, brought on by fatigue, and some great excitement or worriment. 'Pears like she thought she was divorced, or somebody was divorced, for she was talking about it, and showing the ring on her fourth finger. I hope Governor Markham won't mind it. 'Twas none of my doings. She went there herself, and I first found her in the bed in that room where nobody ever slept--the bride's room, I call it, you know."

"Is she there?" Melinda asked, in amazement, while Andy, who had been standing near the door which led up to the next floor, disappeared up the stairs, leaving the women alone.

He knew the way to the room designated, and went hurrying on until he reached the door, and there he paused, his flesh creeping with the intensity of his excitement, and his whole being pervaded with a crushing sense of eager expectancy. He had not put into words what or whom he expected to find on the other side of the door he hardly dared to open. He only knew he should be terribly disappointed if his conjectures proved wrong, and a smothered prayer rose to his lips, "God grant it may be the she I mean."

The she he meant was sleeping now. The brown head which rolled so restlessly all night was lying quietly upon the pillows, the burning cheek resting upon one hand, and the mass of long, bright hair tucked back under one of Mrs. Dobson's own nightcaps, that lady having sought in vain for such an article among her mistress' wardrobe. She did not hear Andy as he stepped softly across the floor to the bedside. Bending cautiously above her, he hesitated a moment, while a great throb of disappointment ran through his veins. Surely that was not Ethie, with the hollow cheeks and the disfiguring frill around her face, giving her more the look of the new and stylish nurse Melinda had got from Chicago--the woman who wore a cap in place of a bonnet, and jabbered half the time in some foreign tongue, which Melinda said was French. The room was very dark, and Andy pushed back a blind, letting in such a flood of light that the sleeper started, and moaned, and turned herself upon the pillow, while with a gasping, sobbing cry, Andy fell upon his knees, and with clasped hands and streaming eyes, exclaimed:

"I thank Thee, Father of mercies, more than I can tell, for it is Ethie--it is Ethie--it is Ethie, our own darling Ethie, come back to us again; and now, dear Lord, bring old Dick home at once, and let us have a time of it."

Ethie's eyes were opened and fixed inquiringly upon Andy. Something in his voice and manner must have penetrated through the mists of delirium clouding her brain, for the glimmer of a smile played round her lips, and her hands moved slowly toward him; then they went back again to her throat and tugged at the nightcap strings which good Mrs. Dobson had tied in a hard knot by way of keeping the cap upon the refractory head. Ethie did not fancy the cap any more than Andy, who, guessing her wishes, lent his own assistance to the untying of the strings.

"You don't like the pesky thing on your head, making you look so like a scarecrow, do you?" he said gently, as with a jerk he broke the strings and then threw the discarded cap upon the floor.

Ethie seemed to know him for a moment, and, "Kiss me, Andy," came feebly from her lips. Winding his arms about her, Andy did kiss her many times, while his tears dropped upon her face and moistened the long hair, which, relieved from its confinement, fell in dark masses about her face, making her look more like the Ethelyn of old than she had at first.

"Was there a divorce?" she whispered, and Andy, in great perplexity, was wondering what she meant, when Melinda's step came along the hall, and Melinda entered the room together with Mrs. Dobson.

"It's she--herself! It's our own Ethie!" Andy exclaimed, standing back a little from the bed, but still holding the feverish hand which had grasped his so firmly, as if in that touch alone was rest and security.

"I thought so," and with a satisfied nod Mrs. Dobson put down her bowl of gruel and went down to communicate the startling news to Hannah, who nearly lost her senses in the first moment of surprise.

"Do you know me, Ethie?" Melinda asked, but in the bright, rolling eyes there was no ray of reason; only the lip quivered slightly, and Ethie said so sadly, so beseechingly, "Don't send me away, when I am so tired and sorry."

She seemed to have a vague idea where she was and who was with her, clinging closer to Andy, as if surest of him, and once when he bent over her, she suddenly wound her arms around his neck and whispered, "Don't leave me--it's nice to know you are with me; and don't let them put that dreadful thing on my head again. Aunt Van Buren said I was a fright. Will Richard think so, too?"

This was the only time she mentioned her husband, though she talked of Clifton and Mrs. Pry, and the story of the divorce, and the dear little chapel where she said God always came, bidding Andy kneel down and pray just as they were doing there when the summer day drew to a close.

"We must send for Dick," Andy said; "but don't let's tell the whole; let's leave something to his imagination;" and so the telegram which went to Governor Markham read simply: "Come home immediately. Don't wait for a single train."

Richard had heard of Miss Bigelow's sudden departure, and had been surprised to find how much he missed the light footsteps and the rustling sound which had come from No. 101. He was a good deal interested in Miss Bigelow, and when Mary told him of her leaving so unexpectedly and appearing so excited, there had for a moment flashed over him the wild thought, "Could it be?" No, it could not, he said; but he questioned Mary as to the appearance of the lady in No. 101. "Was she very handsome, with full, rosy cheeks, and eyes of chestnut brown?"

"She was rather pretty," Mary said; "but her face was thin and pale, and her eyes, she guessed, were black."

It was not Ethie, then--Richard had never believed it was--but he felt sorry that she was gone, whoever she might be, and Clifton was not so pleasant to him now as it had been at first. He was much better, and had been once to the chapel, when up the three flights of stairs Perry came and along the hall till he stopped at Room No. 102. There was a telegram for Richard, who took it with trembling hands and read it with a blur before his eyes and something at his heart like a blow, but which was born of a sudden hope that, after many days and months and years of waiting, God had deigned to be merciful. But only for a brief moment did this hope buoy him up. It could not be, he said; and yet, as he made his hasty preparations for his journey, he found the possibility constantly recurring to his mind, while the nearer he came to Davenport the more probable it seemed, and the more impatient he grew at every little delay. There were several upon the road, and once, only fifty miles from home, there was a detention of four hours. But the long train moved at last, and just as the sun was setting the cars stopped in the Davenport depot, and as the passengers alighted the loungers whispered to each other, "Governor Markham has come home."

CHAPTER XXXVIII: RICHARD AND ETHELYN

Arrived at Davenport, and so near his home that he could discern its roofs and chimneys, the hope which had kept Richard up all through his rapid journey began to give way, and he hardly knew what or whom he expected to find, as he went up the steps to his house and rang the door bell. Certainly not Andy--he had not thought of him--and his pulse quickened with a feeling of eagerness and hope renewed when he caught sight of his brother's beaming face and felt the pressure of his broad hand. In his delight Andy kissed his brother two or three times during the interval it took to get him through the hall into the reception room, where they were alone. Arrived there, Andy fell to capering across the floor, while Richard looked on, puzzled to decide whether his weak brother had gone wholly daft or not. Recollecting himself at last, and assuming a more sober attitude, Andy came close to him and whispered:

"Dick, you ought to be thankful, so thankful and glad that God has been kind at last and heard our prayers, just as I always told you he would. Guess who is upstairs, ravin' crazy by spells, and quiet as a Maltese kitten the rest of the time? I'll bet, though, you'll never guess, it is so strange? Try, now--who do you think it is?"

"Ethelyn," came in a whisper from Richard's lips, and rather crestfallen, the simple Andy said, "Somebody told you, I know; but you are right. Ethie is here--came when we all was gone--said she was a connection of yourn, and so Miss Dobson let her in, and treated her up, and showed her the house, and left her in them rooms you fixed a purpose for her. You see Miss Dobson had some truck she was canning, and she stayed downstairs so long that when she went back she found Ethie had taken possession of that bed where nobody ever slept, and was burnin' up with fever and talkin' the queerest kind of talk about divorces, and all that, and there was something in her face made Miss Dobson mistrust who she was, and she telegraphed for Melinda and me--or rather for Melinda--and I came out with her, for I knew in a minit who the strange woman was. But she won't know you, Dick. She don't know me, though she lays her head on my arm and snugs up to me awful neat. Will you go now to see her?"

The question was superfluous, for Richard was halfway up the stairs, followed close by Andy, who went with him to the door of Ethie's room, and then stood back, thinking it best for Richard to go in alone.

Ethelyn was asleep, and Melinda sat watching her. She knew it was Richard who came in, for she had heard his voice in the hall, and greeting him quickly, arose and left the room, whispering: "If she wakes, don't startle her. Probably she will not know you."

Then she went out, and Richard was alone with the wife he had not seen for more than five weary years. It was very dark in the room, and it took him a moment to accustom himself to the light enough to discover the figure lying so still before him, the pale eyelids closed, and the long eyelashes resting upon the crimson cheek. The lips and forehead were very white, but the rest of the face was purple with fever, and as that gave the cheeks a fuller, rounder look, she did not at first seem greatly changed, but looked much as she did the time he came from Washington and found her so low. The long hair which Andy would not have confined in a cap was pushed back from her brow, and lay in tangled masses upon the pillow, while her hands were folded one within the other and rested outside the covering. And Richard touched her hands first--the little, soft, white hands he used to think so pretty, and which he now kissed so softly as he knelt by the bedside and tried to look closely into Ethie's face.

"My poor, sick darling, God knows how glad I am to have you back," he murmured, and his tears dropped like rain upon the hands he pressed so gently. Then softly caressing the pale forehead, his fingers threaded the mass of tangled hair, and his lips touched the hot, burning ones which quivered for a moment, and then said, brokenly:

"A dream--all a dream. I've had it so many times."

She was waking, and Richard drew back a step or two, while the bright, restless eyes moved round the room as if in quest of someone.

"It's very dark," she said, and turning one of the shutters Richard came back and stood just where the light would fall upon his face as it did on hers.

He saw now how changed she was; but she was none the less dear to him for that, and he spoke to her very tenderly:

"Ethie, darling, don't you know me? I am Richard, your husband, and I am so glad to get you back."

There did seem to be a moment's consciousness, for there crept into the eyes a startled, anxious look as they scanned Richard's face; then the lip quivered again, and Ethie said pleadingly:

"Don't send me away. I am so tired, and the road was so long. I thought I would never get here. Let me stay. I shall not be bad any more."

Then, unmindful of consequences, Richard gathered her in his arms, and held her there an instant in a passionate embrace, which left her pale and panting, but seemed to reassure her, for when he would have laid her back upon the pillow, she said to him, "No, not there--on your arm--so. Yes, that's nice," and an expression of intense satisfaction stole into her face as she nestled her head close to Richard's bosom, and, closing her eyes, seemed to sleep again. And Richard held her thus, forgetting his own fatigue, and refusing to give up his post either to Andy or Melinda, both of whom ventured in at last, and tried to make him take some refreshment and rest.

"I am not hungry," he said, "and it is rest enough to be with Ethelyn."

Much he wondered where she had come from, and Melinda repeated all Ethelyn had said which would throw any light upon the subject.

"She has talked of the Nile, and St. Petersburg, and the Hellespont, and the ship which was bringing her to Richard, and of Chicopee, but it was difficult telling how much was real," Melinda said, adding, "She talked of Clifton, too; and were it possible, I should say she came direct from there, but that could not be. You would have known if she had been there. What was the number of your room?"

"102," Richard replied, a new revelation dawning upon him, while Melinda rejoined:

"That is the number she talks about--that and 101. Can it be that she was there?"

Richard was certain of it. The Miss Bigelow who had interested him so much lay there in his arms, his own wife, who was, if possible, tenfold dearer to him now than when he first held her as his bride. He knew she was very sick, but she would not die, he said to himself. God had not restored her to him just to take her away again, and make his desolation more desolate. Ethie would live. And surely if love, and nursing, and tender care were of any avail to save the life which at times seemed fluttering on the very verge of the grave, Ethelyn would live. Nothing was spared which could avail to save her, and even the physician, who had all along done what he could, seemed to redouble his efforts when he ascertained who his patient was.

Great was the surprise, and numerous the remarks and surmises of the citizens, when it was whispered abroad that the strange woman lying so sick in the governor's house was no other than the governor's wife, about whom the people had speculated so much. Nor was it long ere the news went to Camden, stirring up the people there, and bringing Mrs. Miller at once to Davenport, where she stayed at a hotel until such time as she could be admitted to Ethelyn's presence.

Mrs. Markham, senior, was washing windows when Tim Jones brought her the letter bearing the Davenport postmark. Melinda had purposely abstained from writing home until Richard came; and so the letter was in his handwriting, which his mother recognized at once.

"Why, it's from Richard!" she exclaimed. "I thought he wouldn't stay long at Clifton. I never did believe in swashin' all the time. A bath in the tin washbasin does me very well," and the good woman wiped her window leisurely, and even put it back and fastened the side-slat in its place before she sat down to see what Richard had written.

Tim knew what he had written, for in his hat was another letter from Melinda, for his mother, which he had opened, his feet going off into a kind of double shuffle as he read that Ethelyn had returned. She had been very cold and proud to him; but he had admired her greatly, and remembered her with none but kindly feelings. He was a little anxious to know what Mrs. Markham would say, but as she was in no hurry to open her letter, and he was in a hurry to tell his mother the good news, he bade her good-morning, and mounting his horse, galloped away toward home.

"I hope he's told who the critter was that was took sick in the house," Mrs. Markham said, as she adjusted her glasses and broke the seal.

Mrs. Markham had never fainted in her life, but she came very near it that morning, feeling some as she would if the Daisy, dead, so long, had suddenly walked into the room and taken a seat beside her.

"I am glad for Dick," she said. "I never saw a man change as he has, pinin' for her. I mean to be good to her, if I can," and Mrs. Markham's sun-bonnet was bent low over Richard's letter, on which there were traces of tears when the head was lifted up again. "I must let John know, I never can stand it till dinner time," she said, and a shrill blast from the tin horn, used to bring her sons to dinner, went echoing across the prairie to the lot where John was working.

It was not a single blast, but peal upon peal, a loud, prolonged sound, which startled John greatly, especially as he knew by the sun that it could not be twelve o'clock.

"Blows as if somebody was in a fit," he said, as he took long and rapid strides toward the farmhouse.

His mother met him in the lane, letter in hand, and her face white with excitement as she said below her breath:

"John, John, oh! John, she's come. She's there at Richard's--sick with the fever, and crazy; and Richard is so glad. Read what he says."

She did not say who had come, but John knew, and his eyes were dim with tears as he took the letter from his mother's hand, and read it, walking beside her to the house.

"I presume they doctor her that silly fashion, with little pills the size of a small pin head. Melinda is so set in her way. She ought to have some good French brandy if they want to save her. I'd better go myself and see to it," Mrs. Markham said, after they had reached the house, and John, at her request, had read the letter aloud.

John did not quite fancy his mother's going, particularly as Richard had said nothing about it, but Mrs. Markham was determined.

"It was a good way to make it up with Ethelyn, to be there when she come to," she thought, and so, leaving her house-cleaning to itself, and John to his bread and milk, of which he never tired, she packed a little traveling bag, and taking with her a bottle of brandy, started on the next train for Davenport, where she had never been.

Aunt Barbara was not cleaning house. She was cutting dried caraway seed in the garden, and thinking of Ethie, wondering why she did not write, and hoping that when she did she would say that she had talked with Richard, and made the matter up. Ever since hearing that he was at Clifton, in the next room to Ethie, Aunt Barbara had counted upon a speedy reconciliation, and done many things with a direct reference to that reconciliation. The best chamber was kept constantly aired, with bouquets of flowers in it, in case the happy pair, "as good as just married," should come suddenly upon her. Ethie's favorite loaf cake was constantly kept on hand, and when Betty suggested that they should let Uncle Billy cut down that caraway seed, "and heave it away," the good soul objected, thinking there was no telling what would happen, and it was well enough to save such things as anise and caraway. So, in her big cape bonnet, she was cutting her branches of herbs, when Charlie Howard looked over the garden gate with "Got a letter for you."

"It ain't from her. It's from--why, it's from Richard, and he is in Davenport," Aunt Barbara exclaimed, as she sat down in a garden chair to read the letter which was not from Ethie.

Richard did not say directly to her that she must come, but Aunt Barbara felt an innate conviction that her presence would not be disagreeable, even if Ethie lived, while "if she died," and Aunt Barbara's heart gave a great throb as she thought it, "if Ethie died she must be there," and so her trunk was packed for the third time in Ethie's behalf, and the next day's train from Boston carried the good woman on her way to Davenport.

CHAPTER XXXIX: RECONCILIATION

There had been a succession of rainy days in Davenport--dark, rainy days, which added to the gloom hanging over that house where they watched so intently by Ethie's side, trembling lest the life they prayed for so earnestly might go out at any moment, so high the fever ran, and so wild and restless the patient grew. The friends were all there now--James, and John, and Andy, and Aunt Barbara, with Mrs. Markham, senior, who, at first, felt a little worried, lest her son should be eaten out of house and home, especially as Melinda manifested no disposition to stint the table of any of their accustomed luxuries. As housekeeper, Mrs. Dobson was a little inclined at first to stand in awe of the governor's mother, and so offered no remonstrance when the tea grounds from supper were carefully saved to be boiled up for breakfast, as both Melinda and Aunt Barbara preferred tea to coffee, but when it came to a mackerel and a half for seven people, and four of them men, Mrs. Dobson demurred, and Melinda's opinion in requisition, the result was that three fishes, instead of one and a half smoked upon the breakfast table next morning, together with toast and mutton-chops. After that Mrs. Markham gave up the contest with a groan, saying, "they might go to destruction their own way, for all of her."

Where Ethelyn was concerned, however, she showed no stint. Nothing was too good for her, no expense too great, and next to Richard and Andy, she seemed more anxious, more interested than anyone for the sick girl who lay so insensible of all that was passing around her, save at brief intervals when she seemed for an instant to realize where she was, for her eyes would flash about the room with a frightened, startled look, and then seek Richard's face with a wistful, pleading expression, as if asking not to cast her off, not to send her back into the dreary world where she had wandered so long alone. The sight of so many seemed to worry her, for she often talked of the crowd at the Clifton depot, saying they took her breath away; and once, drawing Andy's face down to her, she whispered to him, "Send them back to the Cure, all but his royal highness"--pointing to Richard--"and Anna, the prophetess, she can stay."

This was Aunt Barbara, to whom Ethelyn clung as a child to its mother, missing her the moment she left the room, and growing quiet as soon as she returned. It was the same with Richard. She seemed to know when he quitted her side, and her eyes watched the door eagerly till he came back to her again. At the doctor's suggestion, all were at last banished from the sick-room except Aunt Barbara, and Richard, and Nick Bottom, as she persisted in calling poor Andy, who was terribly perplexed to know whether he was complimented or not, and who eventually took to studying Shakspere to find out who Bottom was. Those were trying days to Richard, who rarely left Ethie's bedside, except when it was absolutely necessary. She was more quiet with him, and would sometimes sleep for hours upon his arm, with one hand clasped in Aunt Barbara's, and the other held by Andy. At other times, when the fever was on, no arm availed to hold her as she tossed from side to side, talking of things at which a stranger would have marveled, and which made Richard's heart ache to its very core. At times she was a girl in Chicopee, and all the past as connected with Frank Van Buren was lived over again; then she would talk of Richard, and shudder as she recalled the dreary, dreadful day when the honeysuckles were in blossom, and he came to make her his wife.

"It was wrong, all wrong. I did not love him then," she said, "nor afterward, on the prairie, nor anywhere, until I went away, and found what it was to live without him."

"And do you love him now?" Richard asked her once when he sat alone with her.

There was no hesitancy on her part, no waiting to make up an answer. It was ready on her lips, "Yes, oh, yes!" and the weak arms lifted themselves up and were wound around his neck with a pressure almost stifling. How much of this was real Richard could not tell, but he accepted it as such, and waited impatiently for the day when the full light of reason should return and Ethie be restored to him. There was but little of her past life which he did not learn from her ravings, and so there was less for her to tell him when at last the fever abated, and his eyes met hers with a knowing, rational expression. Andy was alone with her when the change first came. The rain, which had fallen so steadily, was over, and out upon the river the sunlight was softly falling. At Andy's earnest entreaty, Richard had gone for a little exercise in the open air, and was walking slowly up and down the broad piazza, while Aunt Barbara slept, and Andy kept his vigils by Ethelyn. She, too, was sleeping quietly, and Andy saw the great drops of perspiration standing upon her brow and beneath her hair. He knew it was a good omen, and on his knees by the bedside, with his face in his hands, he prayed aloud, thanking God for restoring Ethelyn to them, and asking that they might all be taught just how to make her happy. A faint sound between a moan and a sob roused him and, looking up, he saw the great tears rolling down Ethie's cheeks, while her lips moved as if they would speak to him.

"Andy, dear old Andy! is it you, and are you glad to have me back?" she said, and then all Andy's pent-up feelings found vent in a storm of tears and passionate protestations of love and tenderness for his darling sister.

She remembered how she came there, and seemed to understand why Andy was there, too; but the rest was a little confused. Was Aunt Barbara there, or had she only dreamed it?

"Aunt Barbara is here," Andy said, and then, with the same frightened, anxious look her face had so often worn during her illness, Ethie said: "Somebody else has sat by me and held my head and hands, and kissed me! Andy, tell me--was that Richard?--and did he kiss me, and is he glad to find me?"

She was gazing fixedly at Andy, who replied: "Yes, Dick is here. He's glad to have you back. He's kissed you more than forty times. He don't remember nothing."

"And the divorce, Andy--is the story true, and am I not his wife?"

"I never heard of no divorce, only what you said about one in your tantrums. Dick would as soon have cut off his head as got such a thing," Andy replied.

Ethelyn knew she could rely on what Andy said, and a heartfelt "Thank God! It is more than I deserve!" fell from her lips, just as a step was heard in the hall.

"That's Dick,--he's coming," Andy whispered, and hastily withdrawing he left the two alone together.

It was more than an hour before even Aunt Barbara ventured into the room, and when she did she knew by the joy written on Richard's face and the deep peace shining in Ethie's eyes that the reconciliation had been complete and perfect. Every error had been confessed, every fault forgiven, and the husband and wife stood ready now to begin the world anew, with perfect love for and confidence in each other. Ethie had acknowledged all her faults, the greatest of which was the giving her hand to one from whom she withheld her heart.

"But you have that now," she said. "I can truly say that I love you far better than ever frank Van Buren was loved, and I know you to be worthy, too. I have been so wicked, Richard,--so wilful and impatient,--that I wonder you have not learned to hate my very name. I may be wilful still. My old hot temper is not all subdued, though I hope I am a better woman than I used to be when I cared for nothing but myself. God has been so good to me who have forgotten Him so long; but we will serve Him together now."

As Ethie talked she had nestled closer and closer to her husband, whose arms encircled her form and whose face bent itself down to hers, while a rain of tears fell upon her hair and forehead as the strong man,--the grave Judge and the honored Governor,--confessed where he, too, had been in fault, and craving his young wife's pardon, ascribed also to God the praise for bringing them both to feel their dependence on Him, as well as to see this day, the happiest of their lives.

Gradually, as she could bear it, the family came in one by one to see her, Mrs. Markham, Sen., waiting till the very last, and refusing to go until Ethelyn had expressed a wish to see her.

"I was pretty hard on her, I s'pose, and it would not be strange if she laid it up against me," she said to Melinda; but Ethie had nothing against her now.

The deep waters through which she had passed had obliterated all traces of bitterness toward anyone, and when her mother-in-law came in she feebly extended her hand and whispered: "I'm too tired, mother, to talk much, but kiss me once for the sake of what we are going to be to each other."

Mrs. Markham was not naturally a bad or a hard woman, either. She was only unfortunate that her ideas had run in one rut so long without any jolt to throw them out. Circumstances had greatly softened her, and Ethie's words touched her deeply.

"I was mighty mean to you sometimes, Ethelyn, and I've been sorry for it," she said, as she stooped to kiss her daughter-in-law, and then hurried from the room, "Only to think, she called me mother," she said to Melinda, to whom she reported the particulars of her interview with Ethelyn--"me, who had been meaner than dirt to her--called me mother, when I used to mistrust her she didn't think any more of me than if I'd been an old squaw. I shan't forget it right away."

Perhaps the sweetest, most joyful tears Ethelyn shed that day were those which came to her eyes when they brought her Ethelyn, her namesake, the little three-year-old, who pushed her brown curls back from her baby face with such a womanly air, and said:

"I'se glad to see Aunt Ethie. I prays for her ever' night. Uncle Andy told me so. I loves you, Aunt Ethie."

She was a beautiful little creature, and her innocent prattle and engaging manners did much toward bringing the color back to Ethie's cheeks and the brightness to her eyes. Those days of convalescence were blissful ones, for now there was no shadow of a cloud resting on the domestic horizon. Between husband and wife there was perfect love, and in his newly born happiness, Richard forgot the ailments which had sent him an invalid to Clifton, while Ethie, surrounded by every luxury which love could devise or money procure, and made each hour to feel how dear she was to those from whom she had been so long estranged, grew fresh, and young, and pretty again; so that when, early in December, Mrs. Dr. Van Buren came to Davenport to see her niece, she found her more beautiful far than she had been in her early girlhood, when the boyish Frank had paid his court to her. Poor little Nettie was dead. Her life had literally been worried out of her; and during those September days, when Ethelyn was watched and tended so carefully, she had turned herself wearily upon her pillow, and just as the clock was striking the hour of midnight, asked of the attendant:

"Has Frank come yet?"

"Not yet. Do you want anything?"

"No, nothing. Is mother here?"

"She was tired out, and has gone to her room to rest. Shall I call her?"

"No, no matter. Is Ethie in her crib? Please bring her here. Never mind if you do wake her. 'Tis the last time."

And so the little sleeping child was brought to the dying mother, who would fain feel that something she had loved was near her in the last hour of loneliness and anguish she would ever know. Sorrow, disappointment, and cruel neglect had been her lot ever since she became a wife, but at the last these had purified and made her better, and led her to the Saviour's feet, where she laid the little child she held so closely to her bosom, dropping her tears upon its face and pressing her farewell kiss upon its lips. Then she put it from her, and bidding the servant remove the light, which made her eyes ache so, turned again upon her pillow, and folding her little, white, wasted hands upon her bosom, said softly the prayer the Saviour taught, and then glided as softly down the river whose tide is never backward toward the shores of time.

About one Frank came home from the young men's association which he attended so often, his head fuller of champagne and brandy than it was of sense, and every good feeling blunted with dissipation. But the Nettie whose pale face had been to him so constant a reproach was gone forever, and only the lifeless form was left of what he once called his wife. She was buried in Mount Auburn, and they made her a grander funeral than they had given to her first-born, and then the household want on the same as ever until Mrs. Van Buren conceived the idea of visiting her niece, Mrs. Gov. Markham, and taking her grandchild with her. For the sake of the name she was sure the little girl would be welcome, as well as for the sake of the dead mother. And she was welcome, more so even than the stately aunt, whose deep mourning robes seemed to throw a kind of shadowy gloom over the house which she found so handsome, and elegant, and perfectly kept that she would willingly have spent the entire winter there. She was not invited to do this, and some time in January she went back to her home, looking out on Boston Common, but not until she had eaten a Christmas dinner with Mrs. Markham, senior, at whose house the whole family were assembled on that occasion.

There was much good cheer and merriment there, and Ethie, in her rich crimson silk which

Richard had surprised her with, was the queen of all, her wishes deferred to, and her tastes consulted with a delicacy and deference which no one could fail to observe. And Eunice Plympton was there, too, waiting upon the table with Andy, who insisted upon standing at the back of Ethie's chair, just as he had seen the waiters do in Camden, and would have his mother ring the silver bell when anything was wanted. It was a happy family reunion, and a meet harbinger of the peaceful days in store for our heroine--days which came and went so fast, until winter melted into spring, and the spring budded into blushing summer, and the summer faded into the golden autumn, and the autumn floated with feathery snowflakes into the chilly winter and December came again, bringing another meeting of the Markhams. But this time it was at the governor's house in Davenport, and another was added to the number--a pretty little waxen thing, which all through the elaborate dinner slept quietly in its crib, and then in the evening, when the gas was lighted in the parlors, and Mr. Townsend was there in his gown, behaved most admirably, and lay very still in its father Richard's arms, until it was transferred from his to those of the clergyman, who in the name of the Father, the Son, and the Holy Ghost baptized it "Daisy Adelaide Grant."

Made in the USA
Columbia, SC
08 June 2021